Peter Watt has spent time as a soldier, articled clerk, prawn trawler deckhand, builder's labourer, pipe layer, real estate salesman, private investigator, police sergeant and adviser to the Royal Papua New Guinea Constabulary. He speaks, reads and writes Vietnamese and Pidgin. He now lives at Maclean, on the Clarence River in northern New South Wales. Fishing and the vast open spaces of outback Queensland are his main interests in life.

Peter Watt can be contacted at www.peterwatt.com

Excerpts from e-mails sent to Peter Watt since his first novel was published:

'Just finished reading *Papua* . . . Absolutely brilliant. Couldn't put it down.'
BOB

'I have a copy of every Wilbur Smith book out and hang off every word in those books. He has taught me to love the "outback" of South Africa. How exciting then for me to discover an Australian author who writes in the same style about our own wonderful outback and fascinating history.'
JULIE, AUSTRALIA

T0162380

'On reading your fourth novel *Papua* I felt compelled to write to you congratulating you on your work, though I know I shall not be the first nor be the last to do so . . . I have to confess I am an avid reader of Wilbur Smith's work, as well as Jeffrey Archer's, and Bryce Courtenay, and, if I may say without sounding too obligatory, your work sits highly amongst these gentlemen.'
KEN, AUSTRALIA

'I own *Cry of the Curlew*, *Shadow of the Osprey* and *Flight of the Eagle*; I discovered them last year. I read the first book and could not put it down; I had to have the other two to see how the story ended. Imagine my delight when the person who introduced me to your writing in the first place, sent me *Papua* on Saturday!!!! Yee-har.'
FRANCES, AUSTRALIA

'I have previously read your three books of the Duffy and Macintosh families and thoroughly enjoyed them! I have only recently finished *Papua* and am wondering if there will be a continuation of the characters on novels down the track. (I dearly hope so.) Keep up the fantastic work.'
JODIE, AUSTRALIA

PAPUA

PETER WATT

PAN
Pan Macmillan Australia

Also by Peter Watt

The Duffy/Macintosh Series
Cry of the Curlew
Shadow of the Osprey
Flight of the Eagle
To Chase the Storm
To Touch the Clouds
To Ride the Wind
Beyond the Horizon

The Papua Series
Papua
Eden
The Pacific

The Silent Frontier
The Stone Dragon
The Frozen Circle

First published 2002 in Macmillan by Pan Macmillan Australia Pty Limited
This Pan edition published 2003 by Pan Macmillan Australia Pty Limited
1 Market Street, Sydney

Reprinted 2003, 2005, 2006, 2009

National Library of Australia
Cataloguing-in-Publication data:

Watt, Peter, 1949- .
Papua.

ISBN 978 0 330 36422 5.

1. Frontier and pioneer life – Papua New Guinea – Fiction. 2. World War, 1914–1918
– Campaigns – France – Fiction. 3. Male friendship – Fiction. I. Title.

A823.3

Set in 11.5/13 pt Bembo by Post Pre-press Group
Printed by IVE

For Tony Williams
Agent and true friend

ACKNOWLEDGEMENTS

The writing of a novel has a lot in common with the production of a film. Many people have an influence on the final result. In my case I would like to thank a number of people.

Ms Angelika Gassner from Austria who gave good advice on the Germanic aspects of the novel. Phil Murphy from Recognition Australasia in Cairns for his continuing technical advice. Joy and all the wonderful ladies at the Coolangatta Library for providing the resources for research. Robert Bozek and Nadine Vincenc from Sydney whose friendship and wonderful support have meant a lot. Ashley and Amanda Grosser, proprietors of the Sleepy Hill Motor Inn at Raymond Terrace, for their generosity over time to a weary writer on the road. My great brother-in-law Tyrone McKee for giving up his time and sharing the long drive for a regional book tour in 2001. And my sister Kerry who has been there when it counted. To Tony and Chris Pearce at Baulkham Hills for the time I spent in their company while writing this book. To Wilbur Smith, my special thanks for your generous words at a dinner held in Brisbane.

At Pan Macmillan Australia my special thanks to my editor Cate Paterson whose inspiration is, as always, a great part of what the reader sees in the story and characters. To Simone Ford whose attention to editing detail is truly appreciated. My continuing thanks to my publicist Jane Novak whose contact usually means something nice to do other than write books. A big thanks also to Ross Gibb and James Fraser.

My special thanks to some people at Anthony A. Williams Management: Geoffrey Radford, Ingrid Butters, Sonja Patterson and Tony Blair – part of my professional family in the world of writing.

As always, to my family for their support when times got bad.

And Naomi.

PAPUA

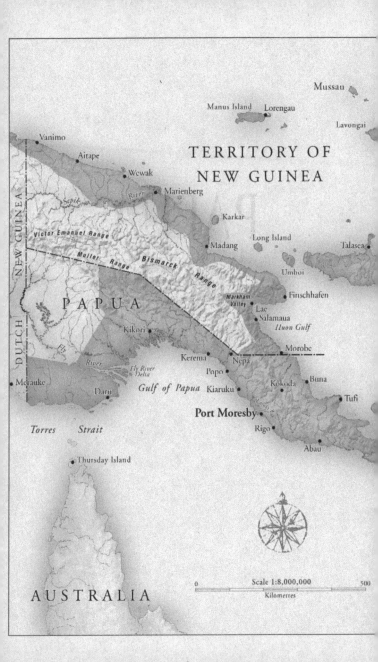

TERRITORY OF
NEW GUINEA
and
PAPUA
circa 1920

Areas in which native population
have been counted or estimated

...ieng
Tabar Islands
Tanga

Namatanai • **New Ireland**
Rabaul

Feni Island

Nissan Island

• Wide Bay

Buka

Buka Passage

New Britain

Bougainville

• Kieta

Buin

Choiseul Island

Solomon

Islands

Yeka Vekalla

Kulambangra

Ysabel

New Georgia

Malaita

Yaugunn

Kiriwina Island
...osuia

Kulumadau

S o l o m o n

Nggela

...gusson Island

Woodlark Island

S e a

... Normanby Island

...ai

Misima Island

Guadalcanal

Adele Island

Tagula Island

C o r a l

S e a

PROLOGUE

A young woman – born in the first year of the twentieth century – stood and gazed as the powerful steam engine hissed and jolted away from her. She knew that it trailed its cargo of grey uniformed men in shabby, overcrowded carriages destined for the carnage of the Western Front. She hardly felt the biting cold flurries of windswept snow around her as the tears streamed down her rosy cheeks. All she could feel was an inconsolable grief as she watched the wan face of the most beloved man in her life fade with distance between them. She could not bear to think that she would never see him again.

Erika Mann stood amongst the small crowd of men, women and children bidding their sons, husbands, fathers and lovers a dreadful farewell. They had tried to be brave and display the stiff upper lip – reputed to their enemies, the British – but the tears of grief had flowed. For in the fourth year of the terrible war none held the optimism of August 1914. This was a war of stalemate bogged down in the stinking mire of barbed wire, trenches, mud and raked by machine guns. This was a war that had at its dark heart the belief that the last man standing was the winner. A war where men used up their enemy's bullets in their bodies and the terrible screaming whistle of an artillery shell randomly fragmented flesh. Erika knew all this and could not believe that her beloved Wolfgang should quit his medical studies to enlist as an infantry officer. Another year and he would have been a doctor. But he had been restless and patriotic despite what he and so many other Germans knew: the war was decimating the youth of a great nation.

The night before he had held her in his arms in the big eiderdown covered bed as she had sobbed after their lovemaking. 'I will be with your brother's regiment,' he had soothed as she desperately clung to him. 'He has survived the war since '14.'

The young officer had attempted to console her and she had wanted to be reassured by his words. She tried to smile bravely for him but the thought of losing his precious body and soul racked her further with sobs. She attempted to sleep, enveloped by the warmth of his love and the thick eiderdown, but watched every tiny shadow in the small room until they were chased away by the pale light of a winter's day outside.

Now she stood and watched the troop train leave Munich in the winter snows of early 1918. When it was gone she turned and walked away. She did not believe in God but she did say a prayer on this occasion just in case she was wrong. Her whispered plea was the same as millions of others being intoned all over Europe and beyond: 'Please bring him home to me.'

The raiding party had set out to avenge the death of Serero's brother. But all had not gone well and the avenging warriors had lost one of their own. Despite the loss of a valued member of the clan, five dark skinned, naked young men squatted around Serero, grinning at his pain.

'It is nothing,' one of the men said as he watched the young warrior tugging the slender wooden arrowhead from his thigh. 'I once had two of the enemy's arrows sticking out of my backside – now that really hurt – but I did not cry when they were pulled out.'

Serero grimaced but did not display discomfort as he yanked the broken bamboo reed shaft protruding from his thigh. The arrowhead emerged, as did a stream of blood to splash the rocks of the mountain stream. He was sweating despite the coolness of the air in the jungle-covered mountains but noticed the newfound respect the older men had for him now reflected in their grim set expressions and head nods.

'It did not hurt,' Serero grunted.

He rose to his feet uncertainly, not sure whether he would be able to walk. The mountain stream had yet to be crossed if they were to keep ahead of their enemies who even now rallied their kinsmen in the rugged mountain valleys looking for payback.

'Stand in the water for a moment,' one of the older warriors said. 'It will help.'

Serero went to protest but the pain of the wound shot through his thigh, almost toppling him. He stepped into the cold mountain stream up to his waist. The water tugged at him but he stood his ground as the rest of his war party waded cautiously across the creek.

Clutching their long bows strung with a sliver of bamboo, the raiding party had crossed and Serero followed them into the great rainforest. Within two days they would reach the village where the women would wail for the loss of a warrior from the clan. But Serero would boast of the two men he had personally killed in the dawn raid on their enemy sleeping in their longhouses. It had been a daring venture and Serero knew that his brother's avenging spirit would be at rest. The story of the raid and the part he played would be told around the cooking fires and his prestige enhanced in its telling.

Serero limped behind his older comrades, beaming with pride for his prowess. A giant butterfly the size of a small bird fluttered in the canopy of the trees above. With any luck they might come across a pig or cassowary on their trek home. To bring such a prize to the village would make the homecoming victory even more sweet. The thought caused the young man to feel less of the pain in his thigh. To be alive in the land of his ancestors on this day was a wondrous thing. His people had a long history of great raids and enemy warriors defeated, going back much further than even the oldest member of the clan could remember.

The young warrior did not count the passage of years as the ancestor spirits did. Had he counted years he would have less than ten before his world was turned upside down forever in the feverish sago swamps of the great Papuan river. That distant day would mark an irreparable rent in the fabric of Paradise and the forests of Eden.

Part One

BARBED WIRE AND JUNGLES

1918–1924

ONE

Major Paul Mann of the Kaiser Alexander Regiment was vaguely aware that the earth no longer shook with the ferocity of a wild animal in its death throes. The terrible onslaught of the British eight-inch shells, that had pummelled his company of helpless and terrified men since five thirty in the morning, was gone from the air around him.

Lying at the bottom of the freshly dug trench, Major Mann could taste blood in his mouth. The big artillery guns behind the British lines had sought targets of human flesh to rip and shred to meaty fragments. He was numb but his whole body shook with the elation of still being alive and untouched by the splinters of searing hot metal that the explosions scattered.

'Major Mann! They are coming!'

The voice sounded as if it had come from another world. A world where he would like to return. A place of happiness and the sweet scents of home. It was the voice of his second in command Captain Wolfgang Betz, the voice of his future brother-in-law, who called to him.

'Sir, they are advancing,' Wolfgang screamed at his shell-deafened commander.

Paul reached out to take his extended hand and scramble to his feet. There was no time to check the state of defences after the heavy artillery barrage. The advancing enemy were already in sight, even though they appeared so small and puny for the moment. But as an experienced soldier of four years on the Western Front, Paul knew many of his younger and less experienced troops would still be stunned into inactivity in the bottom of the trenches, cowered by the awful carnage brought by the barrage. 'Get the men to their posts,' he yelled at his second in command who had already turned his back to move down the line. He too was a veteran of almost a year's trench fighting.

Major Paul Mann studied the advancing troops who moved in scattered groups across the green fields dotted with French farmhouses. The Allies' rapid advances had finally broken the deadlock on the Western Front and forced the German army out of its trenches and back into the relatively unscarred fields around Mont St Quentin. Paul's position forward of the main defences of the Hindenburg Line had been hastily dug and lacked the old, deep fortifications he had known at the Somme. The trench

4

line he commanded had no overhead cover and he knew that some of the shells would have penetrated the soft, early autumn earth to explode, causing cave-ins along the trench line to bury men alive.

Paul also knew that the men advancing on his line of defence were not British or French troops but those of one of Britain's distant former colonies. He would have preferred to face the British. They respected the rules of war. The men advancing on his front had a fearsome reputation as soldiers who asked no quarter and gave none once they engaged in an attack. They were a volunteer army who held the philosophy that if their enemy was prepared to mow them down when they were vulnerable in the open then they had no right to surrender when they had lost. It was not the way of their masters – the British Tommies.

The silence was no more as rifles and machine guns sowed the fields with a deadly crop of metal. Some of the advancing men fell as the bullets ripped through their bodies. Paul Mann felt no pity seeing the young men of another nation fall. He knew that they would not show his men any if they reached his lines. He prayed that the advancing Australian sol-diers' reputation did not affect his men. Germany was fighting for its very survival. Winter was once again coming to Europe and so too were the bitter winter snows to Munich. With the winter would come famine as the British naval blockade had not been broken.

• • •

Captain Jack Kelly also knew acute fear. He was known as one of the 'fair dinkums' by the men he commanded. A soldier who had enlisted after the heavy losses inflicted by the Turkish soldiers on the Australian and New Zealand troops in the Dardenelles at Gallipoli back in 1915, it had taken him some time to travel from the Australian administered territory of Papua where he had lived for some years to enlist in a New South Wales infantry battalion.

Since landing in France he had survived the battles of the Western Front to be promoted through the ranks from private to captain. His natural skills were acknowledged by an army that accepted leadership above authority invested in mere rank alone. Twice wounded, he had been recognised for his courage a year earlier with the Distinguished Conduct Medal and a bar added since then for further courage.

As he now advanced on the German trenches he once again experienced the dread that caused his hands to shake as they gripped the Enfield rifle tipped with a seventeen-inch bayonet. But his fear was more of letting his men down in the attack. This was his first battle as their company commander. His promotion was very recent, the result of his predecessor being killed a month earlier. Until then he had commanded only a platoon. Many of the senior non-commissioned men of the company were mates he had soldiered with as one of their own. His promotion had been popular as he had a reputation for knowing what he was doing in the worst situations.

Jack's colourful past as a gold prospector in the mysterious jungles of British Papua and German New Guinea had honed his abilities to turn things around. Initiative, toughness and a lot of luck had rubbed off onto the men who followed him into hell. He had an easy informal manner that belied his intense reading of tactical situations. He also had an animal instinct for danger that had helped keep the men around him alive. Before the war he had learned to listen to his instincts when living in territory inhabited by warlike tribesmen who sought human heads as trophies to display in the longhouses of their villages.

Jack Kelly stood an inch less than six feet tall and had the build of a finely tuned athlete. His sandy coloured hair had just the faintest first streaks of premature grey. For a man aged twenty-five this was not reassuring. But a consolation was that at least he still had his thick crop of hair, even though he kept it shaved close to his skull to deter the lice ever present on the battlefields. He was not dashingly handsome but had a strong face that inspired a sense of trust in men and willingness on the part of women to engage his company. A woman who met Jack Kelly instinctively knew that his face spoke of an intelligent and mysterious man who could be relied on for protection. But Jack's was also a face that could have an unsettling effect. It was in his hazel eyes – a kind of faraway dreamy look that could suddenly turn cold and dangerous. He was a man who came with no guarantees of being around when the sun rose on a new day.

The German machine guns had been well placed to enfilade the approaches with a deadly crossfire, Jack noted, as he half crouched to check his map. But the Germans had little in the way of barbed wire to disrupt his infantry in the assault. What they did have had been cut in many places by the artillery although its tangles could still snare a man's ankles. It must be a very forward position, he thought as he studied the ground ahead. They would have to be quick to engage the Germans before they could fall back to more fortified positions closing on the Hindenburg Line.

Jack had a great respect for the German soldiers. They were as brave as any and well trained. He even mused that maybe one or two of his mother's family – his cousins – might be in the opposing force. Although his family name was Kelly his mother's maiden name was Schulenburg. She had met his father in the colony of South Australia when she immigrated with her family from a little village on the Rhine to settle amongst the many German expatriates living in that colony. The German immigrants were growing some of the finest wine grapes in the world and had assimilated easily into Australian society with their reputation for hard work, honesty and warm hospitality. Mixed marriages were common and Jack Kelly was the result of Irish Celtic and Teutonic German blood.

Captain Jack Kelly's task was to advance his company on the right flank of the attack. The battalion's CO had decided to attack with all assaulting companies forward but one back in reserve. Jack watched as the forward companies began to take heavy casualties. With a touch of guilt, he was glad it was they and not his own men. But the forward company had gone to ground to return fire as they had rehearsed and he knew it was up to them now.

He raised a whistle to his lips and gave the signal for his platoons to cover the ground with fire and movement as they made the final attack. His lieutenants were to run the battle at their level. He would move with his small company headquarters group at the centre of the attack. They were only three hundred yards out from the line of trenches and Jack could see the face of the enemy.

Major Paul Mann kept his head low. The first line of enemy had gone to ground and were carefully sniping at anything above the level of the parapet. With deadly accuracy an enemy Lewis machine gun had temporarily knocked out the crew of one of his fast firing guns. The crew was quickly replaced and it now became a personal and almost grudging duel between machine gunners.

Paul cursed the new team. They had taken the fire off a company of infantry advancing on his left flank and were coming in fast despite the rifle fire that met them, causing significant casualties in their ranks. If the gun on the left flank did not engage this new company attack then the Australians might break through to within bomb range and their grenades cause havoc in the confinement of his trenches. He looked around desperately for a man to send a message to the gun crew engaged on the flank. But every man was firing desperately into the advancing enemies who were coming on with a terrifying and determined speed. He decided that he would get the message through himself and forced his way up the trench now littered with his dead and dying men. He did not reach the gun crew.

They were running and screaming curses now through a steady rain of spiralling German hand grenades. The tin-like bombs with the long handles could be thrown a greater distance than the dimpled, egg-shaped British Mills bomb before exploding in the ranks of attackers, spraying them with shrapnel.

Jack was screaming with his men as they reached the edge of the trenches. He was hardly aware that shrapnel had torn a long furrow along his arm. As in past attacks he had disassociated himself from his body and experienced nothing other then the blind savagery of a killing machine. Three hundred yards had taken a toll on his men but he had made it to the enemy trenches where the possibility of an impersonal death from bullets and shrapnel was replaced with the very personal form of killing known as hand to hand fighting.

The faces staring up at him were white blurs. Whether they reflected fear or hate was irrelevant as Jack fired point blank into them. Around him the survivors of the attack did the same. Screaming, shouting, grunting, the two forces met as the long bayonets were used to stab through the grey uniforms but the Germans fought back with desperate courage to hold their line.

Major Paul Mann did not see the hand grenade that had landed behind him in the trench. It had been fired from a device fitted to a rifle to further its range. All he remembered was something with the force of a mule knocking him to the ground where he lay in a daze of pain and semi-consciousness. He wanted to go to sleep and wake up under the eiderdown beside Karin in their big double bed, to smell the warmth of her milk white skin and breathe in the sweat of their lovemaking. He wanted to cry for the futility of it all but the tears would not come. He had survived the long years of war despite the odds stacked against him but then his world went black and he knew the war was over for him. He had done his duty to his country as best as he could – only his family might not think that his duty was as important as having him come home alive.

Jack Kelly sensed that the handsome young soldier pointing the Luger pistol at him was an officer. They stood almost toe to toe and stared into each other's eyes. 'Drop it, my friend,' Jack snarled in perfect German.

For a second the younger man seemed startled by his enemy's good grasp of his language, but in the blink of an eye, Jack could see a pride that could get him killed. The young German had hesitated and Jack did not wait for a reply but lunged with the bayonet. His aim was true and the honed point took the German under the rib cage below the sternum. With a savage upward twist Jack caused the maximum amount of internal damage. The young officer attempted to scream but could only gasp in his agony. His eyes rolled and his legs buckled under him as he slid to the ground. The Luger fell from his hand as he died. Jack placed his foot on the chest of his enemy and with all his strength dragged the bayonet from the body without any remorse. Either him or me had always been his philosophy since he had first killed a man with his hands in a trench raid three years earlier.

'Captain Kelly! Jack!' a voice called to him. 'The bastards have packed it in.'

Jack looked down at the dead man at his feet. 'Sorry, Fritz,' he muttered as the still pounding adrenaline surged through his body in waves at the news of the German capitulation in the trenches. 'Just a bit late for you,' he said in German, gazing down at the face of the young officer strangely serene in death.

The voice that had shouted the news down to the trench to him belonged to the company sergeant major, an old friend who had enlisted with him in Sydney, back in 1915. He was an Englishman and had once served with an elite British regiment as an officer but for reasons never spoken of had been forced to resign his commission. He had been in Sydney when the war in Europe broke out and had been in line behind Jack at a recruiting depot when he enlisted with the Australian army. Although he had been offered a commission because of his previous experience he had declined – and continued to decline as the war went on. But he had accepted the position of CSM when it had been offered by Jack who had never raised the issue of why George had resigned his commission. It was a friendship based on a respect for each other's prowess as a soldier. George was an intelligent man who could discuss any subject from Greek drama to geological aspects of mining alluvial gold – the latter a subject near and dear to Jack's heart.

The men of the company accepted the former British officer as their senior NCO because he knew what he was doing. And no one questioned George Spencer's physical courage on the battlefield. He not only wore a DCM riband on his chest but also that of a Military Medal.

George was a tall and slightly stooped man in his late thirties. He had the fine features of an English aristocrat and always seemed to wear an expression of bemusement as if all that occurred around him was nothing more than a bad joke. But now that expression was gone and his face reflected the terror and relief of the past minutes – minutes that had seemed like years to the men who had survived the attack.

He stood in the trench briefing his company commander.

'I've sent a runner to battalion headquarters to report the situation,' he said, wiping his face with the back of a grubby hand. 'We took more prisoners than casualties, Jack,' he added to reassure his friend who had the blank look of a man not comprehending reality. George knew the responsibility of command ultimately balanced the books between how many would die and how much could be achieved in a bat-tle. He did not envy Jack's responsibility for the butcher's bill to be tendered for human lives. 'Looks like you took a hit yourself,' he added. 'I will get someone to look at it.'

'Thanks, George,' Jack replied in a tired voice. 'But I can bind it myself. Didn't even notice it until now so it mustn't be too bad. Definitely not a blighty.'

The strain was showing but had held off until after they had taken their objective. Only Jack's hands shook but he could hide them from an observer. He did not want to bind the wound until his sergeant major was out of sight. To do so now might reveal how badly his nerves were on edge.

'We hold here until the brigade catches up?' George queried. 'Can I tell the men who are not engaged in immediate duties to stand down?'

Jack nodded. 'Give the order to reinforce this trench in case Fritz decides to counter attack,' he said as his world of command came back to him. 'But between you and me, I don't think they will. They seem to be falling back to their main lines. Guess that's where they are going to chew us up as we advance.'

'You realise, old chap,' George said as the look of bemusement began to replace the expression of battle fatigue, 'that the men we fought today are amongst the best regiments the Hun have left. And yet we were able to rout them. That has to say something about German morale at the moment. It may be possible that this war is almost at an end.'

Jack made a feeble attempt at a smile. 'Your British generals have been saying that every year for

14

as long as I can remember. This war is never going to end while their bloody incompetence rules.'

The sergeant major did not reply. Although he had enlisted in the Australian army, the generals Jack disparaged were his by nationality and his loyalty was still primarily to Britain, not to a nation that was only seventeen years old. The mantle of colonialism still hung over the thinking of many in Australia after the Antipodean colonies federated to become a nation but still existed under the British crown.

Along the trench men moaned in their pain and the hostility towards the foe was temporarily put aside to treat those in urgent need of medical attention.

'I will go and check on the boys,' Jack said. 'See how they are bearing up. Tell the platoon commanders I want to see them in twenty minutes for an orders group here.'

'Sir.'

Sergeant Major Spencer also left to carry on with his duties. There was food, water and ammunition to be brought up and the evacuation of wounded and prisoners to the rear to be organised. He snapped at men who were sitting around smoking to go about their duties of fortifying the trench and made mental notes on the condition of the troops still standing. As the company sergeant major his responsibility to the welfare of the men was no less arduous than that of his commanding officer. The onus for keeping the company supplied with the vitals to wage war rested with him. He would talk to the platoon sergeants who would give him their lists of supplies needed to replenish their stocks. Snapping at the men lounging about reasserted his position in the company as their disciplinarian.

Jack made his way down the trench, stepping over the dead and wounded. He was pleased to see that his company was going about its duties as a professional army should. His attention was drawn to one of his men arguing with a badly wounded German officer. The officer was speaking English, but with some difficulty, and lapsed into German to make his point. The soldier tending the wounded man glanced up at Jack when he approached. 'You know what this bugger wants, sir?' he asked.

'He seems to be concerned about someone, Private Casey,' he replied. 'I will talk to him.' The officer was of the rank of major with a finely chiselled face and intelligent eyes. Jack felt a touch of sympathy for the man. The officer seemed to be around his own age and had the handsome appearance of a German aristocrat. Jack could also see that there was more than the pain of his wounds reflected in his eyes. There was also the pain he himself feared most – to lose a fight and lose your men.

'I am Captain Jack Kelly, sir,' Jack said in German. 'How can I help you?'

The officer looked up at him. He seemed surprised. 'I am Major Paul Mann and I must say that you speak German very well.'

'My mother was German,' Jack replied as he squatted beside the wounded officer. 'She couldn't speak very good English so German was my first language when I was growing up.'

Private Casey partly rolled Major Mann onto his side and Jack noticed that the major's back had been shredded by shrapnel although his thick trench coat had helped absorb the shock of the metal fragments. The major did not complain although Jack could see that he was in great pain.

'You are also wounded,' the major said.

Jack shrugged off the observation. 'Nothing to write home about.'

'I would ask a favour, Captain Kelly. There is another officer with me. A captain. Could you tell me if he is still alive?'

'Certainly, Major. What is his name?'

'He is Wolfgang Betz. He is to marry my sister when this is all over.'

Jack glanced around to see a corporal oversighting the reinforcement of the rear edge of the trench. 'Corporal!'

'Sir!'

'Have a look around and see if you can ascertain the whereabouts amongst the prisoners of a Captain Wolfgang Betz. When you find him, send him down here to me.'

'Will do, sir,' the corporal replied.

'Thank you, Captain Kelly,' Paul said. 'I understood what you said to the man.'

'It can only be for a short time, you understand,' Jack cautioned. 'We have to get your lot back behind the lines.'

The major nodded. 'Were you the officer who

17

commanded the attack against us?' he asked.

Jack hesitated. This was a question of tactics but he broke the rule when he realised that the question was asked at a personal level, as if they were two prizefighters introducing themselves in the ring. 'On your section I was the officer who led the attack.'

'I must congratulate you on your professionalism, Captain Kelly. I have survived this war since 1914. I thought I might just make it to the end.'

'You will,' Jack said with the hint of a smile. 'They will probably send you to England to an officer's camp as a prisoner of war. At least you are out of it now.'

'You are not English?'

'No, I'm an Australian, but I wonder about that as home for me has been up north in Papua for the last few years.'

At the mention of Papua the major gripped Jack's hand. 'I was at Finschhafen before the war. I have a copra plantation there although my original home is in Munich.'

'I'll be damned!' Jack uttered in English then switched to German. 'It's a small world, Major.'

Paul released his grip and his face twisted into a grimace of a smile. The pain was bad. 'I wish we were still there, my friend,' he sighed. 'I loved the tropics more than Munich itself and so did my wife. We returned to Germany for the birth of my first child and we have not been back since. The plantation was being managed by one of my men until you Australians landed in New Guinea and seized our properties.'

'My wife chose to stay home in Adelaide when I returned north to find gold after we married,' Jack said, tactfully changing the subject.

Paul's expression suddenly took on a look of recognition. 'You would not be the same Jack Kelly who our police caught in Kaiser Willemsland back in '12 would you?'

Jack's face broke into a broad grin. 'Yeah, that would be me. If I remember rightly your Governor Hahl wasn't very impressed at the time. Tried to tell him his boundaries were in the wrong place and that we were in Papua and not the territory belonging to Germany.'

'I heard about the incident from the boys working on my plantation. They said that the Governor went easy on you because of your German blood.'

'Could have locked us all up but he was a good sport about it. Anyway, that was in a different lifetime when I was pretty young.'

'Are you going back to Papua when the war is over?' Paul asked.

Jack had not thought about Papua for a long time. 'I hope so,' he said quietly and with some hesitation. 'All I have to do is convince my wife to come with me this time but that is going to be hard as we now have a son. He was born while I was away.'

Paul could see the pain in his enemy's face and felt sympathy for the man. 'You have never seen your son,' he said. 'That must be a terrible thing to bear. I have been more fortunate. I once had leave at home in Munich where I was able to see my family again.

But that was a year ago and I worry for them. Things are bad in Germany now.'

'You will see them again,' Jack said. 'My sergeant major tells me the war will be over soon.'

Paul looked away and forced back the tears. The man was not unlike himself, although a man hours before he had been sworn to kill. None of what was happening made any sense. All that mattered now was surviving this hell and going home. 'I hope you make it, Captain Kelly,' he said. 'And I hope we meet again one day.'

Two soldiers appeared with a stretcher and the major was placed on it gently at Jack's bidding. 'When we find Captain Betz I will tell him that you are going to be fine,' he said in parting. But the look of sadness in the major's face reflected that he had already concluded the young man who was to be his future brother-in-law was dead. Jack watched as the stretcher bearers hoisted the wounded man over the trench and off to a hospital enroute as a prisoner of war to England.

The corporal returned to report his findings. 'Found a dead Fritz by the name of Wolfgang Betz down the trench a bit, sir. Had these papers on him,' he said, thrusting a pile of letters into Jack's hand. 'Looks as if one of our boys gave him a touch of steel.'

'Did he have a Luger on him?' Jack asked with a sudden realisation that it might have been he who bayoneted the dead officer.

'No Luger, sir,' the corporal answered in a flat voice. 'He had a Mauser rifle in his hands.' Jack felt an unexpected sense of relief. Of all the men he had personally killed in the war this was one that he was not meant to. 'Thanks, corporal,' he said as the NCO moved away from his company commander.

The corporal had good reason to depart quickly. The Luger concealed under his trench coat was a valuable souvenir and he was not about to hand it over to anyone else.

Jack turned the pile of letters grubby from the dirt of the war over in his hands. All had been written in the same neat hand, he noticed, presuming rightly that they were from the dead German's fiancée – the sister of Major Mann. But Jack had many tasks, including a briefing to his platoon commanders for their next set of objectives, so without much thought he thrust the letters into his pocket. The war was far from over and he had yet to get himself and his men home alive.

TWO

His name was Lukas and he was four years old but to Jack his son was almost a total stranger. They sat opposite each other as the rail carriage bumped and jolted into Sydney, the acrid smell of coal soot filling the compartment.

'Next stop Strathfield,' a bored voice cried down the passageway. Jack stood and reached to the rack above to retrieve his old army duffel bag. 'We get off here, son,' he said gently to the little boy, who was watching his every move with continuing trepidation. 'Your Aunt Mary and Uncle Harry will finally get to meet you.'

Lukas slid from the seat and stood silently awaiting the next instruction. Jack placed a hand on his son's shoulder to steady him as the powerful steam engine hissed its protest at being restrained. The carriage jerked violently as the brakes were applied and faces flashed past the window as the train slowed to a stop. The platform was temporarily covered in a billow of smoke and steam.

Jack held the boy steady until he was sure the carriage would not move again and felt his heart breaking. In the three days of travelling by train from Adelaide to Sydney via Melbourne his son had said little to him. The concept of a father was not something he could comprehend. The people who took care of him after his mother went away to heaven said that his father was coming to fetch him. And suddenly enough the frightening stranger had come into his life to take him away from the home that he had known with his mother, that beautiful, soft creature who had made him feel warm and wanted.

But one day she got sick. She coughed a lot and lay in her bed muttering strange things. The neighbours came and Mrs Roth arrived wearing a mask over her face. With her was a man who was called a doctor. Their murmured voices told him that something was terribly wrong. His mother seemed to be asleep and they ushered him out of the room. Something called the flu had made his mother go to sleep and then go away to heaven, they told him. It was confusing because Mrs Roth said that his father would be home soon but that she would look after Lukas until he arrived.

Now he was in the company of this frighteningly big man who spoke gently to him but was a stranger all the same. Lukas felt a numbness in his life and cried when he tried to go to sleep. He wanted his mother back but the big man said that she was somewhere he could not see her. Now they were in a place of other strangers and the world he once knew was gone forever.

'Jack!' Mary screamed in her delight at seeing her long lost little brother step from the train. She rushed forward and enveloped him with a hug fit to crush a response from a man. Jack accepted the assault as something a sister was entitled to inflict on him. He had last seen her the day he set off for the war in Europe. It was now summer of 1919 and he had not seen Sydney for almost four years.

Mary was now in her late thirties. Tall and serene, she had a pleasant face that seemed never to age. Her husband Harry grinned broadly from behind her as he thrust out his hand, welcoming home his brother-in-law. 'Who is this young fella who looks just like you, Jack?' he said merrily when handshakes had been exchanged.

'That, Harry,' Jack replied, 'is Master Lukas Kelly.' Harry Nesbitt extended his hand to Lukas who stood wide-eyed beside his father. The boy was hesitant but accepted the grasp.

'What he needs is a great big hug – not a handshake,' Mary chided as she scooped Lukas up in her arms. He did not resist and even experienced a faint, warm memory from the embrace. He liked this new stranger and felt safe in her presence. 'I am your Aunt Mary,' she said and suddenly plopped a wet kiss on his cheek which Lukas instinctively wiped at with an exclamation of disgust. Then he did something Jack had not seen the boy do before. He smiled. The tough former soldier who had survived the carnage of the war in Europe quickly looked away lest anyone see the tear that had come to his eye.

'C'mon, Harry,' said Mary. 'Help Jack with his bag and we'll go home to a big roast lamb dinner.'

Harry Nesbitt attempted to grab the duffel bag but Jack slung it over his shoulder. The four made their way to the exit, Lukas remaining by his aunt's side. It appeared that she was not about to let her nephew go.

'I got the news as soon as I disembarked in Adelaide,' Jack said as the three sat at the table after the promised dinner had been consumed. 'I survive a bloody war and Annie dies from the flu only weeks before I get home.'

Mary could see that the beer accompanying the meal had loosened much emotion in her brother. She knew his moods well. Growing up, she had cared for him in lieu of their mother who was often bedridden with recurring illnesses.

'It was a terrible time,' Harry said. 'So many dead from the outbreak. We have never seen anything like it. But we are well and it seems the epidemic has run its course.'

'When was Annie's funeral?' Mary asked.

'Six weeks before I got home. A Mrs Roth looked after Lukas, a nice enough woman. Annie had told her I was coming home so she knew to expect me.'

'You look worn out, Jack,' Mary observed. 'You ought to get a good night's sleep.'

Jack nodded. He wasn't all that sleepy but he did want to be alone to reflect on the future. He excused himself and Mary showed him to his room. She gave her brother a short hug and closed the door behind him.

Jack sat on the edge of the bed and removed his boots, looking around the room. The house was a dark red brick building in a neat tree-lined street. Harry had done well out of the war, providing printed documents for the armed forces. He had tried to enlist when the war broke out but was excluded because he owned a small print shop deemed important to the war effort. He and Mary had been married for twelve years but despite their efforts, Mary remained childless. From the way she took to mothering his son Jack could see that his sister was a woman who should have had children.

The boots fell to the floor and Jack sank back against the bed with its soft eiderdown cover. He stared at the ceiling. He was now a widower with a son who may as well have been a stranger. He had no profession other than that of a gold prospector and his future was unknown. He thought about Annie and felt the guilt of a man who has lost a woman he knew he would have returned to as a stranger. Too many years had passed between them with his service overseas. When it came down to it he had to admit he had not really loved his wife. They had married when she discovered she was pregnant. A country girl from a small town outside Adelaide, they had little in common other than the unexpected arrival of a child. But Jack had done the right thing to appease her family. It was a common enough story. He had come home from Papua to attend his beloved mother's funeral and met Annie at the wake. A short and passionate swirl of events led to a night in the woolshed. Love promised cheaply for the sake of her body and the unappreciated responsibility that followed. But then he had left his pregnant bride immediately after their honeymoon in Adelaide and returned to Papua. When war broke out he enlisted in Sydney and was shipped out immediately. The news that he was a father reached him in France.

Jack sat up and reached for his duffel bag beside the bed. Old army habits died hard and his immediate personal property was always near at hand. He rummaged through the bag until he found the pile of letters. They still had the stains of war. He undid the ribbon that bound them and searched for the small photograph. She caught his eye as she always did. Hers was a noble face with high cheekbones and a thick mass of dark hair tied back and accentuating her deep and enigmatic eyes. 'Erika,' he said as he stared at the photo of the woman who had written the passionate letters to her lover. 'I wonder what you are doing right now.'

Erika Mann was the sister of the German major Jack had met on the Western Front only weeks before the war finally ended. In the turmoil of organising his company for a further advance Jack had forgotten to hand over the letters to the intelligence section. He had later read them out of curiosity and the beauty of the young German woman's words had entranced him. Having decided

27

that the letters had no significance to military matters, he kept them.

At the time he had wondered more about the young German woman than he had about his own wife. Even now he felt the guilt return. Annie was dead but their son remained in his life as a reminder. She was in the little boy's eyes – and in his sad smile. He wanted to love his son, as he knew she had, but for now they were still strangers.

He carefully placed the photograph inside a letter and returned them to the duffel bag.

That night Harry and Mary woke in the early hours of the morning to the sound of Jack's whimpering and his shouted commands to soldiers long dead. But Jack was hardly aware of the commotion. He was in a sleep filled with nightmares of exploding shells and men screaming as they died in a sea of blood.

Neither Harry nor Mary made mention of Jack's disturbing behaviour during the night. They had heard stories from friends of men who had served on the front acting that way in their sleep. Shell-shock, some called it. Mary hoped that Jack's nightmares would fade with time and the happy young brother she remembered from their childhood would return. What she saw now was a man haunted by his immediate past. It was as if he fought to control his very body at times. His hands sometimes shook and he often seemed to be teetering on the edge of an explosion.

'What do you have planned for today, Jack?' Mary asked as she spread jam on bread for Lukas, who was sitting quietly beside her at the kitchen table. He seemed to be avoiding his father who had terrified him one night on the train trip when he started yelling when he looked as if he were asleep. He'd been yelling things about 'fix bayonets' and warning invisible people to 'look out for the bombs'.

'I had planned to see some of the blokes in town,' he replied, sipping a cup of tea. 'You think you could look after Lukas for me?'

'It would be my pleasure,' she said, placing her hand on the boy's shoulder. 'Give us a chance to do things around the house together.'

Jack glanced up at his sister. 'I think he would like that,' he said. 'I think a woman's company is what he needs right now considering everything that has happened.'

'Don't you worry about a thing, Jack,' Mary said with a wan smile. 'Just want to know if you will be home for dinner with us.'

'I don't know. Depends on how things go with the boys.'

He finished the tea and excused himself. The short walk to the train station and the trip to Central in Sydney gave Jack more time to think about the future. George Spencer had elected to return with the battalion to Sydney and he had kept in touch with his commanding officer, agreeing to meet in Sydney after they were demobilised.

. . .

29

The hotel was crowded. Men in uniform jostled with young men in smart suits. It was lunchtime and the weather warm outside. Jack found the tall Englishman easily enough. He stood aloof in a corner of the bar holding a large cold beer in his hand. George looked different in his smart suit and Jack felt just a little shabby in his working man's open-necked shirt and baggy trousers. They were his from pre-war days and he was relieved the moths hadn't got to them.

'George, you old bastard,' Jack greeted his friend. 'Good to see you again.'

George Spencer offered out his free hand and the two men shook enthusiastically.

'I'll get you a beer. Here, hold mine and make sure some son of a convict does not purloin it.'

Jack grinned and took the beer. The others in the bar were strangers. As a South Australian he could not talk football to those around him. They followed the English code of rugby whereas he was a former Australian Rules football player. His only real links in this city – other than his sister – were with a handful of men he had served with. George returned and both men raised their glasses in a mutual toast.

'The old battalion.'

For the first hour they exchanged as much news as they could on the whereabouts of the men of the battalion since their arrival home. It was a conversation many around them were having, as the scars of war were not yet a year old. Jack also talked about his son and how he seemed to be settling down in the care of his sister. It was not normally a subject he would discuss but George was a man with whom he had shared three traumatic years of his life.

'When are you going back to Papua?' George asked across the top of his fourth glass.

'Don't know if I can,' Jack reflected. 'I have responsibilities now and my brother-in-law has offered me a job at his printing business. Besides, I'm broke. Not enough to put together the gear I need to go prospecting again.'

George gazed across Jack's head at the open door. Outside the sun shone with the pale but warm blueness that the Englishman had come to appreciate. 'You are not the kind of man who would be happy working in a factory for the rest of his life,' he said, as if speaking to the sunlight outside. 'You would come to resent your son for tying you down to a life that you are not suited to.'

Jack wanted to protest his friend's observation but knew that he spoke the truth. 'I just can't dump my boy on my sister,' he said. 'It wouldn't be right. The boy and I are meant to be together.'

George looked back at Jack. 'Might he not be better off with your sister?' he asked gently. 'From what you have told me the boy is missing a woman's touch this early in his life.'

Jack thought about the Englishman's statement. What he said made sense. Given the chance to return to Papua he might find enough gold to set himself and his son up for life.

'He is. But why are you so keen on me heading north?'

George frowned at Jack's question. 'Because I want to go with you.'

'To Papua! Why in hell would you want to go to somewhere like Papua after surviving the last few years? It's no tropical paradise. It's a place of malaria, swamps, crocs and blackfellas who would just as much eat you as take your head for a trophy.'

'Ah, dear chap,' George sighed. 'The answer to that is somewhat complex. But it has its roots in a little boy who once read a book written by a Frenchman almost a half century ago. I vividly remember the title: *Adventures in New Guinea: The Narrative of Louis Tregance, a French Sailor. Nine Years in Captivity Among the Orangwoks, a Tribe in the Interior of New Guinea.* That little boy would sit in his father's library and devour every word of the book and pore over the illustrations. And when he survived the trenches he swore that he would go in search of the Orangwoks.'

'That sounds like a simple explanation to me,' Jack grinned, 'except I have heard of the mad Frog's book and it was a total fabrication. His stories of natives riding around on horses and having shields made of solid gold sounds more like *Gulliver's Travels*. There's no bloody Orangwoks in the interior. Nothing but uninhabited mountains and jungle.'

'That may it be,' George conceded, 'but the fact remains that no one knows to this day what *is* in the interior. It's still totally unexplored when even Africa has been mapped.'

'There has to be more reason for putting your life on the line than a whim to go dashing off in search of fictional lost tribes.' Jack took a long swig from his glass. 'It all costs money and I can think of better things to spend it on.'

'In '15 we signed up to go on what we thought was some romantic adventure,' George said. 'Was what we did back then any less romantic?'

'A good point. But we were fighting for the Empire. There was more to what we did than just the adventure.'

'It was not the Empire for you, Jack,' George said quietly. 'You, a German mother and Irish father, fighting for the King. No, you are a man who must seek what is beyond the horizon. The war gave you a chance to travel at the King's expense.'

'Gold is what I seek,' Jack answered. 'And all that it can buy. Not some romantic idealism about the horizon.'

'I will make you an offer here and now,' George said. 'I will pay all expenses to get us to Papua and outfit us for gold prospecting if you will come with me.'

'Why ask me?' Jack questioned. 'I am pretty sure that you could go in search of your Orangwoks without me.'

'Because, old chap, you are the most capable man I have ever known,' George said, fixing Jack with a stare that was so intense it was almost unsettling. 'I have to find the Orangwoks for private reasons concerning my family. For reasons I would rather not talk about in this place – and at this time.'

Jack couldn't question his former company sergeant major's reasons. He knew that all Englishmen were mad. Something in their nature made them want to go to places no sane person would seek out. But it was the same nature that had provided the tiny island nation with one of the greatest empires in history. Mad or not, the offer was generous – and Jack Kelly admired generous men. 'I will think it over,' he replied as he finished his beer. But he had already made up his mind.

The Burns Philp coastal trader was steaming from Sydney to Port Moresby the following week. Jack stood on the wharf with his duffel bag at his feet. It was an awkward moment. Mary was trying not to cry although Jack cynically suspected that her tears would be more of joy than sadness to see him go. Little Lukas stood solemn faced, holding her hand. She had jumped at the opportunity to mind her nephew whilst his father went away.

'He will be looked after as if I were his real mum,' she had reassured Jack who did not doubt her words. Even in the week that he and George waited for the trader to arrive, Lukas had not drawn any closer to his father. They remained virtual strangers and the lack of closeness hurt Jack. He felt so clumsy around his own son. But Mary at least had a rapport with the boy. And leaving Lukas with her helped fill a void in his beloved sister's life. It was not that he was giving him away as much as leaving him in the best care possible.

'Give your father a kiss, Lukas,' Mary said gently.

Jack bent to receive the brief brush against his cheek. Impulsively he grasped his son and hugged him fiercely. 'I love you, son,' he said.

'Well, that's about it, old girl,' Jack said as he straightened. 'Got to join George aboard.'

Mary hugged her brother. This time the tears were for him. 'You be careful, Jack,' she said with a sudden fierceness. 'You always seem to be getting yourself into bad situations.'

'You know me,' Jack grinned. 'Got all my bad ways from Dad.'

Mary stepped back and watched as her brother once again swung the duffel bag over his shoulder and walked away with the step of a man very sure of himself. He was in some ways like Dad, she thought sadly. But at least he was not a drunk.

Jack made his way up the gangplank without looking back. To do so would remind him that the two people he most loved in the world stood on the wharf watching him go. Before him lay the jungles, malaria, hostile natives and the adventure of Papua. Behind him a war, a son and little else. With him was a pile of old letters and a photo of a woman he felt he had fallen in love with, although he had no chance of ever meeting her.

THREE

Hunched against the bitter autumn winds and wearing his old great coat, Major Paul Mann trudged the street he had known so well before the war. What he had feared had come to Germany in her defeat: the famine worsened and with the flurries of the first sleeting rain pestilence had come for his first born. Paul's daughter had died from the terrible influenza pandemic that had swept the world and killed more people in a few weeks than all the soldiers killed in years of war. Theda had only been six years old when death came for her with its high fevers, aches and terrible coughing fits. Paul had received the news through the services of the Red Cross whilst he was still a prisoner of the British in England.

So much had changed in his twenty-eight years of life. The Kaiser and his royal retinue were gone, fled to neutral Holland for safety. The days of family gatherings in his house, which once wafted with the rich aroma of roast stuffed goose, were just a memory. Such thoughts came to him as he made his way to the butcher shop. He was fortunate as his family still had some money, although its value had dramatically decreased with the rampant inflation.

His return from the English prisoner of war camp had been delayed by his visits to the hospital to remove the scraps of iron from the grenade blast. But the British had been humane and he could not complain about the treatment he received at their hands. When he returned to his home in Munich he was met by a family that rejoiced at his survival. To have lived was all his wife Karin had ever wanted – although he was a stranger to his five-year-old son Karl.

Only his sister Erika seemed to resent his survival. Young and beautiful, she harboured, he suspected, a resentment that the Gods of War had not taken his life in lieu of that of her beloved Wolfgang. But her reception was cordial enough. She lived under his roof and respected him as the provider for the family.

When he reached the butcher shop he was not surprised to see that it was closed. A notice in the window read that it would open when a supply of meat came in. That could be never, Paul thought bitterly. The British Royal Navy's blockade of German ports well after the Armistice had guaranteed that. It was rumoured that over half a million civilians had died of starvation as a result of the barbaric blockade. How could he provide for his family? His thoughts turned to a world where the sun was warm and food was plentiful. It was a world of tropical palm trees and a gentle sea breeze wafting off the straits of the Huon Gulf. For just a moment he was back in New Guinea on the family copra plantation and all was well. Christmas there was still the traditional fare of roasts but after the great feast he sat on the verandah, with his shirt sleeves rolled up, while Karin played with the native children amongst the sweet smelling frangipani flowers. But the reality around him now was the silent unsmiling expressions of returned soldiers with pinched faces and gaunt expressions. Of women and children who stared with accusing eyes at the men who had lost the war and brought misery to a once proud nation.

In the distance he could hear a different sound. It was the noise of a crowd rowdy in its expectation of something to come. Paul thought about returning home empty-handed but was curious as to what might be causing such a commotion. Shrugging his shoulders he trudged towards the intersection of the street where a large crowd of men had gathered. It was obviously a political meeting of one kind or another. Such gatherings had become common events on the streets of Munich. Men in their desperate circumstances were attracted to those who might provide the magical answer to their despair at seeing their families starve.

Although Paul had been imprisoned in England at the end of the war he had heard of the Spartacus revolt. It had been an indication of just how much Germany had changed from its days of imperial glory before the war. So named after the revolt by a slave of the Romans, the communists had raised the red flag on the steps of the royal palace. They had dreamed of a socialist state for Germany like that which existed in the new Soviet Union. Weakened by bickering opposing factions from within and right wing opposition from without, the movement had not seized power and ever since the streets had seen violent and bloody clashes.

And along Germany's eastern borders a war continued against the Red Army's aggressive push to seize German territory. Peace had not come to his country with the signing of the Armistice. Just more war, civil unrest and famine while power-hungry men bickered over idealisms to suit their own means of controlling the people. Now it was a time of German killing German. The Bolshevics had been most vocal as they harangued the crowds with promises of a new workers' world underpinned by the equality of mankind. Paul had little faith in their ambitions after speaking to returning German soldiers who had been prisoners in Russia. They told tales that all was not well in Russia under the new order there and that the Allies were currently fighting on that front against the Red Army. It did not take a military man to work out that his former enemies – the British, French and Americans – feared the new force as much as they had feared Germany. For the Allies to commit troops to the Russian front put credence to that fear.

As he approached the crowd he heard his name called. 'Major Mann!'

Paul glanced around the faces in the crowd and vaguely recognised a face from his past. The former soldier stepped forward and saluted.

'We are not in the army anymore, soldier,' Paul said gently, without returning the salute. 'But it is good to see a familiar face. Sadly I regret to say I cannot remember where I know you from.'

'You would not remember me, sir,' the man said.

Paul noticed that the young man was standing with the support of a walking cane. The former soldier was in his early twenties but war had stripped the youth from his rather handsome face. He stared at Paul with the eyes of an old man. 'I was wounded only a few days after I joined your company. Then I was captured by the Tommies and got sent back and ended in a prisoner of war camp at Traunstein. I am Private Gerhardt Stahl.'

'I must apologise for not recognising you,' Paul said. 'You were wounded in the leg?'

'Almost lost it,' the private replied with a grimace. 'The war took a lot more than part of my body though. The damned Allies are crippling Germany as surely as if they had put us all in their prison camps.'

Paul had to agree with the former soldier's opinion. The blame for the war was placed solely on the German people although Paul had long come to the realisation that the war had been the result of family ambitions amongst Europe's royalty. It was they who should have answered to the world for their raw and bloody ambitions for power. He was not unhappy to see that the Kaiser was gone from Germany.

'Ah, but I should introduce you to a remarkable man I was fortunate to meet here in Munich,' Gehardt continued. 'He is one of the speakers at the meeting today for the German Workers' Party.' He turned and beckoned to a man whom Paul guessed was in his late twenties or early thirties. The stranger was of average height and sauntered over to join them. Although the man who joined them wore civilian clothing Paul noticed that he was wearing the high decoration of the Iron Cross First Class.

'This is the officer who I had the honour of serving with when I was wounded,' Gerhardt said to the former soldier who joined them.

'I have heard of you through my comrade in arms,' the man said, without any introduction and somewhat coldly. 'It was fortunate that you survived the war. We are going to need every able-bodied man to build this country back to the greatness it once knew before we were sold out to the enemy.'

Paul stared into the man's eyes and saw the utter conviction in his words. 'You actually think that we can survive this winter coming to us?' he asked.

The former soldier answered without blinking. 'Yes – it will be hard but we will survive.'

The crowd around them stirred and Paul could see that the first speaker was about to address the crowd. There were few women or children, the listeners were mostly former soldiers.

'I must excuse myself,' the man said. 'I am to speak next.'

'Of course,' Paul answered. Alone with Gerhardt, he asked, 'You think that this collection of party

41

people have any of the answers to our problems?'

'I believe that if we do not counter the Bolshevics now then they will take control as they did in Russia. I believe that the German Workers' Party is the best means we have of getting the masses of unemployed back to work without a dictatorship like that existing in Russia. Yes, if we gain enough support from the people we will fight our way back to recovery.'

Paul listened to the words so passionately delivered by his former soldier. It warmed him to see that the courage and tenacity of the battlefield was still alive in the men that the Allies thought they had crushed. 'Not that we have much to offer,' he said, 'but if you and your friend would like to visit me and my family after the meeting I can give you both a hot cup of real coffee. No doubt your friend's inspirational words will be just what we need to keep us warm this winter, but a coffee may help too.'

Gerhardt seemed oblivious to Paul's lighthearted statement and accepted the offer. For Paul it was a matter of honour to provide hospitality to one of his former soldiers, as that was the role of the man who once held their lives in his hands. He did not remain to hear the speeches. Politics had never been an interest to him. It had been, after all, blustering politicians who had put Germany where it was today.

That evening Gerhardt and his companion arrived on the doorstep of Paul's house. His sister Erika answered the door and introduced herself to the two men. 'Paul, we have guests,' she announced, ushering the two men inside.

Gerhardt's companion eyed the young woman as he shook off the cold.

'You are very beautiful, Fraulein,' he said. 'A true daughter of Germany.'

'I notice from your accent that you are Austrian,' Erika countered, blushing under the intense gaze of the man. 'Would I be right?'

'I was born at Braunau-am-Inn. Do you know the town?' he asked.

'It is just on the border,' Erika replied. 'We once visited when I was a little girl.'

'Gerhardt,' Paul said, interrupting, 'would you like to join us for dinner?'

Gerhardt ducked his head. He felt guilty at wanting to accept but suspected from the relatively opulent appearance of the house that his former officer could afford such an invitation. 'I would be honoured, sir . . . if that is acceptable to your wife?'

'My wife is preparing some cold sausage and bread. And we have coffee made from real beans, courtesy of my days in New Guinea. But I must confess that in the events of the day I did not get your friend's name.'

'That is my mistake, Major Mann,' Gerhardt replied apologetically. 'Sir, I would like to introduce my friend Herr Adolf Hitler. He was a corporal with the 16th Bavarian Reserve Infantry Regiment. He was gassed at the Ypres salient and was in hospital when the war ended.'

'Well, Herr Hitler, you are welcome in my home,' Paul said, thrusting out his hand.

'Thank you, Major Mann,' Hitler said, accepting the handshake. 'I will not forget your hospitality.'

That evening the three men sat around the dining room table discussing politics. It bored Paul. Their ideas seemed too idealistic. What people really wanted was food and jobs – not a vague ideal of a new Germany.

'Adolf recruited me to the party,' Gerhardt said. 'He is quite a speaker and a man of many talents.'

'I gather that,' Paul replied politely as Hitler sipped on the rich coffee laced with the little cream that Paul had been able to scrounge on the black market. 'It is not often the Iron Cross First Class is awarded to a non-commissioned officer.'

'Adolf is also a man of culture,' Gerhardt added with a note of pride. 'He was an artist of some renown before the war.'

'You paint?' Paul asked, and Hitler's face clouded.

'I was able to pay my way as an artist,' he replied. 'But I was denied the opportunity to enter the Vienna Academy by men who would stifle creativity.'

Paul did not pursue the subject. He could see that it touched a raw nerve.

Karin had said little during the evening and withdrew early to the bedroom with Karl. The boy still slept in their bed although this annoyed Paul, who thought he was too old for such things. But Karin, despite her joy at his return, had been strangely distant with him. The death of their daughter had somehow put a ghost between them. It was as if Paul was being accused of not being with her when he was needed most. He hoped that time would return what they had together before the war.

Although Paul would have preferred his sister to stay out of their political discussion she made it plain that she would not be deterred. In fact she seemed to be drawn to Hitler's words. Paul, however, found his rhetoric on what was wrong in Germany rather puerile, the ideas of a man who had a terrible need to lay blame on others. What would an Austrian know of the German soul, he thought as he watched his sister engage in lively discussion with Gerhardt's companion. Clearly his sister was attracted to Hitler and his ideas. The hate Erika had for the enemy had boiled to a head and she spoke of her fiancé's death as a martyr.

The night wore on and Paul was pleased to finally see the end of the two men, though Erika was less so. 'Herr Hitler has invited me to attend one of his talks,' she said to her brother. 'I think he has a great future.'

'Go to any street corner,' Paul grumbled, 'and you will hear a thousand disillusioned men like him talking.'

'But Herr Hitler is not a disillusioned man,' Erika responded with a fire in her eyes that Paul had not seen since his return from the war. 'He is a man who knows the future and I also know that if my Wolfgang had survived he would agree with me that we were betrayed by the traitors who profited from our sacrifice.'

'We lost because we were beaten on the battlefield,' Paul responded. 'When the Americans came into the war it was only a matter of when we would have to capitulate. We had fought a war on two fronts and that is too much to ask any country.'

Erika glared at her brother and stomped away. What did he know about the traitors at home when he had been away fighting?

Paul felt his spirits slump. He had never been close to his sister. Their father had spoilt her and she was too aware of her own beauty. Strong willed, she would not bide others' opinions. With a sad sigh he made his way up the stairs to the bedroom.

Karin was already in bed and so too was young Karl. Paul undressed and slid between the sheets. His wife stirred when he placed his hand on her hip.

'Are you asleep?' he whispered in her ear.

'No,' she replied, with just a touch of irritableness.

'Erika seems to be taken by Herr Hitler,' he said. But his wife did not reply. He had been home many weeks but they had not made love. And now her coyness seemed to be turning to resentment. The damned war had destroyed more than bodies and minds. It had destroyed the very thing that they had clung to in the hell of shrapnel and bullets. It had destroyed the memory of a time when all was right between a man and a woman. Was it to be like the ancient Greek warriors who were warned by their women to either come home victorious with their shields above their heads – or come home in defeat lying dead on those same shields?

'Are you like my sister who blames me for losing the war?' he snapped suddenly, without regard for his son sleeping beside his mother. Startled, Karin pulled herself up to the pillows and stared at him with wide eyes.

'I do not blame you because we lost the war,' she said. 'I care only that I have you beside me.'

Paul was taken by her passionate response and was at a loss for words. 'I prayed every day that the war would end and you would come back to me,' she continued. 'I did not care who won so long as we had peace back in our lives.'

'I thought that you detested me,' he said with a lump in his throat. 'I thought that is why we have not made love since I returned.'

Karin placed her hand on his cheek and he looked up into her face. Her pale skin, deep blue eyes and flaxen hair spread across the pillows were memories he had carried in the worst of times between the killing. 'I love you, my husband, with all my body and soul,' she said gently. He felt the warmth of her hand on his skin. 'It is just that . . .' her words tapered away and he could see tears welling in her beautiful eyes.

It was something that he knew he did not understand. Something that only women in all their complexity struggled with. But instinctively he knew that he should be patient. To know that she did not resent him as his own sister did was enough for now. He reached out for her and she moved into his arms. Her tears wet his chest as she sobbed. He rocked her as she clung to him and soothed her pain with gentle words. Karl had not stirred beside them. Paul continued to hold his wife to him until she finally drifted into sleep.

Something remained between them that would have to be rediscovered. He wanted them to have what they had known in far off New Guinea – the laughter and lovemaking in God's last paradise on earth. Germany was in ruins, as was his own life. No work, their money rapidly disappearing with the terrible inflation and men like Hitler viewed by his sister as representing the future of a new Germany. It was up to him to do something to change their lives.

FOUR

The high-pitched wailing of the women and incessant barking of the scurvy dogs irritated the bearded giant. He stood at the edge of the thatched huts built on log bases above the ground, an imposing figure amidst the smaller tribesmen whose village was just on the border of the Central District of Papua. Tim O'Leary stood well over six feet tall and had the powerful shoulders of his Irish warrior ancestors.

'Seems they knew we were coming,' he growled to his smaller companion. 'Looks like we are going to have to use a bit of persuasion to sign up the young bucks.'

The European who stood beside him with his rifle over his shoulder was of swarthy appearance. This was a legacy of his Corsican heritage on an island which had known the invasion of the dark-skinned North Africans in centuries past. Pierre was a French citizen and like the Irish born recruiter of native labour, he was in his late thirties and had lived an equally disreputable life. Both men were at home in their jobs of securing native labourers for the ceaseless demands of plantation and mining operations in the now Australian administered territories of Papua and New Guinea.

O'Leary had left his large family in Ireland just after the turn of the century to run away to sea. A cargo tramp ship had deposited him on the shores of German New Guinea after an altercation with another member of the crew. The young O'Leary had been caught stealing aboard the ship. The end result was that the other man had sustained permanent injuries, crippling him for life. Only the benevolence of the ship's captain had saved O'Leary from the wrath of the other crew members. The captain took into consideration the young man's age and dumped him at a German coastal village in New Guinea. Here he was befriended by a sympathetic government man who sent him to a Chinese recruiter of native labour by the name of Kwong Yu Sen. Sen gave the young Irishman a job recruiting labourers for the German planters, and Tim O'Leary had proved to be brutally efficient at the task. Those natives not compliant with his demands to accompany him back to the coast were more often or not shot, which cowered the living into submission.

His reputation for violence had preceded him through the villages of German New Guinea before the war. But now he was working in post war Papua where the administration of Sir Hubert Murray, under pressure from the missionaries, did not tolerate such brutality. But O'Leary had a knack of finding isolated places beyond missionary influence to recruit his labourers, and had not changed his brutal methods despite the new laws governing native labour in Papua.

Now, with a wary eye on the villagers, the two Europeans led their small force of armed natives into the village. One thing the Irishman had come to learn in his years of recruiting was that the Papuans were first and foremost a warrior people. If they had the advantage they would fight rather than be taken to work indentures far from their traditional territories. They were in a village where the men had little contact with Europeans, but the progress of O'Leary and his party of seven armed natives into the hills had been under observation for some time by clansmen of the tribe.

'Keep a close eye on that bunch over there,' O'Leary hissed to Pierre. 'They look a bit edgy.'

The Frenchman's eyes darted to the large group of almost naked warriors who stood to one side fingering their hardwood bows and stone axes tucked behind thin belts. Pierre licked his lips. He was nervous. The ever-present thought that an ambush and roasting in a native cooking fire could be his fate had little appeal.

One of O'Leary's men who spoke a dialect that could be understood by the clan stepped forward. 'Who is the headman of the village?' he asked.

A broad chested man in his late twenties stepped forward from the group. 'I am,' he answered. 'Why are you here?'

The native interpreter turned to O'Leary.

'Tell the boss man that we want to sign up twenty of his fittest men to come with us to work for the white man,' O'Leary said.

O'Leary did not have to know the dialect to understand that his request had been met with denial. He had expected that. 'Tell the headman that we will give him many gifts for each man he nominates for work with us,' the Irishman countered, indicating to one of his porters to spread the trade gifts of steel axes, sea shells, twists of tobacco and mirrors on the ground.

The assembled villagers stepped back as the blanket containing a sample of the gifts was unrolled on the dusty earth. They were not sure what evil magic was contained here, but despite their fears they soon surged forward to examine the goods with great interest.

'All this to the chief for twenty fit men,' O'Leary said in a loud voice, pointing with his rifle to the goods on display.

The interpreter explained the trade and the warriors muttered amongst themselves. Eventually the warrior leader replied and the interpreter shook his head. 'No deal,' he said.

'Well,' O'Leary sighed. 'It can't be said that I didn't try to be nice. Tell the chief that we will give him time to consider the offer,' he said to his interpreter. 'We will wait outside the village.'

With a wary eye on the assembled warriors Pierre scooped up the trade goods and followed the Irishman to where they would set up a camp a reasonable distance from the village. The Corsican knew what his boss had planned and respected his cunning. They were at a distinct disadvantage so close to the village and the assembled warriors possibly ready for a war with the recruiters.

In a short time some of the more adventuresome villagers came to their campsite where they were met with smiles and small trinkets. Soon a rush was on as the word spread of the white man's generosity and the recruiting party was besieged by men, women and children.

'So far so good,' O'Leary muttered to Pierre as he handed a shy, young girl a mirror. She snatched the present and rushed away followed by a crowd of young women eager to see what magic the hard but water-like object held.

O'Leary had laid out ropes around a tent to indicate the perimeter over which none of the villagers were to cross. His rule was enforced by his porters who pushed back any villager who tried to cross this barrier.

At nightfall the villagers drifted back to their homes and the Europeans placed guards for the night. Neither side trusted the other and with good reason.

But in the morning the villagers returned to be met by the sight of the recruiters sitting down to breakfast. O'Leary hummed an old Irish ballad as he carefully appraised the villagers gathered around them, pressing to the edge of the rope. Already he had noted those he was interested in. Amongst them was the young girl he had presented the mirror to the day before. She was only just entering womanhood and her grass skirt barely concealed what O'Leary wanted as much as the money he would fetch for the reluctant indentured labourers down on the coast.

'I think we will be ready to take our kanakas tomorrow morning,' O'Leary said to Pierre who had joined him to observe the jostling mob. Their prey was being lulled into a sense of security. Already they were bringing yams and pig meat to exchange for the trade goods. The interpreter had again offered to trade even more if twenty of the tribe's fittest men would accompany them back to work for the white man. Again the headman had declined the offer.

He appeared worried now as he stood amongst his warriors, observing the recruiters while his people were gradually accepting their presence. The Irishman could see the concerned expression on the headman's face and smiled at him. The men stared at each other for a moment before the chief finally looked away.

The following day the recruiters followed their routine as the people came again to trade for the precious goods, now almost depleted. O'Leary had briefed his men, and this was not the first time they had used such methods. But the village headman noticed the subtle tension amongst the recruiters as he stood and watched the proceedings of his people with the white men.

'Now!' O'Leary roared and the guns in the hands of his porters spat death into the warriors that stood beside their chief. So sudden and devastating was the attack that those who were witness fell to the ground in terror. O'Leary cursed himself that he had missed killing the chief who had reacted swiftly and ducked behind a group of his men.

With the precision of soldiers in action the porters fell on the unwounded young men with shackles to secure them. They met little resistance from the shocked villagers. One of the porters did not see the headman until it was too late. His rifle lay in the grass beside him as he shackled a young man. Pierre saw the chief's stone axe cleave his head and fired a shot that threw the luckless chief back from his victim. He had chambered a second round and approached the fallen man with great caution. The chief lay on his back moaning from the pain of the bullet, which had entered below the collarbone and smashed a hole through his back. O'Leary strode up to Pierre and glanced at the dead porter. Without a word the Irishman lifted the shoulder butt of his rifle and smashed the fallen chief's face. Again and again O'Leary hammered the man's head with the brass plated butt until the man's head had split open.

He turned and surveyed the carnage. At least ten villagers lay dead or dying. Many had gained their senses and fled to the village. Even the warriors who had not been wounded fled after their people. Here they could regroup to hunt the killers on their trek south across the rolling hills of tall grasses. But this would take time as they had been denied their leadership with the killing of the best warrior amongst them.

O'Leary did not give them time. With his prisoners secured and the young girl bound he ordered half his men to advance on the village. They shot at anything that moved and the people fled even further into the surrounding forests to watch helplessly as their village was put to the torch. O'Leary knew that by doing so, the idea of hunting him would take second place as the warriors recovered as much as they could from the ruins of the smouldering houses.

When he was satisfied that he had eliminated the threat to his rear the Irishman moved out. By the time they reached the planters in the south he knew that his prisoners would have lost all resistance to marking the paper that legally indentured them to the European planters. And the young girl would prove to be a pleasant diversion at night in his bed. It was a pity she would not live to see the bright lights of Port Moresby, he mused, as he watched his men push and shove the shackled prisoners into a column for the march. As they approached the township he would simply cut her throat one night and leave her in the bush to be eaten by the scavenging wild pigs.

Jack Kelly stood at the bow of the Burns Philp steamer gazing at the Port Moresby shoreline. Not much had changed since he was last in the frontier settlement in 1915. It was still a small town of pre-fabricated houses with corrugated tin roofs embraced by the bare, brown hills and the homes of around fourteen hundred Europeans. From the bay he could see the dusty streets and the long wharf jutting out from the land. The thin strip of sand of Ela Beach was lined with tall trees and the town dominated by the Burns Philp tower that marked the company's trading place in the almost forgotten Australian territory and its capital. Hopefully his old friend would be waiting on the wharf after receiving the telegram he had sent from Sydney weeks earlier.

It was mid morning and a haze of smoke hung over the land. The natives were burning off, as was their tradition in the dry season, and the town could have been in outback Australia.

'It does not appear to be as I imagined,' George Spencer said as he joined Jack at the bow. 'I was expecting green jungles and coconut trees.'

Jack grinned as he lit the cigar he had been hoarding to celebrate his return to the mysterious island north of Australia. 'Lot of people think that. But not far from here, around the coast, you will see just that.'

George leaned on the railing and peered beyond the town. 'They don't seem very imposing,' he said gesturing to the hills. 'I was under the impression that they blocked the way inland.'

Jack sucked on the cigar and watched the blue grey smoke whirl away on a gentle tropical breeze. 'A bit deceptive. Go north and you will encounter mountains where ridges, barely wide enough to walk on, exist. Not to mention jungles and wild tribesmen who won't hesitate to kill you for a square meal. Not a place like anywhere else you might know. Anyway, it seems we are about to tie up at the wharf and you will get your first taste of Papua.'

'A shrunken head, old chap?' George asked with a grin.

'A cold beer and an opportunity to meet a real Papuan.'

On the wharf George took the extended hand of the man identified as Jack's old friend. He stood a head shorter then Jack and was of medium height, wearing a clean white suit, tie and matching hat in the tradition of the tropics. He was a real surprise for George.

'Kwong Yu Sen, this is Mr George Spencer,' Jack said, beaming at George's startled expression.

'Pleased to make your acquaintance, Mr Sen,' George mumbled as he shook the smaller man's hand. It was a firm grasp and he calculated Sen to be in his mid thirties. 'I am afraid Jack has told me little of you on our voyage north.'

'Jack has a well-known sense of humour,' Sen beamed. 'He would not tell you about me just so that he could see the expression on your face now.'

'Is it that obvious, Mr Sen?'

'I am a Methodist, Mr Spencer, and my Christian name is Sen. We Chinese use our family name first, unlike you Europeans who place your family name last. I would be honoured if you also called me Sen as my friend Jack does.'

'I must say that you speak English like a native,' George complimented. 'I mean like an Englishman.'

'I was educated by Methodist missionaries in China before I came to Papua.'

'Well, now that you have met your first Papuan,' Jack said, 'I suggest that we adjourn for a cold beer. Sen's boys will look after unloading our kit.'

'Too right,' Sen said. 'I have the sulky waiting for us and the trip to my place will give me a chance to catch up with all that has happened in your life since I last saw you in '15. I heard around the town that you won some medals in the war.'

George was impressed with Sen's residence an hour's journey from the town. A large sprawling house of timber walls and corrugated iron roof, it was raised off the ground and surrounded by a verandah. A mass of well-watered trees, shrubs and ferns shielded the house from the harshness of the dry stunted and drooping vegetation of the countryside. The windows lacked glass panes but were framed by shutters instead. The sweet perfume of frangipani wafted by as they stepped up onto the verandah where a young native man dressed in a clean wrap-around skirt of cotton cloth met them.

'Hey, Dademo,' Jack said. 'Is that you?' The young man's face broke into a broad smile at being recognised. 'You were just a piccaninny when I last saw you.'

'It's me, Mr Jack,' the young man said. 'Mr Sen said you come back.'

'This is Mr George,' Jack said, indicating the tall Englishman following him onto the verandah. 'He's one of those bloody pommies.' Dademo nodded his head shyly.

'There have been a few changes since you left,' Sen said removing his hat. 'I have a wife and sister-in-law living with me.' Jack's expression betrayed his surprise. 'This is my wife My Lee,' Sen continued when a pretty young Chinese woman presented herself with a small bow to the men on the verandah. My Lee wore her jet black hair tied back in a bun and dressed European-style in a long white cotton dress. She appeared fragile like a china doll and her serene beauty immediately impressed both men. 'This is my friend Jack Kelly and his friend Mr George Spencer, My Lee,' Sen said. Both men mumbled their greetings and Sen was pleased to see how impressed they were by his new wife.

'And this is my wife's sister, Iris,' he added when another young woman appeared at the door. Yet again the visitors were stunned. George hoped that he was not gaping. The second woman was an extraordinary Eurasian beauty in her late teens. She stood slightly taller than Sen himself and her eyes were a deep mysterious colour that seemed to be neither dark nor light. Her silky dark hair was bobbed in the European fashion of the day. She did not acknowledge her brother-in-law's visitors with the same diffidence as shown by her half sister but turned back to the coolness of the house.

An ice maiden, George reflected to himself. An ice maiden men would kill for.

Sen could see the confusion on his visitors' faces. 'I will fill you in later, Jack,' he said softly in the

Australian's ear. 'But not now, when I know you both could do with a beer.'

After a sumptuous meal of meat and vegetables prepared in the Chinese style of cooking, Jack retired to the verandah. He leant on the rail and puffed on a cigar.

Sen joined him and stood beside his friend, staring into the warm tropical night of familiar sounds. 'Your friend George seems to be taken by my wife's sister,' he said. 'She is teaching him mah-jong.'

'A beautiful woman,' Jack responded. 'I was rather impressed by her myself. What's her story?'

'Ah, that is a mystery,' Sen sighed. 'All I know is that her father was a European back in China. I suspect a missionary. My wife will not tell me any more.'

'Well, she is in good company with George. He is a bit of a mystery man himself. I still don't know much about him after all the years we served together through the war. All I know is that he seems to have an unlimited source of money from somewhere.'

'I gathered that you could not have purchased all the stores my boys unloaded,' Sen grinned, 'and that your friend was the backer in whatever you are plotting.'

'Plotting!' Jack exclaimed with an expression of feigned shock. 'Plotting is an English word with nefarious overtones, old friend.'

Sen gazed at the soft shadows of the night. 'I remember a story about a man you knew before the war,' he said casually. 'A pretty tough prospector man by the name of Arthur Darling who in 1913 took a whaleboat crewed by Orakaiva boys and slipped past the authorities in the Kaiser's territory up into the mouth of the Markham River in search of gold. It seems from rumours that he did all right until the Kukukukus put five arrows in him and he had to get out after a running battle with them. He was just lucky to survive. Of course you would not be planning to head up into Kukukuku territory, would you Jack?'

The Australian glanced at the Chinese entrepreneur. 'You wouldn't perhaps know of any further attempts to go up into the Markham Valley?'

Sen rolled his eyes and sighed. 'I have heard that Sharkeye Park has been hanging around Morobe way.'

'Park!' Jack spat. 'Darling must have told him something before he died. I heard they had teamed up after Darling got picked up at sea.'

'How did you know about Darling's strike?' Sen asked softly. 'Very few people had any idea.'

'An Orakaiva boy related to another Orakaiva working with Darling told me the story of his gold find,' Jack answered. 'I once did his family a favour.'

Sen nodded. He knew that in such places as Papua and New Guinea – with their small populations of Europeans – it was hard to keep a secret. As a man whose moderate wealth was carefully husbanded through various enterprises on the island, Sen had his own intelligence garnered from a network of scattered native sources. His initial money

had been made as a recruiter for the German plantation owners before the Great War. But he had also
provided native labour to the Australians. He knew
that William 'Sharkeye' Park was a veteran gold
prospector who had worked in the Klondike rush of
Alaska at the turn of the century and had a lot of
experience with minor gold rushes in the tropics. So
if Sharkeye had been seen around the Morobe township in the former German territory it seemed to
confirm that the experienced prospector was onto
something. Sen remembered how, as a young man
before the war, Jack had confided to him that he had
joined a covert expedition of experienced prospectors who had crossed the border into German
territory to seek out geologically promising sites
inland. But the expedition had been intercepted by
the German native police near Salamaua just after
they had landed ashore. The incident had caused
trouble between the German authorities in New
Guinea and the Australians in Papua. Only the personal intervention by the respected chief Australian
administrator Sir Hubert Murray had extricated the
Australian prospectors from languishing in a German
lockup. Sen also knew that Jack's own German heritage had helped them out. His charm and
easy-going nature had helped defuse the situation
with the German administrator, Hahl.

His intuition told him loudly that Jack Kelly was
planning to return and finish what he and others had
started. But the terrain of the country was known for
its rugged, almost vertical mountains. And there was
the high risk of fever, and fierce warriors who would

suddenly appear out of the steaming mists of the jungles to shower arrows on intruders, finishing off their victims with striated stone killing clubs. It was the territory of the dreaded Kukukuku tribesmen.

Sen liked Jack Kelly. He was a man who did not discriminate against him because he was an Oriental and with no rights in European territory. Maybe it was because Jack had himself fought the prejudice of being half-German and half-Irish. Both cultures had taken a battering from the British Empire. Jack, however, had considered himself a South Australian first, but lately just an Australian.

The two men had befriended when Jack had gone to Sen to recruit native porters for a small prospecting expedition in the Kerema region. Sen had been struck by the young man's self-assurance. Jack had expressed an interest in learning how to play mah-jong and from the moment they had built the four walls of ivory and bamboo tiles the friendship had developed to the point where Jack had gained concessions for Sen through his friendship with the Papuan administrator, Sir Hubert Murray. It was a debt Sen recognised. But above all it was a friendship that transcended racial origins.

Sen sighed as the smoke of Jack's cigar wafted pungently around them. 'Maybe you should think twice about what I strongly suspect that you are planning to do, Jack,' he said.

'All I am going to do is look for gold,' Jack replied, turning his attention back to the night shadows. 'No law against that. Anyway, let's see how George is shaping up as a mah-jong player. Maybe

we have someone new who we can convince to put
his money down for a few rounds. Someone we can
both beat.'

George was more interested in the delicate hands of
his teacher than in the instructions she was giving. Iris
had changed into the traditional body-clinging dress
of China. The cheongsam was of cream dyed silk,
brightly patterned with swallows and willow trees.
The swell of her hips, buttocks and breasts seemed to
be accentuated and the tall, normally reserved
Englishman found that he was gazing at her as she
knelt on a coir mat. His face flushed when she glanced
up at him between explanations and caught him staring at her. If his badly hidden and brazen attention had
annoyed her she was careful not to express her
thoughts on the matter. She appeared to ignore his
stolen glances and concentrate on the game.

'I must say, Miss Iris, that you are a most beautiful woman,' George impulsively blurted as he knelt
uncomfortably on the opposite side of the low teak
table. 'And I must apologise if my observation has
caused you any alarm.' Iris avoided his eyes and
looked demurely down at the tiles.

'I take no exception, Mr Spencer,' she replied. 'I
think that you have been away from the pretty ladies
for a long time and your judgment of me is that of a
man who would say any lady was pretty.'

'Not so,' George defended indignantly. 'I have
not long left Australia where there are many beautiful women – in a sort of rough, colonial way – but

65

your beauty is quite extraordinary. Like that of the most exquisite orchid.'

Iris looked up from the table with a hint of a teasing smile. 'I take your compliment as a gracious gesture, Mr Spencer, but you are here in a place of very few women.'

'George, please call me George, Miss Iris,' the Englishman said. 'I would be honoured if you did so.'

The two players had not noticed Jack and Sen close by on the other side of a cotton net curtain dividing the spacious room. Both men looked at each other with a frown. Maybe George might become smitten to the point of forgetting that he was in this mostly unexplored land to search for his fabled Orangwoks, Jack thought. If so he might lose his financial support to search for gold.

For Sen the Englishman's unabashed attraction to his wife's sister was a matter of family honour. Although she may not be of pure blood, she was still Chinese. The thought of a member of his family being romantically involved with a European was unthinkable, they were not a civilised people, an inferior race. He felt a guilty twinge at his recriminations. Beside him stood his friend Jack Kelly who was of European stock. Why would such a thought occur to him when he himself was a Christian Chinese? The answer eluded him, except that he realised that he did not condone mixed race relationships. Was not the ostracising of his sister-in-law by his Chinese relatives an example of the tragedy of such crossings? No good could come of the Englishman's attraction to Iris.

FIVE

The bitter chill of winter permeated the house. Paul Mann hunched against the cold as he sat in the small room that was his retreat from the world. It had once been a library with an impressive collection of books accumulated over the years by his father. But now many of the books had been sold off in lots to collectors for little more than a day's supply of coal for heating. Before him lay the letter he had waited impatiently for. Its contents gave him a warmth that he had not felt in a long time. A new decade was almost upon them and a chance for a new life.

The footsteps on the stairs told him his sister had returned from wherever she had been. He glanced at the clock on the wall and scowled at the time. It was early morning and a time long past the hour any respectable lady should be coming home.

'Erika,' he called softly from the library.

His sister entered the small room, glowering defiantly at her brother seated in a chair frayed by age. 'What do you want me to say?' she demanded as she stood belligerently in the doorway. 'I am no longer a child. And you are not Father.'

'Were you with them tonight?' he accused.

'That is my business,' she replied with a tilt of her chin.

'They are no good. They are little more than thugs and their ideas are dangerous to Germany.'

'Adolf has a vision,' Erika said, with a dreamy expression on her strikingly beautiful face. 'He has the soul of an artist and the heart of a warrior. His words will some day change the world.'

'It was inspired words that got us into this mess,' Paul growled. 'Words of patriotism and Fatherland.'

'You speak like those cursed Jews who have profited from Germany's misery,' she retorted with a snarl. For a moment Paul did not recognise her. Although the war had separated them and disrupted their closeness as brother and sister, he still thought of her as the happy little girl whose smile could melt the coldest of hearts.

'It was not only the Jews who profited from the war,' he replied. 'Look around at the Junkers families. Look at Krupps and men like him. Are they suffering with us? No, they live in their fancy homes and have goose for supper. The rich of any country are to blame if blame is to be apportioned.'

Erika blanched. 'Are you a communist?'

Paul frowned. 'I am not a communist. I am a German and proud of who I am.'

'You swear to me on our parents' honor that you are not a communist?' Erika asked again.

'I damned well told you that I am not,' Paul answered irritably. 'If I was one of them I would tell you.'

The blood returned to Erika's face. She knew her brother would not lie to her. He was a man of honour and his word always held. To be a communist was akin to being a Jew, according to Adolf.

'I am sorry, Paul,' Erika softened. 'It is just that we are in troubled times.'

'I know, that is why I want you to be the first to hear my important news.'

Erika stared at her brother with a quizzical expression. 'Why would you want me to be the first?' she asked. 'I thought that you would tell Karin any important news first.'

'You are my sister,' he replied simply. 'I have a buyer for the house – and a letter from New Guinea.'

The shock registered on Erika's face. She immediately understood the relationship between the two statements. 'We are not leaving Germany to go to New Guinea,' she gasped. 'I will not go with you. Adolf needs me here to help him in his work. I . . .'

'Are you sleeping with Herr Hitler?' Paul snapped as he rose from the chair.

His anger frightened Erika and she took a step back. Very rarely had she seen her brother so angry. 'No. I wish I was his lover,' she blurted. 'Given time I know he will take me to his bed and I will truly share . . .'

'Share what?' Paul exploded. 'Share the thuggery of the streets as we are seeing now? Share another round of sabre rattling by fanatics bent on sending us into another war? Herr Hitler's kind of ideology is not new. It has always been in the European way of thinking. Oh, I know a lot about your Adolf,' he continued with a cold anger. 'He is little different to the men who sent my boys to their deaths on the front. Men who preach the greatness of war and sit safely at home drinking their brandy and complaining that we are not bleeding enough for them.'

Erika was shocked by the explosion of raw emotion in her brother. Since returning from the war he had been so quiet, saying little or nothing of his feelings on any subject. She felt him grip her shoulders and was afraid.

'Do you know what it was like to see the rats in the trenches bloated with human flesh? Do you know what it was like to see school boys sent to the front just to give us the numbers to counter the French and British? To hear them screaming for their mothers as they tried to hold in their bellies ripped by shrapnel? No, you do not, and I pray that you never will see or hear what we did at the front.'

As suddenly as his anger had come it went. He let go of Erika's shoulders and slumped back in his chair. 'We are all going to New Guinea,' he said calmly. 'We are going to start a new life in a new country. I received a letter today from an Australian planter who had taken over our plantation at Finschhafen. He is prepared to sell it back to me at a reasonable price. It seems that the price for copra is not good but I already had plans to diversify the crops before the war put a stop to everything in our lives.'

'I will not go with you,' Erika responded. 'My place is here in Germany.'

'You will go with us,' Paul answered firmly. 'You forget that you cannot inherit any part of our parents' estate until you turn twenty-one. And that by the terms of the will your share is in my control until then. So, as we are all going to New Guinea, you are forced to stay with us until then.'

Erika glared at her brother. He was right, and as she was only a year short of her twenty-first year she would comply. After that she would return to Germany and reclaim her place in the cause of her beloved Adolf. 'One year,' she spat, 'and I will be rid of you, brother.'

Paul nodded. In one year he hoped that she would change her mind with exposure to a new world. She had never been to the tropics and he prayed that the scent of frangipani would hold her to a new life away from a war-ravaged Europe. A year was a lifetime in Paul's experience of war. He hoped that it would be so for his sister.

Paul was pleased with the price that the family house fetched, and he felt little regret in relinquishing it to the new Jewish owners. The man had been an officer on the Russian front and Paul had warmed to him as a fellow soldier who had experienced the brotherhood of fire. They shook hands and the paperwork was drawn up for the transfer.

When the purchaser had departed Paul hurried to Karin with the news. Her enthusiasm was equal to his own. They both knew to leave Germany was to be reborn in a land far from the crises of a nation shattered by war. It was also a chance to leave the terrible ghosts of their pasts behind: for Karin the spirit of her dead daughter, and for Paul the memory of too many happy times before the Great War with friends who had lost their lives on Europe's battlefields.

Only Erika met the news with resentment.

'You sold our parents' house to a Jew!' she shrieked in her anger. 'A dirty Jew who has profited from the sacrifice of our people.'

'The only sacrifice Herr Rosenberg knew was that of his men on the Russian front,' Paul replied calmly. 'There was no profit for him in the last few years unless you call the loss of an eye from shrapnel a profit,' he added bitterly. 'I also believe that it was a dirty Jewish officer who recommended your precious Adolf for his Iron Cross.'

Erika glared at her brother, speechless. Finally she turned her back on him and stomped away.

The incident would have been forgotten in the busy days ahead as Paul and Karin packed and prepared for their journey – first to Australia, then on to Papua and New Guinea – except for a visit from Gerhardt Stahl a week later. He was not alone and when met at the door by Paul invited himself and the two surly men accompanying him inside.

'Herr Mann,' Gerhardt said without a courteous greeting. Paul noticed that the former soldier had not used Paul's old rank of major to address him. 'I have been informed that you have sold your house to a Jew.'

Paul bristled at the man's accusing tone.

'Who I have sold my house to is of no concern to you, Herr Stahl,' Paul replied coldly, glancing at the two men standing silently beside Gerhardt. 'There is no law that dictates who I may – or may not – sell to.'

'I do not wish to offend Herr Mann but you of all people must know of their treachery. You were a fine officer and a man I once trusted with my life. So it does not make sense that you would betray our country to the Jews.'

'Betray our country!' Paul exclaimed with just a hint of amusement at the accusation. 'The war is over, Herr Stahl. How could I betray the country when we no longer have enemies to fight?'

'We still have enemies within,' Gerhardt replied softly. 'Jews, communists and deviants bent on keeping us on our knees. It is a well-known fact that international Jewry is behind a conspiracy to keep us in poverty.'

'If that is all that you have come to say I would be very much pleased if you would now leave,' Paul said, holding the door open to the three men. 'I have much to do before I leave Germany.'

'I believe that you are travelling to New Guinea, as the British have renamed Kaiser Wilhelmsland.'

'That is right,' Paul conceded. 'We leave in five weeks – not that our future plans have anything to do with you.'

'One day we will occupy our lost lands again,' Gerhardt said ominously. 'And when that day occurs I hope that you are not in league with the communists and Jews as it seems you have been here.'

'Selling a house does not constitute a conspiracy, Herr Stahl. Now leave my home.'

Gerhardt nodded to his henchmen and they departed in silence. Paul closed the door behind them and drew in a deep breath. What was happening to Germany when men like Stahl made it their business to threaten him? He glanced up the staircase and saw Karin standing at the top. She was pale and trembling. Obviously she had witnessed the short but menacing confrontation.

'I will be glad when we leave here,' she said. 'The Germany we knew is gone forever.'

Erika sipped at the coffee without tasting it. The dingy coffeehouse was almost empty as Gerhardt sat opposite her.

'I will regret you leaving, Erika,' he said. 'But it will only be for a short time.'

Erika held the cup in both hands with her elbows on the battered table. 'I wish that there was some way I could serve the cause,' she sighed. 'New Guinea is on the other side of the world.'

Gerhardt placed his hand over hers. If only you could see how I truly feel about you, he thought, with an aching feeling for his unspoken love for the beautiful young woman who only had eyes for Adolf. From the moment he had met her he had desired her for himself, but she had attended their meetings and concentrated her attentions on the young man with the fiery speeches and hypnotic eyes. 'I will write to tell you how we are progressing,' he said. 'Then you will return to join us again.'

Erika did not resist his gesture and looked at him. She was vaguely aware that he was a handsome man, but since the death of her beloved Wolfgang on the Hindenburg Line she had entertained the idea of going to only one other man's bed. Her energies were now directed to being a disciple of the new man who had come into her life with words of passion for a greater cause – a cause to resurrect her country from the ashes of defeat. She had been vaguely aware of Gerhardt's attention but did not feel for him as she did for Adolf.

'You can never be with Adolf,' he said as if reading her thoughts. 'He is destined to be a man of the people and human love is something such men can never experience. You should look elsewhere for a man who can love you.'

With a start Erika withdrew her hands and placed her cup on the table. 'I have never considered Adolf in the way you suggest,' she said defensively. 'I see him as the man who can lead us in the future.'

Gerhardt smiled grimly at her lie. 'Then that is good,' he said. 'We have that in common.'

'I would like to return home now, Gerhardt,' Erika said, rising from the table. 'You may accompany me.'

Gerhardt bit his lip in his frustration and anger. But he obeyed Erika's wishes and escorted her through the cold, grey streets to her brother's house. They walked in silence and parted with polite but distant farewells. Erika watched the former soldier stride away down the street until he was out of sight. Gerhardt's parting words echoed in her thoughts: 'If you ever return to Munich, I will be here for you.'

She hoped that she would not meet her brother on her way to bed, where she would allow carnal dreams of Adolf and her in an explosion of mutual lust.

A week later Paul and his small family stood on the docks in Hamburg. Cold sleet whipped around their legs while the ship that was to take them halfway around the world was tied to the wharf. Karin gripped her husband's hand and then turned to take young Karl's. He seemed confused and glanced at his Aunt Erika who stood sullenly a short distance away with her hands encased in a fox skin muff.

'Are we going away for very long?' he questioned his mother.

'I cannot answer that question,' she replied with a sad smile. 'Maybe we will return home one day for holidays.'

Paul glanced at his sister and knew that she was still angry. No matter, he thought. The sea voyage might change her disposition. But deep down he knew he was being overly optimistic. Erika was a strange young woman he had never truly understood. He could only think that their father had spoiled her too much when she was growing up. And there had been almost forgotten disturbing incidents in her past that he dismissed from his thoughts. They were not memories he wished to dwell on. Maybe her attraction to Adolf Hitler had a basis in her past. He frowned. Not that the man would amount to much in the future. By the time Erika turned twenty-one, Herr Hitler would be long gone from the political scene and just a forgotten memory for his beautiful but enigmatic sister.

Paul turned his attention to the ship that was to take them across the sea. For a fleeting moment he thought about a link the war had established with their final destination in New Guinea, the Australian captain he had met on the Hindenburg Line in the last weeks of the fighting. What was his name? It was not German, although he remembered the Australian said his mother was German.

Irish – he had an Irish name, the same or similar to the bushranger he had once read about who wore an iron suit in his battle with police forty years earlier in the Australian colony of Victoria.

Ned Kelly! And Jack Kelly was the Australian captain's name. He wondered if the easy-going Australian had survived the war. And if he had, did he return to the country they both shared in common? He hoped so, as he would very much like to meet up again with his former enemy who had shown such compassion on the battlefield.

SIX

Jack's first night on Papuan soil was not restful. When sleep finally came to him he was once again in a world rent by shell bursts, screams and the pungent smell of cordite. He vaguely remembered a gentle shaking of his shoulder and a disembodied voice soothing him with, 'It's all right, old chap, you are safe, it's all over.' The screams faded and he woke to see the vague outline of his old company sergeant major bending over him.

'Sorry, George,' he apologised. 'I hope I didn't wake the neighbourhood.'

George stood and stretched. 'Couldn't sleep myself,' he sighed. 'Thought I might have a stiff drink to knock myself out.'

'Think I will join you.'

Jack sat up and slipped on a pair of short pants to cover his nakedness. Together the two men moved to the verandah, oblivious of the danger of mosquitoes. They sat side by side on cane chairs and George produced a bottle of black rum. After he had swigged from it he passed it to Jack.

'The nights are a bastard,' Jack said as he wiped his mouth with the back of his hand. 'It all comes back.'

'I know,' George replied. 'I wonder if it will ever go away. Or are we a generation doomed to terrify others with our nocturnal memories of what happened over there?'

'Good thing we're not married. Think our nightmares would cause some consternation with our spouses.'

'Never thought much about marrying,' George said as he swigged at the bottle. 'At least until now.'

Jack glanced sharply at his friend. 'She's Chinese. You know there is no future in that.'

'Iris,' George replied in a dreamy state. 'Iris is only half Chinese – and why do you conclude that I was alluding to her?'

'Pretty obvious – you were like a school boy around her,' Jack scoffed. 'Not like the man I remember who was one of the toughest soldiers I knew.'

'Well, yes, meeting such a divine creature does make one think of settling down,' George conceded. 'I have never met anyone like her in all my life.'

'Not that you have told even me much about your life,' Jack prompted. 'About all I know is that you are a pom with an educated accent. That before the war you were an officer in a British regiment and that you are one of the best men I have ever had the privilege of knowing.'

George seemed to soften at the final compliment. He stared into the darkness and for a moment saw his past in the shadows. 'One day I will tell you who I was, Jack,' he said softly.

Jack was undeterred. 'Obviously there is money in your past – and for that matter in your present, given the supplies you were able to purchase for our expedition.'

'Oh a lot of money, old chap,' George said with a slight smile on his face. 'But money does not buy you happiness. Believe me, I know. What has brought me happiness, in an odd sort of way, has been the friendship of the men I served with in the battalion. And knowing you.'

Jack coughed lightly. In all the time they had served together, through hell and high water, neither had expressed his deepest feelings. It was not the way of tough men to do so and both recognised it was time to discontinue the conversation and seek sleep. But Jack had sensed that the crack in their tough façade had been inserted by the existence of a woman – Iris.

That night Jack sat on the edge of his mattress on the floor and gazed at a now well-worn photo of a beautiful young woman. He would never meet Erika Mann but the thought that she was out there was strangely reassuring.

When sleep did finally come to him he dreamt of a little boy who was at the same time both himself and his son Lukas.

• • •

The following day Jack decided that he and George should visit the hotel in Port Moresby. Sen lent them his horse and buggy and both men dressed in their white suits and hats for a day of drinking and socialising. It was the perfect place to possibly meet with past acquaintances from his days of prospecting before the war and chat about the latest gold news from the old hands.

The journey took them along a dirt road and past villages of natives wearing very little other than cast-off European-style dresses for the women and native skirts from waist to knee for the men. Friendly waves and greetings followed them and Jack could see George was well at home already in a world new to him.

In a quiet dusty street they brought the sulky to a stop outside a primitive looking building of corrugated iron and timber. It was close to midday and the sun was hot overhead. A sign above the door identified the establishment as a hotel although the inside did not beckon with the coolness George remembered as characteristic of hotels in Australia. The hotel sported a billiard table with a sign posted on the wall that read *Men are requested not to sleep on the billiard table with their spurs on*. George was rather alarmed at what appeared to be large bloodstains on the floor. 'They hang a butchered sheep here once a week to bleed,' Jack said when he noticed the Englishman's concerned expression.

'Then it is not just a case of poor losers settling the disputed outcome of a game with knives,' George commented from the corner of his mouth.

'That sometimes,' Jack responded with an evil grin. 'Just don't play for money around here.'

Other than the sweltering conditions once they were inside the main bar, George's impression of an Australian outback pub was confirmed. A handful of men leaned on the bar, a simply hewn wide plank, with their backs to the door. The shade was at least a compensation to the heat outside. One of the men at the bar turned to appraise the strangers. He was a grizzled, bearded man whose sun-blackened face reflected years living a rough outdoor life. He could have been anywhere between thirty and sixty years. For a moment he blinked at Jack then his face split into a slow but broad smile.

'Young Jack Kelly, back from the war,' he roared as he thrust out a dirt-grimed hand. 'Thought the Hun might have done to you what them blackfellas up north failed to,' he said. 'Seems the luck of the Irish is still with ya.'

'How you going, Harry, you old bastard?' Jack replied with a grin, pumping the man's hand vigorously. 'I thought you would be dead by now from some jealous *meri*'s husband out there in the bush.'

The rest of the men at the bar turned their attention to the meeting. A couple of them moved forward to shake Jack's hand in turn. George could see the pleasure in Jack's face at being once again recognised by men he had trekked with in the wilds of the jungle in search of gold. The mere appearance of the men in their ragged shorts and shirts marked them as working men, unlike the few government men he had met on the ship to Moresby. Those men wore clean suits and had clean hands.

'Everyone,' Jack said loudly to call attention to his announcement. 'I want you to meet a real fair dinkum mate of mine, Mr George Spencer. And although he's a bloody pom, he was also the finest company sergeant major Australia ever had sail for France.'

'Pleased to meet yer' followed and a couple of brandies were thrust in their hands. For the next few hours George said little as the conversation spoken in unintelligible prospecting terms flowed with the spirits. Even so, George allowed himself to mellow into the camaraderie of the men. There was talk of the war as two of the prospectors had served in the army, but mostly gossip about the fates of the old hands. But one thing George did note was how Jack would appear to dismiss much of the gossip and hold onto other parts. This was not just a chance to catch up with old mates but an intelligence gathering opportunity.

By the time they were ready to leave towards mid afternoon, Jack had compiled a list of updates ranging from the current price of native labour to where gold may be found, from who was in the country to the availability of permits from the government men who controlled the territory.

For the trip back to Sen's residence George took over the reins. As they passed through the ramshackle town of plain European houses and dusty rutted streets that was Port Moresby, he had noted that he was just a little soberer than his former commanding officer. Jack was sleepy from the effects of the many rounds of strong spirits and mumbled something that attracted George's attention. The Australian appeared either angry or disturbed. It was a name – something like O'Leary. Whoever O'Leary was he was certainly not a friend to Jack Kelly.

Recovering from his hangover, Jack rose from beneath his mosquito net and ambled into the tropical garden dressed in shirt and shorts. George and Iris were admiring the splash of brilliantly coloured flowers. Jack smiled. They were like two young lovers in the way they communicated with subtle body movements. But Iris was rather young, Jack realised. George was at least fifteen years her senior and he was the one acting like a lovesick school boy. Loath to intrude upon them, he was about to return to the house when George glanced in his direction.

'Jack! Thought you were dead,' he greeted warmly. 'It seemed that the bottle did you more damage than Fritz ever could.'

'Alive as you can see,' Jack replied. 'And ready to return to Moresby.'

'The pub?'

'No, a visit to an old friend who I think will impress your English sense of class.'

George's hand brushed Iris's hand and she smiled. Jack noticed the serenity in his former sergeant major's expression. He had never seen him so peaceful and happy. The three strolled back to the house where Sen's wife had prepared a breakfast of a fresh fruit platter. As they ate, the fruit juices helped wash away the remnants of the previous day's excesses.

George was duly impressed, as Jack had predicted, when they arrived at their Moresby destination. The two men were ushered into Sir Hubert Murray's office at Government House by a stiff-necked clerk.

A robust giant of a man in his mid fifties met them from behind his desk. 'Young Jack Kelly,' he said with a broad smile across his still handsome face. 'I heard that you covered yourself in glory for the Empire in the recent Great War.'

'Sir Hubert,' Jack said, a little self-conscious in the presence of the man who was somewhat of a legend in his lifetime. 'It is good to see you again.'

Sir Hubert's eyes came to rest on George. 'We have not had the pleasure, sir,' he said and George shook his hand.

'George Spencer, sir,' he said. 'I assure you that the pleasure and honour is mine.'

'Spencer, you say,' Sir Hubert said with a puzzled expression. 'I knew a Spencer from my days at Oxford. A man who looked very much like you. Lord Spencer I believe he is now.'

Jack noticed that George seemed to be taken by surprise, his normally reserved demeanour shaken for just a moment. 'Possibly a distant relative,' George countered.

'Well, so much for idle chit chat,' Sir Hubert said, clasping his hands behind his back and standing ramrod straight before the two men. 'So I am going to tell you, Jack, before you even ask – as I suspect that you are here for a reason – the answer is no to me granting you permits to go off into the uncontrolled regions prospecting for gold. The military administration in the old German territories has not resolved that matter yet.'

'Sir Hubert,' Jack said throwing up his hands in protest, 'it is not gold that brings me to you personally but the Orangwoks.'

Sir Hubert blinked and for a second gaped. 'Good lord! Surely you don't believe those stories written by that mad Froggy do you?' he exclaimed.

'I do, Sir Hubert,' George said quietly. 'I believe that an island this big must have at its unexplored heart many people living in settlements. Who and what they are I feel is one of the last great questions begging an answer in our modern times. Sir, we know more about the heart of Africa than we know about the heart of this land.'

Sir Hubert turned his attention to George and was silent for a moment as he appraised the Englishman. He was so like the young Irish Catholic Oxford graduate who had won the English heavyweight boxing title years earlier. He searched for a weakness in the aristocratic looking Englishman who stood in his office and talked of Orangwoks. 'What makes you think that there are people living in the unexplored territory?'

'Well, sir,' George reasoned, 'we know that people live along the coastline and into many parts close to the coast. I just believe that it is in the nature of mankind to forever migrate into uninhabited areas.

And thus for thousands of years I believe that the ancestors of the people from the coastal areas must have moved inland to new areas. It is as simple as that.'

Sir Hubert pondered on the answer. 'I have always thought that myself,' he mused in measured tones. 'I have heard rumours that the German Lutheran missionaries have some knowledge of people living beyond our control but they have stayed tight lipped on the subject.' He glanced at Jack with a hint of suspicion. 'And you are not looking for gold?'

'Just Orangwoks,' Jack answered him in his sincerest voice. 'George has kindly requested my services as an old Papua hand to assist his exploratory expedition.'

'Damned if I should believe either of you,' Sir Hubert guffawed. 'But I will see that the proper permits are drawn up – with no gold prospecting and a few other conditions.'

Jack felt his initial enthusiasm wane. 'Conditions, Sir Hubert?' he asked. 'What other conditions?'

'That you take a contingent of police boys with you. And any other conditions that I might think of between now and when I sign the permits.'

'Reasonable enough,' Jack said, and held out his hand to seal the deal. 'I cannot thank you enough, Sir Hubert, for what you are doing to advance man's knowledge of his fellow man.'

'Jack Kelly, you are a rascal, but your exemplary service to the King and Australia in the war has warranted some loss of memory for all the trouble you caused me with my German counterparts years back. I wish you all the best and hope that you do not cross paths with O'Leary again.'

George was quick to pick up on the mention of the name. Who was O'Leary and why was he to be avoided?

The two men politely excused themselves and left the charismatic ruler to continue his day of administering the territory. They were striding back to the buggy under a hot sun and cloudless skies before George asked, 'Who is this mystery man O'Leary?'

'Who is Lord Spencer?' Jack countered.

Neither question was answered and they rode in silence back to Sen's residence. George was not naive enough to believe that Jack was merely interested in his dream of making the last great discovery of the twentieth century – the finding of the Orangwoks. He knew Jack would be searching for gold as they trekked into unexplored country. But at least he had a partner who knew what he was doing. For George, Jack Kelly was the only man alive he truly loved as a brother and trusted with his life. That friendship had been forged in hell. But now they were in a strange and contradictory paradise. Even more important had been the discovery of the most exotic and beautiful of all creatures – Iris. He knew he was hopelessly in love and would eventually ask her to be his wife, even though they had only known each other a few days. That did not matter. He had lived through a time at the Front when life had been often measured in mere minutes and seconds.

'We are going to take a boat from Moresby around the point at Samarai to this river here north of Morobe but south of Lae,' Jack said, jabbing at the map spread on the floor of Sen's house.

George followed Jack's finger around the tail of Papua to a river marked on the coast north of the former German settlement of Morobe in the Huon Gulf. He noted that the map had a red brown colouring close to the coast to indicate areas under government control, but inland an expanse of grey with dotted outlines of a great spine of vaguely mapped mountains with the title Bismarck Range. Somewhere in that grey area George knew they would find the Orangwoks.

'Does Isokihi still have his boats?' Jack asked. Sen was standing above the two men as they crouched over the map spread on the coir mat floor. He nodded and Jack turned back to the map. 'After we land it's going to be a bastard getting up the hills in from the coast,' he added. 'We are going to need porters and it looks like we will have to take whatever we can from Koki gaol for that job.'

George frowned at the suggestion of native prisoners working for them but Jack noted his concern. 'It's okay,' he said. 'It's common practice around here for the boys to work off their sentence and, at the same time, get paid.'

'Why don't we avoid the mountains by taking a course up the Markham Valley?' George asked quietly.

Jack seemed a bit evasive. 'Been done before. If you are going to find your lost tribes you are going to have to look in places less accessible.'

'I was hoping to look up in this region,' George said, pointing to a grey area at the centre of the island between two ranges marked as the Victor Emanuel and Muller ranges. 'That would mean it would be better to follow the Markham Valley.'

Jack looked peeved. 'Why not give this area a try first? It's closer, whereas to try for the place you just pointed out, would require a longer sea voyage. That would put a bit of a strain on our supply line.'

George had to bow to Jack's rationale. Logistics of supply had been his role as a company sergeant major during the war. 'All right, old chap,' he sighed. 'So may it be that we find something in the region you have selected.'

Jack grinned and slapped his friend on the back. 'You won't be disappointed.'

George was acutely aware of what the Australian was really seeking. It did not matter so long as he had the opportunity to blaze a new trail into unexplored country. Should Jack find his gold then they would both find what they sought. For George the lure of gold held little value. Gold merely translated to financial wealth and that was something that no longer mattered in his life. 'If there is nothing else then Sen and I can discuss the finer details of the plan,' Jack said. 'Give you a chance to improve your mah-jong game with Iris while we work on.'

George stood and stretched his legs. He was not offended by being dismissed. Indeed Iris's company was something to look forward to. Especially as the departure date of their expedition was growing close.

George found Iris in the garden amongst the broadleafed monsterios. With the delicate fishbone ferns and colourful waterlilies, it was a cool, pleasant place of tranquillity. A place to sit and talk. A place to express gentle words of love.

It took three weeks to finalise preparations. George left the organising to Jack and spent his time in the company of Iris. She proved to be as intelligent as she was beautiful and George had to admit to himself – with a touch of guilt – that the expedition was taking a secondary place in his life. At times he had forced himself to join in Jack's enthusiasm when in fact he felt depressed at leaving Iris behind. It was ironic that he had travelled to Papua to search for lost tribes and instead found love.

Iris had returned his feelings in a gentle manner. Although George ached to take her to his bed he also knew that this was not the way to prove his love for the mysterious woman. He had seen the same longing in her eyes however, and felt it in the touch of her fingers on his arm.

But the day came when Jack declared they were ready to take one of the Japanese boat builder's modified ketches out of Moresby harbour for the voyage to the Huon Gulf.

'How about we all go to the pub to celebrate?' Jack declared in his usual cheery way. 'Maybe say goodbye to Harry and the boys.'

Sen shook his head and mumbled, 'Not a good idea for me to go with you, Jack. You know how the boys feel about us Chinese.'

'You're with me. No one will give you any trouble.'

'Not a good idea,' Sen reiterated. 'You and George go.'

Jack turned to George who stood a short distance away. 'Well, you old bastard, how about it?'

George smiled weakly and mumbled that he would go with him. He still felt the old duty to protect his friend. It had been like this when they were on leave in France. He knew of Jack's wild ways once he had a few drinks under his belt. If they were to leave in the morning he felt that he should ensure Jack came home in one piece.

Jack scooped up his big floppy hat as Sen placed his hand on his arm. 'Be careful, Jack,' he said with a grim expression. 'I have heard rumours that O'Leary is back in Moresby.'

George noticed the slight shift in the Australian's expression, but his concerned look suddenly shifted back to a broad grin. 'It all happened a long time ago,' he said and turned to walk out the door.

George followed to the buggy. 'About time you told me about this O'Leary chap,' he muttered. 'His name keeps cropping up.'

'Just a bloke who I upset a bit a few years ago,' Jack replied as they walked.

'How upset?' George asked.

'I shot him once,' Jack said mildly. 'But the bastard had it coming. I only wish I had finished the job then because, if he is around Moresby tonight, I have a feeling he is going to upset my drinking.'

'You shot him! And you think he is going to be around tonight?'

'Hard to keep any secrets in Papua,' Jack said when they reached the buggy hitched up by the houseboy. 'Hey, Dademo. What do you think of O'Leary?'

'Bad bastard, Mr Jack,' Dademo replied with a wide grin. 'You killim when you see him, Mr Jack.'

'See, George,' Jack said as he hauled himself up onto the buggy seat. 'Told you O'Leary was a bad bastard.'

George took his place beside his friend who gave a flick on the reins. 'You could at least tell me who to look out for just in case I meet him,' George stated reasonably.

'A really big and ugly man with two scars on his cheeks. The left hand scar is a bit bigger than the right hand one. My bullet blew his teeth through that side of his face. Anything else you want to know?'

'Just a simple explanation as to why you shot him in the first place,' George said, rolling his eyes to the heavens.

'He was raping a native *meri* who was barely eight years old – if that. It seemed the best way to take his mind off what he was doing at the time. Anything else?'

George shook his head and stared at the dusty trail ahead. The sun would soon be below the hills and the dust that filled the air was turning a mauve mist on the horizon. He knew he was on a frontier not too different to the American West. Here the indigenous people could still kill a man with bows and arrows and only the toughest survived in the bush. For Jack to have settled a matter with a gun was just a natural extension in a frontier like Papua.

They had only been in the bar for a hour when George noticed a sudden hush among the normally raucous row of men drinking under the tilley lamps. George turned to see a man framed by the doorway.

'Kelly, you bastard,' the voice boomed and Jack, already half drunk, turned to see O'Leary glowering at him.

'You can't see where I shot him,' Jack slurred to George with a grin. 'Because he has a beard now.'

George paled under his recently acquired tan. The Irishman's eyes were dark like a snake's and yet reflected a danger that George could see. 'Shut up, Jack,' George hissed. He was glad that he had insisted on staying out of the rounds of strong rum being consumed by Jack and his mates. 'I think we have a real spot of bother right now, so don't aggravate the situation.'

O'Leary strode forward. He was truly a huge man with a thick bushy beard to his chest and George guessed him to be in his forties. The men moved aside to allow him passage to the bar where Jack leant back, grinning at him.

'I was hoping you would survive the war,' O'Leary said, thrusting his face up to Jack's. 'So I could settle with you.'

'No trouble in here, O'Leary,' the barman growled, causing the giant to turn his attention to him.

'Kelly and I will be going outside,' he said and the barman nodded.

'Mr Kelly will be going nowhere,' George said quietly.

The big Irishman frowned at him. 'You sound like a bloody pommy,' he snarled and George could smell liquor on his breath. 'I don't like you English bastards any more than I like Kelly here.'

George noted that they were both the same height but the Irishman had many more pounds on him. He was an imposing figure and a life of living in the bush had stripped any fat from the muscle. George felt real fear in close proximity to him. But he had experienced fear many times in the past and was still alive to know what he must do.

'Leave him be, George,' Jack said, straightening himself as best as he could. 'I will go outside with him and finish what I should have done years ago.'

George could see that Jack was in no shape to confront the Irishman.

Contemptuously O'Leary lifted his arm to push George in the chest as if dismissing a slightly bothersome pest. But George had made up his mind. The speed with which he struck was blinding and O'Leary staggered backwards in a spray of blood.

George felt his forehead ache from the collision with the Irishman's now shattered nose. He had used the street brawlers' tactic of the 'Liverpool Kiss' once before against a French pimp when on military leave in Paris. It had worked then – and it worked now.

O'Leary stumbled on a chair and crashed heavily onto the floor. George did not give him a chance to react while he was down. With all the strength he could muster he lashed out with his boot, catching the prone man in the side of his head. O'Leary let out a loud groan, his eyes rolled and he lay still amidst broken glass and wood. But his chest rose and fell, indicating that he was still alive.

'Come along, Jack, there's a dear boy,' George said, grabbing him by the arm. 'I think we should leave before Mr O'Leary wakes up.'

Stunned by the speed and ferocity of the Englishman's actions, Jack just gaped at O'Leary on the floor. 'Best go, Jack,' someone said sympathetically. 'I think we all should go before the big bastard wakes up.'

George hauled Jack after him and guided him out to the buggy. It was dark and George helped Jack up to the seat. 'Jesus, Mary and Joseph,' Jack uttered in his absolute shock. 'I thought I was going to be a dead man tonight until you got in first.'

'Didn't have much choice, old chap,' George replied mildly. 'It was either him or us.'

Jack did not reply but merely shook his head in wonder. What else did he expect than that his best mate would cover his back.

'Oh the whiz bangs go ding-a-ling-a-ling for you, and not for me . . .' Jack sang for no other reason than it was good to be alive.

As the buggy rattled along the dirt track back to Sen's bungalow George joined him in the song.

SEVEN

The tiny craft rocked gently at the wharf and George wondered how they would all fit in. It was not much more than a large whaleboat with a canopy and a thin funnel which indicated that at least she was powered.

Jack bawled orders for the supplies to be carefully loaded. Eight native labourers had been released from the Koki gaol to serve as porters and they grinned as Jack harried them with words that were unintelligible to George. Motu was the language of the coastal people who lived in the vicinity of Port Moresby. Maybe George would pick up a few phrases in the course of the expedition.

Two native police, wearing their uniform lap lap dress and short sleeved collarless shirt, stood by, their single shot .303 rifles slung on their shoulders.

On Sir Hubert's instructions the expedition members had been assigned into Jack's care. The convicts had been gaoled for infractions against their labour contracts to the plantation owners. George marvelled at how shiny black their skin was. He had lived for a short time in Africa but could not remember seeing men as dark before. 'Buka men,' Jack had commented when George asked. 'Good men to have. They come from the Solomon Islands.'

A small but solidly built Oriental man stood in the boat. Isokihi Komine was the Japanese boat-builder and owner of a small fleet of coastal boats that plied the Papua and New Guinea waters with trade supplies. He recruited natives and occasionally collected beche-de-mer, the ugly sea slugs whose flesh was highly sought by the Chinese for their cuisine. George noticed that Sen and the Japanese boat owner avoided each other. 'Monkey men,' Sen had scowled to George. 'True barbarians.'

George was a little surprised. He had expected that, as both men were of Oriental descent, that they would have found common ground.

Towards mid morning the supplies of tents, tinned food, rice, flour, sugar, salt, tea, medical supplies, guns and ammunition were loaded aboard. Despite his misgivings at leaving Iris behind, George was caught up in the air of adventure on the wharf. Curious natives – men, women and children – had gathered to see off the small expedition.

Iris stood with her sister and brother-in-law a short distance away. She wore a dress that fell to just past her knees and held a parasol against the tropical sun. George glanced at her. Her deep and beautiful eyes were watching him with a yearning.

'You will come back to me,' she whispered in his ear as he made ready to board the boat. 'I love you very much.' And with an impulsive gesture she wrapped her arm around the tall man's waist to hold him close.

George felt a lump in his throat. He bent to kiss her on the top of her head. 'I will always love you,' he whispered. 'And we will be wed upon my return.'

Iris disengaged herself, her eyes wide with shock. 'You would marry me?' she gasped. 'But I am Chinese!'

'You are a woman first,' George said gently. 'And I don't care whether you be Chinese, Japanese or Mongolian. All I know is that in my whole lifetime I have never met a woman as beautiful as you.' George turned lest she see the raging emotion in his face. He had grown up in a world where such expression of emotions in public was not the done thing. He strode away to leave Iris standing alone in stunned rapture.

Her brother-in-law glanced sideways at her. He had never seen Iris so stunningly beautiful as now. Whatever the Englishman had whispered to Iris had made her a very happy woman but he hoped it had not been a proposal of marriage. English gentlemen did not marry half-caste women if they ever planned to return to European civilisation. It was a formula for disaster.

George stepped down into the boat and Jack grinned at him. 'Saw what happened on the wharf,' he said with a broad grin from under his floppy bush hat. 'Kind of get the impression you went and did something you will regret for the rest of your life.'

'I was going to ask you to be my best man when we return to Moresby, old chap,' George replied casually. 'Unless you have any objections to a pom marrying a Chink.'

Jack slapped his friend on the back. 'I would be honoured, old cobber,' he replied as the ropes were cast off and the little wooden boat puffed up pressure in her boiler. 'My only objection is that Iris is too good for any pom – let alone you.'

George stood at the stern of the boat and watched Iris standing on the wharf beside Sen and his wife until she was merely a tiny figure with a parasol. He did not take his eyes off her as the boat steamed out into the wide harbour. Soon he could not see her at all. They set a course south east for their meeting with whatever would be their destiny.

Iris was not the only person to watch the boat depart. From Ela Beach Tim O'Leary also observed the departing expedition. Beside him stood a smaller, dark skinned man with black eyes.

'That pommy bastard seems to be pretty chummy with Sen's sister-in-law,' O'Leary grunted through split lips. 'The time to settle with Kelly will start with that pommy bastard first,' he added as he turned away to walk back into the tiny town of Port Moresby. The swarthy Corsican nodded and followed him. Whatever his brooding partner in business was scheming was sure to be brutal. It was the nature of the man. A nature not unlike his own.

As evening approached Isokihi steered into shore. They could camp and leave at first light the next day. The first night of the voyage was spent on a pretty and secluded beach west of Moresby but plagued with minute sandflies. Jack gave orders to his police to be alert throughout the night. He was not familiar with the country they were now in and his vigilance was a result of years on the Western Front. To stay alive meant being careful.

Timber was fetched from the nearby jungle and a fire lit for cooking – and to keep the overly curious giant salt-water crocodiles at a safe distance. The Japanese captain was a taciturn man however and kept to his own company. He sat away from the party eating a meal he prepared himself while the native police and convicts shared rice and tinned fish and Jack prepared a damper loaf of bread and opened a tin of bully beef.

'Does it get any better than this?' Jack asked after they had finished the meal and were lying back on the sandy beach amongst the dried rows of seaweed strewn along the shoreline. The moonless night was clear and balmy and the stars twinkled with a brilliance that almost hurt the eyes.

George did not answer but puffed contentedly on a cigar as he stared upward and listened to the gentle swish of the tropical waters lapping at the edge of the beach. He was trying not to think about the scent of Iris's hair as he had bent to kiss her on the wharf hours earlier. What would his family think when he returned to England with an Oriental woman as his wife? Ah, to imagine the shock on their aristocratic faces, his father all a fluster. Not since his discharge from his father's regiment would there be a scene like it.

But George was not the only one thinking about a woman. Jack stared at the stars and the face of Erika Mann floated before him. Why was it that she should haunt his life when he knew nothing about her? She was merely a two-dimensional image on a piece of paper and yet through the words of her letters to a long dead fiancé she was real to him. Then his thoughts drifted to the sad memory of a little boy watching him board the ship.

'Are you ever going to tell me more about that chap I had the altercation with back in Moresby?' George asked.

'It was back in the year I enlisted,' Jack answered. 'O'Leary was working for Sen as a recruiter of native boys to work on the plantations around Moresby. He and his partner, a sleazy Frenchman, got themselves a bit of a reputation for shooting natives who refused to go with them, to be signed up as labour. Well anyway, I was staying with Sen when O'Leary turned up with a bunch of boys to be signed up. He also had a young girl with him for some reason. I got to find out why he had the girl one night when I went for a walk. He had the girl down in the bushes and was raping her. I kind of got a bit upset and told him to leave her alone. He told me to bugger off so I pulled my revolver and shot at him. When Sen learned of what had happened he fired O'Leary on the spot. O'Leary swore he would kill me one day, and I expect he will try.'

'You did the right thing, Jack,' George said. 'But I have a feeling that Mr O'Leary may have added me to his list of persona non grata.'

'No doubt he has,' Jack agreed. 'Just stay out of his way and everything will be okay. As it is, Sen is also on his dance card. The only thing is that Sen has some good men around him who keep an eye out.'

'Why don't the authorities here curb O'Leary?' George questioned.

Jack laughed. 'This is Papua. This is what the Yanks would call a wild frontier. Here men settle their differences between themselves.'

George was afraid that would be the answer. But years of war in the trenches had taught him that civilisation was a thin veneer. All men had a dark side and frontiers were merely places where it could be expressed without any real fear of retribution.

He was lulled into a sleep by the sounds of soft laughter from around the campfire and the gentle swish of the sea. But sleep did not guarantee peace. In his dreams he was with Iris but they were in the trenches under an artillery barrage. Iris was calling to him and she was covered in blood. George twitched and groaned as he attempted to fight his way through the growing piles of body parts torn asunder by the shards of red hot hissing shrapnel.

• • •

Iris closed the picture frame on the photograph that the houseboy had taken of her and George together in the fernery. Dademo had been given a quick familiarisation of the camera and grinned self-consciously as he lined up his subjects standing side by side. The black and white moment captured in time displayed a stiff-necked, unsmiling Englishman whilst the woman beside leant slightly towards him with a shy smile.

She sighed at seeing George appear so, but considered happily that when he returned, they would be wed. Her sister had expressed her delight at the news, although with some reservation as she knew her husband would not approve. But hopefully Iris would eventually win him over.

It had been three weeks since George had set off on his expedition and Iris had missed his company with the dull ache of yearning that comes with love. At first she had resisted her attraction to him. But his quiet ways and his obvious attraction to her had caused her reservations to crumble. But with the Englishman's sense of decency George had honourably controlled his lust. This enduring quality about him, and along with his slow smile, Iris remembered with a warm glow.

Today she would take her favourite gelding for a ride into the hills to visit a little village some miles away. It was a place where she was known and liked by the native women with whom she would sit and gossip. On the way home she could search for wildflowers for the house as the dry season had been left behind and the rains of the monsoon season had transformed the brown and dusty hills into verdant carpets. Although it was still hot and muggy and she knew she would be stiff and sore from the long ride, the vibrant red colours of the poinciana trees, blooming in the hills with the onset of rains, made the discomfort worthwhile.

She felt no fear in such a ride as she was already known to the local villagers and under their protection. Dademo saddled her horse. Dressed in fashionable English jodhpurs, Iris swung herself into the saddle. She was a good rider and the gelding sensed her confidence. The houseboy watched her ride away and returned to his duties sweeping the verandah. He was to tell Master Sen that his sister-in-law had gone for a ride to the village but would be back before sunset. But Master Sen was in Moresby with his missus and probably would not return until dark anyway. Waiting around to tell him the message would be a waste of time. He would finish early and slip away to the local village markets to buy betel nut.

Iris allowed her gelding his head and they galloped along the flat stretches of land between green rolling hills dotted with umbrella-like, flame coloured trees. She was alone and the exuberance of the ride was a joy to experience. She did not hear the shot for a second and was only vaguely aware that her gelding had shuddered. Then a distant popping sound came to her as the horse reared with an almost human-like scream of pain. He crashed into the earth taking her with him.

Iris grunted in pain as the wind was knocked from her lungs. She fought to get her breath back as she lay on her back, staring up at a blue sky suddenly full of a haze of floating red dots. Feeling the weight of the horse on her leg, she knew that he was dead and in stunned disbelief came to realise that the popping sound was that of a rifle. Her horse had been shot.

O'Leary lowered the rifle with a bitter smile. It had been a clean shot, as intended. The Mauser was a beautifully balanced rifle and its high velocity bullet had been true at four hundred yards.

'Let's go and see if Miss Iris is still alive to provide us with a little amusement,' he spat.

Pierre grinned as he lowered the binoculars. Luck was something he knew a lot about. And it had been sheer luck that had brought the girl within the proximity of their temporary camp outside the village. He had watched her galloping closer to them and his partner had hefted the rifle to his shoulder. Shooting the horse so cleanly was a grand sport. But nothing compared to what was to come.

Iris was struggling painfully to free herself when she noticed the two figures strolling casually towards her down the slope of a nearby hill. At a distance she could see a giant of a man with a rifle slung over his shoulder and a second, smaller man who seemed to scurry rather than stroll.

Her leg came free but when she attempted to stand she cried out in pain. Blood oozed through the tight fitting jodhpurs below her right knee and she could see the unnatural bulge. She knew it was a bad fracture and that she would not be able to escape the two figures looming ever closer. She fell back against the earth. Help was not a concept she could entertain. Only prayer was any consolation.

O'Leary rested the butt of the rifle on the earth and knelt beside Iris. 'In a bit of pain, girlie,' he drawled and his indifference spelt his intention. She glared up at him and did the only thing she could. Despite her fear she spat at him. O'Leary caught her with a vicious, back-handed blow across the face. 'Thought I might remove your trousers,' he said as he lay the rifle on the ground and drew a wicked looking knife from his belt. 'That way we can see how bad your leg is.'

Iris attempted to crawl on her back away from him. The movement caused excruciating pain and she screamed. O'Leary grabbed her by the waist and used the finely honed blade to slice away the jodhpurs down the front. They fell open and with a deft movement, as if skinning an animal, he flipped her on her stomach and sliced down the back of her trousers. They came away revealing her creamy white buttocks. A third determined cut sliced the trousers in two so that he was able to force her legs apart. Pierre licked his lips as he stared down at her nakedness. He knew that he would be second in line to have her, but that did not matter as the line was short.

'Wonder what your pommy boyfriend will think of you having sex with a real man,' O'Leary growled. 'Or how that bastard Kelly will console his pommy mate after Mr George Spencer, Esquire, learns of your desire for old Pierre and meself. Ah, but he is away isn't he? Too bad that he isn't here to see his Chink girlie performing for a couple of real men.'

EIGHT

Time seemed to have lost all meaning apart from night and day for George. He guessed that it had been about three weeks since the Japanese captain of their little craft had put them ashore on a beautiful beach not far from a river mouth in the Huon Gulf. Jack had struck a deal with Isokihi to return in three months when he would pick them up to steam back to Moresby. George carefully checked his cameras and box of photographic film to ensure they were undamaged after the relatively uneventful sea voyage from Moresby into the Huon Gulf.

One day, while they were slashing through the undergrowth of the rainforest with machetes and wading up to their necks in a soggy coastal swamp bordered by prehistoric looking pandanus palms, Jack had announced that it was Christmas. But in the deep of the jungle that meant little to the small party of twelve men and they kept moving to reach dry ground.

Each day was much the same until they reached the majestic tall forests of quondong, laurel and oak, splashed with the beautiful red of the D'Albertis creeper which trailed brilliant colour through the monotone green. Great buttressed trees with broad leaves supported climbing vines overhead and patches of rattans made the party's lives miserable as the clutching, razor sharp thorns ripped away exposed flesh. At the end of each day George would wonder how his friend had such stamina to forge ahead in uncharted country.

Eventually the evergreens gave way to a rainforest perpetually wet from the chilling mists that rose in the mountains that they now climbed. They were in a world of ferns and mosses, a world of exotic orchids growing from the nutrients of the trees themselves. Colourful rhododendrons covered the forest. It was a world of extreme primitive beauty but at the same time eerie in the sudden, unexpected silences that occurred around them as they trekked on. In the daily pitching and breaking of camps George wondered at the sanity in searching for his fabled Orangwoks. They had met no man in the jungle although the carriers and two police boys were nervously certain their progress was being marked by the dreaded Kukukuku tribesmen. By night all were alert to the sounds of the rainforest, listening for any subtle shift in the insect and bird calls.

In the fourth week the jungle covered mountains peaked before them. Jack called for a day to rest and plan the next leg of the trek west into the hinterland. They set up camp in a small clearing created by the fall of a forest giant. They pitched the two tents and Jack made an inventory of supplies. George noticed that he was frowning.

'Not good, old chap?' he asked as he sat down, his back against a tree trunk.

'Not good,' Jack grunted. 'Seems with all your money we still could not have carried any more supplies than we have.'

'How long do you think we can keep going without adding to them?'

'Three weeks at the most,' Jack replied. 'I thought we might have come across a village by now to trade some of our stuff for food, but it seems as if the place is uninhabited. Never struck this when I was here with the boys before the war. We always seemed to come across a village or two.'

George groaned inwardly at Jack's announcement. It appeared that they had achieved nothing – except develop stronger leg muscles. To turn back was admitting defeat. No Orangwoks to photograph for the world to learn of his great find – and no interesting and unique artifacts to take back for the British Museum. 'What do we do?' he asked.

'There is a stream up ahead in a ravine that I spotted when we climbed the last ridge.' Jack slid the bolt of his rifle back to check for rust. Daily cleaning of the firearms was just as much a habit as good sense. 'While you supervise the boys with the camp I am going to go and have a look at it.'

George noticed that Jack scooped up his old gold pan as he sauntered away. At least his friend had something to look for, although the matter of gold mining licences had not been settled on the formerly German side of the border. But that did not exclude gold prospecting. George had never made a comment about Jack's disappearance from the camp whenever they stopped near a river or stream but he well knew what he was up to. But always he would return with a disappointed expression on his sun tanned face and plonk himself down to drink the mug of steaming tea George had waiting for him.

George stretched his legs and set about his tasks around the camp. He was becoming more proficient in Motu and was even able to share a joke with the two police boys.

At first Jack just stared at the dull glimmer in the mountain stream as he stood up to his knees in the icy flow. It lay amongst the river pebbles in a deep hollow. 'God almighty!' he heard himself mutter as he plunged his arm into the water to seize the flattened lump the size of a large knife. It was a joy to feel its wonderful weight in his hand. The sun was rapidly setting in the mountains and Jack was afraid to even move in case any similar nuggets escaped him. He glanced around the water and noticed another smaller piece of gold flattened by eons of wear from the fast flowing waters. Before the night came he had found another five large pieces trapped in rock pools. A rough estimate of its worth told him he already had a working man's wages for a year in his possession. And he had not even had to use his pan!

His heart was pounding as he waded from the stream with the small fortune in the pockets of his shorts. In all his life he had not even dreamed of being so lucky. He was so excited by his find that when he retrieved his rifle from the bank he did not notice the sudden silence of the jungle as he pushed his way back through the undergrowth to the campsite. Nor was he aware of the many dark eyes that watched him with a mix of curiosity, fear and calculation. All he could think of was reaching the campfire he could see a short distance away and carefully plotting their current position on a map. To find such large pieces of gold so easily could mean only one thing. He had found the mother lode of the gold that so many old prospectors in Papua had speculated must exist somewhere in these unexplored mountains.

'Jack!' George called to him as he stood with his Lee Enfield grasped in both hands across his body. 'You see anything out there?' The Australian instinctively glanced over his shoulder into the depths of the forest.

'No. Why?' he answered and quickened his stride.

'The boys feel that something is up.'

By the time Jack reached the campfire the porters were staring fearfully out into the jungle whilst the two police boys nervously fingered the triggers on their rifles.

'You see anything?' Jack asked the older of the two police boys.

'No, mister,' he replied wide eyed. 'But I think the Kukukuku are close by. I just know.'

Jack did not disregard the police constable's intuition. Centuries of living in a permanent state of war with neighbouring tribes had honed the instinct for sensing danger. He placed his hand on the man's shoulder reassuringly. 'I think the Kukukuku will end up in our cooking fire if he comes too close,' Jack said with a grin.

His humour helped settle the nervous police constable. 'Me think so too,' he replied with a sheepish smile.

'We will post guards all night,' Jack said, and the other man vigorously nodded his agreement. There was nothing else they could do except be vigilant. Maybe they were being watched. But maybe the tribesmen – if they were out there – would be interested in trading with them for some of the goods they had brought for such an occasion – a plentiful supply of toia shells which were highly prized by the inland tribes.

George poured a mug of steaming tea from the kettle perched over the red coals of their campfire and handed the mug to Jack who took it gratefully. The chill of the night was upon the mountains and he felt the tension of unseen danger. Years on the battlefield had also honed his instincts. 'You think we are in any danger?' George asked casually as he sipped from his mug but held his rifle in his free hand.

'You never know around here,' Jack said, scanning the darkness outside the glow of the fire. 'Just pays to be bloody careful.'

'You think that it could be these Kukus I hear everyone talk about?'

'Any tribesman outside of Moresby gets called a Kuku,' Jack said. 'For all we know it might be your Orangwoks, and if it is, they are probably more scared of us than we are of them. In the meantime we get on with our routine and see what happens. Might be nothing.'

George agreed with the experienced bushman. Better not to let whoever may be watching them see any fear. If all went well his dream to photograph a tribesman never before seen by a European in this strangely beautiful but primitive garden of paradise might just come true the following day. And with any luck they would be prepared to trade food for the shells they carried as barter.

They went about their evening routine. Meals were prepared and when they were finished, cigars brought out whilst they drank hot tea, laced with a good quantity of sugar. The porters chewed betel nut and were relatively quiet as they huddled together by their fire.

When Jack extinguished the kerosene lamp in the tent he took the precaution of advising George to join him with his blankets outside. They would sleep a distance away, beside a great log from a fallen forest giant. The police boys would be diligent in their duty of standing guard. Fear would make them so. He and George would relieve them just after midnight. One sleeping, one awake when the time came.

'Kind of reminds you of the old days,' Jack said, laying back and pulling the blankets up to his chin. 'When we were at the front.'

'Too much so, old chap,' George answered, as he made himself comfortable on the rainforest floor. 'Thought that was all behind us. I was hoping for a little less excitement in my old age.'

'You mean you are thinking about getting back to Iris and her bed,' Jack teased. 'Thinking like that takes the edge off the old warrior that I once knew in France.'

George smiled and stared up at a patch of stars rapidly disappearing behind a scudding cloud. Jack was right. There was not a moment since he left Iris that he was not counting the days, hours and minutes of returning to her. So this terrible ache of wanting to be with someone must be love. 'Did you love your wife, Jack?' he asked softly.

Jack turned his head towards him. 'I don't know,' he replied after a short silence. 'I suppose I did. We had a kid together.'

'Do you miss her – now that she is gone?'

'The conversation is getting a bit deep and philosophical for this time of night,' Jack said lightly.

'Sorry, old chap,' George apologised. 'I was not meaning to pry into your personal affairs.'

'I didn't take it that way,' Jack countered, and fell into a guilty silence. No, I don't think I loved her, he thought. It was just one of those things that happens between two people too young to know better.

Instinctively he touched the waterproof wallet in his pocket where Erika's photograph was carefully protected from the tropics. But how could he be so attracted to a woman he had never met? A woman he knew nothing about except the passion she revealed in her words to a long dead soldier lover. He felt the spatter of rain on his face as the stars disappeared and groaned at his decision to sleep away from the tent. But he and George had shared worse in the falls of snow on the battlefields of France.

The skies broke and the downpour felt like a torrential weeping of heaven, as if for the loss of so many young men whom they had known in their past and who now slept for eternity.

And the dark eyes continued to watch from the depths of the forest.

NINE

Cloying sweat soaked the sheets. Paul Mann lay on his back, wearing only a pair of long johns whilst his wife lay beside him in the sensible, light cotton shift she had purchased in Sydney. Her back was to him and he could vaguely see the shapely, curved outline of her hip where it folded into her waist.

The heat in the small hotel room was almost suffocating and Paul felt guilty that he did not have the money to rent larger more airy accommodation for him and his wife, while Erika and young Karl were forced to share a room and bed.

Although it was dark the sound of men drinking downstairs in the public bar dampened their prospects of getting any sleep. But soon they would drift home and possibly the heat would even dissipate in the hours before sunrise.

They had reached Townsville, the tropical northern port in Queensland, en route to New Guinea when the bad news had been delivered by telegram to the ship. The Australian who had originally agreed to sell the family's plantation at Finschhafen back to Paul had reneged on the deal. Paul made the decision that he would leave his family in Townsville until he was assured of employment in New Guinea. When he was settled he would have them join him. To those ends they had taken the time to find a suitable house and were fortunate when an Australian of German descent rented them a little place on a small lot of land just outside town. They were due to move in within the week, after Paul had sailed for Port Moresby.

Erika scowled when she saw the house. It was too far from the bright lights of the tropical town where there was sure to be at least some distraction. But Karin had loved the house at first sight. Although small, it was surrounded by a well-kept garden of exotic, tropical flowers and stood high on a frame to catch the occasional breezes. It even had a verandah on which to sit at the end of the day.

'Paul?'

'Yes?' Paul had sensed that his wife was awake, as she had known he was.

'What will we do? Does it make sense to continue to New Guinea?'

Paul did not answer immediately, as he did not have an answer. They had sold everything and burned their bridges back to Europe. The money had been transferred into a British bank account for

119

transfer to Australia. It was a reasonable amount to live on for at least a year. But after that . . . .

'I could possibly get employment as a manager on a plantation around Finschhafen,' he answered, staring at the black space above his head. 'I have the experience and know the natives.'

'I have read that the Australian administration hates Germans. That when they invaded New Guinea at the beginning of the war they had our men whipped for no reason.'

'That was war,' Paul said softly. 'A lot of bad things were committed by good men. But the war is over and I know that all nations will need to rebuild with the few of us left with experience.'

Karin rolled on her side to face her husband. 'The people in Sydney did not appear very friendly when they learned that we were German.'

'They lost a lot of their men in the war for the British. You must realise that it will take time for the wounds to heal and leave only the scars.'

'Do you think that all Australians will hate us for being German?' she asked, as a child would a parent.

Paul felt a surge of love for this woman who had followed his decisions without question. He reached out and touched her gently on the cheek and felt her hand close over his. 'Not all Australians,' he said softly. 'I once met an Australian officer at the front who was from Papua before the war. He spoke fluent German and told me his mother was German. He was a good, kind man who I hope survived. And I hope that he returned to his wife and son, as I have been fortunate to with you and Karl. I often wonder where he is today, now that we can be friends and not enemies sworn to kill each other.'

Despite the heat of the tiny room Karin nestled closer to her husband and Paul was vaguely aware that it was not just the stifling room generating all the heat. He slid his hand down Karen's shoulder and continued his journey of exploration to her hip. He held his breath. They still had not made love since his return from the prisoner of war camp and that had been many long months past. But here in the tropics of Australia with Karl in another room, they were alone. His wife had not resisted his exploration and he was almost stunned by her move to lift the cotton shift above her waist. She took his hand and placed it between her legs where he felt her wetness.

'I want you, my darling husband,' she said as she drew her legs apart for him to explore her more intimately. 'It has been too long for us both to be apart this way.'

The strength of Paul's arousal made him feel as if he were a young school boy again. He recalled the time that he had accidentally seen a naked lady for the first time. She was bathing in the Rhine one summer's day, long before the trumpets of war had called him to military service.

Paul gripped Karin's wonderfully full buttocks and pulled her to him. It took only a moment to slip his undergarments off and hurriedly enter his wife. Karin gasped, whether from pleasure or pain it did not matter, as for the next hour they coupled like two animals in heat. It was as if the world would end and they must love as they would have lived.

When it was over Karin collapsed back against the sheets and cared little that the moistness was now a wetness. Nor did she feel the heat of the room as she slipped into a deep and untroubled sleep. What the future held was uncertain. What was certain was the present reality of her husband's strong body and arms that held her in a tender embrace.

Paul however did not slip easily into sleep. He held her until he was sure she was oblivious to their uncomfortable surroundings then eased his arm from under her. He was still overcome by the euphoria that Karin's body had brought to him and hardly noticed that tears splashed down his face. He wiped them away with the back of his hand and was glad that Karin was not awake to see his unmanly display. Throughout the war he had not cried once. It took the love of his wife to touch his soul which he had guarded so carefully in the horror of the trenches. Whatever the future held for them, their strongest roots had been rediscovered here in a stuffy hotel room in an obscure town, somewhere on the tropical coast of eastern Australia.

Down the corridor in her own room, Erika lay on her back in a swelter of sweat. Her six-year-old nephew Karl tossed restlessly beside her in the big double bed. The heat was unbearable – an experience new to her, although their brief stopover on the island of Ceylon had provided a taste of what was to come, as they lay in their cabins perspiring. But at least then she had been able to go on deck and feel the kiss of a gentle tropical sea breeze. Here the heat was everywhere and it was a walk to the Townsville harbour.

Like her brother Erika was pondering the future. Once again he had blundered into a situation that had caused his family distress, she thought bitterly. They were twelve thousand miles from home in a land as alien as if they had been on the moon. Ahead of them was the uncertainty that was New Guinea whilst behind her the memories of gentle falls of white snow. Then it had been more of a nuisance but now she would have given anything to feel its cooling embrace.

What was happening in her absence? Was Adolf recruiting more and more true believers to their cause? The memory of the handsome young former soldier with the mesmerising voice and eyes caused her to temporarily forget the stifling heat. For a moment she was in his arms and he was tearing at her clothes.

The thought caused her to squeeze her legs together as the unbearable ache crept through her body. She was aware that she was swelling and that a moistness was oozing from her. She groaned in her frustration, causing Karl beside her to ask in a startled voice, 'Are you unwell, Aunt Erika?'

'No, Karl,' she replied with a touch of guilt. 'I just had a small tummy ache.' She wished he would go to sleep. Then she could relieve the agony of desire. She would think of Adolf, the fantasies of being with her fiancé long forgotten. They had been romantic memories of their stolen moments in summer fields where she had first experienced the meaning of a man and woman being one. Wolfgang had been a wonderful lover, but she now admitted that his memory could not truly give her what she wanted.

But what did she want? She puzzled. Something brutal and exciting that crouched in the dark and hidden places of her mind. As a young girl she had experienced her first taste of sexual desire watching animals mating, the brutality of the stallion taking the mare. Sex devoid of love, free to indulge the most forbidden desires. Somehow she sensed that Adolf was that terrible and unspoken god of her most forbidden desires. The agony grew and she knew she desperately needed relief. Nothing else mattered in the world except to feel the explosion that would follow.

'Karl?' she asked in a husky whisper. 'Are you awake?'

The boy remained silent and Erika moaned softly as she sought her pleasure in the only way she could. But Karl was not asleep. He lay very still in his fear and confusion as the sounds of his aunt's self-induced pleasure filled the room.

During the family breakfast together in the hotel dining room, Paul frowned at his son's strange silence. He was normally a talkative boy but this morning he poked at his fried eggs in a distracted manner. Karin glowed, oblivious to what her husband had noticed. Her appetite was good and she ate the fried steak that had been served with the eggs along with two slices of toasted bread and butter. The abundance of good food was something that even Erika had grudgingly admitted was much better than back in Germany.

Paul glanced at his sister who had said little during breakfast. She normally complained about anything and everything. But this morning she was also quiet, eating her breakfast with a good appetite.

'It is a beautiful day,' Paul said in English, as he wanted his family to improve their fluency in the language that was second to them. 'I think the Burns Philp steamer will be a pleasant voyage to Port Moresby for me.'

'I think so too,' Karin agreed cheerily and reached over to touch her son on the cheek. She frowned when he seemed to wince from her touch and withdrew her hand with a hurt feeling. Maybe it was that he was growing up, she consoled herself.

'What will you do when you reach Papua?' Erika asked, and her tone was accusing.

'I will make enquiries as to whether any of the plantation owners need a manager,' Paul answered calmly and firmly in order to curtail his sister's recriminations. 'I am sure with the experience that I have I will get a job until we are in a position in the future to possibly invest in our own plantation. Times will change, and many of the less experienced owners who took up our plantations will be pleased to sell out.'

'So we will be stuck in this hell hole while you hope that someone will take pity on a former enemy and give him a job,' Erika said bitterly. 'I have heard what some of the passengers on the ship from

Sydney have said about living this far from civilisation. Do you not care for the safety of your wife and son?'

'I do,' Paul growled. 'But I would not take any of you to some place on earth where I could not protect and provide for my family. And sadly, dear sister, that includes you.'

'You really do hate me,' Erika spat. She rose from the table, almost spilling her plate on the floor. 'You have always been jealous that father preferred me to you when we were growing up.'

'Sit down!' Paul ordered as he folded a linen table napkin. 'That is not true, and until you are twenty-one, you will do as I say.'

Erika resumed her seat. Yes, she would do as she was told but when she turned twenty-one she would take her share of the family estate and return to Germany. Her brother had always been a man who was not capable of understanding the destiny of Germany. He was a man who thought that family came before country. A fool.

The breakfast continued in silence. Karin felt the rich food curdle in her stomach. She had always found her sister-in-law to be a strange young woman, prone to explosions of temper. But they had shared the loneliness of the war years in Munich and a bond had formed between them despite their differences of opinion. She glanced at her husband and saw pain in his face. She did not doubt him. Her love was something that grew stronger with each day they were together. No matter what lay ahead, he would find a way. Besides, she was looking forward to once again smelling the sweet perfume of the tropical flowers and seeing the lush foliage of the rainforest trees. She knew they would not be apart for long. Paul was a very capable man who would soon find employment and have them join him in New Guinea. Like her husband, she truly felt that they were going home. Germany was but a memory of despair and ruin.

TEN

The dawn mists swirled in ominous fingers around the campsite. The sun was burning off the coolness of the morning and soon the humidity would bring clinging sweat and thirst to be slaked with brackish warm water from the canteens.

George woke with a feeling that all was not right. He had stood guard until three in the morning when Jack relieved him, then gratefully crawled under his blankets to fall into an exhausted sleep. But now he awoke to notice that something was happening around him. Or that something was not happening!

He sat up and rubbed the sleep from his eyes. He could see Jack standing in a huddle with the two police boys and by the way he held his rifle George knew that his former officer was tense with the expectation of a coming action.

Glancing around the campsite, he noticed that the fire had not been lit for the breakfast meal, and that the native porters squatted, looking out at the dense rainforest cloaked in a still, grey mist.

Jack disengaged himself from the two police and walked over to George. 'No doubt that they are out there,' he said. 'The boys are sure. It's all too bloody quiet for my liking. No bird sounds.'

'What do you think will happen?'

And as if to answer his question an ululating sound rose in the forest. George felt the hair on the back of his neck stand up. The call was answered by many and came from all around them. He had never heard such a strange, eerie sound before.

'Better get yourself ready,' Jack said quietly. 'I know that sound and it's not good.'

The porters cast fearful looks in the direction of the two Europeans as they fingered machetes. The police boys raised their rifles to their shoulders.

A swishing sound filled the air and a porter cried out in agony as a long, thin bamboo arrow struck him in the chest. And even before he had fallen to the ground three others pierced his body. He screamed as he groped at the deadly shafts.

The crash of Jack's rifle beside George's head almost deafened him as he snatched his own rifle from the ground beside him. When he rolled into a kneeling stance he saw Jack's target.

Three short but solidly built dark skinned men had appeared out of the mist. They sported bird of paradise plumes above their heads. Around their waists they wore bark cloth skirts and they had strung short black palm bows with arrows. One of the men fell back when Jack's well-aimed shot took him in the throat. His two companions hesitated at the sound of the rifle's blast. It was obvious that they had never encountered a firearm before.

'Looks like we found your Orangwoks,' Jack muttered as he flung back the bolt and chambered a second round.

But as the arrows continued to rain down out of the mist one thunked into George's side just above his waist belt. 'I'm hit!' he gasped.

Jack fired again and dropped a second warrior before he could charge them, wielding a lethal looking stone axe. The mist swirled away on an eddy of morning breeze and it was Jack's turn to gasp. Advancing on them and firing their arrows were at least a hundred warriors. Jack knew that they were completely surrounded as the men of the rainforest closed in. In unison the police boys wildly fired into the advancing warriors. Another warrior fell and this time the advance hesitated. The fact that members of their war party had mysteriously fallen at the sound of the thunder proved that these were surely evil spirits of the forest. Their power was awesome. Blood oozed from the dead and wounded men. One of the dead men had his flesh minced from a bullet exit wound. Such an injury was terrifying to behold. As one, the warriors broke off the fight, leaving their dead behind. The grey swirling mists swallowed them and left the campsite a haunted place of silence.

Jack bent to examine his friend. George lay on his side, tugging at the arrow. It was lodged firmly, having penetrated a good six inches.

'God it hurts, old chap,' George groaned. 'Didn't even see it coming.'

'Just take it easy,' Jack said gently. 'I will give you a good slug of the rum and pull it out when you are a bit under the weather. It's still going to hurt like hell though. But first I've got to see how we stand just in case your Orangwoks decide to return, so start sipping on the bottle.'

George nodded and raised himself to his feet to go to the tent and find the bottle in the medical supplies. It was the only thing close to an anaesthetic they had. The ground around him was littered with hundreds of arrows, protruding from the earth and riddling the tent. The number certainly gave credit to the war party's expertise.

George swigged from the bottle until it was almost empty. The rum quickly took effect. He sighed and slumped down inside the tent.

Jack returned with blood on his hands. 'They killed two of the boys and wounded three others,' he said. 'But the police boys were lucky – no injuries.' He knelt beside George and examined the shaft. 'I am hoping that isn't barbed,' he muttered. George winced when Jack tugged on it gently. 'Sorry old mate, but I am going to have to cut you so that I can make the wound wide enough to allow me to pull the bastard out.'

'Got to do it,' George slurred and Jack chuckled. 'Was funny?' George asked.

'Never seen you this pissed before. It's a bit of an experience.'

'Just get the bloody thing out you colonial hooligan so I can get sober.'

'Never heard you swear before either,' Jack added as he slid his skinning knife from a sheath on his belt. George eyed the blade and Jack could see the fear in his face. He was not a coward but the systematic cutting into his body held a personal fear.

'You have to close your eyes,' Jack said.

'Why, old chap?'

'Because I am going to say a little prayer, and I don't want you to see me praying.' George squinted at his friend. Jack was not a religious man and he wondered why he would be saying a prayer now. For whatever reason he obeyed and closed his eyes as he heard Jack mutter under his breath, 'Dear Lord, who looks after wayward prospectors and mad pommies, gird my arm that I may do your work.'

'Was that . . .' George did not finish his sentence as the blackness came to him in a blinding shower of red stars. He had not seen Jack wrap the handkerchief around his fist. Nor did he see the powerful blow coming.

'Hey Karius, Lipo – get over here,' Jack called to the two police boys who hurried to the tent. 'If Mr George wake up I want you to hold him down.' They nodded and stood by with their rifles as Jack commenced his first incision.

Mercifully George did not feel the cut but he did feel the arrow being tugged from his side. He woke with a shout but found himself held firmly to the ground by the two police boys. Jack struggled to release the cane shaft from George's flesh. With a mighty yank it finally slid from the Englishman. George's body arched as the arrow was removed but only a gasp of air exploding from his lungs revealed any sign of his trauma. A copious flow of blackish blood seeped in a small rivulet from the wound.

'How do you feel?' Jack asked gently when George was sufficiently recovered.

'Pretty awful, old chap,' George replied and rolled on his side to promptly vomit up the contents of his stomach. With a rising horror Jack noticed that there was the dark stain of blood in the vomit; the arrow had pieced his friend's stomach. From experience, such a wound on the battlefield usually meant a slow and agonising death unless immediate medical help was sought. And even then it was touch and go.

'Sit back and take it easy,' Jack said, helping George to lean against a low set camp stretcher.

'Got a terrible thirst,' George slurred. 'And a bloody headache like the chimes of Big Ben are going off in my head. Need to have some water.'

'Maybe not a good idea for the moment,' Jack said and avoided the Englishman's eyes. 'Just get some rest.'

'It's a stomach wound isn't it, Jack?' George had tasted the blood in his mouth.

'Afraid so. But we will get you to a mission station down on the coast where they usually have a good supply of medicines.'

'That's not going to happen as you and I well know,' George sighed. 'We both know that I will not live long enough to survive a stomach wound. I may be dead before the sun sets.'

'We are going to try. The rest is up to you. We've been in worse spots before. Like that time . . .'

'You don't have to patronise me,' George said softly. 'At least I got to see my Orangwoks.'

'Listen, you pommy bastard, I am not going to let you die out here. We didn't survive all those years of war for you to die from an arrow fired by some Stone Age kanaka, when the best of German industry thrown at us failed.'

'Jack?'

'What?'

'I am going to tell you some things before I die. Might shut you up for a while.'

'Nothing that would be of much interest to me.'

'I think what I am going to tell now has everything to do with you,' George said as a wave of pain swamped him. 'I have to tell you things about my past and who I am. I want you to give Iris some letters that I have been writing to her since we left Moresby.'

'When we are having a drink back in Moresby you can tell me and personally hand over the letters to Iris.'

Before George could continue speaking the air was filled with the voices of many men keening a song that rose and fell with an unmistakable beauty in its simplicity. It was a wailing song, and its tone was sad rather than threatening.

'The little bastards are back,' Jack said.

· The two police boys had already exited the tent to face another onslaught. Their courage was equal to that of the overwhelming numbers of warriors facing them. Jack stood with his men and the wounded porters – although fearful – gripped their machetes in a resolute manner.

They came from the forest with their wooden shields held high above their heads and their bows unstrung. Jack sensed that their wailing was not that of men preparing to attack. Their posture was like that of the Roman soldiers Jack had once read about in a history book. They were asking for a truce to retrieve their dead from the battleground. 'Lower your guns,' Jack ordered, by way of signalling to the slowly approaching warriors that he understood their motives were peaceful.

They retrieved the bodies of their fallen comrades and, still wailing their song, retreated to the cover of the jungle.

Jack walked back to the tent and stepped inside. 'Damnedest . . .' He froze as the words died in his throat. His friend was slumped back against the camp stretcher. Jack had seen death many times and knew that George was gone.

He knelt beside his old friend and the tears rolled down his cheeks. 'Now why did you go and leave me,' he whispered hoarsely as he choked back his terrible grief. George was closer than any brother he could have had. They had shared such experiences in the horrors of the Western Front, things that neither could tell to anyone who had not been there.

And even when the guns had fallen silent, George had followed Jack to Australia rather than returning to the greener fields of his home in

England. But in doing so he had been led to his death. Jack was selfishly seeking riches for himself. But George's noble search to enrich mankind's knowledge was something that would endure in memory long after the gold was melted down and sold for the material comforts it could bring.

Jack rose from his knees and faced his small party. They too had reason to grieve. They knew that they would be leaving their fallen in foreign territory a long way from their ancestral lands.

The dead were buried and they struck camp. The confrontation with the tribesmen had decimated the expedition, but Jack had carefully marked his find for a future claim. It was time to return to Port Moresby.

Before they retraced their steps back to the Huon Gulf Jack stood over his old friend's grave, his rifle slung on his shoulder and his battered hat in hand.

'Don't matter about who you were and what you did before the war,' he said quietly. 'All I know, is that you were the bloody best company sergeant major the Australian army ever had, and the best friend I ever knew. I won't forget you George, and I will tell Iris that you had her name on your lips before you died.'

From the shadows of the forest many eyes watched the white demon and his servants preparing to leave. They had succeeded in killing one of the white demons but his partner was able to elude their arrows. They would go to the graves and dig them up as soon as the demon left their territory. That night they would feast on the flesh of the men they had slain.

ELEVEN

The Japanese boat captain was true to his word. His boat was anchored in the bay waiting for Jack and his party, now diminished to just himself, the two police boys and the two Buka porters who had survived the fight weeks earlier in the mountains. The other porters had died from their wounds, from arrows Jack suspected had been dipped in poison.

They had arrived on the beach after a forced march. The drums that had been silent for Jack's trek into the dreaded warriors' territory now pounded in the forests with their unreadable messages. Their eerie sound was unnerving but the threat of another attack faded as they grew closer to the coast – although Jack never allowed his men to drop their guard. It was possible that the warriors had passed word back down to any coastal natives that the white demons could be killed like normal men.

But what Jack did not know was that the warriors who had attacked them had no knowledge of any other persons whatsoever living beyond their rainforest territory. George had been right when he had concluded that they had met their Orangwoks, although they did not ride on horses nor were they covered in gold armour.

The sea voyage back to Port Moresby was as uneventful as the voyage out and within a couple of weeks Jack arrived in the frontier town. His first stop was Government House to report to Sir Hubert Murray on the tragic consequences of their limited exploration into the Huon Gulf hinterland. Sir Hubert listened sympathetically and expressed his condolences on the loss of George and the Buka men who had accompanied them.

'I have even worse news for you, Jack,' he said leaning forward at his desk. 'We received a letter for you some days ago. As it was actually addressed care of the administration my people took the liberty of reading it. The letter came from your brother-in-law. It seems that your sister Mary in Sydney is critically ill.'

Jack felt his shoulders slump at the news. In such a short space of time he had lost his best friend and his men. Now he might lose his beloved sister back in Sydney.

'When was the letter dated?' he asked wearily.

'It was posted four weeks ago from Sydney. We have had no other news since then.'

Jack rose. He would need to submit an official report to the Papuan administration on the events of the past few weeks, but now he had to make his way out to Sen's house and tell Iris the sad news concerning George's death. In a way this was not something new to Jack. He had written many letters to next of kin of soldiers killed or missing in action during the war. Sometimes missing in action was nothing more than the official description for men who had taken a direct hit from a high explosive artillery shell and their bodies blasted into a thousand tiny pieces of flesh with nothing left to identify them or acknowledge that they even existed except for the fact they had been in the army. But he had never before personally delivered the message to the next of kin or a loved one. To do so was something he wished he could avoid. Jack knew his first stop before going to Iris would be to the hotel for a long, hard-earned drink.

'What are you going to do about your sister?' Sir Hubert asked as Jack picked up his big floppy bush hat from the floor beside his chair.

'I will be arranging to catch a steamer south to Sydney,' he replied. 'Mary is looking after my son.'

Sir Hubert glanced in surprise at Jack. 'I was not aware that you were married,' he said.

'Married and widowed – but with a son.'

'I am sorry for your circumstances,' Sir Hubert said gently. 'It must be hard leaving a son behind.' Jack did not reply.

When Jack thought it could not get worse – it did.

Sen explained that Iris's horse had been found dead with an arrow in its chest about a month after the time that he and George had departed on their expedition. Iris was missing without any trace and the police had been investigating the circumstances of her disappearance. Their conclusion was that some renegade natives from around Moresby had taken advantage of the isolated area and a lone girl and had ambushed her.

'Jesus,' Jack swore softly and bowed his head as he sat on the verandah steps of Sen's residence. 'A single arrow killed her horse you say.'

'It may have been a poisoned arrow,' Sen said. 'No other explanation.'

'At least I have been spared the task of telling her that George is dead,' Jack said bitterly. 'And it is a kind of mercy that George did not live to learn of Iris's fate. I think it would have killed George if he had known.'

'What are your plans now?' Sen asked.

Jack looked up from the fernery to stare at the blue sky above. 'Use some of the money I know you will give me for the gold I found and head back to Sydney for a spell. My sister is pretty crook and I need to be away from here for a while. Just one of those things . . .' He trailed off, at a loss for words to describe the crushing feeling of despair and guilt. Despair for George's death – and guilt for leading him to that cruel fate.

'You are always welcome in my house,' Sen said, placing his hand on his friend's shoulder. 'We have both lost people close to us.'

'Thanks, old cobber,' Jack said as he rose from the steps. 'But I will catch the first steamer south I can.

In the meantime I need to go back to Moresby and have another drink at the pub. With any luck I might bump into O'Leary while I'm still sober and finish what George started for me before we went north.'

'O'Leary is not around these ways,' Sen said with a touch of relief. He knew Jack was in a mood to take out his pent-up emotions in a display of violence. He was aware of the Australian's pre-war reputation for being prepared to take on any man who dared challenge him to a fight. It was the Irish in him, some said. 'O'Leary and his partner went west to the Fly River region on a recruiting drive about the time you went north.'

'Pity,' Jack growled. 'It's not going to be over between us until I make him know that I will not take any rubbish from him. Anyway, I will accept your kind offer and head back to put my head down here tonight. I should be able to get the boat leaving the day after tomorrow. You will find the gold in my duffel bag,' he added as he rose from his cane chair. 'I don't have to say that I can trust you to arrange its sale with your Chinese contacts and take your commission.'

Sen glanced at his friend with just a touch of surprise. But why should he be surprised? Jack Kelly was indeed a trusting man when it came to friends. He knew that he could trust Sen and he also knew that Sen would not let him down. He watched him stride away but noticed his friend seemed to carry a sad load on his shoulders. His gaze lingered on Jack and Sen felt the surge of guilt turn to a wave of despair for those things about his own past years in the territories of Papua and New Guinea he knew he could never tell his good friend, who had fought so courageously for his country. It had been so simple to fool the Australians. They were a trusting people who saw him as just another Oriental who had worked hard to make his fortune. If only they had known how he had been given his stake to build his fortune he might now be a dead man. Such was the punishment for the offences he had committed during the war years. And as for O'Leary and Jack's suspicions – Sen knew a lot more than he could tell.

Jack strode towards the stables. He would take the sulky into town and get roaring drunk and bury his old friend again in the manner they both knew so well. The horse would make its own way back to Sen's with him as a passenger once the alcohol had helped numb his grief. Or was the alcohol a means of numbing guilt, Jack wondered bitterly.

Dademo was standing beside the sulky stroking the big chestnut's forehead as it stood patiently waiting between the harness rails.

'Hey, Mr Jack, me got something you want to buy,' he said and held out his hand. In the palm of his hand nestled an empty rifle cartridge. 'You buy this fella stuff.' Jack knew that empty brass rifle cartridges could be reloaded and so too did the natives who worked with Europeans. Bullets cost money and a reloaded bullet cut back on cost of ammunition.

Jack took the brass cartridge and frowned. It was not the standard .303 case used in the Lee Enfield rifles common throughout the British Empire. He recognised it immediately as a German 7.92 case as used in Mauser rifles.

'Where did you find it, Dademo?' he asked. The houseboy suddenly appeared sheepish, moving from foot to foot in a manner that Jack knew meant he was reluctant to speak. 'You tell me quick smart where you found this bullet.'

Under Jack's withering stare, Dademo relented. What harm could come from telling Mr Jack, who was a good man? 'Found it in the hills near where missus Iris horse got killed,' he mumbled. 'When we went out to look for her with Master Sen.'

'You didn't tell Master Sen about your find because you figured a white man would buy it from you.' Jack spoke without rancour. It was the way of the local people to remain aloof from European matters not of their concern and he did not expect a reply from Dademo. 'You think that one arrow could kill a horse?' he asked and Dademo now frowned.

'No, Mr Jack.'

'Nor do I,' Jack replied pocketing the empty case. From the expression on the white man's face Dademo knew better than to ask for payment.

Jack hauled himself into the sulky and took the reins from Dademo. The ruse of placing an arrow in a bullet wound was as old as the Palmer River days, almost half a century before. Jack remembered how the old timers who had worked the dangerous gold fields of northern Queensland told stories of unscrupulous men who killed Chinese miners for their gold, then placed souvenired spears in the resulting wounds to make it appear that the

143

Aboriginal warriors had killed the Chinese. This memory was fresh when Sen had told him that a single arrow had killed the horse. He had considered poison but that would still be slow acting – and from what Sen had told him, when they found Iris's horse it was clear it had crashed into the ground very heavily.

The find of the rifle case was purely circumstantial. It could have been ejected at any time, but the fact that it was a Mauser case made Jack think of O'Leary. He was the only man he knew in Moresby who preferred the German rifle to the British Lee Enfield most commonly used by prospectors and police. But even a suspicion required proof. The rogue Irishman was the lowest of men, Jack knew, but surely not stupid enough to kill a woman related to a man with considerable influence in Papua. Jack remembered how Sen had told him that O'Leary left the Moresby district about the same time as Iris went missing. Sen *thought* that O'Leary had left a month earlier. But whilst Jack had been at the pub earlier after his audience with Sir Hubert he had been informed by one of his old gummy, prospector mates that O'Leary had stolen a good set of false teeth from him. When Jack had ceased laughing he had asked idly when the theft had occurred and the old prospector grumbled the date, which he had obvious reason to remember: three days before Iris went missing.

Before he flicked the reins Jack turned to Dademo. 'That arrow that killed Miss Iris's horse, I will pay two bob for it if you know where it is.'

Dademo looked startled at Jack's offer of a reward. He did know where it was. It was in the possession of an old and feared *masalai meri* – a witch the Europeans would have called her. She lived in Dademo's village and paid well for items that had been used to kill. Such items held strong magic and in a land where all misfortunes were attributed to acts of magic the arrow was a potent item. Her powers must be strong, as she was still alive in a land where a bloody vengeance was often sought against those identified as practitioners of the dark arts.

'I know where the arrow is, Mr Jack,' he replied. 'But it belongs to *masalai meri* who is the witch of my village.'

'Tell her that I will buy the arrow off her for five bob,' Jack said, 'and I will throw in a couple of bob more for you if you get it to me tonight.'

Dademo whistled. Such an amount of wealth must mean that the arrow was truly powerful and he now regretted selling it to her for the price of a blessing against the curses of his enemies.

'I will, Mr Jack. But I will need some money to buy another blessing against the evil spirits.'

The reward he had offered was generous and Jack knew he would get the arrow when he returned from the hotel that evening. Dademo would be leaving only a trail of dust back to his village a short distance away to retrieve the item. 'Tell her she only gets the money when I get the arrow.'

Dademo nodded and Jack flicked the reins.

• • •

In the town Jack submitted his written report to an official at Sir Hubert's office then went to purchase his fare for the voyage back to Sydney. The exchange of gold for cash had left him with a considerable amount of spending money, which he took from Sen in Australian currency. Rolled in a wad it felt good in his pocket. But he was also aware that it was not enough to properly outfit another expedition back to the river where he had found his gold, nor enough to bring in the equipment and supplies to set up a large scale mining operation. To do that he would require a vast amount of capital, and Sydney was the place to try and raise it. For the venture he envisaged, this would not be just a case of grubbing a staked out lot. It would give him a chance at his long held dream of owning a mining company and becoming a very rich man.

Jack was deep in thought as he crossed the street to walk to the hotel where he had left his horse and sulky. Now it was time to have a drink in George's memory. To raise a glass to him in the bar where George had so efficiently dispatched O'Leary and earned a place in local folklore for his efforts.

'Captain Kelly! Is that you?'

Jack froze. Not because someone had recognised him – there were many former soldiers of the war who had travelled to find a new life on this wild frontier – but because the person who had questioned his identity had spoken to him in German. Jack turned to see a face that brought back memories of a terrible day of hand to hand fighting in the trenches of the Hindenburg Line three years earlier.

'Major Mann!'

'It is you, Captain Kelly,' Paul said as he stumbled forward, almost in a daze of disbelief. 'I always hoped that you had survived.'

Jack's expression of shock thawed to a slow, warm smile of welcome. 'I am pleased to see that you made it,' he said as he thrust out his hand. 'But I never thought I would ever see you again. Especially back here.'

Paul took Jack's offered hand and pumped it enthusiastically. 'It is good to see you again, my friend.'

'So what the hell are you doing in these parts?' Jack asked. 'I thought that our government took all your lands from you up in New Guinea.'

'They did,' Paul replied with a frown. 'But I was to buy back my plantation from one of your countrymen. However he pulled out of the deal at the last moment. So here I am in Port Moresby on my way up to Finschhafen to see if I can get work as a plantation manager.'

Jack suddenly realised that in their conversation they had been switching from German to English. He was surprised how fluent he still was in his mother's language. 'Why don't you join me at the pub for a drink?' he beamed. 'Tell me how things have been since I last saw you.'

'I would, my friend, except that I have noticed that I am not welcomed by many of your countrymen in the hotel. I was there yesterday and they asked me to leave.'

'Like bloody hell they will when they know you are with me,' Jack swore. 'C'mon, old cobber, I'll buy the first round.'

'What is a cobber?' Paul asked in English.

'Cobber is a mate – a friend, an amigo,' Jack laughed.

Paul smiled. He had not smiled very much since leaving his wife and son on the wharf at Townsville with his petulant sister. But the Australian had an infectious friendliness about him and the air of a man confident that he was bullet proof to the world.

As Jack stormed into the bar heads turned curiously to greet him. Without any further fanfare Jack roared above the low babble of men steeped in drink. 'This is Major Paul Mann, formerly of the German army, and formerly a man who did his best to kill me on the Hindenburg Line. But now he is here with me and prepared to buy the first round. Any man who objects to him being in here can tell me personally of his grievance. But, for the sake of propriety, that will be done outside the pub where civilised men settle their differences. Are there any objections?'

'No, Jack,' old Harry the prospector said. 'If he is a cobber of yours and you don't object to the fact that he tried to kill ya, then he is okay with us.'

A mumbled ripple of agreement went through the room and Jack guided Paul across the pub to a place at the bar beside Harry.

That evening Şen was disturbed in the office of his house by the sound of drunken men. The voices

148

were coming from a distance and he was puzzled by the foreign words. Although he did not speak German, he did recognise the language.

He rose and went to the verandah to see the chestnut come to a halt and two men spill out of the sulky. Jack collapsed on the ground but rose to his feet with the help of a stranger.

'I am sorry, my friend,' Paul said, addressing Sen as he helped Jack by half dragging and half walking him towards the verandah, 'but we have not met. You must be Mr Sen as Jack has told me much about you. I am Paul Mann from Munich but formerly of Finschhafen in New Guinea.'

The stranger appeared less drunk than Jack and Sen stepped down from the verandah to assist. The German held out his hand. 'I am Sen,' he replied as he took Paul's hand. 'I must thank you for getting Jack back to my place in one piece. I am not surprised to see him this way. He has had a lot of bad things happen to him recently.'

When Paul let him go Jack crumpled on the step. 'Good man, this Kraut,' Jack slurred as he tried to focus the world around him. 'A bit like old George in many ways. Tried his best to kill me once though. But now he is a fair dinkum cobber. A Papuan like you and me, Sen.'

'We will get him inside and onto his bed,' Sen grunted. 'I think he will be a very sick man in the morning.'

They dropped Jack on his camp stretcher under a mosquito net and left. Sen invited Paul to join him in a drink but the German politely declined the offer with the explanation that he had to get back to his boarding house in Moresby.

'It is very late and you would be better off staying here for the night, Mr Mann,' Sen said. 'I have room and my wife will arrange to make up a bed for you near Jack.'

'That is very kind of you, Mr Sen,' Paul replied.

Sen did not correct Paul's use of his name. He had long realised that Europeans tended to be embarrassed when they were told of their mistake in addressing him. It was similar to the Asian loss of face. So he would remain 'Mr Sen' to the German.

'It is the least I can do for a man who once tried to kill Jack,' Sen replied with just the hint of a wicked smile. 'But that was when you Europeans were doing your best to destroy your own civilisation.'

Paul nodded. Jack had told him about Sen and now he was able to see for himself just how remarkable the Chinese man was. His English was fluent with little trace of an accent and Paul sensed that Sen was very much in tune with European thinking. This was strange to Paul, as the only Chinese he had known before the war were labourers or recruiters of native labour, so very different to Sen who could easily be at home in any European house – except that he was Chinese. Paul suddenly had a fleeting thought for the Jewish people of his own land. They were the Chinese of Germany, he thought. 'I will accept your kind offer to stay overnight,' Paul said, and once again shook Sen's hand. 'It is very late and I am not familiar with the country around Port Moresby.'

'That is good,' Sen said. 'And knowing Jack I will presume that you have not eaten as yet.'

'No, but I do not wish to impose any further on your hospitality,' Paul said. 'You have done enough.'

'I know most of what happens around Moresby,' Sen said. 'But I have not heard of you before.'

'I am only in Moresby on my way back to Finschhafen,' Paul replied. 'I am not from around here.'

'So what is there in Finschhafen for you?' Sen asked bluntly. He was warming to the German, there was something about him. Besides, Sen had known many Germans from his time in New Guinea before the war and respected the efficient way that they had governed the northern part of the island under the Kaiser's jurisdiction.

Paul told Sen his story; of how he had returned to New Guinea with the hope of starting a new life for his family away from the ruins of a war ravaged Germany. By the time Sen's wife had served up a light meal of steamed vegetables and pork cooked in the Oriental style, Sen had offered Paul a job to help get him on his feet. Paul was stunned by the offer – especially since Sen's accompanying offer of pay was more than generous.

'Are you sure that I could be of use?' Paul asked. 'I am not familiar with the country you talk about.'

'Your general knowledge of New Guinea will be a great help to me,' Sen assured him as they sat on the floor either side of the low table spread with food bowls and condiments. 'The mission I have in mind is dangerous and most probably will come to nothing.

But it is something I must do to appease my wife's ancestors. I have a feeling that short of Jack Kelly you are the right man to lead the expedition. But I do not want Jack to know what you are to do. If he knew he would insist on going himself and I think it is time that he went south to see his son and make arrangements for his mining operation.'

Paul shook Sen's hand for the third time that night and sealed the deal. It certainly was a strange and most probably futile mission, but he could not afford to walk away from it. Meeting Jack Kelly under the circumstances of war had been a strange event in his life, and here they were again in the land that they had shared before the war. For Paul it had been New Guinea. For Jack it had been Papua. But both had survived the horror that had been the Western Front. Two men from opposing armies were now strangely bonded in peace.

TWELVE

Dademo shook Jack awake. The Australian felt as if his head would crack and he had trouble focussing on the houseboy standing over him. He was vaguely aware that it was morning. He could hear Sen's wife's singsong voice in lilting Chinese chiding a *haus meri* in the kitchen. Jack attempted to smile. The Papuan girl would not understand a word of the rebuke.

'I got the arrow.' Dademo stated it nervously. Possession of such an item provoked fears for its malevolent power. 'It's outside, Mr Jack.'

Jack heaved himself into a sitting position. 'Give me a couple of minutes and I will meet you down in the fernery,' he groaned, holding his head. He had a nagging feeling that something had happened the previous day and he was not yet sure what it was.

'I thought you might like a strong cup of tea,' said a vaguely familiar voice. Jack turned his blurry vision on Paul who had entered the room as Dademo left.

'Thanks,' Jack replied, taking the mug of steaming tea from the German. 'I just hope it clears a few cobwebs.'

'I have news for you, my friend,' Paul said with a beaming smile to hide the lie he must tell. 'Your friend Mr Sen has given me a job working for his enterprises as a recruiter of native labourers.'

'That's good,' Jack replied less than enthusiastically as he took his first sip. 'Guess you will be around Papua a bit longer than you first figured.'

'At least now I may be able to get accommodation for my wife and son and my sister Erika.'

At the mention of Erika's name Jack almost spilled the hot tea on his bare chest. During their drinking session the day before the two men had recounted their personal experiences on the Western Front but family had not been mentioned. 'Did you say your sister was also with you?' Jack asked, trying to sound nonchalant. 'I thought she may have remained in Germany. There is not much to offer out here.'

'Ah no,' Paul sighed. 'My sister will remain with me until she turns twenty-one. I do not think that she should be in Germany during these troubled times. I am afraid that she was falling into bad company. So she is with my wife and son in Townsville. I rented a house for them until I am settled here. Then they can join me in Papua or New Guinea.'

The fog in Jack's head was rapidly clearing as he remembered the beautiful and angelic face in the

154

photograph that had been with him since the Hindenburg Line. His heart rate had suddenly doubled at the mention of how geographically close he was to her even now. Townsville was a stop for the Burns Philp steamer on its way south. 'You know, I could drop in and pass on your regards to your family in Townsville on my way back to Sydney,' he said. 'Tell them that you are well and looking forward to them joining you soon.'

'That would be nice,' Paul replied. 'I have spoken of you to my wife and I know she would be pleased to finally make your acquaintance. It would be a good omen to have you meet my family – for them to learn that there are Australians who are prepared to extend the hand of friendship to former enemies.'

'Well, got to try and see if I can walk,' Jack said putting the mug aside and heaving himself to his feet. 'Have a lot to do today.'

'Thank you, my friend,' Paul said, grasping Jack's hand.

'For what?' Jack replied.

'For being a cobber.'

Jack burst into a deep laugh. 'You are learning,' he said. 'You will be a fair dinkum Aussie before you know it.'

'What is fair dinkum?' Paul questioned with a frown.

'I will give you language lessons some time,' Jack grinned. 'You see, the way we Australians speak English is a bit different to the way the poms speak the language.'

Paul thought he understood. The Australians spoke a dialect of the language just as people did in his homeland in the different regions of Germany.

Jack skipped breakfast. His stomach was not up to food. He found Dademo hovering in the fernery. 'Okay, where is it?' Jack asked.

Dademo retrieved the arrow from a niche in the rockery and handed it to Jack. He stared at the blood stained shaft.

'This is a Kuku arrow,' he said. 'It's not an arrow from around here.'

'No, Mr Jack,' Dademo agreed. 'Looks like an arrow from the wild men up in the hill country.'

'You think that they would have been down around Moresby at any time recently?' Jack questioned.

'Not the wild men from the hills,' the houseboy replied, shaking his head. 'I would know if they had.'

'So it's a plant, like I figured,' Jack muttered as he turned the arrow over in his hands. 'Thank you, Dademo, you did good.'

Dademo beamed at the praise. Maybe the arrow did have strong magic.

There was something Jack knew he must do before leaving for Sydney. He found Sen later that morning. The Chinese entrepreneur was overseeing a stock-take of stores for an expedition to be led by the German. He glanced with some curiosity as Jack approached with the arrow in his hand.

'I don't think your sister-in-law was murdered by local natives,' Jack said by way of greeting. 'In fact, I think there might be a slight chance that she is still alive.'

Sen let out a long breath of air. 'I have had my suspicions,' he said. 'We did not find her body.'

'This arrow was found in Iris's horse,' Jack said, 'and it's not from around here. And one arrow will not kill a horse. My bet is that we would find a bullet in the horse if we went looking. A bullet to match this casing.'

Jack produced the Mauser cartridge case which Sen recognised.

'O'Leary,' Sen stated and Jack nodded.

'As good as any.'

'But we do not have proof,' Sen said, shaking his head. 'He was last reported going west into the Fly River delta on a recruiting drive.'

'That doesn't discount the fact he may have done his mischief before he left.'

Sen fell silent and turned away to stare at the pile of trade goods spread out on the floor of his shed. 'I think I would prefer that Iris be dead rather than in the hands of that man,' he finally said.

Jack knew what he meant. O'Leary and his partner were men capable of unspeakable cruelty. 'We have the means to find her,' he said. 'O'Leary will return to Moresby and I will get the truth out of him one way or the other.'

When Sen glanced up Jack could see uncertainty etched in his face. 'Maybe,' he replied. 'Would you like to partake of tea?' he offered, suddenly changing the subject. 'I think you have something else to talk to me about before you go south.'

Jack pulled a pained expression. Sen was a very perceptive man. 'There *is* something I want to talk to you about.'

Sen sighed in relief. He did not want Jack to doggedly pursue the subject of O'Leary. The evening before he had shared his secret with Paul Mann and sworn him to total silence on the events of his past. There were some matters that he could not include Jack Kelly in and this was one of them.

On the verandah Jack sipped from his mug of steaming black tea. Sen held a dainty china cup filled with what looked like pale green water. He much preferred his green tea to the black brew from India.

'You think that you have found enough gold to make a large scale mining operation feasible?' Sen asked.

'I think I found a mother lode,' Jack replied. 'But I am going to need a lot of money to get it out.'

Sen sipped his tea and stared towards the gardens. 'I know of a man in Sydney who might be able to help you out if all else fails.'

'That would be appreciated,' Jack answered.

'But only if all else fails,' Sen cautioned. 'He is a man who has a bad reputation for taking advantage of situations to satisfy his own ends.'

'Is he Chinese?' Jack asked and Sen chuckled at his friend's less than tactful slur on his race.

'No, he is an Australian like you,' he replied and Jack felt embarrassed by his thoughtless question. He understood, however, that Sen was warning him.

'Sorry,' Jack mumbled. But Sen did not hold any animosity. Jack's remark was simply a slip between friends.

Before he left for Moresby, Jack said goodbye to Paul who handed over his family's address in Townsville and a letter for them. As they shook hands Jack realised just how much he owed the Chinese businessman for the hospitality and friendship he extended – to himself as well as Paul. He also knew that he owed it to his old friend George to find the truth about Iris. The guilt of leading the quiet and brave Englishman to his death in the densely forested mountains of Papua haunted the Australian more than he could confide to anyone.

He stood on the wharf with his swag at his feet. Returning to Sydney meant confronting a little boy he felt that he had selfishly deserted. He had been able to console himself with the knowledge that Lukas was better left with his sister who could give him motherly love. But now the last news of Mary was that she was critically ill. To have her die would be bad enough. But for his son to lose a second mother would be worse.

The gangplank rattled down to the wharf. Europeans milled on board. Men from the government service and their families jostled in the queue, happily looking forward to some leave at home.

Home for Jack however was the place he was leaving, not the one he was going to. He hefted his swag and made his way to the gangplank.

THIRTEEN

She was as beautiful as he had always imagined. And there was no doubt that the young woman in the photograph that Jack had carried through the short years since the Great War was the same woman who now absent-mindedly scattered seed to the hens in the dusty yard.

'Good morning, Miss Mann,' Jack said. Erika snapped from her chore to look sharply at the man who had addressed her in her native tongue. She had not noticed his approach along the track – few people visited the temporary home she shared with her sister-in-law and nephew. 'My name is Jack Kelly and I am a friend of your brother,' Jack said as he removed his hat and brushed it against the side of his trousers.

'You speak German although I suspect that you are an Australian from your accent,' she replied with a frown.

'My mother was German,' Jack answered, taking in the graceful curve of her cheekbones. He felt a weakness in his stomach akin to that he had experienced in the trenches. It was called fear and he knew why. He was standing with his hat in his hand looking upon the vision of someone he had not imagined he would ever actually meet – the woman of his dreams. 'I last saw your brother in Port Moresby a short while ago and he asked that I tell you all that he was well. He misses you all very much.'

'Jack Kelly,' Erika mused. 'You were the enemy soldier who my brother told us about when we left Munich,' she said as if remembering another time and place. 'He said you were kind to him when he was wounded.'

Jack hardly heard her words as he stared at the young woman. She was wearing an ankle length dress with a tight waist, a style popular in Europe before the war. Her long black hair was piled on her head in a tight bun that had been unable to control all her lustrous locks. Wisps fell across her face in a way that made her look vulnerable. She was not wearing a hat and the hot tropical sun was already touching her skin with rosiness akin to a blush.

'We did meet under less than kind circumstances,' he finally said, after taking in her dark beauty. He was aware that she was also appraising him in an enigmatic way. 'I have a letter from Paul for Mrs Mann,' he said, breaking the strange moment between them.

'Then you should come inside to meet her,' Erika said as she emptied the last of the seed from her apron onto the ground. The scrawny hens scrabbled in a frenzy around her dress to peck at the feed. She turned her back and Jack followed her to the high-set wood plank house built in the tropical style. It was a simple dwelling with a fenced garden of vegetables that had been lovingly attended to from what Jack could observe.

'Karin,' Erika called inside when they had climbed the rickety staircase. 'There is a man to see us who has just come down from the north. He has a letter from Paul.'

An older woman who looked to be in her late twenties emerged from the cool gloom of the house. She was covered in a thin film of flour and Jack guessed she had been in the process of making bread. What struck Jack most about Paul's wife was the beautiful serenity of her welcoming smile. She held her hand out to him then withdrew it to wipe the excess flour from her hands on her apron.

'I am Karin Mann,' she said, embarrassed for being caught in a less than dainty condition.

Jack beamed a broad smile to set her at ease. 'My name is Jack Kelly and it is nice to see bread being made the way it was meant to be baked,' he added. 'A bit of a change from the damper I make in the bush.'

Like Erika, Karin was impressed by Jack's fluency in German, although his accent was somewhat amusing. It had a slight twang to it and his pronunciation of some words was rather quaint.

'Mr Kelly's mother was German,' Erika reminded her sister-in-law. 'That is how he speaks our language. Mr Kelly says he has news of Paul.'

As if on a prompt, Jack reached into his pocket then passed the letter to Karin, who avidly read the contents. Jack stood patiently in the doorway while Karin finished reading the six-page expression of love and yearning.

Finally she glanced up at Jack. 'I am sorry, Mr Kelly, for my neglect,' she said as if coming out of a trance. 'I am rude in not inviting you inside for a coffee. Or is it tea you would prefer?'

'Coffee would be fine,' Jack said, stepping inside the sparsely furnished house. It was strange, Jack thought, that Paul's sister had not expressed a desire to know what was in the letter her brother had written. But he dismissed the thought as Karin bustled around the wood burning stove to place a big, blackened coffee pot on the hot plate.

'Paul has already told me about you, Mr Kelly,' Karin said with her back to him. 'I think you must be a very good man. He has written in his letter how you were able to get him employment with a friend of yours in Port Moresby. I am very grateful for your kindness.'

'Nothing much in what I did, Mrs Mann,' Jack said, parrying the expression of gratitude. 'Just something mates do for each other around this part of the world.'

Jack had translated the word 'mates' into German but it did not coincide with what Karin could understand in the Australian context. He could see her confusion and hurried to explain the meaning. 'Mates are men who we look after. Not in the way of mates between animals.'

Karin smiled and nodded her understanding of his clumsy explanation. 'What we would call a deep friendship between men.'

Now it was Jack's turn to nod. He had to admit to himself that Paul's wife was also a beautiful woman. He felt a touch of guilt. Such things were not usually admitted to, even to one's self, when it came to a mate's wife. That was the bush code of chivalry. But privately Karin was the kind of woman a man would be glad to live with – or die for. But then there was Erika, who seemed to be at the edge of their conversation. She had suddenly left the room with a muttered apology. There were tasks to attend to and Jack was disappointed to see her go. But he had noticed the fleeting scowl on Karin's face.

'I must apologise for Erika's rudeness,' she sighed as she poured the thick black coffee into two teacups, taking a seat at the simple plank table opposite Jack. 'She has not taken to this land as I had hoped she would. I must also apologise that I do not have milk for your coffee.'

'Tough country,' Jack said as he stirred in a generous spoonful of sugar and took a sip. 'But the coffee is good.'

'You must not consider that Paul's sister is normally like this with guests, but I am afraid she knows that you met my husband at the same time her beloved fiancé Wolfgang was killed. I sometimes think that she holds all Australians responsible for his death.'

'I was sorry to learn of his death at the time,' Jack said gently, 'but that was war. I also lost a lot of friends to German bullets but I do not hold that against individual men who were only doing what the bloody politicians ordered us to do.'

'I understand this also,' Karin said. 'With time I think Erika will come to understand the same. Now she is a young woman with the passion of her convictions. I do not think that she holds you personally responsible for Wolfgang's death. It is just still fresh in her memories. She did not want to come to this country but Paul felt that he could better look after us over here rather than in Germany where things are not well. There is a deep bitterness that I fear is eating my country like an ogre.'

Jack was about to express the opinion that Germany deserved her fate for starting the war in the first place. But he looked at the gentle face wracked with anguish for things past and present and bit his tongue. No, Karin Mann and her husband were truly decent people who did not need any more suffering. The war was over and so too should be the wasted search for causes. What did it matter who had started the bloody war? What was more important was that it was over.

'I believe you have a son,' Jack said, by way of changing the subject.

'Yes,' Karin replied with a wan smile. 'Karl is currently attending school in Townsville. Her smile darkened. 'The other children are cruel to him. They call him a dirty Hun.'

'Kids are like that,' Jack attempted to console her when he noticed tears welling in her eyes. She looked away. 'But given time kids also have a way of sorting out differences,' he hastily added.

'I pray that you are right, Mr Kelly,' she replied as she wiped at her eyes with the back of her flour covered hand. Instinctively Jack reached across the table to take hold of her hand. It was a gesture prompted by the depth of her hurt and one that surprised him. Normal feelings for such perceived trivial problems had been long blasted out of him on the battlefields of France – or so he thought.

'Things will work out,' he said as he held Karin's hand gently in his.

She gazed at him with an expression of gratitude and allowed the ghost of a smile. 'I think you are right,' she replied. 'Oh, I miss Paul. I pray that we will all be together soon. I am afraid I have not been as good a wife to my husband in the past as I should have been.'

Jack withdrew his hand. 'I doubt that. From what I have seen in even this short space of time I think Paul has to be the luckiest man alive to have a wife as good as you.'

Karin unconsciously brushed at a strand of loose hair hanging across her face and sniffed. 'I thank you for your kind words. Paul is lucky to have you as a friend. But tell me, Mr Kelly, what brings you to Townsville?'

Jack was taken aback by her bluntly delivered question. How could he tell her that he had only stopped over so that he could meet the woman of his dreams? That delivering the letter was merely an excuse to do so?

'Just on my way to Sydney and I thought I might drop in to tell you that Paul is doing well,' he answered as convincingly as he could. 'I will be leaving tomorrow on the train south to Brisbane and then on to Sydney from there. I received a telegram when I landed yesterday that my sister has died. My son was staying with her.'

'Oh, I am sorry. But you are married?' Karin said with a note of surprise. 'And you have a son?'

'Was married,' Jack replied. 'But my wife died in the flu epidemic a couple of years ago. I am afraid I hardly know my son. He was born while I was serving overseas. His name is Lukas and he is around five now. They say he looks like me.'

'Paul is almost a stranger to our son too,' Karin said. 'The war took more from us than we know. Our son is only a year older than yours.'

'Think I know what you mean. Lukas is like a stranger to me and I feel bad that I am not a better father. I just dumped him on my sister so that I could go gold prospecting back in Papua and New Guinea.' Jack fell silent and stared across his coffee at an almost translucent gecko perched high up on the wall in a dark corner of the kitchen. 'I don't know what I am going to do.'

'I am sorry for your loss,' Karin repeated gently. 'Death still comes to us.'

Jack nodded and his sadness was thick in the room. 'My last correspondence on her health was that she was not expected to live long. She got some kind of infection when she cut herself pruning flowers or something. Doctors said that they could not stop it eating her up.'

'What will you do about your son?' Karin asked. As if to answer her own question she added, 'I could look after him if you wish.'

Startled by the simplicity of the suggestion, Jack stared at her. 'You would do that?'

She smiled with a warmth that Jack could not remember in a long time. It reminded him of his sister's wonderful smile. 'I may require just a little money to pay for his expenses but I have room in my life for one more boy. It is a simple way of repaying your kindness towards my husband.'

A massive weight seemed to lift from Jack's shoulders. If he was to return to Papua, he knew that his brother-in-law was not really capable of rearing Lukas on his own. The boy needed the attention of a woman at such an early stage in his life. Now Karin was offering to give his son a home where the wonderful and earthy aromas of baking bread and brewed coffee might give stability to a little boy's life. Sometimes fate had a strange way of repaying acts of compassion.

'If that is not a trouble to you, Mrs Mann, I would gladly pay for his board and keep. I know he would be looked after under your roof.'

'Please call me Karin,' she said. 'And may I call you Jack?'

'Meant to say that before,' Jack said with a feeling of euphoria for the sudden answer to the problem of his son's welfare. 'I guess we are kind of family now,' he added with a short laugh which made Karin smile.

'He will be treated as if he were my own son – and Karl's younger brother.'

'I cannot thank you enough for your offer. I hope that the young fellow does not cause any trouble.'

'Oh, I am sure if the son is like the father he will prove to be a boy any woman would be proud to have under her roof.'

Jack sensed the honesty of her statement and in it a gentleness that he had not known for a long time. He felt a lump in his throat and decided it was time to leave. He did not finish his coffee but said his farewells to Karin at the door, arranging to bring Lukas with him on his way back to Papua.

Karin watched him walk away, waving when he was at the head of the track that led back to Townsville. When the big gum trees swallowed him in the distance she turned back to the kitchen to finish making the dumplings for the stew.

Although Jack was disappointed that he did not get the opportunity to bid Erika a farewell, he walked back to town feeling that something good had come to his life. Karin was just the right sort of woman to care for Lukas. He was not aware however that Erika had also watched him depart, as she stood beside the water tank pondering. She would ask Karin questions about this strange Australian who had a German mother and who had met her brother in the trenches of the Western Front the day her beloved Wolfgang had been killed. She too watched him walk away until he was hidden by the dignified old trees that lined the track. But somehow she knew that he was not gone from her life. Fortune had brought Jack Kelly to their front door as the answer to her aspirations to find a way out of this god-forsaken country of heat, dust and dangerous snakes.

FOURTEEN

The eerie glow of phosphorus laced fungi and the darting flickers of fireflies brought back vivid memories of the battlefield. Paul lay in the sago swamp of primeval plants and swigged at the phial of laudanum. The expedition deep into the Fly River delta was not going well. Paul knew the symptoms of malaria and the dreaded disease was racking his body.

Dademo had quarrelled with the three native carriers who were insisting on returning home to Moresby. The white mister was dying and there was no sense in staying. But Dademo used bluff and threats to make them remain.

Paul eased himself into a sitting position with his back against a huge tree. The jungle was like a brick wall – unrelenting and impenetrable. All around them frogs croaked incessantly whilst night birds shrieked with almost human-like cries. It was unnerving and flashes of the battlefield came to the very ill German.

'They are going to stay,' Dademo said as he knelt over Paul and offered him a pannikin of mushy sago paste. 'I told them that if they didn't stay I had your permission to shoot them.'

Paul tried to grin at the former houseboy's determination and loyalty. 'You have my permission to shoot them if they try to leave,' he sighed, and sank back as another wave of the fever hit him. How many weeks had he been in the delta since Sen had commissioned him to go in search of Iris in the far flung province of Papua? Three, four? It was all a blur now.

And Dademo had begged for permission to be head boy in the expedition. Paul had opposed his inclusion in the recruiting party; he was a houseboy and not used to the gruelling hardships that went with such forays into the jungles. But Dademo had his reasons which he confided to Master Sen, who was at first angry but then agreed the houseboy should go. Dademo had confessed that the day Miss Iris went missing he had failed to tell the master where she was going. He felt responsible for her loss and needed to do something to make up for his negligence.

Thus the party of Paul, Dademo and three porters recruited from a village near Moresby had loaded their provisions aboard the Japanese captain's little coastal boat and chugged west towards the gaping mouth of the Fly River. They were heading into a region barely touched by Europeans, unknown territory inhabited by unknown tribesmen. But Sen ascertained it was the last known destination of O'Leary and his recruiting party.

'The governor does not know of your destination,' Sen had cautioned Paul before leaving. 'But I am sure you have the experience to be successful in determining whether my sister-in-law is alive, and perhaps also opening up new areas for recruiting labourers.'

Sen had upheld his nagging suspicion that local natives had not ambushed and killed Iris. His wife would wake at night and cry out to her half sister in the dark corners of the room. 'She is calling to me,' she would utter in a wide-eyed sweat, and when Sen looked into her dark eyes he could see the conviction she held that Iris was somewhere out in the jungle alive. When Jack had confronted him with his evidence it confirmed to Sen that for his own peace of mind he must attempt to search for Iris. She had always been a strange woman but one he liked very much. Her parentage was still a mystery but My Lee had shared the rumour with Sen that she was the product of an illicit affair between a Chinese woman and a European missionary, that in fact she was not his wife's half sister but had been adopted by his wife's mother to cover the indiscretion.

Sen had briefed Paul on his covert mission. He was to say that he was recruiting native labour, should he ever be questioned by the Australian authorities. When he had employed the German Sen sensed in the man a strong character prepared to take on the risks of this mission. When the briefing had concluded Paul had turned to walk away with his newly acquired .303 rifle on his shoulder. 'If you find O'Leary,' Sen added, 'be prepared to kill him. If you do not, he will kill you.' With that warning echoing in his ears Paul set off on a journey that took him far from all that Europeans called civilisation.

The boat voyage had not given Dademo a real opportunity to exercise his authority over the three porters, but he did have a Lee Enfield single shot rifle and the authority of the white man to enforce the law. Now that they were ashore Paul was glad that Sen had overruled him on the choice of Dademo as his head boy. The young man had proved to be as brave as any soldier Paul had known. He had a cheerful determination to win against all odds and a keen sense of humour.

'Any sign of natives today?' Paul sighed as the malarial attack abated a little.

'Some footprints down near the river,' Dademo answered. He was reluctant to sleep just in case the three men, all from a village not far from his own home near Moresby, attempted to slip away under cover of darkness. And he had kept their stores close by and guarded. 'I heard drums when we were cutting a track to the river.'

'Got to come across a village sooner or later,' Paul muttered as he closed his eyes against the flashes that reminded him of the battlefront. 'When we do we get as many of the boys to come with us as we can and head back out of here.'

When Paul woke a few hours later he noticed that the cloying mists had wrapped themselves around the sleeping figures in the very small clearing. He counted heads and was satisfied that Dademo had done his job. Then the morning came and so did a change of luck.

It was a large man-made clearing. Felled trees indicated that it had been recently used to make canoes, and fresh wood chips beside a partially hollowed out log gave a strong indication that the canoe maker would be back.

'We hide here and wait until someone comes,' Paul said quietly. Dademo issued the orders and the men concealed themselves in the surrounding jungle. They did not have to wait long before a native sauntered from the forest with a stone axe. Dademo stepped into the clearing and the canoe builder gave immediate fright. He cried out in his fear and attempted to flee but the native porters tackled him to the ground. Greater was the man's terror when Paul loomed over him.

'Do you understand what he is saying?' Paul asked and Dademo frowned.

'No savvy this man,' he replied.

Paul smiled and held out his hand to the fear stricken native. 'I will give you a gift that will help you build your canoe,' he said, although he knew the man did not understand him. He took one of the trade axes from their supplies and walked over to the canoe.

The native pinned on the ground realised the futility of struggling against his captors and turned his head to observe the strange white man suddenly start hacking at his canoe. Wood chips flew as the man sweated.

Paul stopped and motioned to the porters to bring the man over so he could observe what he was doing. They held the terrified canoe builder between them as Paul continued to hollow out the log. The captive native watched in awe as the shiny hard stone carved away the wood with an ease he had not seen before.

'Let him go,' Paul ordered as he proffered the trade axe to the canoe builder. The man stood for just a moment before suddenly turning on his heel and fleeing for the safety of the forest. Paul cautioned his men to let the man escape but Dademo had an expression of concern across his face.

'Maybe the bugger will get a war party together to come back and kill us,' he grumbled.

But Paul ignored his natural fears. He placed enough credence in the fact that they had not harmed the man and allowed him to flee without hindering his escape. The man would return to his village and discuss what had occurred in the clearing. That they had not harmed him. It was just a matter of waiting.

And wait they did.

Paul insisted that they set up camp in the clearing and go about their routine without any sign of fear or animosity. If he were right about the man returning to his village he had no doubt that even now men were returning to spy on the strange intruders into their territory.

Just before sunset they came – a party of around twenty men armed with the long bows and arrows of the warrior.

'They are here,' Dademo hissed as he fingered the trigger guard of his rifle nervously.

'I can see them,' Paul said calmly as he applied a burning twig to his pipe and puffed at it. 'Just ignore them and see what happens.'

'They will kill us,' Dademo muttered as his eyes took in the scene.

The warriors were standing at the edge of the clearing. But they had not strung their bows and Dademo recognised the man they had captured earlier that day standing at the front gesturing in their direction.

Paul eventually rose from a log where he had been sitting with his pipe and scooped up a half dozen small trade hatchets. As he slowly walked towards the gathered party he was thoughtful of the Webley & Scott revolver slung at his hip. He could see that the men were all in their prime and truly warriors. They wore grass skirts, cassowary bones through their noses and little else. All were heavily armed with bows and stone axes. They watched him from a distance with curious and brooding expressions. He could see fear but also sensed a dangerous tension and knew he should go no further. He placed his offerings on the ground, and walked casually back to Dademo and the porters standing by the fallen tree and partially built canoe.

The man they had captured moved forward to pick up an axe. He held it above his head and Paul could hear him deliver an oratory to his kinsmen who listened without making any move. Then an older man in the group moved forward to pick up one of the axes. Paul could see that the metal puzzled him as he turned it over in his hands. These were truly a primitive people. Their technology ran to wood and stone alone, he thought.

The canoe builder continued to deliver his oratory in a high voice to his kinsmen but this time he was slowly approaching Paul as he spoke. Paul casually rested his hand on the butt of his revolver but sensed that the man meant him no real harm. When he came up to Paul he continued his dialogue in his high warbling voice. Then he stopped and fearlessly reached out to touch Paul's shirt. He said something and the German guessed that he was being examined.

'I don't think that the man is a demon,' the canoe builder was saying to his comrades, who had watched with some trepidation as the canoe builder dared go towards the strange creature with the pale skin. 'I think that he might be an ancestor spirit who has come with this strange stone so that we may better build canoes. He has brought us more of the axes made like the clear waters but harder. I think he is the spirit of my dead brother Mekeore who was killed when I was young.'

Muttering and head nodding from the warriors confirmed the canoe builder's observation. It was a strange thing that the ancestors should return in such garb. But if the canoe builder who was a respected member of the clan said the stranger was the long dead Mekeore, then it must be so.

Paul was startled when the native man much shorter than himself flung his arms around him in an obviously friendly embrace. Tears flowed down the man's dark cheeks and he continued passionately with his monologue. Paul was being welcomed back into the land of the living. Seeing that he did not harm their kinsman, the other warriors approached cautiously and gazed with interest at the remaining trade goods piled at the centre of the clearing. Paul glanced at Dademo who appeared a little more relaxed as the tension subsided. 'I think we can begin trading,' he said as the canoe builder finally released him from the embrace and went to retrieve what goods might be of use to him. After all, they were a gift from his dead brother.

Soon more of the people from the nearby village streamed out to see the miraculous return of the canoe builder's long dead brother for themselves. Paul found that he had trouble keeping his dwindling supply of trade goods together. One brazen warrior decided to take a mirror for himself. He had watched the ancestor spirit using it when he scraped away the stubble of his beard in the morning. Instead of offering pork meat or sago for it he snatched up the hand mirror when Paul placed it beside his tent in a pannikin of suds. However, Dademo saw the theft and called to the German.

Paul grabbed the warrior and snatched back the stolen item. The man reacted by swinging on Paul with his axe. The explosive crack of Dademo's rifle was followed by a sudden change in the gathered villagers. The man spun as the .303 round smashed through his shoulder. Terror-stricken at the sound of the rifle and the wounded man's wailing they fell on their faces. Everything had changed but Paul did not know how to remedy the rapport he had established with the villagers.

It was the canoe builder who saved the moment. He rose from the ground and began another warbling monologue, denouncing the wounded man's action in taking the property from his brother. Unconvinced, the villagers rose from the grassy clearing and drifted back to their village with the wounded man. Only the canoe builder remained to chastise his brother for bringing the forces of thunder and lightning down upon them.

What Paul did not know was that the canoe builder had heard stories from upriver of another couple of ancestor spirits who had passed them by to inflict many deaths on the people of a neighbouring tribe. The other two spirits were evil and had a white woman spirit with them. But those ancestor spirits must have been from a tribe even further up the river and had come to avenge the death of one of their kin. Such was the logic of the canoe builder who was wise enough to understand such vagaries and bad tempers. His brother had been generous and his action in bringing down the thunder and lightning to smite the troublesome and greedy warrior only right.

. . .

For the next four days Paul insisted on remaining at their present campsite. Every day the villagers would come and squat to watch the ancestor spirit go about his daily duties. Nothing Paul did went unnoticed. When he threw out the shaving water the villagers scrabbled to retrieve the remains. It was discussed that possession of any part of the ancestor spirit was strong magic against other more malevolent spirits of the forest.

The canoe builder was a constant companion and it was Dademo who made the language break-through with him. He learned that his name was Serero and that he was a respected member of his clan for his skills in oratory and boat building. With patience and a mix of pantomime and words, a story unfolded that other white ancestor spirits had been reported further upstream. But these spirits were wrathful. They had killed many villagers and put able men into bondage against their will with ropes made of the same strange shiny stone as the axe heads. When Dademo related the story to Paul in his tent he listened and spat, 'O'Leary. Does the canoe builder know of a white woman with O'Leary?'

'He thinks that there was a white missus with the ancestor spirits.'

Paul stared through the tent flap at the giant rain-forest trees that reared up at the edge of the clearing. Beyond the trees was the river. The malarial bouts had been fewer and fewer and his strength had returned. The porters were in good spirits and Dademo had proved to be a better than expected head boy. In fact Paul had grown to admire and respect the cheerful and competent young man from Port Moresby much as he would a competent senior non-commissioned officer of the old German army. If only the Australians had not overrun New Guinea in the early part of the war then the German army might have been able to recruit such men into their ranks. But he also knew the European aversion to arming natives. Such an act might give them future ideas as regards their colonial masters.

Paul and his party were well supplied with sago, pork and other vegetables by the local natives who had forgiven him the wounded warrior's condition. Compensation had been heavy however. The trade goods were dwindling. It was this fact that influenced Paul's decision. He must make one last attempt to track O'Leary's party down and ascertain whether Iris was in his company – or even alive for that matter.

Dademo stood patiently while Paul filled his old briar pipe – a souvenir taken from a dead British officer – and lit the tobacco. He puffed a couple of times then finally spoke. 'See if the canoe builder will take us upriver in one of his boats. Tell him we will give him the rest of the trade goods for doing so.'

'I will tell him this,' Dademo replied with a broad grin, revealing his teeth blackened by years of chewing betel nut. 'He thinks that you are his dead brother come back to be with him.'

Paul almost choked on the thick smoke of his pipe. 'He what?!'

'Yes, Mr Paul,' Dademo roared laughing. 'You are a ghost.'

'Why is it that your people do not believe that we are ghosts then?'

'Because we are smarter than these bush natives,' Dademo replied. 'We are smarter than you think.'

Paul grinned at his cheeky attitude. Let him have his fun, he thought. After all, the natives would never be able to govern themselves. They needed the white man's superior intellect to guide them.

Dademo found Serero hacking away at the great log. His canoe had been built to carry six people thanks to this new technology of the iron axe. They haggled over the proposal and Dademo finally returned to Paul. 'He says that he will only take us upriver if you give him your pipe.'

'Why my pipe?' Paul asked puzzled by such a simple request.

'He thinks that the nice tasting smoke is the secret to your magic.'

Paul remembered how their supply of tobacco had clinched the uneasy friendship with the local tribe's people. But the missionaries to the tropics had long known that secret, and many a soul for the Christian God had been gathered to the fold with tobacco as the inducement. Paul handed the still smoldering pipe to Dademo. 'Tell him that he can have some of my magic – and I will supply him with enough magic tobacco to keep him puffing for at least half a year.'

Dademo gave the pipe to Serero who immediately stuck it in his mouth and drew back. He inhaled the strong smoke and his eyes watered. He coughed and smiled contentedly. The pact was sealed.

Paul gave orders to break camp. The canoe was almost finished and he would organise to cut a trail to the river so that it could be launched. Then maybe they would find O'Leary. Paul also remembered Sen's warning. Killing a man was often easy, but from what he had heard of the Irishman and his Corsican partner it would not be so in this case. No doubt they outnumbered and outgunned his own party. It would take every skill he had learned in war to carry out the task.

FIFTEEN

Although the Townsville Hotel provided an oasis of lazy conversation and cold beer, Jack Kelly had little time to indulge in either. He downed the glass and wiped the froth from his lip, then heaved his swag on his shoulder and stepped outside into the still sweltering heat of the mid afternoon. He had a train to catch for Brisbane, almost a thousand miles south. It took a second to adjust his eyes to the white heat and when he did he was surprised to see Erika standing before him with a small suitcase.

'I wish to accompany you south to Sydney,' she said by way of greeting.

Jack took a moment to take in her statement. 'Won't you be missed by your family?' he asked with a frown.

'My sister-in-law is better off without another mouth to feed and I have planned to leave for some time. Whether I accompany you or not I am leaving on the next train to go south to Sydney.'

Jack shook his head. 'I suppose if you are that determined to leave home I may as well make sure you get to Sydney safely.' Although he had expressed his concern for her decision he was secretly pleased to have her travel with him. It would provide an opportunity to get to know the woman who had haunted his dreams since before the war even ended. He bent and picked up her suitcase. 'C'mon, or we will be late. Do you have a ticket?'

'I do and I have enough money to pay my way for some time. I expect to get work when I reach Sydney.'

'Determined miss,' Jack chuckled as she struggled to keep pace with his long strides. 'Reckon you will get work with an attitude like that.'

The train pulled away from Townsville with a jolting rattle and long hiss of steam. Erika stared out the window at the heat shrouded gum trees that dotted the landscape. It had been so easy. She had known from the way he had looked at her when they met that her beauty had captivated him. That he could speak her language fluently and was bound to know people in Sydney was the deciding factor for her leaving the hellhole her brother had dumped her in. She had left a letter for Karin to find but did not think that her sister-in-law would object. Just because Karin was one of those *haus frau* types contented to sit at home waiting for her husband did not mean that she had to live the same life. No, the world had changed since the war and it was now a place for the young to live the hedonistic life promised with the peace. She had read women's magazines to improve her English and along the way gazed at the latest in fashions, social news and the life she was missing by being stuck at the edge of a wild frontier.

She turned away from the dusty scenery and examined the Australian. It was not that he was unattractive but she felt nothing towards this man. She knew that he had been with the enemy when Wolfgang was killed and her brother wounded. She had long sworn that she would never forget Wolfgang until the day she died. But she also sensed that she was in the company of a man who she knew would care for her until she no longer needed him. Erika was an ambitious woman. Sydney would be merely a stopover on her way home to Munich. There she would be able to convince Adolf that he needed her in his life as his partner.

Erika closed her eyes and fell into a deep sleep. Her head fell against Jack's shoulder as the train bumped and screeched south. He did not move lest he wake her and wondered how his luck could have changed so dramatically for the better. Maybe it was an omen for his chances of raising a loan to capitalise the mining venture. He already had a name for the small river where he had found the gold. He would call it Spencer Creek to honour the memory of his best friend. And Spencer Creek would become an international name known to gold miners around the world.

By the time they had reached Sydney some days later, Jack was a little less convinced about Erika coming into his life. On the long trip she had proved to be taciturn to the stage of surly and he had wondered at what he had done wrong. He knew that he was smitten by the beautiful young woman and was convinced that smitten meant in love with her. It had to be when he had cherished the thought of her every time he had gazed upon her visage in the now well-worn photograph. From the trenches of the Western Front in the latter days of the war, on the ship voyage home to Australia and even into the jungles of Papua he had carried her in his heart. But now that he had met her it all seemed different. It was as if she was another woman, not the one he thought he knew from the passionate prose of her letters to Wolfgang. Where was the intensity of spirit? Where was the love she was capable of giving?

As they stood on a platform at Central Railway Station amidst the early morning passengers, Jack was reminded of why he preferred the tropics. Cold driving rain whipped around them. And not only did Jack hate cities but Sydney epitomised all that he hated about them: crowded places of unsmiling people locked in grey jobs and living too close to each other.

Erika however seemed to come alive the moment she stepped off the train. 'Isn't it wonderful,' she exclaimed at the first flurry of cold drizzling rain to greet her.

Jack muttered under his breath and picked up her suitcase. 'We need to catch the train to Strathfield,' he said. He had not slept well on the train south and his ill temper at being confined in Sydney was evident.

On the train journey Erika marvelled at the clusters of red roofed houses in the suburbs. They had only stopped one night in the harbour before continuing north to Brisbane. This had not allowed any time to explore the harbour city. Now she asked many questions about Sydney and Jack attempted to answer them. She seemed to have a great interest in what forms of entertainment the city provided. Jack thought this strange. She could have asked about working conditions and employment.

Jack's sister's house was only a short walk from the railway station. Jack was taken aback at Harry's deterioration. Mary's death had aged his brother-in-law and he had the appearance of a man who had given up on life. When he introduced Erika he hardly seemed to notice the beautiful young woman with Jack.

'Where is Lukas?' Jack asked after offering his condolences to Harry. Jack had come to grips with the fact that he would never see his sister again. He felt grief but the war had hardened him to any public display of emotion. Too many times before he had buried good friends. Even the loss of his beloved sister had been a private outpouring of his feelings. He had read the telegram from Harry in Townsville on the footpath outside the post office and gone to his hotel room where he wept uncontrollably for a time. Then he had gathered his feelings and headed straight to the public bar where he drunk himself into a stupor before being helped back up the stairs by the publican to sleep off his private despair.

'Young Lukas is next door being looked after by Mrs Casey,' Harry replied. 'What are you going to do about him?' Jack did not bridle at the bluntly delivered question. Harry was a good man but he was not responsible for raising someone else's son.

'I've made arrangements to take him north with me to be looked after by a lady in Townsville. She has a son about the same age as Lukas and I think she will do a good job until I get myself settled.'

Harry nodded vaguely. 'God, I miss her, Jack,' he said, and tears tumbled down his cheeks. 'I took leave to get myself together but I don't think I can,' he sobbed softly.

Jack leaned forward and put his hand on his brother-in-law's shoulder. 'You will cope, old fella. Time heals all wounds.'

Harry wiped away the tears and tried to smile. 'I suppose of all people you would know,' he said. 'You must have lost a lot of mates during the war.'

'A few,' Jack said as he sat back in his chair. 'We all have.'

'If you want a place to flop for a while you can stay here,' Harry said. 'Plenty of room for yourself and the young lady.'

'Thanks, Harry. I need a week or two to get some business done before I go back north. I appreciate your hospitality.'

'It's no less than when Mary was with me,' Harry replied. 'I'll go and see Mrs Casey and have her send over Lukas. You must have missed him a lot while you were away.'

Jack nodded, as he could not bring himself to say that he had not missed Lukas as much as he was missing George from his life. He felt guilty that his son had not figured more importantly in his thoughts.

Erika had sat silently, trying to follow the conversation while the two men consoled each other. She understood most of the words and already knew about Jack's sister's death. The mention of Lukas intrigued her. Karin had told her about him having a son but he did not seem to be the kind of man who would be tied down by a wife and family.

When Harry ushered Lukas inside, the reactions of father and son seemed to confirm to Erika that she was right about Jack. The little boy appeared serious and distant with the man who was his father. For Jack, being reunited with his son was wrapped in the formality of meeting a stranger. They shook hands. Harry seemed oblivious to the tension.

'How have you been?' Jack asked his son.

Lukas looked at Harry and then back at his father. 'Good,' he replied in a solemn tone.

'That's good,' Jack said awkwardly. 'You and I will be going on a wonderful trip up to a place called Townsville soon. It's a great town that I know you will really like.'

Lukas once again looked to Harry who nodded to confirm Jack's words.

'This is Miss Mann,' Jack said, turning to Erika who smiled sweetly and held out her hand.

'You are a very nice young boy,' she said in English. 'You will like Townsville when you go there.'

But Lukas was not convinced. The stranger who was his father was not someone he knew. So many people seemed to come and go in his short life, and some did not come back – like his mother and Aunt Mary.

That afternoon Jack decided to retire to the local hotel, leaving Erika to rest. He had hoped to bump into one or two former soldiers. This he did, as many returned soldiers were out of work. He established a rapport with a couple of former infantrymen who had also fought on battlefronts that Jack had served. The conversation fluctuated between the rights and wrongs of the English government banning the Australian Catholic archbishop Doctor Daniel Mannix from visiting Ireland to the recent release of the members of the International Workers of the World from prison. One of Jack's drinking partners was of Irish descent and the religious argument with his English drinking mate escalated to the point of a possible punch-up. But the perceived injustice of releasing into society those who were seen by many in the armed forces to have been out to undermine an Allied victory in the Great War united them. All was peaceful – if not fruitful – in the company.

Jack bid them goodbye at closing time and staggered home. He was not stupefied drunk but the alcohol had helped him feel better about everything that seemed to go wrong in his life.

Harry had gone to church to light a candle for Mary and Erika met Jack at the door. He beamed her a crooked smile by way of greeting and slumped into a chair in the kitchen where she poured him a beer from a bottle. His first question was as to his son's whereabouts. Erika told him that the boy was staying next door at Mrs Casey's house. Under the circumstances Harry had felt that Mrs Casey should look after the lad until things got settled. She had five children of her own and an extra child was no bother. Her husband had not returned from the war and she had long learned to cope without him. Jack reminded himself to give Mrs Casey some money to help out. He appreciated her unstinting kindness but also knew that a war pension did not go far in a large family.

Jack raised his glass to Erika who sat opposite him with a small glass of sweet sherry from a bottle she had found in the kitchen cupboard. 'Here's to winning the war and losing the peace for Jack Kelly and his mates,' he said bitterly, and downed the contents.

Erika stared across the short distance with an enigmatic smile as she raised her own glass. 'To a new Germany,' she toasted and Jack stared at her. It was not a toast he had expected on Australian soil.

'Germany is finished,' he responded quietly. 'The League of Nations has made sure of that.'

Erika stared back defiantly. 'There are men and women in my country who do not believe so. I know, I have met such a man who is destined to make us a great nation again, one that the world will respect.'

'And who is this man?' Jack asked as he poured himself another glass of beer.

'His name is Adolf Hitler and he holds the promise to raise my country from the ashes.'

'Never heard of him,' Jack snorted. 'Not a male friend of any consequence is he?' Jack challenged, leaning towards Erika.

He felt jealous at the mention of another man's name so passionately uttered by the woman that he desired. Erika realised this and felt cornered. She could not afford to lose Jack Kelly yet, as she had not established her independence on this foreign soil. But she had also been aware that her distant behaviour towards him had tempered his desire for her. She knew she must do something about the situation or she risked losing his attention.

'He is just a man I have heard speak in Munich – nothing more,' she lied.

It seemed to appease the Australian and she relaxed. Already she knew what her next move would be.

'I will make you something to eat,' she offered.

Her gentle manner surprised Jack. It was as if the wall between them had come down and he muttered his thanks. Erika found some lamb chops and eggs in the icebox. She fried them in the way she had seen Australians eat their food. Jack was hungry and the food was cooked well. Erika did not eat with him but they conversed in a relaxed way, much as lovers or married couples might. Erika talked about winter in Munich and the holidays she enjoyed in the hills of Bavaria before the war, wistful and nostalgic talk that made Jack realise how homesick the young woman was.

He listened and when the meal was over he felt the weariness of the long day come upon him. He excused himself and went to the bedroom that Harry had set aside for him next to Erika's. In a short time he fell into a deep and troubled sleep filled with shell bursts and dying men. It was the same old dream and the night deepened over Sydney as he twitched and sweated back in the trenches.

He was not aware of Erika's naked body next to his when he was forced awake by a nightmare shell burst. He only became aware when a soft hand covered his mouth as the sleep rapidly fell away.

'Be silent or your brother-in-law will hear us,' Erika whispered in his ear as she slid her hand down his chest and onto his stomach. Stunned, Jack obeyed as he fully awoke.

In the early hours of the morning they came together in an embrace of violent, passionate lovemaking. Erika was in every way as exciting as Jack imagined she would be. For her part, Erika knew that when they lay together after their passion was spent that Jack Kelly was hers to command. And it had not been an unpleasant experience, she realised, when she remembered the strength and gentleness with which he entered her. Oh, but if it had only been Adolf in her arms, she thought, and felt the tears on her cheek as Jack slept soundly beside her. But the man that she loved was oceans away.

However, the man who now slept beside her would inadvertently help her return to Germany. She had only to wait for the right opportunity and recognise it when it came.

Here the chieftain who now sent forth her wraith, remorselessly from the realm of the dead, king, she had only now for the passing minute and eternity everlasting.

SIXTEEN

Serero's canoe took them upstream. Paul was able to shoot a big bush pig, which provided them with meat, and they found a sand spit off the river-bank to camp on for the night. They travelled light. All but essential supplies went in the canoe. For Paul, that meant little more than the two rifles, the machetes and all the ammunition they had.

Towards late afternoon the next day the garru-lous canoe builder indicated that they were nearing the village of his upriver kinsmen. He did not expect trouble once he explained that the white man was the reincarnation of his dead brother. But when the canoe rounded a jungle-entangled bend in the river, Serero went suddenly quiet – as quiet as the appar-ently deserted village. The canoe glided to a stop on a shallow bank and the party disembarked, their weapons at the ready. For the nervous porters armed with their machetes it was a case of sticking close to the head boy and boss with the guns.

Paul waded ashore with the muddy water splashing around his knees as Serero called in a wailing voice to his kinsmen. But no one answered and as they cautiously walked into the village they could see that it had been the scene of a terrible carnage. Blood had blackened on the thatch in some places and Dademo found a spent cartridge case lodged in a slatted floor of reeds. Paul recognised the shell casing as that of a Mauser rifle.

Serero squatted in the centre of the village and wailed his grief. Was it that the other evil ancestor spirits had killed his wife's family and all his cousins? Not even their enemies had ever succeeded in accomplishing that in their interminable raids and ambushes over the years. Already the forest was reclaiming the vegetable gardens. In time nothing would exist except rotting logs to give a home to the deadly scorpions.

'How long ago do you think O'Leary was here?' Paul asked his head boy. Dademo stared around him and shrugged. 'Don't know, boss,' he replied and turned to Serero who was still squatting and wailing. Dademo had learned many important words of Serero's dialect and asked the question. Serero ceased wailing and sniffed. He then launched into one of his warbling monologues and at the end indicated about three weeks in European terms. Dademo relayed the answer.

'Too bloody long ago,' Paul muttered, realising that he had used an expression he had learned from Jack. English was the language he now used, the language of the new masters of Papua and New Guinea. 'I think we are chasing phantoms if we continue to search,' he spat with frustration.

The jungle, malaria and close calls with the local natives had all come to this. They were in unexplored territory along the Fly River with no charts to aid them in finding the route possibly used by O'Leary's party. But then the Irishman probably had no charts either, Paul thought. He too must have used the river as his road into the jungle. The deduction came in a flash. All he had to do was follow the river back down to the delta and trust there was a chance that he would find O'Leary. Unless O'Leary had already reached the sea and any boat that was scheduled to pick him up.

'Mr Paul!'

Paul swung his rifle in the direction Dademo was staring. An old woman had appeared on the edge of the village and was calling with a note of desperation to Serero. The canoe builder answered and she hobbled towards him.

'Obvious he knows her,' Paul said as the two greeted each other with a form of handholding. Her face was screwed up in anguish and it appeared that she was pleading with him.

'I think she is a kinswoman,' Dademo said as he lowered his rifle. 'I think she is telling him what happened here.'

Dademo's guess was right. The old woman had been left behind when the survivors of the small village fled the evil white spirits that brought the thunder and lightning death to them. But the evil spirits had taken some of the young men and women and their fate was not known although she presumed that they had been taken for their meat.

Soon enough Dademo had gleaned the story. Serero convinced the old woman that the white man was his dead brother come to protect him and supply him with bounteous and wondrous gifts from the world beyond death. Paul directed that the old woman be given food but she would still tremble uncontrollably whenever he or his men approached her. Squatting in the dirt of the village she dared not look upon the ghosts and continued to warn her nephew that he should not trust the white man. But Serero ignored her warnings and strutted about the clearing with the pipe in his mouth.

'What could you get out of the canoe builder?' Paul asked.

Dademo told him that as far as he could understand there was a white woman with the evil spirits. But from the way they treated her it appeared that she too was a prisoner.

'What else did you understand from the old woman?'

'She thinks that when the . . . Mr O'Leary and his native boys started to chain the young men and women the others tried to stop him and that's when the shooting started. When the young men saw their dead kinsmen they did not try to resist and were taken away in chains.' Dademo screwed up his face and Paul could see that he was thinking about something that Serero had told him. After some time he continued. 'The old woman said that the white woman got away when the shooting started and ran away to the forest.'

Paul looked sharply at his head boy to see if he was lying. But he could not see any suggestion of untruth in his open expression. 'Does the old woman know where she is now?'

Dademo stared at the ground. He knew that he would be asked the question and was reluctant to disappoint Mr Paul. 'She does not know where Miss Iris is.' It was the first time he had used her name, such was the shame he still felt at his negligence in keeping her safe. Paul stared over his shoulder at the old woman who squatted in the dirt. He could continue his search of the jungle but doubted that he would find Iris. Only the local villagers might know of her whereabouts. It was worth a try and he sent Dademo to further question Serero. From the expression on Dademo's face when he returned, however, Paul knew the answer was not good.

'All the villagers are gone,' he said. 'No one can help. Miss Iris is gone.'

Paul sighed and hefted his rifle over his shoulder. 'Leave the old woman some food and tell the boys we are going home.'

Dademo hurried to pass on the good news and the canoe builder left his aunt wailing a dirge for the dead. They launched the canoe and used the sluggish current to aid them on their way downstream to Serero's village.

They arrived early next morning after a night camping on the riverbank. The canoe was run ashore and the party set out along the trail for Serero's village. Serero was the first to feel the dread. All did not sound right in the forest. He could not hear the chatter of children or the usual sounds of the villagers going about their daily routine. There was not even the grunting of the domestic pigs rooting for grubs and tubers.

As soon as he noticed the canoe builder unsling his bow and notch one of the long arrows, Paul felt for the safety catch on his rifle and signalled to his men to be wary. Serero moved forward stealthily until he could see the fringe of his small village enclosed by the jungle.

'God in heaven!' Paul swore. 'O'Leary must have been here while we were at the canoe builder's kinsman's village. But how in hell could that be when the other village was raided weeks ago?'

O'Leary and his party, Paul deduced, had been searching the jungles for villages and had decided to come down to this one on the way downstream to their rendezvous point in the delta. That meant they could still be very close. A chill ran through Paul at the thought. Had they scoured the jungle after the first raid upriver and recaptured Iris? If so, she was most probably still with them. But furthermore, the enemy was possibly only a few hours to a couple of days away. Who would lie dead in the steamy forests of the Fly River when the inevitable meeting took place? Paul considered the devastation of the village and looked towards his very small party of men. He did not like the odds. Unlike O'Leary's, his men were not proven killers.

• • •

When Paul gave the order to paddle downstream Serero volunteered his services, with his village and kinsmen gone it was time for payback. The hunter and canoe builder was now the grim faced warrior. His wife and children were amongst the dead and their spirits would not know peace until he exacted vengeance.

Paul resorted to tactics as old as warfare itself. He gave his order to launch the canoe just on dusk and the party of seven men used the cover of night to paddle quietly downstream. Serero guided them in the dark. It was a moonless night and occasionally they bumped sandbanks or fallen trees as they made their precarious way down the slow-moving stream.

Paul had based his plan on the premise that O'Leary would be camped close to the river as the jungle and adjoining swamps would have blocked him from going very far inland. And if so, it was more than probable that the Irishman would have lit a campfire. They paddled for hours in silence with the night calls of birds and insects covering the sound of the canoe. Many times Paul considered the other possibility that O'Leary had already reached the mouth of the delta and was well on his way back to Moresby.

On one occasion the canoe slid onto a sandbank and the oarsmen were forced to wade up to their waists, dragging the canoe across. The great salt-water crocodiles were active by night, they knew, and Paul prayed that any that might be about were not hungry this night. He gripped his rifle, ready to fire in the event of one approaching nonetheless. He knew from his previous experience in New Guinea however that crocodiles struck with such speed and strength that if they snatched a man they would immediately make their death roll and snap his back. Paul had once seen a native at Finschhafen encounter a giant croc which had snatched him by the arm whilst he was fishing by a river. It had rolled with such speed that it had ripped the man's arm cleanly from the shoulder socket. The memory of that incident chilled Paul. He was worried too that a rifle shot might alert O'Leary's men and the element of surprise be lost.

The water was cold as Paul slid into the dark waters. His boots found the riverbed and the waters swirled around his knees. Although they were in a shallow section of the river he was still acutely aware that a croc could take any one of them as they gripped the canoe and forced it into deeper water. The boat came clear and suddenly Paul felt the edge of the sandbank disappear from beneath his feet. He found himself sliding into the depths as the water rose to his chest and had a fleeting but terrifying thought that one of the man-eaters was just inches from snatching him. The toe of his boot caught the edge of the sandbank and he scrambled with desperation to clamber aboard the canoe as it began to drift away.

'Puk puk!' a voice cried from the dark.

Paul knew the native word for crocodile. His desperation was rapidly turning to panic. He expected any moment to feel the great toothed jaws enclose his body and take him down to the bottom.

He was not sure whether he imagined the swirl of water beneath him or whether it was real. A hand gripped his arm and he was hauled aboard the rocking canoe. For a second he saw a flash of white as eyes wide with fright greeted him in the dark.

They had been lucky and only seconds from what Paul had feared. A great croc had bumped the canoe as it turned to swim away. Paul's heart was still pounding as he glanced at the pale green glow of his watch dial. It was close to midnight and weariness was a cloak on not just himself but also his crew. Only Serero seemed impervious to fatigue. He sat at the front of the canoe, guiding the rowers as he puffed on his prized pipe. The sweet but acrid smell drifted on the night air. Paul sat in the stern of the sturdy log canoe. He now wished that he had not been so hasty in trading his pipe to the canoe builder and wondered what the dead British officer might have thought if he had known that his pipe was now being used by a Stone Age man.

'Mr Paul!' Dademo hissed. 'Over there!'

Paul snapped out of his reverie to scan the shoreline. Sure enough, the dull glow of a fire flickered between the distant trees. They were on a broad stretch of the stream and the German made a rough estimate that the light was around four hundred metres distant. 'I see it,' he whispered his reply. 'Get the canoe into the shore now.'

With their acute night vision the rowers had already spotted the campfire and changed direction on command. The current tended to push them closer to the location of the campfire as they rowed towards the shore. But eventually they found the river's edge and struggled up the heavily forested bank.

In the dark amidst the overgrowth Paul made a quick head count and checked that his party was intact. 'You will conceal the canoe here when you have just enough light to do so,' he briefed Dademo. 'I am going to follow the river until I come across the campfire – I want to know what we are up against. I will make my way back to you here just on last light tomorrow. You understand?'

'But why don't we attack them now?' Dademo queried. 'They do not expect us.'

Paul understood Dademo's point of view but he was a man who was meticulous in planning. A good reconnaissance during the war had proved its worth in absolute success. He did not expect Dademo to understand his past experience. 'We will make the raid but we will do so on our terms. Not just go charging in like a bunch of cowboys.'

'What are cowboys?' Dademo puzzled.

Paul grinned. 'Men like us – but men who know what they are doing.'

Dademo shook his head, still perplexed. 'I think I savvy,' he replied, trying to dismiss his confusion.

Once Dademo had passed on Paul's instructions he left them settling down for the night. Serero had bridled at being forced to stay behind. He did not understand why they should wait. The razor points of his arrows were impatient for enemy blood. But he obeyed his dead brother's orders. Maybe his dead brother was seeking extra powers from the spirits of the forest and that is why he had to go alone. He shrugged and settled down with the men from another tribe. This was a strange thing for him. He had never cooperated with anyone outside his own clan before.

For a couple of hours Paul stealthily approached the camp. He had been guided by the river and eventually came within range of his target. His first indication of its proximity was the distinctive scent of burning wood, then the muffled sounds of a camp at rest and glimpses of the fire through the scrub. He confirmed that he had found his man when he saw the tents pitched at the centre of a clearing that had once been a native garden. And then he saw O'Leary himself.

SEVENTEEN

Jack knew he was in love. Erika was everything he ever imagined: beautiful, smart and charming, like one of the erotic Celtic goddesses revered by the Druids in the ancient dark oak forests of Germany.

And Erika knew she could command the tough former soldier as if he were one of her private troops. She was fond of him but she had also determined to use whatever means were within her power to get out of Australia and return to Munich.

Being rejected by a string of staid and conservative bankers was easier to accept when Jack returned to Strathfield and Erika's passionate, unrestrained lovemaking each night. They kept their secret from his brother-in-law. Jack knew he would not approve of any sexual practice outside of wedlock. Each night Erika would come to his bed and leave for her own room before the sun rose over Sydney.

But the numerous rejections for finance rankled Jack. The same reasons were given by all the stodgy grey men in dark suits who peered across their desks at the tough looking adventurer down from Papua: was it not unlawful in the newly mandated territory to mine for gold? Finding the gold was not illegal but mining it was until the New Guinea administration got itself together to issue such licences, Jack would accede. The more far sighted bankers would add the impossible provision of Jack producing considerable collateral to secure any kind of loan. Jack had laid out his case convincingly across their highly polished desks, but the grey men had no real sense of risk. But then, what banker did?

In the end Jack had exhausted his last avenue of raising the capital and grudgingly admitted to himself that he was more gold prospector than businessman. But he also knew what he had discovered in the Morobe mountain stream had the potential to make himself and any investors who might back him very rich men. The fools have no spine, Jack thought as he stood on the footpath with his collar up against the biting wind.

'Bloody idiots,' he cursed as he hunched against the chill as cold as the feeling in his heart. At worst he could probably return and grub for gold on a pegged lot when the New Guinea administration finally organised the granting of mining licences. He had heard the rumours around the bar of the Moresby hotel before he returned to Australia that there were other prospectors sniffing in the same region as himself – men with reputations of knowing where to find the precious metal.

Time was of the essence and Jack had just one last card up his sleeve. He turned over the elegant business card that Sen had given him and read the name and address. It was only two blocks away in Bridge Street and Jack knew what he must do. He hoped his last card would be an ace.

The offices of Quentin Arrowsmith were impressive. That had to be a good sign, Jack thought as he stood before a desk in an anteroom of marble and polished teak inlay. He did not look like a successful business-man. The suit he wore was probably out of fashion now in 1920. Jack had purchased it years back when he got married. It still fitted but had been in moth-balls during his absence overseas. Maybe it even smelt of camphor, Jack thought, and was tempted to sniff the sleeve.

'Do you have an appointment with Mr Arrowsmith?' a severe looking woman in her fifties asked, as if addressing an errant schoolboy.

'I am afraid that I do not,' Jack replied politely. 'But I would like to make one if that is possible.'

The woman glanced down at the leather bound appointments diary. She held an expensive fountain pen with a gold nib poised above the pages. 'If you could state your business I will see if I am able to give you an appointment, Mr . . . ?'

'The name's Jack Kelly and Mr Arrowsmith was recommended to me by a Mr Sen from Port

Moresby. It's about a large gold strike made up there.'

The mention of gold got the reserved woman's attention, as Jack knew it would. Nothing like the mention of gold to stimulate a little greed, he thought. Even matronly secretaries can be flustered by the word. She glanced up at Jack with undisguised interest in her pale eyes.

'If you will excuse me for a moment, Mr Kelly,' she said as she rose from behind her desk. 'I will have a word with Mr Arrowsmith and see if he is prepared to speak to you.'

Jack nodded and watched as she knocked lightly on a cedar door behind her desk. A muffled voice bid her enter. Now it was only a matter of waiting.

Jack hardly had a moment to gaze around the anteroom when the door opened and the secretary stood to one side. 'Mr Arrowsmith seems to have a short amount of time to speak to you,' she said, holding the door open. 'You may go in.'

Jack flashed her a smile as he stepped past. As she closed the door behind him, Jack quickly took in the trappings of old money in the sombre oiled timbers that furnished the room and the expensive carpet on the floor. There was a gloomy ambience about the office and the rows of leather bound books in the glass fronted bookcases were no doubt collections of rare and expensive journals and first editions. But it was the man sitting behind the desk that gave the room its meaning. Jack guessed him to be in his mid thirties. He was tall with aristocratic features and the look of a man used to power and money. Jack sensed in the man a dangerous ruthlessness too. Sen had been right to warn him.

'My secretary has told me that you are an acquaintance of Mr Sen, and that you have something to do with a gold strike,' he said without bothering to rise and introduce himself.

It was time for Jack to seek an advantage before they settled down to any talks. 'You remind me of someone I met in France during the war,' he lied.

'I am afraid you have the wrong man, Mr Kelly,' Arrowsmith replied as he steepled his fingers under his chin. 'My service to my country was here providing the necessities required to wage war. However my brother served with some distinction . . . possibly you have us confused.'

'My mistake,' Jack replied.

At least he knew that Arrowsmith was not of the brotherhood of returned soldiers. But Arrowsmith must have known why Jack had asked the question. He appeared to soften his arrogant manner by stepping away from the barrier of his desk. 'My name is Quentin Arrowsmith, Mr Kelly, and if you have something important for me, I am in a position to make decisions. I am sure that you have done your homework with Sen and know that I control a rather substantial base of companies – here and overseas.'

'I suppose it all depends on whether you are a man prepared to stick his neck out, Mr Arrowsmith,' Jack said, determined not to be intimidated by the man and his wealth. 'What I have may not be of interest to you.'

Arrowsmith flipped the lid of a silver cigar box and without offering one to Jack withdrew a large Havana cigar and proceeded to light it. Jack had already formed the opinion that he could never like this arrogant and self-centred man. But business was business.

Arrowsmith took a long draw and blew the smoke into the confines of the office. It hung in the still air like a blue mist between them. 'What do you have, Mr Kelly?'

'I have discovered a source of gold that I know has the potential to produce enough to rival some of the biggest mining operations in the western hemisphere. But naturally I want to see it exploited to its full value, and not just extract a few nuggets and grams of weight by panning alone. I need capital.'

Arrowsmith studied Jack through the smoke without making any immediate comment. It was unnerving and Jack felt the pressure. He was about to bid the man a cold goodbye when Arrowsmith finally spoke.

'I am sure that what you say has a truth behind it, but such an enterprise requires a lot of capital and a great deal of risk, as I'm sure you are aware. I concede that if you are right then the return would be worth the risk. But at the moment I need time to make some inquiries about you, Mr Kelly. I am sure you would do the same if you were in my position.'

'You would consider a proposal?' Jack asked, feeling a little lightheaded. Someone was actually considering to grub stake him!

'If your credentials stand up to scrutiny I will consider your proposal and give you a decision next week. I have a place at Point Piper on the harbour shore and my wife has organised some friends to come over for tennis and tea next week. Do you play tennis, Mr Kelly?'

'I am afraid not,' Jack answered reluctantly.

Tennis was the sport played by the rich when he was growing up in South Australia. For Jack boxing, football and cricket had been his games. He was a natural sportsman and a strong swimmer and athlete. But not a tennis player.

'No matter,' Arrowsmith continued. 'Bring your spouse if you have one. I am sure she will be impressed by the view. Mrs Phillips will give you the particulars on the way out.'

On the street Jack did not feel the cold. Things were finally starting to look up. If all went well he would have his capital and a chance to establish a future for himself, Erika and Lukas.

He did not stop off at the hotel on the way home. Instead he went to Erika, swept her up in his arms and told her the news. She appeared happy for him and he naturally concluded her happiness was yet another sign of her love for him. But then Jack was not a good judge of a woman's moods – only those of men.

EIGHTEEN

All day Paul Mann lay in the dank undergrowth observing O'Leary's camp. Covered in dry mud he blended with the earth, and his camouflage had been completed with the insertion of branches and twigs into his clothing.

O'Leary had twenty-three prisoners chained in a line to a tree. The dispirited young men and women sat silently all day in the sun and were fed once in the middle of the day with stodgy sago paste. Paul counted seven native porters in O'Leary's party. All were armed with old but effective French rifles. O'Leary himself had a pistol holstered at his waist as well as his Mauser slung over his shoulder. His French companion carried a Mauser pistol with a broomstick-type rifle butt.

The mood of the camp appeared relaxed – almost festive – and Paul was under the opinion that they were fairly settled, as if waiting for someone or something. Probably the boat to return them to Moresby, he guessed, as the camp was located close to a deep and broad stretch of river, capable of allowing a large coastal boat to anchor close offshore and take aboard cargo.

As he watched and waited for dusk he attempted to gather more information: where the porters were likely to bed down for the night, which of the two tents O'Leary would use to sleep in, and if he would post guards. As it was, he did not notice any particular guard post on the prisoners and guessed that O'Leary had faith in the strength of the chains.

Even as he made his observations Paul was already formulating a plan of attack. It was important that he neutralise O'Leary and the Frenchman first. With any luck he could make the porters think that they were under a heavy attack and cause them to panic – especially if the two white men were killed from the outset. He might not be able to bring Iris back to Sen but at least he could report back that vengeance had been exacted. That would give the expedition some meaning.

Paul felt a scorpion crawl across his hand. He did not disturb the tiny but venomous creature, just lay still and watched it warily as it went on its way in search of smaller creatures to eat. When he glanced up he was staring directly into the bearded face of O'Leary. For a terrifying few seconds he thought that he had been spotted, as he was a mere fifty yards out from the camp. But O'Leary looked away and

Paul was certain that he was merely looking around the jungle in an idle way.

Paul knew that justice had to be dispensed. He was not only doing this for Sen but also for his new friend Jack Kelly. Sen had told him how O'Leary had sworn to kill Jack at the first opportunity that presented itself; with any luck that opportunity would never come.

The only real concern Paul had was the armed native porters. What if they did not panic? What if O'Leary had instilled in them a sense of discipline? The German was slowly appreciating the fighting prowess of Papuan warriors. Should he call off the attack considering the dangerous variable of the greater number of arms arrayed against his own party?

One option was to work as a sniper would and just shoot O'Leary from cover. Paul slowly inched his rifle into a firm position where it rested easily in his grip. He slowly pulled back the rear site until the gradient read fifty yards. In the foresight, O'Leary was an easy target – a big man with a broad chest.

He lowered the rifle. Not a good option. He might kill O'Leary but it was daylight and he would soon be discovered. He had survived the trenches and was not going to get himself killed in some god-forsaken territory that did not have a map to mark his grave. As a rescue mission he could justify his actions and a court of law would probably exonerate him if he were ever brought to trial – which he strongly doubted. He had right on his side. But then, Germany had God on its side in the war, and God had forsaken their just cause. It was not a comforting thought.

The more he thought about an attack at night the less convinced he was of its success. Sure, they might get a few of them but he could lose some or all of his own men. It was frustrating to come to the conclusion that O'Leary could possibly get out of the jungle alive. There had to be another option. All it needed was some thought. But night was close and in the tropics it came fast. Time was running out. He sighed and waited for darkness to come.

Just on sunset, as Paul was making his preparations to slither from his hide, he hesitated for a moment. The camp seemed to have come suddenly alive with activity. There was much shouting and his attention was drawn to movement at the edge of the tall forest.

He turned his head cautiously and with a sinking feeling saw that four more armed native porters had appeared from the bush, with what appeared to be another prisoner. He well knew that the appearance of the extra men further shifted the balance of arms. Paul focused on the prisoner through the undergrowth and felt his heart beat jump. The prisoner was a white woman! A Eurasian, to be exact! He gasped in his surprise. It had to be Iris. The young woman appeared gaunt and had obviously suffered in the jungle since her escape. But she did not appear cowered by her captors.

O'Leary strode across the clearing and with a powerful backhanded blow sent her crashing into the ground. Paul's instinctive reaction was to raise his rifle

219

and kill the man. But he checked himself. He still had the advantage of surprise and knew that he must keep it until he was in a position to strike at a time of his choosing. He watched as O'Leary bent down to grasp Iris by the hair and drag her to his tent.

Paul was pleased that they had not launched any rash assault on O'Leary's camp the night before. To do so would have been to lose the reason for the expedition in the first place. But if the option of pulling back and allowing O'Leary to leave had been a consideration at any stage, it was not now. No matter what it took Paul knew that he must get Iris out of the Irishman's hands.

When the sudden darkness came to the jungle Paul withdrew from his hide and made his way back to where Dademo and the rest of his small party had waited patiently, concealed in the dense jungle by the river. Paul had formulated a desperate plan and it involved dividing the considerable force arrayed against him and his small party. His plan required patience and the key element of surprise. But there was also something that niggled the former German officer's thoughts. As he had crouched in hiding all that day and observed the enemy camp there were matters regarding the situation that did not seem to make sense. Something about some of the native porters was not right. There were unanswered questions, questions that defied any logical answer. How did O'Leary expect to take his captives back to Port Moresby without questions being raised as to how he had recruited them? And how could he keep secret the abduction of a woman related to a prominent

Chinese businessman in the Port Moresby community? Paul would soon enough get the answers.

Dademo listened to Mr Paul outline his plan of action for the next day. It had a certain simplicity but Dademo still felt apprehensive. They would move into positions not far from O'Leary's campsite and conceal themselves, then wait until either O'Leary struck camp to make a march or until the boat that he seemed to be expecting turned up. Paul suspected that the latter would occur first because he had overheard mention of a boat rendezvous. The prisoners would have to be loaded aboard. The guards would be preoccupied and less alert to an attack. Paul would swap his Enfield with its attached magazine of ten rounds for Dademo's single shot rifle. He issued his pistol to a porter nominated by Dademo as the man most capable of using it. Paul doubted that he would be very effective but it did give his small party more firepower – and it bolstered spirits. He was pleased to see that his men seemed not to be afraid of the coming action. Whatever Dademo had told them seemed to have worked. Or was it that Paul had underestimated their innate courage?

'I will shoot O'Leary and then the Frenchman,' Paul briefed. 'You will shoot as many of the armed native boys that you can,' he told Dademo. 'The canoe builder and the rest of the boys will use the canoe to attack whoever turns up in a boat. They will use their machetes. I have seen a place they can paddle to tonight and hide until they hear my first shot. Then they must paddle as fast as they can to the river side of the boat and cause as much damage as possible. Just try and avoid shooting any of the prisoners and make sure that Serero does not act until he hears my first shot. You savvy?'

Dademo grinned his understanding and briefed the others who sat in the dark fingering their machetes. It was a desperate plan, as Paul well knew, but history had shown that sometimes desperate plans come off. Sometimes small bands of determined men could inflict casualties disproportionally beyond their numbers.

Paul went over the plan again and again until he was satisfied that his men knew what they must do. Then they snatched a couple of hours of sleep until Paul roused them.

Just after midnight Paul and Dademo made their way down the river, while Serero and the remaining porters paddled quietly into the hide on the river bank a short distance from the campsite. All was in place. Paul prayed that he had not overestimated the fighting prowess of his small army. He also knew that he would have to use every ounce of his skills as a tactical commander to take advantage of any opportunities that may present themselves during the execution of the plan.

As they lay in wait at the edge of the camp the night seemed to go on forever. Never before as a commander had Paul Mann faced such daunting odds. He was once again a soldier fighting what seemed to be a hopeless war. But he had his orders – and loyalty was his forte.

• • •

The mists from the river swirled around the clearing as the sun rose over the green canopy of interlocked forest giants. The camp was stirring and Paul rubbed away the weariness from his eyes after what seemed to be one of the longest nights of his life. He strained to see Iris but she was not manacled with the captives.

The flap to O'Leary's tent flew open and he emerged to stretch and scratch his crotch as he gazed over his camp. Behind him Iris emerged in a simple cotton dress. Paul could see how the young woman could enchant a man with her exotic beauty. It was no wonder Jack Kelly's English friend had been in love with her. Although a captive, she carried herself with dignity.

'The boat comes,' Paul heard one of the native porters from O'Leary's camp say softly. He had spoken French, something Paul thought unusual.

The boat appeared from around a bend in the river and suddenly all Paul's questions were answered. A large wooden sailing ship with a high stern and sweeping, triangular lateen sails came into view. She had a sharp bow and her appearance in the Fly River struck him as completely out of place. Paul had only seen such craft in the Indian Ocean sailing off Ceylon on his voyage to Australia. 'God almighty,' he hissed in his dawning horror. 'She's an Arab dhow!'

Dademo stirred beside Paul and glanced at him for an explanation. 'O'Leary isn't recruiting labourers – he's taking slaves!'

'Slaves' was not a word Dademo understood but from the shocked expression on Mr Paul's face he guessed it was something very evil. Paul had heard rumours that slavery still existed in some Middle Eastern countries and when he now more closely examined the porters he realised that the majority of them were in fact Africans – not Papuans.

The dhow sailed confidently towards the shore, her decks bristling with heavily armed Arab and African crew. Paul knew that his plan was doomed to failure as soon as a gangplank was dropped on the riverbank and the crew met with their comrades on the shore. The former soldier knew that he would be spitting into a cyclone. To open fire and kill O'Leary now would gain nothing.

He watched helplessly as the prisoners were hustled aboard and groaned with frustration as Iris was taken below decks. O'Leary was last to board. Paul kept him in the tip of his rifle sights all the time, so badly he wanted to pull the trigger. But he resisted the temptation for more than one reason. As far as he was concerned his mission was not over yet. Sooner or later O'Leary would return to Moresby as he always did. And when he returned Paul would be waiting for him. There were ways to get a man to tell. He would find out where the dhow had sailed.

By midday the Arab slaver had gone. Paul stood and stretched his legs. At least he could return to Sen and tell him Iris was indeed alive.

NINETEEN

When Erika learned of Arrowsmith's invitation to his harbour house she was intrigued. From what Jack had mentioned of the man he sounded like someone she would want to meet. After all, it did not hurt a young lady's social opportunities to be seen in the right company. And she had been bored sitting around the house while Jack had gone into town each day in his attempts to raise capital.

At first he seemed reluctant to allow her to accompany him to the Point Piper house. He was there on business and Arrowsmith was not the sort of man anyone would want to know, he argued. But she persisted and he relented when she accused him of being ashamed to be seen with her in public because she was German.

The day arrived and Erika disappeared into her bedroom to prepare for the visit. When she emerged

Jack was stunned. She wore a fashionable new dress that clung to her body, accentuating its curvaceous lines. It was in the current style, flowing to just below the knees, and the young woman had the looks to turn any man's head.

Jack whistled softly, more out of surprise than admiration for the transformation. 'You could pass muster for Buckingham Palace,' he said with a smile. 'Reckon you will be the most beautiful woman in Sydney today.'

Erika made a small pirouette that caused her dress to swirl, flashing brilliant coloured sequins sewn in the hem. Besides the new dress Erika had used lipstick and rouge to accentuate her beauty. 'Do you think I will impress Mr Arrowsmith and his wife?' she asked with an appealing smile.

Jack nodded and they left for his rendezvous with destiny. Today he would learn if the dream he harboured for their future would be realised.

The house was impressive, a great white stuccoed mansion that seemed to sprawl down to the harbour's edge. Its lawns were perfectly manicured and a wide, open patio curved around to take in a spectacular view of the harbour, east to west.

'You must be Mr Jack Kelly,' a slim young woman said when the butler ushered them inside. 'I am Caroline Arrowsmith.' Jack shook hands with the very attractive woman whose hair was bobbed in the new style. She also wore the latest in body clinging dresses. Both women made subtle appraisals of each other before introduction and Caroline passed a complimentary comment on Erika's appearance. Jack could see that Erika was also impressed by Caroline.

'Pleased to meet you, Mrs Arrowsmith,' Jack replied. 'May I introduce Miss Erika Mann. Miss Mann is recently from Germany and a friend of mine.'

'I am pleased to make your acquaintance,' Caroline said in reasonably good German.

'You speak German, Mrs Arrowsmith,' Erika said as Caroline took her hand and held it. 'I am surprised that an Australian would speak my language.'

'My husband is quite fluent in German although I am still learning,' Caroline replied modestly. 'The knowledge of German has long been a tradition of the Arrowsmith family. I attended my final years of school in Switzerland. French was my preferred language but we did speak a reasonable amount of German.'

Erika immediately warmed to Caroline and was momentarily reluctant to let go of her hand when Caroline turned to escort them to the patio outside, where a mix of elegantly dressed men and women were sipping cocktails. Jack knew he stood out in his old suit and felt uneasy. He would have liked to impress the Arrowsmith guests. He noticed that one or two of the guests wore white flannels and guessed they had been playing tennis. Caroline steered Erika away when her husband pushed his way through his guests to Jack. Toe to toe, Jack noticed that Arrowsmith was a couple of inches taller than himself.

'Mr Kelly, what is your drink?' Arrowsmith asked, and held out his hand by way of greeting.

Jack was surprised at the gesture although he noted the other man's handshake was limp and fleeting. 'I'll have a beer if there is one going.'

Jack glanced over his shoulder to ensure that Erika had not been left alone and was surprised to see her in a bright and animated conversation with Caroline. When he turned back to Arrowsmith a waiter was approaching with a glass of beer on a silver tray.

'As I said I would, I have made some considerable checks on you, Mr Kelly, and it seems you are quite a remarkable man.' Jack was not sure whether Arrowsmith was being facetious or praising him. The man was an enigma. 'I heard that at one stage during the war that you were recommended for the Victoria Cross but granted a DCM in lieu of our highest award for bravery. And that you rose through the ranks to become an officer. That before the war you worked in Papua gold prospecting. Also of interest is that you are fluent in German – that happens to be of interest to me as I also admire the language,' he continued in German. 'I overheard my wife introducing your lovely lady friend as German. I presume she is a lady friend, as I also learned that you are a widower with a young son and not known to be remarried at last report.'

'You seem to have a good source of intelligence,' Jack said as he took a mouthful of cold beer. The afternoon was warm after days of drizzling rain and the ale tasted good. 'I doubt that you will tell me where your information comes from.'

'Not really a matter of interest to you,' Arrowsmith said. 'More of interest to you is whether I am prepared to bankroll you. You are yet to convince me that your proposal has financial merit.'

'Whenever you have the time, I have the proposal.'

'Right now is as good a time as any, Mr Kelly,' Arrowsmith replied. 'We can go to my library where we won't be disturbed. I will have a bottle of beer sent to us, so that you do not go thirsty.'

Jack followed Arrowsmith into the house and to a room not unlike the man's office in town. Arrowsmith slumped into a great leather armchair while Jack outlined his scheme. He spoke in mining language with military style logistics, and finally estimated what it would all cost.

Arrowsmith raised his eyebrows at the figure. 'One thing you failed to mention in all your talk, Mr Kelly, was exactly where your strike was made.'

Jack had expected the question. 'If I told you where I made my strike you might not need me. You might bypass me with a team of your own geologists and claim the field for yourself.'

Arrowsmith made the faintest of smiles. 'You have a valid point there,' he said. 'I could do exactly what you suggest. But I am a man who adheres to the expression of not killing the goose that lays the golden egg. I would still have to employ a competent man to manage my enterprise.'

'I did not come here to offer my services as a manager,' Jack stated firmly. 'I came here to see if you would want to invest in the mining project – not buy me out and then let me run the show while you and your companies raked off the cream.'

Arrowsmith raised his hand in protest. 'I did not intend to suggest that you would be my employee, Mr Kelly. I hope you did not get that idea.'

Jack was no fool and knew exactly what Arrowsmith meant. For a reasonable amount of money, he expected Jack to hand over his discovery and then allow the Arrowsmith companies to assume control. But this was definitely not in Jack's plan.

Arrowsmith attempted a counter. 'It seems that at this stage it is unlawful to make gold claims in the former German territory, if that is your proposed location.'

'Have you ever visited Papua or New Guinea?' Jack asked quietly.

'I am afraid the place has never held much appeal to my company interests,' he replied. 'No, I have not.'

'I can tell you something about the place and its problems. It is probably the most inhospitable island on earth. Mountains that reach to the sky covered in almost impenetrable jungle. No roads, and just a few native tracks along narrow ridges that a man can hardly traverse. The climate will suck a man dry and what is left the local natives will eat. I think I can safely say that only a handful of men alive are capable of finding where I made my strike – and they are all in Papua. No, Mr Arrowsmith, even if you *think* you know where my strike was made, I doubt that you would find anyone stupid enough to go in and end up like my good friend George Spencer. He died with a Kuku arrow in him.'

'I take your point,' Arrowsmith said. 'I might offer you a partnership in the enterprise.'

'Investment or nothing,' Jack responded stubbornly. 'Or I go elsewhere.'

'You have already,' Arrowsmith smirked, 'and they all knocked you back. So consider my offer. That is, if it still stands in a week's time.'

'You are giving me a week?'

'A week – no more.'

'Thank you for your time,' Jack said, wanting to be out of the house. 'I will bid you a good day.'

'Don't be so hasty, Mr Kelly,' Arrowsmith said quickly. 'You may as well stay and chat with some of my guests. I believe Hugh Hopkins served in your theatre of the war. I have no doubt that you and he could reminisce about old times together over a beer or two.'

'The war is not something I want to remember,' Jack replied with a bitter note in his voice. 'I get enough of it every time I lay down to sleep.'

Arrowsmith shrugged. 'So be it,' he said as Jack turned to leave the library. 'It does not pay any man to be my competitor – or enemy.'

The echoing threat did not worry Jack. Many men had made them before, but he was still standing.

He found Erika still in Caroline's company at the edge of the patio. They were laughing together with the backdrop of the magnificent harbour behind them. Erika held a cocktail glass delicately in her hand and leaned forward to place her hand on Caroline's knee. They hardly noticed Jack's approach.

'We are leaving, Erika,' Jack said gruffly, and she glanced up at him with surprise.

'But I am having so much fun, Jack,' she protested. 'Why can't we stay longer? Caroline was telling me about her time in Germany before the war. We have so much in common.'

'Why don't you let Erika stay with us for a little longer, Mr Kelly,' Caroline said smoothly. 'I can get our chauffeur to run her home when she is ready to leave.'

Jack was not in a mood to argue but when he gazed into Erika's eyes he saw her desperate plea and softened. She had not been out much with him and to force her to return to Strathfield now would be cruel. 'I will see you when you get home tonight,' he said, and Erika beamed him a grateful smile.

Jack left the house preoccupied and frustrated at not getting a straight answer from Arrowsmith. The raising of money seemed to be an unsolvable problem for him. His problems grew when Erika did not return that night.

The next morning he telephoned the Arrowsmith house. Caroline explained that Erika had decided to stay over. She was sorry that she had caused Jack any worry but would ask Erika to call him back when she returned from shopping. The phone clicked and Jack stood with the mouthpiece in his hand, wondering why he felt apprehensive. After all, the explanation was perfectly sound.

Erika finally telephoned Jack that evening. She explained that she would like to spend some more time with her new friends. Caroline was going to take her up to their summer house at Palm Beach. She hinted that her growing friendship with the Arrowsmiths could be very helpful to Jack's cause and grudgingly he had to admit that she was right. So he bowed to her wish to spend the rest of the week with Caroline and her husband.

While he was marking time, hoping that Arrowsmith would fold on his conditions for financial backing, Jack spent some more time with Lukas. At first they felt awkward together, but a trip to Taronga Park Zoo and a ride on the elephant – along with copious quantities of boiled lollies – started to thaw the coldness between them.

On the train trip home, Lukas fell asleep with his head in Jack's lap. Jack carried the dozing boy home and returned him once again to Mrs Casey's maternal care. He put Lukas to bed, stooping to kiss his son on the forehead. 'Good night, young fella,' he whispered as he crept out of the bedroom shared by three of the Casey boys, none of them much older than Lukas.

'He's a very good young fella,' Mrs Casey told Jack as she saw him out. 'But he's had a rough time first losing his mother, and then Mary, God bless her.'

Jack agreed and despite her protests left a five-pound note on the kitchen table before walking down to the hotel. He again shared the company and conversation of the two argumentative ex-servicemen he had befriended. This time they were in agreement that those who had been eligible for military service – but chose to stay at home in civilian jobs rather than face the dangers of the battlefield –

should now give up their jobs for the men who had fought for King and country. Jack listened to his comrades and was in sympathy with them, but did not enter the conversation. His mind was on Erika and her silence since the telephone call asking to stay on with the Arrowsmiths. He brooded on his decision and realised just how much he missed her in his bed. Love had never been mentioned between them but he presumed she knew how he felt about her. He had never told her of the letters or the photo he had taken from her dead fiancé and wondered if he should ever let her know. Maybe she would see his possession of them as robbing the dead.

When closing time came, Jack staggered back to his brother-in-law's house and shared a bottle with him before collapsing into bed. He hoped that for once his dreams would be of Erika and not of men he had shared life with until a hideous death came to claim them.

The next morning a young man arrived on the doorstep with a telegram from Papua. Jack hardly had time to digest the contents when the mailman arrived with an important looking letter. Both pieces of paper were about to turn his life upside down.

The sign read *Sullivan, Levi & Duffy, Solicitors* and the offices in a three-storeyed sandstone building just off Circular Quay seemed to be bursting at the seams with wads of legal papers stuffed in manila folders and tied with pale pink ribbon.

Jack was ushered into an office marked *Thomas Sullivan MC*. He was pleased to note that the solicitor had obviously seen war service and been awarded a Military Cross. A strongly built man about his own age greeted him across an untidy desk strewn with papers. It was when he stood that Jack noticed the brawny lawyer had lost a leg.

'Mont St Quentin,' he grunted at Jack's obvious glance at his wooden limb. 'Bloody war was almost over when the Fritzes stitched me up with one of their bloody machine guns. Hear you saw a bit yourself in France.'

Jack warmed to the man despite a great dislike for lawyers generally. 'Yeah, enlisted just after the Dardenelles campaign.'

'I read that in the report about yourself and the late Lord Spencer. Seems he held you in the same esteem as he might a blood relation. But come to think about it George Spencer was not very close to his family after he resigned his commission. Seems that he was accused of diddling mess funds and looked like he might face a court martial at the time. His father's regiment and all that. But the culprit was caught red handed and the army did not apologise for their mistake. The stiff upper lip – or something, I suppose.'

'So that was it,' Jack mused as he made himself comfortable in a chair.

'Would you like a whisky or gin?' Tom Sullivan asked when he was seated. He turned to the bottles stashed behind a pile of documents in the corner of his small office. 'Think you will need a stiff drink for what I am about to tell you,' he grinned.

'If you think it's a good idea, I will have a gin.'

Sullivan reached over and retrieved a bottle. He placed two glasses on his desk and poured liberal tots into each. 'Sorry, I haven't got any tonic,' he apologised as he pushed Jack's glass across the table between reams of papers. 'Place is always like this. Got to hate the neat and tidy ways of the army so I suppose this is my way of staging my own mutiny to everything that reminds me of those days.' He raised his glass. 'To the late Lord George Spencer.'

Jack responded by raising his glass in a silent salute to his old friend. He was bursting with curiosity as to why he had received the summons to the solicitor's office. All the letter had said was that as a beneficiary of the will he was required to be at its reading on this appointed day.

The lawyer placed his glass to one side and produced a formal looking document. 'We were appointed Lord Spencer's executors while he was in Sydney. Then we received his will by mail some months ago when he went north to Papua. It seems that he did not have much faith in the more expensive and English dominated law firms here. My family's firm has always had a tradition of being a thorn in the side of the Australian establishment. I think that he was wise in his choice considering the beneficiaries of the will. In the hands of a more respectable firm of solicitors – not that we aren't respectable,' Tom hurried to justify, 'but a more conservative firm, especially British linked, might have wanted to have the English aristocracy dispute the terms of the will. But as Lord Spencer was the very last of his line it seems they would probably have to drag out some poor half-witted imbecile from the dungeon where he was locked away to avoid a family scandal. Anyway, I gather from the shock you have exhibited on learning that your former friend was of noble birth – in a pommy sort of way – that you require some more explanation.'

'It would help,' Jack said taking a swig from the bitter clear liquid. 'I always suspected George had some surprises in his background – but a title was not one of those things I suspected.'

'He was only Lord Spencer for a short time whilst he was in Papua,' Tom explained. 'Up until then his older brother had inherited the title from his father who died in '19. But his brother was a serving officer, a family tradition of the Spencers, and was killed last year fighting at Archangel in Russia against the Reds. George automatically inherited the title – not that it seems to have helped him any from the report I read that was sent to us with his death certificate. I see that you were with him in his last hours.'

Jack stared at the wall behind the solicitor for a brief moment as the memory of the attack came back to him. 'George was a fair dinkum mate. Best pom I ever knew,' he said finishing the contents of the glass in one swallow.

'You don't get the title,' Tom said with a smile, 'but you get the whole shooting match of estates and accounts held in the Spencer name. And that amounts to a lordship's fortune.'

'Is that what George said in his will?' Jack asked as the shock wore off.

'Well, not precisely,' Tom Sullivan said as he shuffled the papers before him. 'It seems that the terms of the will specified that in the event of his death his estate was to be equally divided between yourself and a young lady called Iris. From a report sent to me by the Papuan administration it appears that Miss Iris was unfortunately killed.'

'She is not dead,' Jack said. 'I received a telegram from Port Moresby to say that she had been sighted still alive by a reputable witness.'

'Ahh . . . that somewhat complicates matters then,' the solicitor replied. 'You see, under the conditions of the will we cannot release any of the estate until the lady signs for her share.'

'Well, easy come, easy go,' Jack laughed bitterly. The chance to independently bankroll himself had existed for the time it took him to finish a glass of gin. 'I doubt that getting her signature will be that easy.'

'Why is that?'

'I don't have all the facts and have to wait for a letter that will brief me on the situation. But about all I do know is that she is out of reach.'

The pained expression on Tom Sullivan's face said it all. The will was at a stalemate. 'I am sorry – there is nothing else we can do for you for the moment. We require confirmation that either the young lady is dead – or her signature. Sorry, old chap.'

'I hope you get Iris's signature,' Jack said as he rose from the chair. 'I owe that to my old mate.'

• • •

When Jack returned to Strathfield he was met by Harry who said that Erika had returned home in a chauffeur driven car to pick up the last of her things. She had told him that she was not coming back. Jack stood on the doorstep, stunned by the news. Maybe Harry had got it wrong.

'Did she actually say she was leaving us?' he asked in a strained voice.

'Afraid so,' Harry replied sympathetically. 'I don't think you will be seeing your young lady again.'

Jack felt numb. What had gone wrong? This was worse than the old dreams of war. 'Tell young Lukas that I won't be able to take him to the park today to play cricket. And I am not sure when I will be in tonight.'

Harry could see that his brother-in-law had a set expression that was disturbing. 'Don't do anything rash,' he warned, but Jack ignored him as he spun on his heel and strode down the footpath. Jack knew where he was going – and knew what he must do.

Jack stood at the front of the Point Piper mansion and rapped sharply on the door.

'I am sorry, Mr Kelly, but you cannot enter,' the butler said firmly as he blocked the entrance. 'I have orders from Mrs Arrowsmith.'

He was not a young man and Jack felt a twinge of guilt as he forced his way past him. 'Mrs Arrowsmith,' he called out, planting himself in the large airy chamber below a set of marbled stairs that led to the upstairs living area.

He was about to climb the stairs when Caroline appeared at the top wearing little more than a cream silk chemise. Behind her stood Erika in a similarly short undergarment with the addition of a black suspender belt and stockings.

'You are not welcome here, Mr Kelly,' Caroline stated in a commanding voice. 'If you do not leave immediately I will call the police and inform my husband of your uninvited intrusion into our home.'

'I am here to speak to Erika,' Jack said, staring past Caroline to Erika, who appeared pale and frightened.

'Say your piece and leave,' Caroline conceded coldly. 'I hope that it will be brief.'

'Are you coming home?' Jack asked, directing his question to Erika.

'I am sorry, Jack,' she replied, almost in a whisper, 'but my life is here. Not with you. Caroline has arranged for me to take a position in her house.'

'Are you and she . . . ?' Jack could not find the words but Erika knew what he wanted to ask.

'That is not of your concern,' she replied with a defiant tilt of her chin. 'My life is my own. And after what I have now learned about you, I never ever want to see you again.'

'What are you talking about?' Jack asked in confusion.

Erika glared at him. 'The letters,' she said in a trembling voice. 'I found them when I was packing to leave. I was not prying into your affairs, I found them by accident. How could you be in possession of my words to Wolfgang? They were sacred and private. Did you kill Wolfgang?'

Jack paled. He did not know how to respond. He had meant to tell Erika about the letters and how they had come into his possession, but every time he had considered doing so he always felt a touch of guilt. Now he wished he had destroyed them.

'I did not kill your fiancé,' he replied softly. 'I swear on the life of my son that it was not me who killed Wolfgang.' And Jack uttered the words in the genuine belief that they were true. He did not know that all for the sake of a war souvenir a soldier had lied to him that day.

Erika stared at him for a short time then turned to walk into the room behind her. She was not sure whether she could believe him but felt that Jack was not the kind of man to lie. It did not seem to be in his forthright nature. But doubt was something she also harboured in her feelings. She knew that she was not likely to ever turn to him again.

Jack watched Erika walk from his life and stood helplessly swamped by his sorrow for what could have been. Somehow the matter of the letters was not a thing he could explain in simple terms. But Jack was not a man to beg.

That afternoon Jack got blinding drunk. This time his two erstwhile drinking companions had to help him home, holding him between them as they had helped wounded comrades from the battlefields. Jack was no less wounded now than he had been at times on the Western Front. At least his physical wounds had healed. This was a different kind of wound, one that he doubted would ever heal.

Jack remained in Sydney for another three months. He was reluctant to leave whilst Erika was in the city, hoping against all hope that she might return to him. But it was not to be.

Soon the money he had made from his find was almost gone and he knew that he must make a decision. He could remain with his brother-in-law and seek employment with his printing firm or return to the land that he loved. Jack purchased two railway tickets for Townsville en route to the mysterious island to Australia's north. Whatever was to be his destiny still lay in those wild, unexplored mountains.

TWENTY

'**N**ext stop Townsville,' the conductor called as he walked down the carriage past the weary travellers.

Jack glanced at Lukas sitting by the window, peering out at the landscape of the new place his father said would be his home. The paddocks were green and the spindly gum trees seemed to have taken on a new lease of life. The Wet had come to the north and Townsville had benefitted.

Christmas of 1920 was almost upon them and Jack wondered if his dwindling supply of money could stretch to buy his son a decent gift to go under the tree. He stared out the window at the paddocks and felt their welcome. He was back in the country, away from the grey city people and their suits. His only regret was that he hadn't smashed the smirk from Arrowsmith's face when he confronted him in his office. At least he had the satisfaction of telling him where he could stick his suggestion of a partnership when he still refused to invest. He remembered how the bigger man had trembled when Jack got past his secretary and burst into his office demanding an answer and still angry about Erika's defection. Jack had stated that one day he would come looking for Arrowsmith and that when he did, he would settle scores with him. What that meant he left to Arrowsmith's imagination. Quentin had led a privileged life of luxury and was not used to dealing with men who did not think twice about putting their lives on the line on a daily basis.

'Almost there,' Jack said gently to Lukas. At least the Sydney to Townsville train trip over the last few days had helped Jack develop something of a paternal bond with his son. It dawned on Jack one night out of Brisbane that he was looking at himself as a young boy when he gazed upon the sleeping face of his son. And it also occurred to Jack that his son was now the only living relative in his life. Both awesome realisations that made him appreciate how important it was to succeed, that he must leave something of substance behind when he finally joined his old comrades in the eternal sleep of death.

A letter had arrived from Papua in which Paul Mann gave Jack an account of his expedition into the Fly River delta in search of Iris. He was sketchy in his description of sighting her, but Jack got the picture. He also mentioned that he would be back in Townsville for Christmas to be with his family. He hoped that Jack could join them, should he be in the area at the time. Jack accepted the invitation. It would be good to share a Christmas with his son in a family atmosphere. So he telegrammed his acceptance to Karin and they were all standing on the railway station as the train pulled in.

Their greeting was warm and Karin made a big fuss over Lukas. Jack was pleased to see that his son seemed to take to her and their boy Karl. Although young Karl's English was not perfect, he was learning fast at school and the two boys immediately struck up a conversation about the animals of the region. Jack could see that Paul had suffered a severe bout of fever as he was gaunt and hollow-eyed.

'Sen was good to me,' he said, as they walked to a horse and sulky that Paul had been able to buy. 'He paid me well and purchased my ticket home for Christmas.'

'Smart bastard,' Jack said with a grin as he slapped Paul on the back. 'Knows he won't get a better man than you.'

'I have you to thank for that,' Paul replied modestly. 'I think fate meant us to meet that terrible day.'

'Maybe,' Jack mused. 'Kind of need a good mate right now.'

As they approached the little house outside of town Jack was amazed to see how Karin's garden had sprouted a cornucopia of fresh vegetables. When he commented on it Karin scowled. 'Those damned kangaroos have tried to eat all my vegetables,' she said.

'You sound like an Aussie already,' Jack laughed.

Karin seemed pleased by the comment.

'It is a good country,' Paul added. 'Lots of sunshine and food. And the people are proving to be a little more friendly – well, most of them.'

Paul brought the sulky to a stop and the two boys immediately jumped off to run and see something that Karl had told Lukas about.

'Karl!' Paul called in a commanding voice. 'Help me with the horse before you go off to play.'

'Yes, Papa,' he replied, obediently scooting to a stop and idling back to his father with his hands in his pockets.

Karin showed Jack through to a gauzed-in verandah at the back of the house. It had a simple iron bed with clean sheets. 'You can sleep here,' she said, patting the bed. 'Lukas can sleep in with Karl.'

Jack dropped his swag on the bed.

'I have heard from Erika,' Karin continued as if reading Jack's mind. Being in the house had reminded him of the first time he had set eyes on her. 'She wrote me a letter to wish us well for Christmas and she said that you were good to her in Sydney.' She paused. 'I think you were a little in love with her.'

'How did you know?' he asked.

Karin smiled. 'I saw it in your eyes the day you came to visit us. Men are so easy to read in such matters but complicated in all other ways.'

'Not that complicated,' Jack replied with a sad smile. 'Just naive.'

'She was not meant for you, Jack,' Karin said sympathetically. 'She is not a good woman despite the fact that she is my sister-in-law. I think she would destroy any man in her life. But I should not say such things to you as I can see she has hurt you already.' Jack nodded and sat on the bed. 'I have something for you and Lukas to eat. I have made a stew with dumplings. I hope you like it.'

Flavoured with herbs and spices, the stew was delicious and both Kelly men had a second helping.

'Great tucker,' Jack grunted as he ladled the rich dark meat and gravies into his mouth. 'Can't quite figure out if it is beef or lamb though.'

'Neither,' Paul grinned. 'It's one of those pesky kangaroos.'

Jack laughed. 'Takes someone new to this country to make something out of a bloody nuisance. Got to get the recipe from you, Karin,' he added and she beamed with happiness. How lucky Paul was, Jack thought, when he looked at Karin. She was everything a man wanted in a woman.

That evening Jack and Paul sat outside the house on a log and shared a couple of bottles of beer under the constellation of the Southern Cross. It was time to swap their experiences since they had last seen each other at Sen's house on the outskirts of Port Moresby. The night had a balmy breeze and Jack felt at complete ease. How ironic life was – a little over two years earlier they were at war and would have tried to kill each other to satisfy the whims of power hungry politicians. Now they sat together sharing a beautiful night in the tropics of Australia.

Paul recounted his expedition in search of Iris. After relating the events of his planned attack on O'Leary he became subdued.

'You made the right decision not to play your hand,' Jack said, guessing Paul's sense of failure. 'The odds were against getting yourself and your men out alive. O'Leary will turn up again and when he does we will find out where Iris was shipped to.'

Paul nodded. 'I do not want to pry, my friend,' Paul said quietly, 'but I fear you must be low on funds by now. Sen told me that the gold you found would only keep you for a while.'

'Bit like that,' Jack answered, and took a long swig from the large beer bottle. The fizzy ale felt good in his throat. 'But I will get back to Papua and see if I can do anything about making the best of the strike.'

'That will cost money,' Paul said. 'I wish I were in a position to help you.'

'My old mate George Spencer – sorry, Lord Spencer – was almost in a position to help me,' Jack said. 'But it all hinged on finding Iris to satisfy the terms of his will. I doubt that will be easy until we get our hands on O'Leary.'

'What will you do?'

'Work for Sen for a while until I have enough to put together some stores and a couple of boys to go back into New Guinea. It can only be a matter of time before the administration up there start issuing licences to mine leases.'

Paul said no more. He had a surprise for his friend, but that would wait until Christmas Day. His present was also intended for his family. He smiled in the dark and gazed up at the Southern Cross twinkling overhead in the crystal clear skies. Australia was a new land of bounty and opportunity. And so too was Papua.

Christmas day soon came with the patter of four very excited feet in the early hours before dawn. There were presents under the scraggly young gum sapling Paul and Jack had dragged from the bush. It had been adorned with coloured paper cut from women's magazines by Karin and shaped into stars and angels. The previous evening they had all sat up singing carols in German. Karin had left the men by the tree to reminisce about their days at the Front. Although on different sides, the conditions were basically the same for both men: mud, barbed wire and hideous death.

A highly agitated Lukas shook his hungover father awake and dragged him to the decorated tree to see what Father Christmas had left for him during the night. Stumbling after his son, Jack felt the throb of each footfall on the timber floor. Karin was already sitting by the tree in her long nightdress with her legs tucked under her knees, her hair like a golden fountain down her back. She smiled up at him when he entered the room.

'A happy Christmas to you, Jack Kelly,' she said sweetly.

Jack responded, wishing the clanging of Christmas bells would leave his head.

'Look Daddy,' Lukas shouted. 'Father Christmas has left me a real cowboy gun and hat.'

Jack peered curiously at the present Lukas held up to him. He had not been able to buy Lukas a present but a knowing look from Karin explained it all. He mouthed a thank you and she looked away. Karl had also received a cowboy outfit and the two boys blazed away at each other in the small living room dominated by the sapling, which already had wilted in the heat of the hot Australian Christmas morning.

And so Christmas 1920 was one of the best Jack could remember in a long time. Not since he was a boy growing up in the colony of South Australia could he recall experiencing such warmth and happiness.

But Christmas got even better over a lunch of a roast haunch of beef with baked vegetables, followed by custard and fresh fruit. Then, after the meal, Paul announced that he had been able to purchase a copra plantation just down the coast from Port Moresby. Sen had helped him with the red tape and after Christmas they would all return to live on their new property. 'And I will need a manager, Jack,' he said leaning onto the table. 'How would you like the job?'

Jack glanced at Lukas. 'If the offer is open, you have your man.'

As they shook each other's hands Karin served coffee. The day couldn't have been happier, Jack thought. Not only had Lukas been part of a real Christmas but now Jack could spend more time with his son. Next time he would make sure he put the present under the tree himself. Maybe 1921 would prove to be a better year than the one that had passed.

TWENTY-ONE

Q uentin Arrowsmith always ate sparely at breakfast. The hard-boiled egg and fingers of toast were his limit although he had a busy day ahead of him with meetings and documents to peruse and sign at his office in the city.

Already 1921 looked to be a promising year. Consumer spending was rising and the land development side of the companies was turning a good profit. Men were returning to civilian life and government contracts were being filled. His competitors felt the established power behind the ruthless giant that was Arrowsmith enterprises and fell like nine pins.

'We have a small problem,' Caroline sighed as she poked at her own hard-boiled egg with a small silver spoon.

'What problem?' Arrowsmith grunted from behind his morning paper. He kept his eye to the

troubles still being stirred by the army of unemployed former servicemen.

'I am afraid Erika is pregnant.'

Arrowsmith stopped reading and stared belligerently at his wife. 'She is your plaything. I expect that
you can take her to someone who knows how to
dispose of such problems.'

'I have already attempted to convince the poor
girl that is her only alternative but she has a dread of
termination. She told me of friends who died under
the most terrible of circumstances as a result of such
procedures. And I fear she is already too advanced for
an abortion to be attempted anyway.'

'Well, it's not my bastard,' Arrowsmith growled.
'She has been your exclusive property, despite what
you may be thinking.'

'I am not accusing you of being the father. Erika
has told me that she knows beyond any doubt that
the father has to be that man Jack Kelly.'

'You do realise, of course, the scandal that her
pregnancy would cause me? A woman living under
my roof suddenly gets pregnant. It is obvious that our
friends would think that I was the father.'

'Well, Quentin,' Caroline replied smugly, 'you can
see that the problem is not mine alone and that I
need your help in finding a solution to *our* problem.'

Arrowsmith pondered his wife's words. 'We could
send her away with some money to keep her quiet.'

'I have become rather attached to my little kit-
ten,' Caroline said. 'I would not like to see her in dire
straits despite her stupidity. She should have known
better, however.'

'I could telegram that bastard Kelly in Papua and tell him what he has done,' Arrowsmith muttered savagely.

Months had passed but he still smarted from the confrontation in his office when Kelly had forced his way in. Quentin Arrowsmith had never before been exposed to a threat where he actually feared for his personal safety. Such had been the rage blazing in the former soldier's eyes that for a moment he thought the man might kill him. The memory was a cancer eating at him. Oh, how he wished he had challenged Kelly's rage. But the man had shown him up and it had somehow become known around the companies that he had backed down to the challenge. For that he would do everything in his power to crush the man.

Arrowsmith had been fortunate in marrying a woman from a highly respected family who encouraged his ruthless desire to be the richest and most powerful man in Australia. Caroline was the only daughter in a family not unlike his own. The Arrowsmiths had a line of noble ancestors. He and Caroline had recognised in each other a dark side. In their unbridled pleasure seeking he had catered to her sexual whims.

His consideration to now telegram the administration in Papua and inform them that Mr Jack Kelly had left a poor young girl pregnant back in Australia appealed to his twisted sense of vengeance. What would the conservative administration think about one of their respected citizens then? Quentin Arrowsmith had learned in his private inquiries about Jack Kelly that he was a man respected by Sir Hubert as a man of honour. Was it honourable to leave a young girl pregnant to face the streets in a country foreign to her?

'I would rather not have you even tell that horrible man,' Caroline cut across his brooding thoughts of revenge. 'Although I'm loath to see her go, I think that it would be easier to allow the girl to have her way and return to Germany. She has expressed that desire to me.'

Arrowsmith had not known of Erika's desire to return to Germany but now considered the solution to their problem had been found. Germany was a long way from Australia and out of sight was out of mind. What happened to her there was not his problem.

'You should have told me that first,' he said. 'I can arrange to buy her passage on one of our ships to Europe. It is as simple as that.'

'We must give her enough money to tide her over during the pregnancy,' Caroline said across the table. 'She deserves at least that much from us and I know you can well and truly afford. Oh, and she travels first class to Europe on a passenger ship and not one of your cargo steamers.'

'You are asking a lot, Caroline,' Quentin said in a pained voice. 'She is of little consequence. A young and confused girl who has got herself knocked up by a man of no significance.'

'Don't be so boorish,' Caroline retorted. 'She has been devoted to us these last few months. She deserves just a little consideration.'

'I will make the arrangements,' Quentin sighed as he made his first business decision of the day. 'She will be gone from our lives this time next week.'

'Good. And when are we next going to visit Europe?' Caroline asked sweetly as she pushed her silver egg cup aside. 'I would love to visit Paris sometime soon.'

'That is another matter,' Quentin grunted.

He had more important things on his mind than sharing space with garlic eating Frogs – he had a financial empire to run. An empire he had hoped one day to hand on to a son and heir. But that aspiration was already doomed, as he well knew. He stared at his beautiful wife and considered the cruel irony of life. All his money could not buy him an heir.

Erika was ushered to her cabin by a smartly dressed steward for her first class passage to Hamburg via the Suez Canal. Caroline had not bothered to come to the pier and bid her farewell. Instead the chauffeur had driven her to Circular Quay and promptly left her on the wharf to fend for herself.

When the steward placed her single bag by her bunk and left, the young woman finally broke down and collapsed on her bed. How had it all gone so wrong, she thought, as the sobbing racked her body? She had always wanted to return to her true home but not pregnant and possibly destitute. The money was generous but not enough to keep a woman without a husband. For a fleeting moment she thought about Jack. She had even considered trying to contact him and informing him of her circumstances. But that option was rejected once her suspicions that he had killed her beloved Wolfgang were recalled.

From the wharf Erika could hear people bidding friends and relations a bon voyage. Would there be anyone to welcome her when she finally reached Munich? And what would she do with the child of the man who had murdered her fiancé?

She dried her tears away with the back of her hand and sat up. She was returning to Munich and to the man she had replaced Wolfgang with in her life. She wondered what Adolf would be doing at this very moment. In a few weeks she would again join him in his struggles to make Germany a great nation once more.

TWENTY-TWO

Just over two years had passed in relative peace for Jack on Paul Mann's plantation. He had adapted well to managing the operations of the copra plantation alongside Paul. The sweet white flesh of the coconut was usually in demand on the overseas markets, although it fluctuated at times. Jack now had the pleasure of Lukas in his life on a daily basis and the little boy had grown to love the man who had once been a stranger to him.

Jack and Lukas lived in a comfortable tin and timber hut not far from the main house occupied by Paul and his family. They had a commanding view of the Coral Sea through the rows of stately coconut palms. For Lukas, growing up in the tropical paradise could not have been better. He had everything a boy could want in life: a best mate in Karl, the ocean to swim in, a horse to ride and a .22

rifle to shoot pigeons for the dinner table.

Jack appreciated Karin's maternal concern for Lukas. He was very close to her and called her Aunt Karin. She had taken to the old life in the tropics much as Paul remembered her as his young wife in the pre-war days at Finschhafen. Her days passed with a routine of tutoring the boys in their schooling – much to their dismay when the time, in their opinion, could have been better utilised fishing, swimming and hunting with the native boys from a nearby village. She had the assistance of a girl from the local village with the cooking and cleaning and an old native villager assisted with other chores around the house.

The years passed in serenity, following the Wet and Dry seasons of the monsoon climate. Karin loved the Wet because it meant that her two men would be at home sitting on the wide verandah and waiting out the torrential downpours. Paul and Jack would sit in silence, puffing on their pipes, as the deafening roar of the rain on the tin roof made any semblance of a conversation difficult. Karin would sit beside them and sew or read. It was a time of peace, a time to reflect on the fruits of friendship.

And when the heavy clouds were replaced by the gentle powder puffs in the vast blue skies, the birds of paradise with their brilliant plumage sang and the villagers at work filled the coconut groves with their lazy laughter. Karin hardly even remembered her life before their return to the paradise they had left behind in the terrible year of 1914.

Karin's announcement in early 1923 that she was pregnant disrupted the two boys' idyllic existence. They would sit on the beach and discuss how a girl might come into their lives and ruin everything. It was agreed that she would want to hang around them and be a pest. But it was also mooted that another boy might arrive and that would not be so bad.

Both Paul and Jack got resoundingly drunk when Karin announced the news, and Paul broke out a supply of big, thick cigars to celebrate. He and Jack sat under the stars – as they had often done before – to take in the beauty of the clear night sky with its magnificent display of twinkling lights. Like the two boys, the men had grown as close as brothers in the time they had sweated beside their Papuan plantation workers, bringing in the coconuts for processing.

It was not a big plantation, however, and its future as a commercial concern had always been dubious. Copra prices had been falling and as Paul sat at a rickety desk made from wooden crates in the corner of a packing shed he stared forlornly at the neat row of figures in his battered accounts ledger. Outgoing costs outnumbered incoming profits. He did not have the heart to tell Karin in her time of expectant joy that they were facing bankruptcy. She had never been happier in all the years he had known her. He too had finally found peace in their tropical paradise, but the meagre savings left from his family estate in Munich were decreasing as quickly as the price of copra.

Paul sighed and flipped the accounts book closed. He gazed across the dusty yard to the flat blue sea beyond. Maybe he would talk to Jack and warn him that he might be better off seeking employment elsewhere soon, but how did he break such news to a man he had grown to accept and love as family? He even suspected that Karin was a little enamoured of the Australian. He had often observed how she fussed around him when he was sick and Paul had smiled at how his wife treated Jack as she would her husband, while Jack would unconsciously respond as Paul himself did. But Paul was not jealous. He knew that Jack would never consider making any improper advances. It was not in the nature of the man.

'Paul!'

Paul could see that Jack was flustered as he hurried across the yard from his quarters.

'Paul you old bastard, where are you?' Jack called as he waved a paper around his head.

'Here, Jack,' Paul answered from his makeshift office in a corner of the packing sheds. 'What is the matter?'

Jack made a beeline for the desk and dropped the government paper on Paul's ledger. Paul glanced at the official looking document and noticed that it was a copy of the *New Guinea Gazette*.

'They found the bloody mother lode,' Jack exploded. 'Just west of where George and I were back in '20.'

'Who's they?' Paul asked, bemused by Jack's indignation. It was rare to see the Australian in such an agitated state.

'Bloody Park, Sloane, Nettleton and Dover have made lease applications up in the Morobe district to mine gold. I should have known something was up when I heard old Sharkeye Park and Jack Nettleton had disappeared up that way. If anyone, other than myself was capable of finding a big strike, it had to be Park. I would bet everything I have that they are onto something really big. We have to get up there by any means we can,' Jack added. 'Just drop everything and get there to peg claims before the word gets out and we end up at the end of the rush with nothing more than a bad bout of malaria and a Kuku arrow in our arses.'

Paul was surprised that Jack had so quickly included him in his plans of going to the Morobe district to peg claims. He was not a prospector and Jack knew that.

'We have no other choice,' Jack said as he calmed down. 'I'm no fool, I have read about the falling prices of copra and I would not be much of a manager if I didn't know what was going on around here. I was getting ready to hand in my resignation before you were forced to ask and go and see if Sen had any work for me. I know you have kept me on for longer than you should have and for that you have my thanks, old friend.'

Paul was stunned. He thought he had kept the truth of his dire circumstances a close secret. Even with Jack gone it was only a matter of time before he would have to cut his costs and walk off the plantation.

'I don't know what to say,' he replied. 'Just that I have always valued your friendship more than you would know.'

'Trust me, Paul, and we will make a fortune,' Jack said with a passion. 'I know where the gold is and I know how to get it out before the rush starts. But we have to be there before the hordes come and take the surface pickings. After that it will be the big companies with their machinery.'

'I am no miner,' Paul responded. 'You would be better off with a partner who knows what he is doing.'

'So, you are considering my offer,' Jack said with an edge of triumph. 'You don't need to be a miner for what is ahead of us. I need a mate who is good in the bush, and you proved that with your expedition to find Iris.'

'Do you really want me along?' Paul asked. 'Do you think we could make some money out of such an expedition?'

'To both questions the answer is yes. I need a mate who I know will watch my back. Besides, we are going to have to do this with a lot of haste and a little bit of rule bending.'

'Rule bending?' Paul asked suspiciously. 'What do you mean?'

'The priority is to actually get in where Sharkeye Park and his mates are staking claims. We're not going to have much time to chase permits or mining leases. What counts is getting our hands on weight before anything else. We can stake our claims through the legal channels with the administration in Rabaul once we have got the gold out.'

Paul groaned inwardly. His friend was asking him to risk legal prosecution should things go wrong. He was a German citizen and he did not think that the Australian authorities would be very sympathetic towards him. 'How much risk is there, Jack?' he asked with a pained expression.

'Not a real lot,' Jack grinned widely. 'I doubt that any government men would be wanting to head into Kuku country in a hurry. I heard in Moresby that the district officer up that way, Cecil Levien, copped an arrow in the chest early this year when he was on a patrol out in the Morobe area not far from where George and I were camped. It's rough country and crawling with those dangerous little bastards. But I know between us we can handle them if they get a bit pesky.'

Paul rose from his desk. 'I will speak to Karin tonight,' he said rubbing his forehead. 'I will give you a decision in the morning.'

'Every day counts,' Jack warned. 'We need to be getting supplies together as quickly as we can.'

Paul nodded and walked towards the house. Jack watched him go and was glad that he was not married. As a single man he could pack up and leave. For a moment he reflected guiltily on the existence of his son. But he was able to console himself that if anything were to happen to him, he knew that Karin would look after Lukas.

That evening, as Paul and Karin lay side by side under the mosquito net, Paul confessed the dire financial straits that they were in and the losses the plantation was incurring. He could sense how tense

Karin was at the prospect that they may have to walk off the plantation, and the knowledge that their savings were almost gone.

'What will we do?' she asked tearfully. 'I love this place.'

'Jack has a plan,' Paul said after taking a deep breath. 'It is guaranteed to make a small fortune for us all.'

Immediately he had planted the seed, Karin sat up and stared at her husband in the dark.

'What plan?' she asked in a tone that left Paul in no doubt that he would have to be very careful how he answered. As much as Karin liked Jack, she was still a female protecting those she loved.

'There is a gold lease that Jack has back in New Guinea,' Paul lied. 'He thinks that, with a bit of effort, we could make it pay. But he needs my help, and whatever supplies we can get together, to mine it.'

'Why hasn't Jack mentioned this before?'

'It never came up before,' Paul replied lamely, hoping that Karin would not cross-examine him any further. He knew he could not continue lying to her. She had a knack of knowing when he was not telling her the truth. 'But it could be the answer to all our problems.'

In her despair Karin fell back against the sheets. 'How long would you be gone for?' she asked quietly.

Paul breathed a sigh of relief, hoping that his wife did not hear it. Her question implied that she had conceded to his suggestion. 'I would say we would be gone for four to six months,' he guessed.

'That is a long time,' Karin replied and hugged Paul to her. 'I did not imagine that we would ever be apart again. The war was terrible enough but I suspect that this is also dangerous.'

'Not really,' Paul said holding Karin gently against his chest. 'We will be home before Christmas and you can roast a goose for us.'

'We don't have any geese,' Karin half laughed and half cried. 'It will have to be a roast pig.'

'Then I can tell Jack first thing in the morning that I have your blessing on our venture?'

'You know that I trust your decisions, my husband,' she said. 'I just wanted you to be around when our child is born. But I also know that our child will not have a home unless you do what you must do.'

Paul stroked his wife's hair until she fell asleep in his arms. He dreaded the thought of going back into the jungle but at the same time felt the strange lure of the gold. The very word was calling to him in irresistibly seductive tones. What was it about the yellow metal that caused men and women to risk everything to seek it? He was just learning the answer now. He knew that he would miss his family with an aching heart. But he also knew that Jack would miss his son in the same way. The lure of gold or not, this was their only chance to stave off losing what little he had left in his life. It was a desperate gamble under any circumstances. But he trusted Jack and knew that Jack trusted him. They were mates and would watch each other's backs.

It took two days to arrange stores for the expedition: flour, tinned meat, sugar, tea, salt and coffee (at Paul's insistence). Then there were medical supplies, ammunition for the rifles and shotguns as well as adzes, axes and a few trade goods. The final task was to find a boat to convey them around the eastern tip of Papua and into the Huon Gulf. Jack rode to Port Moresby and returned a few days later in a whale-boat powered by a small steam engine. It had once belonged to a Lutheran missionary before the war. He'd sold the horse to help pay for it.

One of the native labourers spotted the whale-boat chugging towards the shore and shouted to Karin who was watering her precious flowers beside the house. She dropped the watering can and walked down to the beach, shielding her eyes against the glare on the calm seas. She could just make out Jack. And beside him was a tall, well-built young Papuan.

'All I could get was this,' Jack shouted as the boat slid onto the beach below the plantation. 'She'll be right. It will get us to the Gulf okay.'

Karin prayed that he was right. Jack was always optimistic and cheerful in contrast to her more pes-simistic and dour husband. It made for a good partnership, she grudgingly admitted to herself, as Jack bounded up the beach and kissed her lightly on the cheek.

'Don't look so worried,' he laughed. 'I wouldn't dare let anything happen to Paul or I would have to account to you. This is Dademo,' he added as the young man clambered from the boat with a shy but broad smile. 'He is going to keep an eye on things while Paul and I are off making our fortunes.'

'You are right, Mr Kelly,' Karin replied in a stern voice. 'If anything happens to Paul . . .' Her voice quavered on the verge of tears and Jack felt awkward.

'It's going to be all right, old girl,' he said gently. 'We will come back as the kings of Papua.'

Paul strode down to join them at the beach and greeted Dademo with an affectionate handshake and slap on the back. He then scrutinised the whaleboat. Jack tentatively stood aside and waited for his opinion.

'We will be able to stow our supplies but will need a tarpaulin to protect them against the sea.' Almost completely ignoring the Australian he turned to Dademo. 'I see that Sen let you go for a while,' he said and the two men walked up the beach, discussing what Dademo's duties would be when they were gone. He had been expecting the Papuan as Jack had said before he left for Moresby that he would talk to Sen about borrowing Dademo's ser-vices while they were away. But as Paul walked away with Dademo, Jack knew all was not well. He turned to Karin.

'He is worried about me,' she said to his unspoken question. 'But I have faith in you, Jack, to look after my husband.'

With this weight thrust upon his shoulders, Jack Kelly experienced a sudden surge of doubt. He had not kept George Spencer alive. How would this situation be any different? Karin followed her husband up the white sands, leaving Jack alone to wonder just what they were getting themselves into.

• • •

The following day Jack and Paul put to sea. Karin and the two boys watched from the beach until the little boat steamed around a small headland and out of sight. Taking the two boys by the hand she walked slowly back to the house.

'When will Dad be back?' Lukas asked, as he looked up at the woman whom he had come to accept as the most important female in his life.

'That is in God's hands,' Karin replied quietly, and looked away lest the boys see her tears and sense her uncertainty. It seemed that she was always saying goodbye to the man she most loved in the world. And every time he left she was never sure if she would see him again. This time was no different. She could feel the baby growing inside her, and burst into tears. What if her child was born without knowing the tender love of the man who had survived so much only to be killed on this wild, uncivilised frontier at the end of the world? The two boys glanced at each other and crept away. They did not understand why Karin should be so upset. They had seen their fathers' cheerful smiles and waves as the boat pulled away from the beach. To Lukas and Karl such men were indestructible.

TWENTY-THREE

Months passed and there was no news from the two men. Not that Karin expected any as she knew that Paul and Jack were well beyond the frontiers. But each night she would pray for their safety, pleading to God to bring them home soon. It did not matter that they may fail in their endeavours. More important was that Lukas had a father and she a husband for her son and unborn child.

Her confinement was near and she knew it was time for Dademo to take over the running of the plantation whilst she took the day's buggy journey to Port Moresby to have her baby delivered. She had grown to rely more and more on Dademo. He had proved an excellent manager and was respected by the local villagers who made up the labour force for the plantation. He was intelligent and had a basic but competent grasp of figures. He was also liked by the two boys who would beg him to recount the adventure he had with Paul in their search for Iris.

Lukas felt just a little jealous of Karl whose father had so bravely gone into the jungle to search for the beautiful lady. Dademo had told them that Iris was a princess taken captive by an evil pirate. He wished that his own father could have been on the quest. Dademo had once heard a story of such an adventure and was a natural storyteller himself. But his embellishments were eagerly accepted by the two boys. In Dademo's version Paul had actually fought with the evil pirate captain but he escaped. Needless to say he also had fought with the pirate captain's lieutenant and killed him.

Dademo had expressed the view that he should go with Karin on the potentially perilous journey to Port Moresby. But she had reminded him that he had the care of the plantation and the two boys to consider. He understood and helped her pack just a few personal items, and food and water for the difficult journey. The last thing Karin placed in her swag of items was Paul's Webley & Scott revolver.

With a final briefing to Dademo just before dawn – and dire warnings to the two boys to do what the young Papuan overseer said – she was helped into the buggy and drove from the plantation. All going well, she would see the lights of Moresby just after nightfall.

Right on schedule three days later she gave birth to a baby girl.

'Angelika,' she murmured as she lay back in her bed in the newly constructed hospital in Moresby. 'You are my precious little angel.'

Three days later Karin felt strong enough to travel back to the plantation with her baby despite the warnings of the stern matron who had acted as midwife and brought Angelika into the world. Karin had told her she was temporarily without her husband because he was, as she put it, 'somewhere up bush'. That was the way of life for women who came with their men onto the Papuan frontier. They had to be just as tough and resourceful to cope with a life so far from civilisation with its running water, stores and medical services.

When Karin returned to the plantation she was met not only by the male workers but also their women who fussed over the little jewel with the tuft of golden hair like her mother. The baby lay crying in Karin's arms with her little fists balled. It was a time of celebration for the labourers. The villagers killed a pig for a feast. Dademo had quietly supplied it from the master's small herd. He did not think that Master Paul would mind it being killed before Christmas which was not long away. Karin did not go to the feast but retired to her house after the boys had poked at the little thing they most dreaded – a sister! And a very ugly one at that they both agreed.

As she lay on her bed with her daughter beside her, it occurred to Karin that Angelika had been born on the soil of this foreign land called Papua. Her daughter was not a German but a Papuan.

• • •

Christmas came and went without any news of Paul and Jack. Life went on and Angelika continued to thrive in the tropical environment. The two boys – when they were at home – grew used to the fact that she was the centre of attention in Karin's life. School lessons continued whenever Karin could find the boys. And each day Karin would walk to the edge of the beach to gaze out to sea and intone her oft-repeated prayer: 'Dear God, be merciful and bring my husband and Jack Kelly home to me.'

Five months to the day since Paul and Jack left on their expedition into the Morobe province of New Guinea, Dademo came rushing to the house. 'Missus,' he yelled breathlessly, 'Master's boat comes.'

Karin had been breastfeeding Angelika and immediately buttoned her blouse. She swept from the house with the confused, hungry baby bawling in her arms and hurried to the beach. Dademo and three of the plantation workers followed her. It was just on sunset and in the distance she could see the whaleboat puttering towards the shore. Karin's blood ran cold. She could only see one figure standing at the helm, but it was too far to ascertain whether it was her husband or Jack. Two had gone out but only one returned – the words echoed in her thoughts. She gripped Angelika to her breast, almost smothering the baby until she bawled in her discomfort.

The boat drew nearer and finally Karin could make out that the lone, bearded figure was Paul, waving his hat over his head and shouting his greetings. Karin felt the relief of having her prayers answered. But she also experienced a terrible fear that Lukas had lost his father to the wild and savage jungles.

Unable to constrain her impatience to once again touch the face of her husband and with the baby still in her arms, Karin waded into the warm tropical waters until the sea was around her thighs, soaking the long dress she wore.

Paul did not wait for the engine to stop and leapt into the sea, leaving the old whaleboat to find its own way to the beach. Dademo and the three workers followed Karin into the gentle surf and guided the boat to shore. Paul surfaced and waded with all his strength towards his wife. His face was an expression of absolute joy as they came together and Paul enveloped Karin and their baby daughter in his arms. They were alternately laughing and crying as they stood in the calm seas, waves lapping around them.

'Your daughter's name is Angelika,' Karin finally got out between hugs and kisses as they babbled their love to each other.

When finally they disengaged themselves from the embrace Paul could see the cloud come down over his wife's face. He burst into laughter when he realised why she should be looking so glum. 'I left Jack in Moresby,' he said. 'He will be back in a couple of days after he does some business with Sen.' Karin's expression of happiness returned. 'And if you are wondering, you are now looking at one of the new kings of Papua,' he added. 'Jack did it! We are wealthier beyond your wildest imagination, my beautiful wife. You can buy a golden tiara for my little princess and a dress of silk embroidered with pearls fit for a queen such as yourself.'

They were indeed amongst the wealthiest people in Papua. The gold was exactly where Jack knew it would be and they had wrested a small fortune from the rugged mountain creeks. In a short time the rush was on but they had been amongst the first to pick up the prize, along with a handful of other canny men of Papua.

Two days later Jack returned to the plantation. He came with a bag full of Christmas presents for them all. It did not matter that Christmas was two months gone. They celebrated his return with a coconut frond for a Christmas tree. But for Lukas the best present of all was that his father had returned to his life.

Part Two

STONE
AND STEEL

1932–1934

TWENTY-FOUR

T he view of Port Moresby from the deck of the Burns Philp steamer had changed very little in the years since Jack and Paul had arrived to grub out their small fortune from the Morobe gold fields almost a decade ago. Jack stood at the bow of the ship as it ploughed through the calm blue-green waters and gazed at the hills nestling the little frontier town. It was still a place of government administrators, planters, gold prospectors, missionaries and a few misfits.

For a brief moment he thought about the time when the tall, quietly spoken Englishman George Spencer had stood on the deck of this same ship and observed the town as they had steamed in. They were both younger men then, with separate dreams of finding something meaningful in their lives. George hadn't had the chance to find his. For Jack, his dream had to wait until he and Paul Mann had forged into the jungles of the Morobe province to sluice the rivers and creeks rich in alluvial gold. And how they had found it! Anything that could be used to carry the precious nuggets and specks was utilised: empty bully beef tins, socks and as much as they could jam into their pockets. Up the rivers, Sharkeye Park and his compatriots had been doing the same, unaware of the interlopers downriver.

The gold that had come out with Jack and Paul was smuggled back to the canny businessman Sen, who was able to convert it to cash on the black market in Singapore without the Australian authorities knowing of its existence. All told, they cleared around fifty thousand English pounds each from the transactions, with Sen taking a small percentage.

'Father?'

Jack turned to see his son striding across the deck towards him. How grown up he looked at seventeen, Jack thought with a swelling of pride. Tall like his mother's family but with the breadth in his shoulders of his own people. He had hazel eyes and a thick crop of unruly brown hair. Although not handsome in the fashion of the Hollywood movie stars, whose faces now flickered in the film palaces of the major cities, he still had the appearance of a young man who would break a woman's heart. But Lukas had inherited his father's restlessness, and boarding at St Ignatius college in Sydney under the disciplined care of the Jesuit priests had not tempered his wild ways. The occasional infractions had been conveniently forgiven by his performance on the rugby field. Lukas played with a brilliance that was spoken of as having the potential for him to one day play against England and the bone crushing All Blacks of New Zealand. Jack did not understand rugby. He had grown up playing Australian Rules, a game that had much in common with the rugged Irish brand of football. But he had come to appreciate the skill required in evading a team of young men intent on grinding their opponent with the oval ball into the turf.

'Do you think Uncle Paul and Aunt Karin will be waiting for us when we dock?' Lukas asked.

'I think so,' Jack replied as he lit his battered old pipe and puffed until a thick plume of smoke was blown away on a gentle sea breeze. It would be a hot and still day ashore. There was not a sign of a cloud in the pale blue skies. 'Your Uncle Paul replied to my telegram when we were at Elston.'

En route to Port Moresby, the two had travelled south from Brisbane for a break in their journey, to a small coastal village called Elston. They had stayed at the Surfers Paradise hotel and spent three days swimming in the rolling breakers of the Pacific Ocean, fishing off Main Beach and sitting around at night playing cards with the other guests. Apart from soaking up the South Seas atmosphere of the hotel, Jack had also caught the train south to take a look at property in the towns of Coolangatta and Tweed Heads that straddled the borders of Queensland and New South Wales. He liked the area so much that he had purchased a block of land on a steep hill in Tweed Heads, planning to one day build a house there as a retreat from Sydney.

Lukas took a position at the bow beside his father and leant on the rail. The town rose and fell gently on the horizon. The land was a dusty brown tapestry dotted with native villages along the shore-line at Koki located to the east, while the tower of the Burns Philp office dominated the little township on the edge of the Papuan frontier. He was looking forward to his break from school to revisit the land that held so many fond memories for him. It had been four years since he'd been here, as his holidays had usually been spent in Sydney with his father at home in Mosman.

A few months earlier the opening of the Sydney Harbour Bridge, the largest single span bridge in the world, had dramatically changed things for citizens on Sydney's North Shore. No longer did the har-bour ferry provide most of the transport between the two shores. Jack, however, still preferred to travel by ferry to his Macquarie Street office, from where he managed his small financial empire. His enter-prises took in real estate acquisition and development as well as his far off gold mining oper-ations in New Guinea.

His charitable work for the families of the men who had not returned from the war was noted by many in power. And in the Sydney community Jack Kelly was quickly establishing a reputation as a bene-factor among those families suffering the terrible displacement brought by the Great Depression. He had befriended the colourful premier of New South Wales, Jack Lang, known to his friends and enemies alike as the 'Big Fella' because of his imposing size. It was with the premier's influence that places at the prestigious Catholic college of St Ignatius had been obtained for both Lukas and Karl. The two 'wild boys from the north' had stuck together and, like Lukas, Karl had also established a reputation as a top rugby player. The two were inseparable and considered more as brothers than just mere friends. Their partnership was strengthened in the close hierarchy of boarding schools, with more than one fist fight against the older boys to establish their credentials. Most of the time they won the bloody, slogging matches, but even if they lost, they won the respect of the junior and senior students for their courage. Neither boy was known to back down against even the toughest of the seniors. And both were prepared to take risks that endeared them to the school as a whole, if not always to the staff.

Karl had grown to be a powerfully built young man. Both boys were bigger than their fathers and Karl also had Paul's suave looks. He no longer spoke with a trace of a German accent and under the tutelage of the priests both boys had acquired the educated tones of polished radio announcers. More important to both fathers was that Lukas and Karl had sat their Leaving Certificates to complete their secondary education. Hopefully, the boys' results would be good enough to gain them places in a university.

Jack turned to his son whose unruly hair was being whipped by the wind. 'Have you any plans for the future when we return from Papua?' he asked gruffly.

The years had slipped by in his busy life and he was about to lose his only child to the world. Lukas would take his place soon as a man. Jack suddenly felt the cold chills of loneliness. Since the day Erika had left him all those years before he had directed all his love and attention to his son.

'I was rather hoping that you would use a bit of that money of yours to send me to Germany with Karl,' Lukas replied with a cheeky grin. 'You know that his old man is paying for him to visit the old country next year.'

'And pigs will fly,' Jack growled good-naturedly. 'For a start you are too young and secondly you have to earn your own way there.'

'I could work for you as one of your managers,' Lukas continued in the same playful tone. 'Start at the top and work my way down.'

'That would be about the sum of it,' Jack chuckled. 'But I can give you something while we are here, working around the mines.'

Lukas raised his eyebrows. He knew that the work was dirty and dangerous, and the mine in an isolated location on the island's frontier. For his father to suggest such an enterprise spoke of his confidence in his abilities. 'Well, actually Father,' he replied in a more serious tone, 'I was thinking of going into law. Mr Sullivan has said that there was always a place in his firm as an articled clerk if my exam results were good – which they will be.'

'When did all this come about?' his father asked. 'Just after you met young Sarah Sullivan by any chance?'

Lukas sucked in his breath. 'How did you know?'

'Kind of hard not to see how gawky you were whenever we were over at the Sullivans',' his father said as he puffed on his pipe and stared at the shoreline growing ever closer.

Tom Sullivan had become Jack's chief solicitor and a good friend since their first meeting to discuss the will George Spencer had drafted. Tom's sixteen-year-old daughter was a dark eyed beauty with grace and poise. She had aspirations to study medicine when she completed her secondary schooling at a prestigious convent. A bit on herself, Jack had thought when he had met Sarah Sullivan, but still a daughter any father would be proud of. He had also noticed that his son was well and truly under her thumb whenever they were together. But choosing a career in law meant that his son could also pursue his other great love in life, rugby union. It was a sport strong in the circles of law students. 'I will talk to Sullivan when we return,' Jack sighed. 'In the meantime you and Karl stay out of trouble while we are in Moresby.'

Lukas feigned affront at the suggestion that he and his mate would get into any trouble. 'Father, did you not pay all those expensive fees to see your one and only son become a gentleman, unlike my wonderful father who made his fortune grubbing gold without the proper permits?'

Jack glanced at his son and frowned. Was he being mocked – or was his son's statement delivered with great affection? It was hard to say with the younger generation. They had lived in a world of relative peace and not had to experience the harshest realities of life. Lukas placed his arm around his father's shoulders and Jack knew that his statement had been delivered with love.

'It will be good to be home,' he said, and Jack agreed with him.

Paul, Karin, Karl and little Angelika were all waiting on the wharf at Moresby to greet them. Karin hugged Lukas and cried with joy. Her other son was home. Paul shook Jack's hand with a strong grip. 'You are getting soft, old friend,' he said with a friendly jab at Jack's stomach under his immaculate white suit. He himself wore his work clothes of old pants and a many times repaired shirt. Jack noticed how strong and healthy his old friend looked and felt just a little embarrassed at how unfit he had become working from his office. 'I have heard that you own Sydney now and plan to buy the rest of Australia within the next year or two,' Paul continued as he turned to Lukas. 'How are you young man?' he asked in German.

'Very well, Uncle Paul,' Lukas replied in kind.

'Ja, it is good you have not forgotten your German. It is the language of your grandmother's people.'

Angelika stood beside her mother and frowned. She only vaguely remembered the young man from a long time ago when she was a very little girl. But she did recall that he was not a mean teaser like her brother Karl. Lukas grinned at her and the frown turned to a shy smile.

'Don't you remember me?' he asked as he bent to look directly into her eyes. She appeared a little confused. A lot had happened in her nine years on earth.

'You are Lukas,' she replied slowly. 'You and Karl got into trouble for taking Mummy's dumplings.'

Lukas laughed at the incident that he had almost forgotten from six years earlier. Finally Karl stepped forward and both boys engaged in a feigned exchange of blows.

'How are you?' Karl asked. 'It's been pretty quiet around Moresby without you,' he continued. 'You should have come back early with me instead of hanging around Sydney with Sarah Sullivan.'

Lukas was about to protest that she was not his girl but instead countered, 'And which of the *meris* have you been chasing, you big Kraut lughead?'

This brought on another bout of sparring. Their respective fathers shook their heads and walked down the wharf with Karin and Angelika beside them.

'It is good to have you home,' Karin said as she touched Jack's arm with a gesture of affection. 'Paul and I have missed you.'

'Good to be back,' Jack responded. 'The place has a lot of memories for me. Both good and bad.'

A noticeable difference for Jack was that Paul drove them from the town to the plantation along a recently constructed track in his new Ford truck. The ride was bumpy but the track and truck turned the trip from what was a good day's drive to just a few hours. The boys and Angelika sat in the back tray with the luggage. They called out in greeting to the villagers they passed, making their way to the market in Moresby. Conversation was limited as the noisy grinding of the transmission drowned out words as Paul constantly changed up and down the gears to negotiate the bends and bumps. All were glad when they reached the plantation after the long hot drive. Red dust had turned Jack's immaculate white suit a pale pink. He stepped from the cabin and helped Karin down.

Dademo stood barefooted, wearing a starched lap lap around his waist on the verandah of the house. 'Mr Jack, good thing you come back,' he greeted with a flash of betel nut stained teeth. 'I get the boys to bring your luggage.'

Jack thanked him and turned to Paul. 'Sen decided that I could have him as my boss boy,' Paul answered the unspoken question. 'Paid the old Chinese pirate a good price to indenture him to me, but he has been worth it. Knows the business better than I do,' he added.

Inside the house Jack noticed the improvements Paul's share of the money had brought to the Mann family. A gramophone record player took pride of place beside a new piano and one wall was filled with book shelves and a good supply of novels, both in German and English. Jack had offered Paul a part-nership in his mining enterprise but he had declined on the grounds that his life was tied to the land and not under it, as in mining operations. And so he had used his share to bolster his plantation, pay for Karl's education, buy some luxuries for Karin and Angelika as well as put aside an amount in the bank for a rainy day. He had also purchased a little land in Townsville as a family retreat from Papua. In all he was happy with his simple life. A 'rainy day' had recently come in the form of the terrible financial depression, but his savings had kept the family afloat as the bottom fell out of the price of primary produce.

'We have extended the house,' Paul said as Jack followed him. 'You now have a room to yourself. Lukas can sleep in Karl's room. Get yourself settled in. Maybe go for a swim before dinner.'

Jack thanked his old friend and took his advice. He found the tropical water refreshing and stroked out strongly in the placid sea for a quarter of a mile, before making his way back to the beach where he collapsed on the gritty sand to soak up the last of the setting sun. Lying back, he could hear the gentle hiss of water rushing over the hot sand and the distant laughter of the plantation workers. A great feeling of peace descended on him as he stared up at the sky that was taking on a dark mauve colour.

When the sun was a great red orb on the horizon he rose and walked back to the house, now lit with electric light since Paul had also invested in a generator system.

The boys had hearty appetites and so too did Jack. He had missed Karin's wonderful cooking. Fresh fruit followed and then the two men retired to the verandah whilst Karin relaxed with the magazines Jack had brought from Australia. The two boys disappeared into Karl's room where they swapped stories of what they'd been doing since the last time they had been together in Sydney some weeks earlier.

Jack tapped his pipe on the edge of the verandah and refilled it with a plug of tobacco. Paul puffed on a cigar that he had been saving for Jack's return. For a short while both men simply gazed out into the soft tropical night.

'How are you coping?' Jack finally asked, breaking the meditative silence.

'Times have been better but we are coping well enough,' Paul answered, watching the smoke curl lazily on the still air. 'I have thought about diversifying into tobacco growing. I met a young man in Moresby a while ago who was giving it a go over on the Laloki River just north of here. He'd done a bit of prospecting up in Morobe on the fields. Last I heard of him he was back to work a claim he won in a ballot.'

'Anyone I know?' Jack asked.

'I don't think so. He is from Tasmania. A young fellow by the name of Errol Flynn. He came here in '27 or thereabouts. Worked for a while chartering a schooner and I heard he had a run-in with the Dutch up around the Sepik when he went poaching bird of paradise for their feathers. He even starred in a film made in Tahiti by the Americans. *In the Wake of the Bounty*, I think it was called. He's a character with a reputation around Moresby for having an eye for the ladies.'

'Better keep the lads away from him then,' Jack grinned. 'They seem to be at that age where trouble can start with just the whiff of perfume.'

'Ahh . . . but to be young again,' Paul sighed. 'Those days up in Finschhafen and Munich before the war.'

'Know what you mean,' Jack responded quietly.

Where had the time gone, he thought sadly. He was approaching middle age and was to all appearances a successful man. But there was a loneliness in his life. He was losing Lukas to manhood and had no one else to share his life and dreams with. Oh, there had been short interludes with some very desirable women in Sydney, but in the end they had left him either because they found him too absorbed in his work or sensed that he was not with them in spirit. It was as if he lived with the ghost of a love that haunted not only him but anyone else who tried to get close to him. And the nights were still hell. The nightmares came less often but he would still feel his hands shake when something reminded him of the terrible war. Would it ever really go away? Almost fifteen years had passed and yet it was all still fresh in his memories.

At length Paul decided that he must retire. The copra ship was due and he would have an early start with Dademo to ensure all went smoothly in the loading. He bid Jack goodnight and left him alone on the verandah. He was not alone for long. Karin came out on the verandah and sat in the cane chair vacated by her husband.

'Would you like coffee before retiring?' she asked.

Jack tapped his pipe. 'I have never told you what a wonderful woman you are,' he said quietly. 'You have raised Lukas to be the man I always wanted him to be.'

Karin sat very still listening to the words that poured from his heart. 'You have a wonderful son,' she said with a choke in her voice. 'I would have been proud to be his mother.'

'You were,' Jack replied. 'More than you will ever really know. All those years that Lukas grew up on the plantation he knew your love. A love as good as any mother could have given a boy in need of one.'

Karin leant across and touched Jack on the arm. 'I will always treasure every letter that he has sent to me from school, every hug he ever gave me, every time he and Karl were naughty little boys. And now we are about to let our sons go out into the world and learn to be men. Oh Jack, I only wish that you had found the love that Paul and I have.'

'I nearly did.'

'Erika,' Karin scowled. 'She was never meant for you. She was not the person that you imagined, Jack. Although, as the sister of my husband I shouldn't say it, Erika was a disturbed young woman. I think that even Paul knew that an evil existed in her that no one spoke of in his family.'

Jack took in a deep breath and sighed. Karin could sense his pain and wanted to reach out and take it from the man she had come to love, a wild and reckless foil for her Paul. 'You still miss her.'

'Not a day goes past when something doesn't remind me of her,' Jack said. 'Not a woman I meet who I don't search for Erika in. It's been almost ten years and I still find myself wondering where she is and what she is doing.'

Karin fell into a silence as she struggled with what she knew. 'I can answer some of your questions,' she finally said, and Jack looked at her sharply. 'Erika is married and living in Munich. She has a daughter just a little older than Angelika.'

'Has she contacted you?' he asked in a calm voice, attempting to hide what he felt.

And for a moment Karin regretted telling the Australian what she knew when she saw the pain etched in his face. 'Paul received a letter some weeks ago,' Karin replied. 'It is from an old friend of his in Munich.'

'Who is she married to?' he asked.

'A young man she met just before we left for Australia.'

'Definitely not this Adolf Hitler who the papers are all talking about,' Jack said with a short, bitter laugh. 'She mentioned that she knew him when we were in Sydney and I suspected at the time that she was a bit taken by the bastard.'

Karin's face clouded. She vaguely remembered Hitler when he had visited their home in Munich during the winter of 1919. She had instinctively not liked him but had never imagined in her wildest thoughts that the man would rise to such prominence. 'Her husband's name is Gerhardt Stahl. He is very high in this Nazi party that I have read about.'

'Never heard her mention his name,' Jack muttered. 'Must be a mate of Herr Hitler. But how did Paul get the letter all the way out here?'

'Through the office of Sir Hubert,' Karin answered. 'It was simply addressed to him via the Australian authorities here. Paul feels that his sister is in some kind of trouble.'

'Like what?' Jack frowned.

'As much as Erika appeared to dislike Paul, it is not in her nature to remain so silent for so long. He has what you would call a gut feeling that his sister needs him.'

Jack could see the pained expression in Karin's face. It was as if she were struggling with unpalatable facts. 'Do you think that she is in serious trouble?'

Karin turned to stare directly into his eyes. 'I think so – and I think it has something to do with the events unfolding in Germany. I fear that the things that we left behind in the old country will drag Paul into a dangerous situation, one beyond our control.'

'I would never let anything happen to Paul,' Jack consoled gently. 'He's my mate and mates stick together, no matter what.'

Tears glistened in Karin's eyes. 'He has not told you yet but he plans to return to Germany to see Erika. I cannot tell him that I fear his life is in danger if he returns to Munich. I am his wife and I love him. And I know that even if you were to try and convince him not to go he would still return because he loves his sister and feels responsible for her.'

Jack stared up at the Southern Cross. He had missed its brilliance when he had served in France. If he died he wanted to do so under its crystalline comfort and nowhere else. 'If he goes to Germany,' he said quietly, 'then I will go with him.'

'Thank you, Jack,' Karin said and wiped away the tears that spilled down her face. 'I know that my husband will always be safe in your company. You were born to be brothers.'

Jack broke into one of his broad smiles. 'Tried to kill each other once,' he reminded her. 'But what else would you expect between brothers? Kind of a family thing, I suppose.'

Karin laughed at his twisted reflection on the bond between the two men. Jack was truly the other half of the man she loved. And in loving her husband she also loved the Australian in ways she knew she could never tell him.

That night Jack lay back on his bed and stared at the ceiling. Outside a full moon glowed over the plantation. His thoughts were in turmoil: Erika and Germany, Lukas and losing him. Sleep came in the early hours and his terrible dreams returned, but this time Lukas stood by him in the trenches. He could hear his son screaming one word: 'Why?' Jack woke with a start and felt the sweat clinging to him. He sat up and propped himself against the bedhead. This had been the first time that he had dreamed of his son. Maybe he was unconsciously accepting that his son was now a man and it was natural that he should share a part of his nightmare. At least there would be no more wars such as that. The Great War had proved how futile it was to use science and technology to wage a war no one really won. Admittedly armed conflicts were even now being waged across the globe but they were restricted by national boundaries. Surely no truly civilised nation could ever entertain the idea of starting another global conflict? Jack rose from his bed and found his pipe. He lit it and sat on a chair in his bedroom to watch the sun rise over the coconut trees.

The following day an incident occurred that was to mar Lukas's stay at the plantation. Isokihi the Japanese boat builder arrived in one of his launches to drop off supplies for the Manns. Dademo sighted the wooden craft puttering into the bay and went down to assist with the unloading. Karl and Lukas were lounging around on the verandah, taking in the early morning sun.

'Isokihi comes in his boat,' Dademo called to them as he passed the two boys. 'You want to come down to the beach?' The boys glanced at each other and rose from their comfortable cane chairs. 'What the heck,' Lukas shrugged and they followed the boss boy.

Isokihi had already launched a dinghy with a large pile of goods balanced in the stern. When the two boys reached the beach they noticed a tall, well-built young Japanese man with the solid, little Japanese skipper.

'Fuji,' Karl said quietly. 'That bastard is working with his old man now.'

Lukas squinted against the shimmering seas and focused on the figures. He too recognised the man in the boat staring back at them from his days at the primary school in Port Moresby. Fuji had been a fellow student who neither boy liked, always surly and refusing to make friends with the others. It was as if he carried an air of superiority towards those not of Japanese blood. And now here he was years later with the same sneering expression on his face.

Dademo waded into the sea and helped guide the boat to the beach. Fuji jumped from the boat and turned to stare at the two boys a few yards away.

'G'day, Fuji,' Karl said by way of greeting, but the young man simply stared at him with an expression of contempt. 'See you haven't changed,' Karl added with the slightest trace of a grin.

Without a word Fuji turned his back to take the anchor rope and secure the dinghy to the beach. His father clambered over the side to stand beside his son. Dademo carried on, unloading the boxes and parcels of supplies.

'Better give a hand,' Karl said and the boys walked towards the boat. As Dademo worked one of the parcels fell from his hands and splashed into the surf. Isokihi swung on Dademo with amazing speed for a man of his age and the Papuan went down in the water. It happened so fast neither Karl nor Lukas had time to intervene. When Dademo struggled to his feet gasping for air, blood ran down his face. Isokihi had his fists raised again to strike, but this time Karl leapt forward. With all his strength he swung at the side of the Japanese boat builder's head. The blow was true and the solidly built man staggered, his ear ringing from the impact. Fuji spun to deliver a kick to Karl but missed as the heavily built young man moved with unexpected speed for one so big. He retaliated by moving in on the young

Japanese man before he could regain his balance and hammering his face and body with hard, stinging blows, driving Fuji into the sand.

'Your old man doesn't have the right to hit Dademo,' Karl gasped. 'What happened was an accident, you bloody Jap bastard,' he continued as he stood over the young man. 'No one has a right to maltreat Dademo.'

Fuji glared up at Karl. The battering had felt like a series of steam pistons pounding his body. Already one of his eyes was swelling to the point of almost closing. Fuji turned to seek out his father who stood in the surf, holding his damaged ear. The impact had burst a drum and the pain was acute. Lukas stood between Fuji and his father, obviously covering Karl's back against a possible retaliation.

'I think you should drop off the supplies and leave immediately,' Lukas said calmly. 'What has happened here will remain on the beach. There are no hard feelings but you have to understand that, as Karl said, no one goes around hitting Dademo. He's a bit like family here.'

Fuji rose warily from the sand to assist his father. Dademo had also recovered and quickly unloaded the last couple of boxes from the boat, the blood still streaming down his face from his smashed nose. Fuji went to his father who greeted him with a silent glare of pure contempt. Fuji recoiled from the unspoken rejection for not saving face in front of the barbarians. With his head lowered he commenced to push the dinghy out to sea. 'I will come back one day and kill you, Mann,' he spat as he clambered aboard followed by his father. 'I will never forget this.'

Both boys gave the Japanese boat builder and his son distance as they departed. Watching as Fuji guided the boat back to the small coastal trader anchored in the bay. 'What do you think will happen now?' Lukas asked.

'Nothing,' Karl replied as he rubbed one badly swollen knuckle. 'Fuji is all talk and I doubt that his old man is going to complain about being done by a kid like me.'

Lukas smiled at Karl's description of himself. He was hardly a kid and he had the build of a young bull.

Dademo glanced up the beach. 'I think Master Paul is coming down,' he said quietly. 'Thank you, Mr Karl,' he added quickly, but Karl's shrug dismissed any more need for thanks. It was just something that was expected when defending the honour of friends and family.

Paul frowned when he came close enough to see Dademo's injuries. He could sense from the quiet behaviour of the two boys that something had occurred. 'What happened?' he asked calmly. 'How is it that Dademo has blood on his face?'

'Dademo fell over and hit his face on the side of Isokihi's boat when he was unloading stores,' Karl replied, wanting to nurse his hand as it throbbed with pain. 'Nothing much else.'

Paul glanced at his boss boy to confirm Karl's story. 'That is all, Master Paul,' Dademo said but could not look Paul straight in the eye.

Paul turned his attention to the coastal trader in the bay. Whatever had happened on the beach had been settled here, he thought. If Karl was concealing the truth it was because he was old enough to make such decisions. There was nothing to be gained by pursuing the matter – at least not for the moment. 'Well, let's fetch some of the boys from the shed to come down and get these supplies up to the house,' he finally said.

Only that evening did Paul learn all that had happened on the beach when Dademo came to him with the truth in case Isokihi laid a formal complaint with the authorities in Port Moresby. Paul listened quietly and thanked Dademo for his honesty before dismissing the boss boy for the evening. It had taken a lot for him to come forward but Dademo's concern was for Karl who had intervened on his behalf. Paul would let the matter drop. What was done, was done.

TWENTY-FIVE

Jack's leave with Lukas in Papua went all too quickly. Although Lukas was missing the beautiful Miss Sarah Sullivan he found plenty to entertain himself with in the company of Karl. They spent their days riding into the hills, swimming in the warm waters of the Gulf of Papua and hunting pigeons. And there was also the distraction of the Moresby social set to tempt two young men from any thoughts of fidelity to their respective girlfriends in Sydney. Visits were made to neighbouring plantations where the young ladies wore formal dresses and danced to popular songs on the gramophone, passing the night amidst the frangipanis and hibiscus that filled every room with their heady fragrance.

In the men's tennis doubles the young men teamed up and proved unbeatable. The singles competition was a cliffhanger as the boys were pitted against each other and both fought hard to win. In the end Karl was declared winner with a final ace in front of an audience of admiring young ladies, the daughters of planters and government administrators. Lukas accepted his defeat with grace. Although he had lost at tennis he won in love and danced that night away in the arms of the prettiest of the spectators.

Meanwhile Jack had taken time out from the tennis tournament to visit his old friend Kwong Yu Sen at his house on the outskirts of Moresby. He was greeted warmly and surprised to see that the Chinese businessman was now the proud father of twin girls and a son. Although he had lost contact with his old friend, he thought that such important events would have been transmitted to him. The girls were aged six and Sen's baby son gurgled contentedly from his cradle.

'When they are older I will return to China,' Sen said with a sigh as Jack poked at the chubby little pride of his father.

'You have everything here,' Jack replied in his surprise. 'Why would you want to leave?'

'Everything but the respect of you Europeans,' he answered with an edge of bitterness. 'All the money I have cannot buy respect here.' Jack accepted what his friend said. Sen was wealthier than most Europeans in the Moresby district and they resented him for that as much as for his race. 'And this country has taken Iris from our lives. My wife has never been the same since we received the news that she was O'Leary's captive all those years ago. She insists that her sister still calls to her from over the oceans for her help. It has caused a rift between us,' he added sadly.

At the mention of Iris's name Jack ceased playfully prodding Sen's son. He too often had recriminations on the matter. 'You should have told me what you were planning when you sent Paul on that expedition up the Fly River. I should have been with him. Didn't you have any faith in me to find her?'

'I could not tell you, Jack. I feared that you might be killed,' Sen replied, hanging his head. 'Mr Mann was not as close to me as you and I rightly judged him to be a very competent man capable of carrying out the mission.'

Jack had to concede to his point about Paul's competence and was touched by Sen's concern for his welfare. So much for the inscrutable reputation of the Chinese, he thought. 'You haven't heard if O'Leary ever returned to Papua?'

'Not a word,' Sen replied. 'I suppose he knew that if he came back Sir Hubert would have hauled him in for questioning about his recruiting methods. The missionaries received reports on the way he was going about it and have a lot of pull with Sir Hubert in such matters as the welfare of the natives.'

'Maybe one day we will get lucky,' Jack mused. 'And when that day comes O'Leary will answer for what he has done in the past.'

'Maybe,' Sen echoed, but without much conviction. He would still have to live with an emotionally disturbed wife who continued to speak to her half sister as if she were in the room. For all that he knew Iris could be dead. 'Come, we will have tea,' he said to distract them from their gloomy thoughts.

Jack followed him to the verandah where they were served tea by a *haus meri*. They sat and drank for a while in contemplative silence. Finally Sen opened the conversation with what was on his mind.

'I have had word from Sydney that Quentin Arrowsmith is out to get you, Jack.'

Jack merely smiled. 'We have crossed swords on more than one or two occasions,' he replied. 'It seems that Arrowsmith is a man who keeps a grudge.'

'You must have caused him a great loss of face to be so intent on destroying you.'

'I think I once made him feel real fear. I don't know that he had ever before considered his fate at the hands of a man with nothing to lose.'

'Then be careful,' Sen said quietly. 'He is a man who will stop at nothing to destroy those who he dislikes. And it seems that you are his number one enemy.'

'Probably because I have cost him a lot of money in our latest transactions. I went under him in a big purchase that it seems he had spent quite a bit of money on. He thought he had it in the bag until I used a couple of my own contacts in government to cut him out.'

Sen nodded. He feared for his friend. Quentin Arrowsmith was also a man with contacts. He even suspected that Arrowsmith was capable of considering murder as a business option.

Jack bid his old friend farewell and was driven back to Moresby. There he stopped off at the hotel and shouted a round of drinks for all in the bar. He was cheered and repaid in shouts by the old timers who remembered the brash young man who had crossed the border into German territory before the Great War. And now he was a successful miner and generous to friends to boot.

Jack was very drunk and happy when he was dropped off at Paul's plantation the next day by a couple of prospectors in their truck. He sported a black eye and a split lip but could not remember whether he had fallen over or had been knocked down in a fight at the hotel. Karin shook her head and called Dademo to fetch a couple of the boys to take Jack down to the surf for an involuntary swim.

Many hours later he sat on the verandah with Paul who grinned at his friend's sorry state. 'Would you like a schnapps?' he asked mischievously.

Jack leaned forward in his cane chair with a groan. 'Bugger off,' he replied ungraciously.

'You were just unlucky that Karin saw you first when you got home,' Paul said as he lit the most pungent cigar in his possession. The thick and acrid smoke drifted towards Jack.

'No sympathy for a dying war veteran,' he said. 'Just gave me a ten minute dressing down about setting a good example to the boys after Dademo had been given instructions to drown me. Hell, I would rather face a bunch of enraged Kukus with poisoned arrows than your wife again.'

Paul burst into a gale of laughter that hurt Jack's head. 'My friend,' he finally said, 'why do you think you have never seen me drunk?'

'What's this I hear about you planning to go to Germany?' Jack countered. He was not sharing his friend's good humour in his present state and got the response he wanted. Paul grew serious and stared at the coconut trees, waving in the last onshore breeze for the day.

'Karin told you,' he said. 'I have to go. I know that Erika is in some sort of trouble and she is still my sister, despite everything.'

'You know that I will be going with you,' Jack said quietly. 'And Karin thinks that is a bloody good idea.'

'What reason would you have for going with me?' Paul asked with the raise of an eyebrow.

'Always wanted to see the country of my mother's people,' Jack answered. 'And I promised that I would take Lukas to see it too.' He was lying but knew that his son would be ecstatic at the opportunity to visit Europe. 'Might even drop over to Ireland to visit my old man's relatives while we are at it.'

'That the only reason you would go with me? Or is it that you would want to see Erika again?'

'Karin said she is married with a kid,' Jack casually countered. 'Nothing more than that.'

'It would be good to see the old country one more time,' Paul reflected. 'Good for the boys too. I have read that there are great changes in Germany today. It seems that Germany has once again taken its rightful place with the other western nations of the world.'

'What about this Hitler bloke in Berlin and his Nazi party?' Jack asked.

Paul frowned. He had followed the former German corporal's rise to power with some interest. 'He and his ideas concern me a bit,' Paul said. 'I met him once when I was just back from the war. He came to my place and we sat one evening discussing the future of Germany. I got the impression that the man was a very disturbed individual. But possibly I was wrong. He seems to have the people on his side. I read that his party took a lot of seats in the Reichstag in the July elections this year. He must be giving the people what they want.'

'From what I have read about him, the bloke worries me a lot,' Jack said.

Paul looked away. He did not totally agree with his friend. How could he know what it had been like for ordinary German citizens at the end of the war? The world did not care about the starvation and humiliation at the hands of the arrogant French, British and Americans. Despite his personal misgivings about Hitler, Paul conceded that the man had returned pride to the German people. And if he did eventually gain power but failed to deliver on his promised slogan of 'Germany Awake!' then the people would vote him out. After all, no German would ever allow a man to rule as a despot again, not after the bitter experiences of the Great War at the Kaiser's hands.

Jack realised that he had touched a raw nerve. It was a subject he and Paul had never broached before.

He dropped it and sat quietly in his alcohol-induced pain. Christmas was just around the corner and he looked forward to being with the only people who he could call family – the Manns.

Christmas 1932 came and went. In true festive tropical style a suckling pig was roasted on a spit and the tender white meat served up with baked yams, pumpkin and a spinach-like vegetable known as abika. It was all washed down with beer and schnapps to the blaring of the gramophone. Karin danced the foxtrot and tango with both Jack and Paul until she was exhausted. The boys disappeared after the gargantuan lunch to visit a neighbouring plantation that had as its main attraction two very pretty sisters about their own age.

Ten days later Jack and Lukas stood on the deck of a coastal steamer to travel to the port town of Salamaua in the Huon Gulf. There Jack had arranged a meeting with one of his trusted employees who was returning from Christmas leave in the north Queensland town of Cairns. Jack was reflective on the journey, knowing this was a meeting of such importance that his – and his son's – futures may be decided by its outcome.

Lukas was impressed by the town of Salamaua on its sandy finger of land flanked by Bayern and Samoa bays. Stately palms and colourful but prickly bougainvillea added colour to the tropical jungles backing the township. Since the establishment of the gold fields inland, the little coastal hamlet had provided both comforts and necessities for the miners returning from the inland fields. It even sported a hotel: a long tin roofed building with a comfortable verandah to take in the cooling tropical breezes of an afternoon. Salamaua was an oasis of European tropical culture providing facilities not common in this new land.

After docking, Jack booked into the hotel and got settled. Sitting on the verandah that evening with Lukas, he could not help thinking how much gold had changed this part of the world. Years earlier he and George had made their landing nearby on the Morobe coast to trek inland in search of George's fabled Orangwoks and Jack's real gold. Then the coast had been without any established signs of western civilisation, just the occasional isolated police outpost or missionary station. But amongst many things, gold had brought a meat freezer and cold beer to the coast – welcome fixtures at the Salamaua Hotel.

Lukas badgered his father for a beer.

'You have hardly started shaving,' his father growled gently. 'I don't think that gives you the right to start drinking.'

'How old were you when you started?' his son shot back with a cheeky grin.

Jack shifted uncomfortably. His father had been a heavy drinker and Jack had well and truly acquired a taste for beer by fifteen. 'Go and order a beer for me and you can have a shandy.'

Lukas leapt to his feet and went off to the bar. Returning with his lemonade and an added dash of beer for flavouring, he was not about to admit that he and Karl had indulged in a bout of drinking at a friend's house during a break from school just before the final examinations. The result had been two very sick boys who had looked with some newfound respect upon the sermons concerning the evils of alcohol.

'Ah, Dougal has arrived,' Jack said as a stocky red haired man in his forties walked down the verandah towards them. 'How was your Christmas leave, Mr MacTavish?' he asked as he held his hand out to the Scottish engineer.

'Canna get a good drop of malt whisky in Cairns,' he snorted in his thick Glaswegian burr as he gripped Jack's hand. 'But it's good to see you, mon. And who would this wee lad be then?' he said with a grin.

Lukas stood straight and took the Scot's hand as it was offered. 'Lukas Kelly, sir,' he replied and felt the crushing strength of the Scot's powerful clasp. 'I am Jack's son.'

'Thought as much,' MacTavish said when he let go Lukas's hand. 'Has the same blarney as his old man.'

'Got you something when I was down in Sydney,' Jack said, producing a bottle of expensive aged whisky from beside his chair. 'Knew you might want a drink for what you have to tell me.'

Dougal accepted the gift with a grateful sigh. It was his boss's way to know what his employees' needs were. 'Is it all right to talk in front of the lad?' he asked as he lovingly turned the bottle over in his hands to read the label.

'Said he wanted to work his way down in my companies,' Jack replied with a wry grin. 'Sounds like from your reports last year that's what we might all be doing if it is as bad as you say.'

'It's that bad,' Dougal said as he took a seat and Lukas was sent to fetch an appropriate glass so the Scot could partake of his country's traditional drink. 'To put it in a nutshell, the gold has run out on the company's leases and we are dredging mud and nothing else.'

Jack felt as though the weight of that same mud was bearing down on him. When the New Guinea administration had finally granted mining leases Jack was quick to stake his claims along the stretch of river he and Paul had originally panned illegally. It was a rich stretch, promising many years of production with the right equipment. He had not expected the gold to run out so early and had invested a lot of money back in 1925 in purchasing the expensive heavy dredging plant required to exploit the type of gold field he had leased. The machinery had to be flown in bit by bit by aircraft, technology which had opened up island transport like nothing else before.

At first the assembled dredge had produced gold in payable amounts, but each year since MacTavish's reports had been more pessimistic, until the one just before Christmas that said he needed to brief his boss personally. Dougal understood loyalty and knew that if the news got out that the gold lease was drowning investors' money in the mud of the jungle, Jack might go under. He would not trust his report to paper but instead wanted to speak to Jack in person before any decisions were made.

Lukas returned with a glass and Dougal immediately poured himself a generous tot then leaned over to pour one into Jack's empty beer glass. 'To the good ship Hindenburg and all who sail with her,' he said as he raised his glass.

Jack responded accordingly. They had named the dredge the Hindenburg to honour the men who had died fighting on that part of the frontline in 1918. 'To better times.'

'What are you going to do, Jack?' the Scot asked bluntly when he had refilled his empty glass.

'You don't think there is any chance of coming good?'

'None. It's been played out.'

Lukas was not aware of the course of the meeting but he could see the stricken expression on his father's face. He had never seen such barely concealed anguish before and wanted to ask what was wrong. But he knew it was not his place to do so for the moment.

'We continue mining for at least another couple of months,' Jack said quietly. 'By then I hope to be able to transfer funds to pay out the operations up here. I have something going down in Sydney and all going well it will get us out of trouble. Just so long as the investors don't get a whiff of anything wrong I will be able to keep up the supposed returns for their money. Then at the right moment, close down and sell off the equipment.'

'Do you think you are in a position to pull it off?' Dougal asked.

'Like I said, so long as the word does not get out that the mining operations have gone belly up.'

'I'm your boss man up here and I swear on the Cross of St Andrew, and the finest breweries in Scotland, that not a word will come from me.'

'Thanks, Dougal,' Jack said, as he slapped his mining manager on the shoulder. 'I can promise that you will be well looked after when we get clear of this mess.'

Dougal nodded and the three sat on the verandah as the heavy rain clouds overhead opened, drowning out conversation.

The next day Jack and Lukas checked out of the hotel and sailed south for Australia. Jack well knew the fortune that had its basis in the gold of New Guinea now relied on his skills as a businessman rather than those of a prospector. Just so long as there was no leak. Otherwise how easily it could all come tumbling down around him.

TWENTY-SIX

Gerhardt Stahl closed the door against the bitter winds of a Munich winter and slumped in the big leather chair that smelt strongly of tobacco. He badly wanted a drink but was too tired to go to the cabinet to pour one. The January elections of 1933 had secured yet more seats in the Reichstag for Adolf. And yet his friend of their earlier days would not even see him anymore!

The rebuffs he had received made Gerhardt seethe with anger. He and Adolf had shared the hardest times over the last decade before his so-called former comrade in the struggle had risen to his present powerful position in German politics. Had he not been a friend and devoted follower of Adolf's from the day they had met, just after the war? On the streets back in '23, had they not faced the bullets together, and had fled for their lives? And had he not visited Adolf in his cell after his arrest, and listened to his tedious dictation of his book *Mein Kampf* to that odd and colourless man Rudolf Hess? But over the years he had been quietly shuffled off to low ranked jobs in the party. His current job in the SA's Intelligence Unit amounted to little more than procuring homosexual partners from the Gisela high school for Adolf's good friend Ernst Rohm. Gerhardt did not like Rohm one bit but he feared him greatly too. He was a coarse, brutal, battle scarred man whose desire for young boys was well known to all. He even openly boasted of his wickedness and yet Adolf not only tolerated him but also took him into his inner circle.

It was as if Adolf wanted Gerhardt out of his life altogether. He shuddered, although a coal fire warmed the room. Was it possible that he may end up with a bullet in the head, that he knew too much about the party's leader should Adolf acquire total control of Germany? The former German soldier who had fought for his country in the Great War was now in his mid thirties and at the prime of his life. For it to end now was not an option he wanted to entertain.

He had another good reason to fear the future too. Although Ilsa was not his daughter by blood, he had grown to love her as if she were. She was twelve now, and so different in temperament to her mother, who had made it plain from the day she was born that she wanted nothing to do with the girl. And it had been so since. The young girl grew up in the care of nannies whilst her mother – his wife – had lived a wild life of parties and picnics with high ranking party members.

Gerhardt rued the day that he had married Erika but she had appeared so vulnerable and desperate when she stepped off the boat in Hamburg. She told him about the baby and he had kindly sworn that it would never come between them. They had married in a quiet civil service in Munich and Ilsa was born three months later. At first he had to force himself to accept the child. All he knew about her heritage on her paternal side was that she was the daughter of some former Australian soldier who had raped Erika when she had been in Sydney. When she had recovered from the birth his wife was constantly out at night and had a steady supply of expensive presents from men she met as a result of the services she provided. It was well beyond his humble means to purchase the jewellery and new dresses she required to present herself at the lavish parties where, on behalf of the party, she solicited support from the industrialists to finance Nazi coffers. Gerhardt now doubted that his wife's story about being raped was true. She was a born liar. But her striking beauty and innate sensuality had carried her further up the party ladder than his own loyalty to his friend Adolf.

Gerhardt had long desisted from becoming enraged and engaging in shouting matches over his wife's obvious infidelities. He tolerated her now merely for the fact that she had contacts and if he continued as her husband she would ensure that he was at least employed by the party. This she had promised him during a truce a few years earlier. It had in fact been Erika who suggested that the job in the Intelligence Unit of the SA would be a good place to be when Adolf finally came to power. Now it seemed to be proving the opposite and sometimes Gerhardt wondered if his wife was actually setting him up for his own execution, horrifying as the thought was. It was time to consider a plan to ensure his very survival.

'Papa, are you home?' he heard Ilsa call from the bedroom upstairs in their modest detached house in the city.

'Yes, my little love,' he replied in a tired voice. 'I am downstairs.'

He heard the patter of feet on the stairs and then Ilsa entered the room. She always took his breath away with her beauty, a physical replica of her mother but with a gentle soul and loving nature.

'You look tired, Papa,' she said and hugged him where he sat in his big comfortable chair. 'I don't suppose Mama will be home tonight,' she sighed.

Gerhardt felt her gentle love momentarily wash away his brooding thoughts. 'Is she ever?' he answered with a weak smile.

Ilsa sighed again in sympathy for her father who had always been there for her whenever he could spare time from his important duties. 'I don't suppose so.'

But Erika did return later that evening. Gerhardt had revived himself with a half bottle of schnapps, providing him with enough belligerence to confront her as she stood by the fire in a body clinging black sequined dress, her hand glittering with diamonds and rubies. In one hand she held a slender cigarette holder, in the other a flute of champagne.

'There has been talk that your loyalty is in question,' she said coldly as she sipped the bubbling wine.

Gerhardt could see that she was in one of her moods where he would be belittled. 'Who is questioning my loyalty?' he asked in a tired voice. 'One of your many lovers during some pillow talk?'

'Don't be so coarse,' Erika flared, as he knew she would. 'I was only telling you for your own good.'

'Why don't you just divorce me?' Gerhardt said, quickly regretting his question. Despite all her faults he still desired her above all other women.

'It suits us both that I am your wife,' she retorted. 'Until otherwise I will remain so. I will decide when that will be,' she added in an icy, cruel tone.

Gerhardt did not know what happened next except that a red rage came over him. Too many years of his wife's contempt and infidelity had accumulated. She was on the floor and he was standing over her as she held her hand to her face, red and swollen from the savage backhanded slap. The champagne glass had shattered into a thousand crystal shards against the fireplace. 'You want a lover? You can have me,' he snarled as he bent to haul her to her feet, ripping the front of her dress to reveal her small but perfectly formed breasts.

The sudden explosion of Gerhardt's temper had come as a complete surprise to Erika. For years he had been the butt of her scorn as a man she recognised as having no real future in the new Germany of Adolf. He had often expressed the opinion that what they had set out to achieve was going terribly wrong. There was no place in her life for an idealist. She was hungry for the trappings of power and had realised that it was through her links with the rising star of Adolf and his party that she would receive them. But Gerhardt was becoming a burden to her ambitions and she had often thought about how he could be removed.

Gerhardt hurled Erika's dress across the room and gripped her by the throat. She was gasping from lack of air and shock. He was not surprised to see that she only wore long silk stockings and a suspender belt under the dress. He could see the fear in her eyes and felt a savage elation. Where was the scorn now? He thrust his hand between her legs and felt a wetness that was not hers alone.

'Papa! Papa! What are you doing?'

He heard his daughter's cry and felt the anger replaced by shame. As he released his grip Erika slumped to the floor. 'You are an animal and I will see you dead if you ever touch me again,' she gasped.

'No more of an animal than most of the men you sleep with,' Gerhardt said, rubbing his forehead to ease the throbbing. 'I know the corruption, deceit and cruelty that has got your precious Adolf this far. I know that if we gain power Germany will not know peace in the next generation, that my daughter will become just like you and all the rest of the thugs who call themselves patriots.'

'She's not even your daughter,' Erika said as she stood unsteadily. 'She's the daughter of a man twelve thousand miles from here.'

Ilsa had remained in the doorway and her mother's statement now hit her. With a stricken expression she turned to her father. 'What does Mama mean?'

'Your mother is trying to hurt you,' he pleaded. 'She doesn't mean what she has said.'

'He is not your real father,' Erika sneered at her daughter. 'Your real father is not even a German.'

'A Jew!' Ilsa uttered, wide-eyed in her horror.

'No, an Australian,' Erika quickly countered. Even she could not let her daughter think such an unspeakable thing. 'He was an enemy soldier who raped me.'

Ilsa turned on her heel and rushed upstairs to her room in tears. Gerhardt turned to his wife and for a moment she felt the terrible fear return when she saw the murderous expression in his eyes.

'For that you will burn in hell.'

His tone frightened Erika. She shrunk away from him as he took a step forward. She had badly underestimated his tolerance for her ongoing jibes.

'Touch me and I can promise you that you will never see Ilsa again,' she spat defiantly. 'I have enough power to ensure that.'

Gerhardt hesitated. His reasoning was returning and he stepped back. Time was running out for him and this violent confrontation had brought matters to a head. All he could hope for was that his ruse to lure her brother to Germany had worked. It was Ilsa's only chance for a normal life away from what his beloved Germany was rapidly spiralling into.

• • •

A week passed and Erika remained bitter and aloof towards Gerhardt. And although Gerhardt had explained to his daughter that her mother had lied about her parentage, Ilsa had changed. No longer was she the warm young woman he had grown to love. Now she was withdrawn, but still cordial in all other matters. Furthermore, time was indeed running out in more ways than one, as Gerhardt was to learn when he was taken aside by a fellow worker in the Intelligence department.

'Be careful, my friend,' the colleague had warned in a meeting in the corridors. 'There is some talk of your lack of commitment to the cause.' The warning had been furtive and whispered. 'It seems that your wife has been expressing her thoughts to people in high places about your opinions.'

The Intelligence man was also a former soldier who had fought on the Eastern Front against the Russians and then later against the Poles on the frontier after the war. He was a good man at heart but also a pragmatist. However, the goodness of his soul had won out against his fear of being seen to be on the side of a man whose loyalty to Adolf was in question.

The warning left Gerhardt with a sick feeling in the pit of his stomach. How long did he have? And how did they plan to do away with him? His intimate knowledge of the probable future leader of Germany meant that he knew too much. He knew that Hitler, who was so vehemently anti-communist, had once been an active worker for the communist cause after the war. That it was only through threats from the army that he had been planted as a spy in the very party that he manipulated and now controlled. And there was more that could embarrass the future chancellor.

Yes, he knew far too much. He doubted that the police, so cleverly infiltrated by the Nazi party, would be meticulous in investigating his 'accidental death'. All he had was Ilsa and the hope that somewhere in a land hardly known to the world a letter had arrived causing enough intrigue to make a former soldier return to his country. If so, he could get Ilsa out and then it did not matter what they did to him.

TWENTY-SEVEN

When Jack and Lukas arrived in Sydney Jack opted to stay in one of the city's best hotels for the night rather than make their way home to Mosman. Exhausted from the trip, Lukas remained in the room whilst Jack went downstairs to have a nightcap. He knew sleep would not come easily now he was back. The unstable state of his finances weighed heavily on him and his future seemed to be tottering. He ordered a beer and sat in the lounge. It was late, and other than a party of late night revellers dressed in evening wear, he was alone to brood on his circumstances.

'Jack, old boy!' one of the group exclaimed. 'Come and join us for a drink.'

Jack recognised the man as an officer he had served with during the war. He now sold property in the suburbs blossoming around the city, and they had business dealings from time to time. Jack gave a thought to politely declining the invitation but then the offer was renewed by a vaguely familiar voice.

'Mr Kelly, you must join us.'

'Mrs Arrowsmith,' Jack said with a nod of his head.

Caroline rose from a lounge seat where she was surrounded by the three men of her party and walked towards Jack. Time had not changed her sensual looks and her evening gown accentuated her body. Jack's first reaction was to despise the woman who had taken Erika from him, but he felt an unexpected desire for her at the same time. Her eyes met his and a slight smile curled the corners of her moist red lips. She approached and held out her hand and Jack found himself accepting her invitation. He rose and took her hand as she led him back to her companions.

'Ah, I see it took Caroline to get the hard working, hard drinking Jack Kelly to join us,' the former army acquaintance said.

'G'day, Dave,' Jack responded before being introduced to his companions.

Dave was slightly younger than Jack and had slick, suave looks. He appeared to emulate a Hollywood movie star with his pencil-thin moustache. He had only joined the battalion in the last months of the war and Jack had not particularly liked him then. But fate had thrown them together in peacetime through property dealings.

Jack could feel Caroline standing very close to him and could smell her expensive perfume. When he moved her hand brushed his.

'You know, Jack was one of the wildest men in the old battalion,' Dave said to his friends, both bankers from Melbourne. 'I think he personally killed more Fritzes with the bayonet than any other officer we had.' Jack flinched at the reference to his wartime experiences and wished that the drunken former officer had not spotted him. 'He should have got the Victoria Cross for one action where he singlehandedly took out five Germans and a machine gun post. We thought he had copped it when we found him amongst the dead Fritzes he was covered in so much blood. Oh, I am sorry, Caroline,' Dave added. 'Such talk is not for a lady's ears.'

'Don't worry about me,' she said sweetly. 'I think it is good to be reminded of what you brave gentlemen did for your country.'

'Well, Jack and I were the real heroes,' Dave said drunkenly, throwing his arm around Jack's shoulder in a comradely fashion.

As Jack eased himself out from under the arm, one of the bankers suggested that it was time to leave. He was obviously unimpressed by the drunken boasting of this man who they were forced to endure for business reasons. They were polite, however, when they shook hands with Jack. Dave stood alone for a moment until Caroline guided him to the entrance and hailed a taxi.

Jack was pleased to have got away so easily and decided it was time to join his son. 'Mr Kelly, don't be so quick to leave,' he heard Caroline say as she returned to the lounge. 'I was hoping that we could have a drink together before retiring.' Jack's confused expression invited an explanation. 'I am staying here for a couple of days while Quentin is out of town. I presume that you are also a guest?'

'I am, but I thought you were with Dave and his friends.'

'Oh, we were just out at a club for the evening. Come to think of it, I don't think that I have ever seen you on the club scene.'

'Not much time for socialising,' Jack replied gruffly. He could smell her heady perfume again and wanted to distance himself.

'Why don't you order us a drink and sit down and tell me about your wartime experiences,' she said in a sweet tone, taking a seat on a lounge chair. 'I have heard much about you over the last few years. You seem to be a rather remarkable man to have achieved all that you have.'

Jack motioned to a waiter who took their order. 'I have to say, Mrs Arrowsmith,' he said, turning back to face Caroline, 'that I am surprised you would have the presumption to speak to me considering what occurred in the past.'

'Please call me Caroline,' she replied. 'And I hope that I may call you Jack.'

Jack nodded to her request, falling silent as the drinks arrived. He paid the waiter and as the man returned to the bar Jack noticed that he and Caroline were the only two patrons remaining in the lounge. He raised his glass of beer in a mock salute. 'To strange meetings in strange times.'

Caroline frowned. 'I am not sure what you mean,' she said as she took a sip of her cocktail. 'But it was interesting.'

'The meaning is of no relevance to you. Just something in my life.'

'But you have had a very interesting life from what I have heard,' Caroline continued, with a frank look that bespoke her genuine interest. 'In my husband's circle of friends men such as yourself are rare.'

'What circle would that be?' Jack asked quietly.

'Oh, men who followed their duty to support the war from the home front.'

'You mean blokes who made fortunes staying home and staying out of uniform. Like your husband.'

Caroline slightly tilted her head to acknowledge his observation. 'My husband is a very remarkable man whose destiny is to carry on the traditions of a great and noble dynasty. To have volunteered might have put that destiny in danger. Quentin is a man above all that.'

'A lot of destinies were cut short by the war but that did not stop those men from fighting.'

'I did not intend to speak about my husband,' Caroline said. 'I would like to hear about your experiences.'

'If you want me to go on like Dave,' Jack said with a tight smile, 'then I am afraid you will be disappointed. I put the war behind me the day I got out of uniform. And that seems a lifetime ago now.'

'In this day and age it is rare to meet a man other cultures might call a true warrior.' Caroline leaned forward. 'It is important that I know something about you for reasons only I know. I trust you will not ask me what they are.'

Jack frowned. Her behaviour was odd but he could sense from her demeanour that she was not toying with him. There was an intensity in her eyes that was almost a plea and he found himself feeling less resentful towards her. Perhaps it was his weariness after the sea voyage, but somehow her presence was revitalising. 'If that is what you want then I will respect your wishes,' he said.

'Please tell me about the killing,' she asked.

Jack stared at her for a brief moment. 'Not much to tell,' he replied after a long swig on his beer. 'Just something we did to stay alive.'

'What did it feel like to see a man die at the end of your bayonet?'

Jack felt suddenly uncomfortable. He did not want to remember. 'Both sickening and good at the same time. I am no philosopher to analyse how it felt.'

'You have answered a question that is very important to me,' Caroline said.

For a moment Jack thought he saw relief in the expressive eyes that had never left his. 'I don't want to talk anymore about the war,' he said quietly, staring past Caroline's shoulder.

'I am sorry if I was so rude to you when we first met,' Caroline said. 'I was different then, and much too young and selfish.'

'Past is past,' Jack replied. 'We all have something to regret at one time or another.'

'What do you regret, Jack?' Caroline asked softly.

'Maybe you can answer that question,' he replied. 'You took her from me.'

'Erika was a lovely young thing but I do not think you know who she really was.'

'You do?' he countered.

'I think so,' Caroline sighed. 'She was just like me, with a need to have all she desired.' Jack laughed softly and shook his head. 'You may have a reputation with men as a born leader, courageous and strong, but you know very little about the way a woman thinks, Jack Kelly. We have had to be much smarter than men to survive in this world.'

'I am sorry if I insulted you,' he apologised. 'But you may be right. I am afraid my whole world has been with men.'

Caroline's smile was warm and gentle and Jack found that he was actually getting to like the wife of a sworn enemy. It was a strange feeling, even unnatural.

'Would you do me the honour of escorting me to my room?' Caroline suddenly asked.

'If that is what you would like,' he replied. 'It's about time I hit the hay.'

Jack followed Caroline to the lift. When they arrived at her door Caroline found her key and stepped inside.

'Well, goodnight,' Jack said.

He was about to turn and walk away when Caroline suddenly threw her arms around him, drawing him into a deep passionate kiss. Stunned and resistant at first, the sweetness of her mouth and the probing of her tongue soon melted any reluctance that he may have had. Under all circumstances he had avoided liaisons with married women. It was a matter of honour to him, reinforced by bitter memories of men he knew at the front whose wives had been unfaithful to them. But this was somehow different.

Caroline drew him into the room and he did not resist. In the dark she pulled him down onto the bed. He could feel her breasts pressing against his naked chest. Nothing mattered for the moment other than being inside her. Caroline moaned in her pleasure and he felt her nails rake his back. She was like a beautiful sleek cat, their lovemaking little more than her being serviced.

Jack did not know how right he was in this impression; he was indeed providing a service for her, for Caroline needed to provide an heir to the Arrowsmith dynasty, a child to inherit the companies. She had once come close to providing an heir after learning of Quentin's inability to father children. She had found a suitable young man but that pregnancy had ended in a miscarriage. For years afterwards she had shied away from repeating the tragic experience. But her child bearing time was now running out. She would try one more time and this night the handsome property man had been her unwitting target, hence her decision to book into the hotel. The unexpected appearance of Jack Kelly had changed everything. She had long been fascinated by the man who had made Erika pregnant, particularly with his meteoric rise to fame in Sydney. Instinctively she knew that Jack Kelly could father a child with all the traits desired in an heir to her husband's companies.

Caroline sensed Jack's warmth flood her womb and sighed with pleasure. Oh, how strangely this night had turned out, she thought and lay back with a contented smile that Jack could not see. 'Just stay where you are,' she whispered, as he was about to release his weight from her. 'I like feeling you inside me.'

Moments later Caroline gently pushed him off and they lay side by side until the exhaustion of his voyage sent Jack into a deep sleep. When he woke in the morning she was gone, with nothing left in the room to suggest that she had even been there. Jack wondered if he had been dreaming. He dressed and made his way back to the room he had intended to share with his son. Lukas was up and dressed.

'Where were you last night?' he asked with a grin.

'None of your bloody business,' his father growled. 'But it wasn't here.'

Back at his office that day Jack knew from the stricken expression on his faithful, hard working secretary's face that the worst of his fears had occurred. Doris was a widow from the war and a woman who Jack trusted to run all his enterprises. For the five years she had been in his employ he had been able to spend less time in the office and more time improving his serve on the tennis court.

'Mr Kelly,' she said as she rose from behind her desk and stumbled towards him. 'I have been trying to contact you for the last two days. I have terrible news . . .' She burst into tears and Jack handed a clean handkerchief to her. She blew her nose and shook her head in her sorrow.

'It's all fallen through,' he said flatly as she blew her nose. 'Kind of felt something was wrong.'

'The banks have telephoned every day. I told them that you were away in Papua. I didn't know what to do,' she wailed.

'That's okay, Doris,' Jack said kindly as she clung to him. 'I was half expecting the worst.'

'Is it true that the Hindenburg mine is not paying?' she asked as she composed herself. 'They said that they had news the mine was not producing.'

'I'm afraid the news is correct but I don't know how in hell anyone back here could have known,' Jack growled. 'I doubt that Dougal would have broken his word to me.'

'What are you going to do? What are we going to do?' Doris asked.

She had two children in their teens and had hoped her job might provide them with an education and a better life. Jobs were hard to come by during the terrible economic recession that had descended on the industrial nations of the world. Homeless families roamed the country in search of work or handouts and she imagined how that she would be joining their ranks. Jack's nightmare was also hers.

'I will talk to the banks and see if they will extend a bit of credit until the contract goes through with the subdevelopment.'

Doris gasped and flung her hands to her face. 'You haven't heard!'

'Heard what, Doris? I just walked in.'

'The Arrowsmith companies made a last minute bid and went over you to get the contract.'

'God almighty!' Jack felt his stomach churn. He had put all his reserve of cash into the deal going through. A quick sale with another developer was meant to finance his cash short companies, including the mine, until they could ease out of the crisis. But the large sum of cash he had invested was on a high interest loan from the banks. Jack knew it was now lost to the dubious political fund of the local council that controlled the bid. It had been to all intents and purposes a bribe, one not honoured by unscrupulous men. Jack knew that he was in real trouble. 'No, I didn't know,' he said, sitting down to recover his balance. It had been as easy as that to lose a fortune he had risked his life to obtain. And now it was all gone. Every penny plus a few more if the banks wanted their pecuniary interest.

Jack excused himself after giving Doris the rest of the day off on full pay. If nothing else he would ensure that she received every penny due to her and a bonus. With the office unstaffed it would make it harder for the creditors to find him and he needed just one afternoon to get rolling drunk before a ferry took him across the harbour to his home. After that he did not know what he would do.

The creditors moved in quickly. Within three weeks Jack was penniless except for his comfortable home and some personal property that was not listed under his company's assets. Lukas had taken the news well, but telling him bad news was one of the hardest things he had ever had to do.

'What will we do, Dad?' his son had asked as he sat with his father in their cosy living room with a view of the Mosman inlet. Jack noticed that his normally polished son had dropped the title of 'Father' for 'Dad' – something he had not called Jack since he was a boy in Papua, growing up on the plantation with the Manns.

'I've let you down,' Jack said softly as he hung his head. 'I always planned that you would have the best money could buy.'

'You did, Dad,' Lukas said as he put his arm around his father's shoulders. 'You got me a posh education and a chance at life. But better than that, you were always there for me – even when you were away on business trips.'

Jack glanced up at Lukas and saw a slow, sad smile appearing. He was just as disappointed that they had lost it all but he had the spirit to accept adversity with optimism. Maybe he could teach me something, Jack thought when he looked into his son's face. 'Well,' he said. 'I will not be able to pay your university fees.'

'I was only joking when I said that I wanted to be a solicitor,' Lukas lied. 'I really want to be like you.'

'Like hell you will be,' Jack growled affectionately as he tousled his son's hair. 'The last thing I want you to experience is the life I have had.'

Lukas rose from the chair and walked to their kitchen. He returned with two bottles of beer and Jack cast him a questioning look.

'I thought we should have a real drink together,' Lukas said as he opened the bottles. 'Before they come and take everything.'

Jack was about to protest at his son drinking but realised he himself had done the same thing with his father so many years earlier before he left home to travel to Papua in search of gold. When he thought about it he had been younger than his son was now. He took the glass of beer from Lukas. 'What are your plans for the future?' he asked as Lukas sat down.

'Get drunk with my old man,' he said. 'Then go and see Miss Sarah Sullivan and tell her that the man in her life can no longer hope to keep her in the manner that she aspires to. Then I will decide after that.'

Jack raised his glass and his son followed suit. 'To better days,' Jack said.

When Lukas next saw Sarah Sullivan he told her the news. Within a couple of days she found excuses not to see him anymore. Lukas had learned his first cruel lesson about some women. He sat on the ferry crossing the harbour after his final visit. She had refused to receive him. Mr Sullivan had been sympathetic to the point of annoyance at his daughter's haughty dismissal of the likeable young man, and even reaffirmed that there would always be a place for him in the firm. Lukas had been polite in his thanks but said he had other plans. What they were he was not quite sure, but he was not about to show his anxiety to a man he admired so and who in different circumstances might have been his father-in-law.

Being broke was easier to accept than being shunned by Sarah, Lukas thought. How could she do that to him when he was still the same person, with or without money? A graceful schooner slid past the ferry, heading for the twin sandstone cliffs that guarded the magnificent harbour. It caught Lukas's eye and he watched its sails unfurl to blossom in the breeze. On the schooner's deck, a suntanned young man was at the helm. Lukas almost smiled as a thought dawned. One thing his father's money had bought him was a circle of well-heeled mates who owned yachts. He had proved a very competent sailor himself on the weekends he had sailed the blue waters of Sydney Harbour. To hell with Sarah, he thought fiercely. He knew how he would prove to her and her snobby friends that he was not a failure.

Overhead a small biplane seemed to float in the air. Lukas looked up and sighed. Flying was what he really wanted to do but that was now merely a dream. To realise his dream he would have to leave his father on the ground to fend for himself. The desire to fly had been with him since he had watched a film about the Great War fighter pilots. He had left the cinema determined to one day learn to fly and soar with the eagles. Had matters turned out differently then he would have asked his father to support his dream. But that was not to be so. The opportunity was gone. But perhaps with a boat he and his father could face the future.

TWENTY-EIGHT

TWENTY-EIGHT

There was a definite change in the reaction of Gerhardt's colleagues whenever he was in their vicinity. In the corridors they would fall silent as he approached them, and friends called less often to the house. He recognised the signals. It was time to act.

Gerhardt knew that his superior officer Colonel Spier held the list of persons deemed by the party to be a possible threat to any government that may be formed when they gained a majority. Hitler's ultimate aim was to rule alone without the coalition of other parties. To date the list contained the names of known communist party members, intellectuals who may query the ideals of the Nazis, church leaders, unionists, government employees, teachers and others.

No one in Gerhardt's department had access to the list except his boss, and the list was kept in a safe to which only Spier knew the combination. But

Spier had a weakness. Gerhardt knew his boss had no mind for numbers. An intelligent man but poor with arithmetic. Such a weakness may lead a man to record the safe combination and carry it with him, Gerhardt concluded. If he was right, Gerhardt knew his boss was smarter than to leave any such record lying around his office in a bureau or desk drawer. To test his theory, one day when he brought him a file that he knew would be secured in the safe, Gerhardt found an excuse to engage his boss in idle talk as Spier went about opening the safe. Gerhardt noticed that his boss perused a scrap of paper that he had slipped from his trouser pocket.

The trouble now was getting hold of the combination numbers on the paper – to do so would require the man to take his clothes off. Gerhardt stood in the corridor between offices, puzzling over how to achieve the next stage of his plan. 'Erika!' he uttered under his breath as the answer came to him. But obtaining her assistance in the matter would be almost impossible. She had no interest in his future – alive or dead. But if any woman could get a man to take off his clothes, she would be the one.

He had to wait two days before she returned to the house. Her absences were growing longer and he felt less like a husband, more like a landlord. He was awake and weary when she returned one morning in the early hours before sunrise. He heard the sound of a car engine and laughter. A door slammed and another opened. Sleep had not come to him during the night. Every hour that passed was an hour wasted. He desperately needed her help, but wondered how he could convince her; he knew pleading was useless.

The bedroom door opened and he could see Erika silhouetted in the hallway light.

'I am awake,' he said.

At least Erika had a touch of consideration when she returned from her nights out. She would leave the light off as she undressed and slipped into the bed. 'I did not mean to wake you,' she said, and for just a moment he thought he detected a slight softening of her usual hard contempt for him. 'I would like to talk to you.'

Gerhardt was surprised by her tone. He pulled himself up in the bed as she turned on the light. God, how beautiful she was, he thought bitterly. How had it all gone so wrong?

'I want a divorce,' she stated bluntly. 'I am sure that is what you also want. I will not contest you for Ilsa.'

Gerhardt blinked. Something had changed in her life. Obviously she had met the man she wanted to be with. 'Who is he?' he asked 'Anyone I know?'

'That is not important,' she retorted. 'I would hope that you agree we do not have a marriage.'

'And you have no maternal feelings,' Gerhardt countered. 'I will take Ilsa with me. She is my daughter.'

Erika's laughter at his statement of parentage caused him to see the red haze of anger. 'You!' she said. 'You are not her father, as we both well know. I

338

only married you because I needed someone to take care of her and provide me with a means of support. I am surprised you were not aware of that from the very start. I thought it was understood that I did not love you.'

Her words still hurt although he had rapidly become aware of her real reasons for marrying him only weeks after the ceremony.

'I will give you a divorce,' Gerhardt said.

Erika was surprised. She had expected him to resist the idea. Maybe she had underestimated him.

'Well, then,' she said, 'I think I will have a coffee before I retire.'

Gerhardt watched her leave the room. He now dismissed the idea of gaining her voluntary assistance but there were other ways. His latest plot would bring with it a sweet revenge, although he knew that he must be patient. He only wondered at who had prompted her request for a divorce. It did not matter. What mattered now was that not only must he get Ilsa out of the country but also himself. The writing was on the wall.

When Gerhardt reached the offices of the party's intelligence service that morning he put the first stage of his plan into place. Gerhardt went to a colleague's office and greeted him as he did every day. He picked up the pile of papers in the out tray. 'I will go through these this morning, Herr Neumann,' he said.

'Yes, sir.'

Neumann's job was to report any information that might be telephoned to his section from disgruntled citizens or party branches. There were now many members in the party from all walks of life and the line was often busy. Most of the intelligence was useless, but occasionally something came through that was noted by Gerhardt as potentially useful. Now it was time to add another name to the list of persons considered a threat to Adolf Hitler. Papers in hand, he entered the office of Colonel Spier and placed the night file on his desk. To the wad of papers he added an extra sheet he had composed. There was no turning back now.

Gerhardt sat in his office, fiddling with a pencil, his attention continually drawn to the clock on the wall. The waiting was terrible and he found himself jumping every time someone laughed or a door slammed in the winter wind. He was incapable of starting on the paperwork piled on his desk. Four hours passed and finally he heard his name called by Colonel Spier from the office next door. Gerhardt tried to compose himself as best he could but felt the unsteady beat of his heart thump in his chest as he rose.

Spier sat at his desk stuffing sausage and bread into his mouth as he thumbed through the sheets of paper Gerhardt recognised as those he had delivered that morning.

'I presume you have read the reports from Herr Neumann?' he asked as some crumbs of bread spilled onto the papers.

'Yes, sir,' Gerhardt answered in a strained voice.

'Then you have read this report on your wife?'

'Yes, sir.'

Spier finally looked up at his subordinate. 'I find it strange that you would not do the normal human thing and lose the report, Herr Stahl.'

Gerhardt had anticipated the question. 'I was torn by my duty to the party and my love for my wife,' he replied, feigning agony. 'But I believe that my duty must come first as it did when I was a soldier in the Kaiser's army. I have made no comment on the adverse words from what appears to be a reliable source. I thought it was better that you do that, sir.'

Spier frowned and glanced back at the report, apparently scribbled in Neumann's hand. He was aware of his subordinate's less than happy marriage to Erika – and of her reputation as a lover of many high ranking party officials. He himself envied those men as he had met Erika Stahl from time to time and she was a very desirable woman. The report seemed out of character, but there had been a woman in the last war by the name of Mata Hari who also fooled a lot of high-ranking generals on both sides. Gerhardt watched the expression on his boss's face and knew that he must carry out his plan now or never. He made his move.

'Sir, considering the delicate circumstances, do you think that you should discreetly question my wife about the accusations of her disloyalty to the party?'

'That would be hard,' Spier mused. 'She has very powerful friends who might take exception to that.'

'May I suggest that you arrange to drop in at my house and question her in what would appear to be a friendly manner . . . you know . . . just a visit to one of your subordinates after work,' Gerhardt suggested, hoping that Spier would detect the desperate pleading of a husband torn in his tone.

'I could do that,' Spier pondered. 'One way or the other I must take this report seriously. If any of the facts here are true then I should pass on the information to those above me.'

'I agree, sir,' Gerhardt concurred as his heartbeat steadied. He knew he was playing a deadly game but the stakes were high. So far things were playing out as he hoped. 'When do you think that will be?'

Spier frowned. He had a meeting with the young Heinrich Himmler who was in charge of Adolf's bodyguard units, now given the title of SS. Spier did not like the prim little man and resented the fact that someone with no experience of war should have such a senior position, when he, who had served in the army for his country, did not. But it was the leader's policy to encourage the youth of Germany to join in his ideals. 'I will not be able to visit your house for at least two days,' he finally said. 'Then I will determine whether the report is malicious or has some grounds for further investigation. Until then I trust you will not mention this matter to your wife.'

'No, sir,' Gerhardt answered, pretending a terrible sadness in his reply. 'I know my duty.'

'You are dismissed, Herr Stahl,' Spier said as he reached for the remainder of the sausage. 'Go about your work.'

Gerhardt turned and walked smartly from the office. In the corridor he felt his hands tremble as he contemplated what he had done. He had virtually condemned his wife to death and now all he had to do was force Erika to realise that she needed to cooperate with him if she wanted to survive. It was called blackmail but that was the game of intelligence: to know your enemies' weaknesses and exploit them. He had lived long enough with Erika to know her fears. If he failed he knew without doubt that he would become a name on a police report as a man who had fallen foul of persons unknown. His body may or may not be found.

Spier however was no fool. He had watched his subordinate depart and scowled. Stahl's name was also on a secret list of those considered as undesirable persons. Spier knew that he must soon do something to remove him from the sensitive portfolio he held. Although Spier privately believed that Gerhardt Stahl was loyal to the ideals of the party, the word had come down that the man could prove an embarrassment to Adolf, should he gain political power at the elections. Spier knew that it was not wise to know a lot about certain people in the party – particularly the leader. If he wanted to keep his job then he must act soon and transfer Stahl until other arrangements could be made to silence him. He bit off and chewed the last portion of sausage. Swallowing it, he scribbled notes for his meeting with Herr Himmler.

• • •

Erika's disbelief was written on her face. Gerhardt stood with his hands behind his back, warming them on the coal fire. He waited for her to digest the news of her reported treachery with a solemn face of a husband whose loyalty to his undeserving wife still existed.

'None of it is true,' she exploded. 'I have not given any information to foreign journalists about the party.'

'Erika, I believe you,' Gerhardt said easily, as that was at least true. 'But the report came from a reliable source. Maybe one of the foreigners you did not sleep with is out for revenge against you.'

'And Herr Spier is going to interrogate me here?' she continued. 'I will set him straight about this pack of lies!'

'I think that you will have to do more than that,' Gerhardt offered calmly. 'I think that you will have to appease him the best way you know.'

She swung on him with an expression of incredulity. 'I choose with whom I sleep,' she hissed. 'Not some middle aged, low ranking party official.'

'Put it this way,' Gerhardt said mildly. 'It's either that or I am sure Herr Spier is going to be a very bitter man with a grudge against the party's whore. And as low ranking as he may be, I can assure you that those above him listen to what he says. And don't think that I don't know how you have entertained other men in my bed while I have been at work,' he added. 'But this time I will turn a blind eye.'

'Why is it that you are suddenly so concerned for my welfare?' she asked. 'It is you behind this,' she uttered. 'You made the report against me!'

'It does not matter where the report came from,' Gerhardt answered with a sigh. 'What matters is that others believe it has some substance and requires investigation.'

'I will tell Herr Spier that you are behind this.'

'It will do you no good,' Gerhardt countered calmly. 'In these times the slightest whiff of a scandal within the party can destroy one's reputation forever.'

Erika slumped into a chair and stared at the glow of the burning fire. She knew her husband was right. To be innocent of any report that went through his office was almost irrelevant. She had begun to rue the day she had obtained him a position in Intelligence. Now it was up to her to convince her husband's boss to lose the report. Yes, she had very much underestimated Gerhardt.

'I will do it,' she whispered.

I will do it, she thought. But you will wish I had not. You will pay for this in ways that you could not in your worst nightmares imagine. Already she had formulated a plan to turn events her way – and against the man she had grown to despise for no other reason than she had been forced to rely on him in their early years together. Oh, how it should have been Adolf and not this under achieving man full of nothing but ideals.

TWENTY-NINE

Jack Kelly shook his head as he stood on the jetty. The briny smell of the harbour water was strong, as was the lingering odour of long dead fish. But he was also laughing.

Lukas knew that was a good sign. 'I know she is the answer to all our problems, Dad,' he said eagerly as Jack walked backwards to better appraise the lines of the old lugger, rocking at her moorings just off shore. She looked old but sturdy. A bit like himself, he thought. 'And the owner wants to sell her as soon as possible.'

'What would we do with a lugger?' Jack asked, slipping his pipe from his pocket. 'Sail around the world so that my creditors can't find me?'

'I was thinking that we could sail her up to Papua and use her in charters – or transport goods back to Queensland. Anything that comes up.'

'More money in her if we sailed her to America and ran grog for the Yank bootleggers from Canada,' Jack said with a twinkle in his eye.

In his eagerness to convince his father that the lugger was their way to make a fortune, Lukas fell for the suggestion. 'We could do that but . . .' Then he realised that his father was joking and broke into a broad smile. 'Or we could sail to Papua.'

'I will think about it,' Jack said, as he stuffed his pipe with a plug of tobacco.

'We don't have much time,' Lukas warned with the impatience of youth. 'They are taking everything we have.'

'But not the house,' Jack reminded firmly. 'We still have that as an asset – along with the land in Queensland.'

'I'm sorry, Dad,' Lukas apologised, realising he was pushing his father into making a decision. He knew his father would think it out.

And Jack did think about it as they drove home. He had pondered on his future for some time. What could he do as he approached his middle years? Crocodile shooting? Maybe even working for Paul Mann back on the plantation near Moresby. But he had learned that searching for gold was a job for much younger men with unshakeable dreams and no family commitments. Not that he had to worry about Lukas. He was old enough to look after his own future. If nothing else, he had provided him with an education that could take him anywhere. Not to mention his natural charm and good manners – acquired more from the Jesuit priests than Jack's own example.

The trouble with this plan was that boats were as foreign to Jack as going to the moon. Lukas seemed to have a reasonable knowledge of sailing but only in skiffs on the harbour with his rich friends. This was a totally new venture in his life. But hadn't going north to Papua and New Guinea been a totally new venture for Jack when he was around his son's age? He glanced at Lukas who sat staring at the passing gum trees as they drove along the bumpy dirt track from the jetty.

'We will buy her,' he said with the pipe clenched in his teeth.

'Really, Dad?' Lukas exploded. 'We will really buy her and sail to Papua to make our fortunes?'

Jack felt warmed by the sudden change in his son's demeanour. 'Probably cost us a fortune,' he grunted but with a smile. 'And we will have to give her a name I suppose. I believe that is part of the tradition of the sea.'

'I thought about calling her the *Sarah*,' Lukas said. 'A reminder of a girl I once knew.'

'The one that did you wrong,' his father observed. He had spoken to Tom Sullivan who had told him the news about his foolish daughter's behaviour towards Lukas, though Tom and Jack remained close friends. 'In that case we will christen her the *Erika Sarah* to honour a lady who once did me wrong,' he added.

'It has a kind of ring to it,' Lukas conceded. 'The *Erika Sarah* she will be.'

• • •

348

Caroline Arrowsmith sat opposite her husband, knitting as the sun shone warmly down upon them in the garden. Like most men he was blissfully unaware of the change that had come to her life. He had his head buried in the papers and was muttering curses about unionists, seeing them as a threat to all God fearing industrialists. They were just trying to make enough to buy another beach house or trip to France on a luxury liner. The stark photographs portraying the bleak poverty in the lines of the unemployed did not touch him. As he glanced up to reach for his cup of tea from the silver salver ornately embossed with the Arrowsmith coat of arms his wife caught his eye.

'What are you doing?' he asked in a puzzled voice. He had never seen Caroline in any domestic pursuit other than mixing a cocktail when the manservant was not available.

'Knitting booties for our baby,' she said, waiting with a sly smile for his reaction.

'You mean . . .' he blustered.

It was not often that she had seen Quentin look so confused. 'Yes, according to Doctor Vinefield the baby is due around early next year.'

Quentin Arrowsmith realised that his hand was still poised to reach for the tea. 'Congratulations,' he said in a flat voice. 'Do I know the father?'

Caroline ceased knitting to gaze at him. 'I don't think it matters except to say I believe he has qualities you would approve of.'

Quentin was not convinced. One part of him wanted to know what bloodline would inherit his fortunes whilst the other half dreaded the thought that it might be a close friend, smug in the fact that he had cuckolded him.

For Caroline the choice of Jack Kelly had been perfect. Not only did the man have all the qualities desired in a future heir – courage, intelligence and ambition – but he was also definitely not a friend of her husband. The irony of Jack Kelly being the father was not lost on her nonetheless, and she smiled at the thought. But she also knew that no one other than herself must ever know her secret.

Quentin once again buried his head in his paper and continued reading about the traumatic effects the economic depression was having on the masses of ordinary Australians. Of slight interest outside the financial situation was an item about Australian Jews meeting at the Melbourne Town Hall to protest at the treatment of Jews in Germany. He moved on from the article with a grunt. Bloody Jews were always unhappy about one thing or the other. Maybe Herr Hitler would stop their whining one day, he thought. An article about Australian beef exporters making complaints to Britain regarding the Argentinian practice of exporting beef under the guise of offal – now that was of a lot more importance than the bloody whining Jews. The birth of a child in his family was another item of lesser interest, at least for the moment. It would all depend on whether Caroline bore a son or daughter.

* * *

'Well,' Jack said as his son tossed the last of their provisions aboard the *Erika Sarah*. 'Time to cast off, I suppose.'

Lukas leapt aboard with the agility of a cat and patted the great spoked teak wheel. The sun was still below the horizon and other than the gentle lapping of the calm waters around the hull and the sad call of a curlew on a sandy spit nearby, the morning was silent. Like a hush of expectation for the great adventure before them, Jack idly thought, gazing out over the harbour's waters. There was a chill in the late winter air. Soon would come spring, and then the heat of summer with its bushfires encircling the city.

He had settled all his affairs with creditors and the sale of the house had provided a stake in the lugger along with provisions and a few luxuries. He had to admit when he had gone to buy the boat that there was a real appeal in being free of the office he had come to resent. One by one his enterprises folded and he had done his best to ensure employees were placed in other jobs. In this he had mostly been successful on account of his charitable work for the families of servicemen who had died for their country – and one or two of his political contacts had not deserted him in his quest for help.

He had only a few regrets when the house was sold. It had been the place where his son had spent the latter part of his teenage years when on leave from school. It was a place of laughter and good times together. And now here they stood, on the deck of a lugger. Neither knew much about sailing, although Lukas would not admit it. He had devoured every book and journal on navigation as well as taking every opportunity to go sailing in the time they had waited for the house to sell. And what he had learned was to be admired – unfortunately, it was all theory. Now it was time to see if what was in the lad's head could be transmitted into the hands. But Jack trusted his son.

What lay ahead was unknown but at least they were sailing home to Papua. Maybe they could do a bit of fishing and swimming on the way through, Jack thought with a smile. It was the holiday he had always denied himself because all his time had been spent just keeping the intricacies of his business running smoothly. And how easily it had all disappeared.

Under her engine the lugger puttered out of the harbour with Lukas at the helm. By early morning as the sun began its ascent and the city was waking to another day at the office or factory, the *Erika Sarah* was through the great sandstone cliffs that protected the harbour from the rolling Pacific Ocean and steering a course due north, a brisk wind speeding her progress. She was now under full sail and Jack was quickly discovering muscles that had remained long dormant. But for a couple of amateurs, he thought that they were doing okay so far.

The *Erika Sarah* sailed well and Jack took a back seat to observe his son's superb handling of the big boat. Within a few short days, Jack ascertained from the charts that they were approaching the scenic towns of Tweed Heads and Coolangatta which straddled the state borders. It was time to go ashore and stretch their legs.

They sailed into the Tweed River and anchored just off the main street of the New South Wales town of Tweed Heads. It was a Saturday and the town was busy with visitors, many of whom had travelled down from Brisbane by railway train to enjoy the vast stretches of beautiful surfing beaches. Jack still liked the feel of the place; it was lively and sported all the facilities of a major city. Over the border in Queensland, Coolangatta even boasted the finest picture theatre anywhere between the major cities of Brisbane in the north and Newcastle in the south.

They spent a week more than they had planned for in the coastal resort. 'This place has a lot of potential,' Jack said one evening as he and Lukas sat on the aft deck of the lugger, sipping mugs of tea. The boat rocked gently on a rising tide and overhead a full moon bathed the surrounding hills in a silver light. 'Wouldn't mind retiring here one day.'

'I thought you would want to retire in South Australia,' Lukas said.

'I've been too long in the tropics to ever go back south,' Jack said, as a big fish leapt from the water near the lugger and plopped back into the river. 'Kind of got used to the warm winters. Besides, I don't have any family back there now. The only family I have is you, son.'

Lukas fell silent and gazed at the tall, craggy ridge known as the Razorback. He knew his father had purchased a lot of land on the slope, with a panoramic view out to the ocean as well as south and

353

north along the stretches of beaches. It was hard to imagine his father sitting on the verandah of a house, wearing slippers and puffing on his pipe. He was such a dynamic and adventurous man. Lukas had come to understand what the medals were that his father kept in an old cigar box. For years the Great War had been just dull accounts in his history books, yet his father had actually fought in those old battles. He felt his heart swell with love for this man who seemed to have always been a part of his life. He could hardly remember his mother, apart from a vivid and disturbing vision of her lying in an eternal sleep, and adults speaking in hushed tones as if they did not want to wake her. But there was still a lingering sadness for something taken too early from his life.

'I love you, Dad,' Lukas suddenly blurted and Jack ducked his head. He had not heard his son say that since he was nine years old. 'I love you, son,' he said softly and the two men went back to gazing upon the tranquillity of the sub-tropical night as they sipped their mugs of tea.

After a week that had turned into a holiday, the next day they set sail. Lukas seemed to mope as they put the headland of Point Danger behind them and sailed over into Queensland waters, en route to Papua via the Great Barrier Reef.

'A girl, was it?' Jack said as he nudged Lukas in the ribs with the end of his pipe.

'I met her at the flickers the night you were at the pub,' Lukas sighed, gripping the helm. 'She was a really nice sheila.'

Jack chuckled. 'You know the old saying about having a girl in every port. Well, you are only following the tradition of sailors in such matters.'

Lukas cast his father a sad smile. It could have been love if they had stayed longer, he thought with just a touch of regret. But to stay longer would have meant deserting his dream of adventure and he brightened somewhat from his melancholy. Could life get better than it was when he was the master of his own fate and had the man he loved not only as a father but also his best mate beside him, a man of infinite wisdom and courage – even if his luck in business had failed him?

THIRTY

Gerhardt had told his superior that he would not be at home the evening he went to question Erika and was not surprised at the pleased expression on Spier's face. Not even the dour Colonel Spier could resist her after a few brandies and Gerhardt was able to search his superior's discarded clothing as he slept soundly beside Erika.

Gerhardt's late night visit did not seem to raise the suspicions of the nightwatchman at the Intelligence headquarters. After all, Gerhardt had worked back before to complete his reports so a casually offered explanation gave him access to the guarded corridors. He avoided the night duty officer dozing in his office when he was meant to be alert to any early morning telephone calls; the less people who were aware of his presence the better.

The safe door swung open and Gerhardt quickly

went through the neatly stacked colour coded files. Finding the one he sought, he scanned the lists of names until he found his own. Worse still, he noted that his dismissal had been given a priority on the list and he well knew what that meant.

His eye was caught by one of the other files, its title referring to German nationals abroad. Gerhardt was curious as he planned to become a national abroad as soon as he could. He opened the file and found a categorised column of names divided into occupations. It was a file, Gerhardt knew from experience, that also marked the men for death, and under the heading 'Scientists' one name in particular caught his attention. It was of a German–Jewish scientist now resident in the United States of America whose brilliance had caused media interest around the world. He was obviously to be eliminated should conflict occur between the two nations. German paid agents abroad would be activated to carry out executions.

The name of the scientist was Albert Einstein. Gerhardt realised the sensitivity of such a file personally signed by Himmler and also realised that the file could be his passport to a new identity in another country. To take the file and be discovered with it in his possession would surely sign his death warrant but the information was far too valuable as a key to opening doors to the British or Americans. He also knew that he could not smuggle the file itself safely out of Germany – too many customs officials and border guards were in the party and might recognise its importance. The only thing he could do was take the file, photograph it with his new Leica camera and then destroy it. An attempt to return the file to the safe would be pushing his luck too far. Besides, the unexposed film would be a lot easier to conceal than a bulky file.

Gerhardt could hear the nightwatchman doing his rounds and knew he must decide now. It was a gamble that Spier would not notice the file missing immediately as there were so many in the safe. Gerhardt snatched the file and thrust it down the front of his jacket. With shaking hands he carefully replaced the other files in their order. Spier was a very observant man. He closed the safe and felt quite giddy. Now he must get home and pray that Spier was still sleeping off the combined effects of alcohol and sex.

Gerhardt could not remember another time when he had been so frightened except for his days at the front. At least then his enemies were foreigners and not his own people. He crept up the stairs to the bedroom and was relieved to hear a loud snoring. Very cautiously he replaced the crumpled paper in the pocket of Spier's trousers. Satisfied, he walked downstairs to the living room where Erika stood by the fire, with a cigarette in her hand.

'Well, I have done my part,' Erika said. 'What did you learn?'

'That I am also on the list,' he said, his weariness apparent. 'You will get your divorce for the part that you have played so well.'

'What are you going to do?' Erika asked.

For just a moment Gerhardt thought that he heard a trace of concern in her question. 'I would rather not tell you as it might endanger your life,' he replied. 'What you don't know will be your safest ticket.'

Erika frowned as she examined her husband's face for signs of deceit. But there were none. 'I truly wish you well,' she said in a gentle tone he had not heard her utter since the day she had accepted his proposal of marriage. 'I have not been a good wife or mother.'

'That does not matter anymore,' Gerhardt said. He placed his hands gently on her bare shoulders in a tender gesture. She gazed up into his face, eyes glistening. 'What matters is that I take measures to protect our daughter from the madness that I know will come to Germany if Adolf gains power. The democracy that we have will be gone forever and we will be part of a terrible machine which will suppress all that is good. I was a fool to think that he truly cared for the people. The man behind the fanfare of parades and flag dedications to so-called martyrs is a liar and bully on a grand scale.'

'I thought that Adolf would lead the way,' Erika said. 'But now I share your doubts. I wanted to divorce you because I thought that you were weak, but I can see that they have used you. You are a good man. I am sorry for the pain I have caused you and Ilsa.'

'You could come with us,' Gerhardt suggested gently. Despite all that his wife had done to him, he thought, he still loved her in a perverse sort of way. 'We could leave Germany and start a new life some-where safe,' he continued optimistically.

'Where?' Erika asked.

Gerhardt could hardly believe his ears at such a simple question. It was as if she was actually consid-ering his offer. 'Not Europe,' he replied. 'I fear war will eventually come to Europe. Maybe America is the place to go.'

'We could not obtain immigration status,' Erika countered. 'The party would block any application as it cannot afford to have you leave with what you know about Adolf.'

Gerhardt knew that she was right. 'We could apply to visit your brother in Papua,' he offered with a note of hope. 'That would not look suspicious. All I have to do is keep up a pretence of being a loyal member of the party. Maybe Spier would consider a proposal to initiate contacts with loyal Germans still in that country. I think I can convince him that intel-ligence gathering in the Pacific region may be of importance to us in the future should war come to Europe.'

Erika was sceptical but Gerhardt's plan seemed the best of the very few options they had. To take leave in Europe still placed them within range of the shadowy men of the SS and SA who enforced orders with brutal efficiency, silencing those who may prove to be an embarrassment abroad. The deaths of one or two German nationals considered outspoken against the ideals of the Nazi party in foreign lands had already occurred – unexplained accidents that the

German authorities did not insist being investigated to the fullest by French or Polish police.

'I will contact my brother,' she finally said as the snoring from upstairs turned into a grunting. 'You had better hide until Colonel Spier leaves,' she whispered.

Gerhardt made himself scarce as his superior officer dressed to return home to his wife. He could hear Erika laughing with the man at the front door and he crooning soft words of love. Gerhardt suddenly felt sick. He hated himself for what he had blackmailed his wife into doing, but that was before she expressed a softness he had not known in many years. Maybe they could start again in a foreign country. He did not know much about Papua and New Guinea except that it was a mostly unexplored land of cannibals and headhunters and under Australian mandate since the war. Whatever it was like it could not be worse than what he was facing in Germany. Now he had to continue with his careful plan. He knew that he would need money if they were to establish a future in a foreign land and that was a problem equal to convincing Colonel Spier to release him for espionage duties.

Erika was bitter. She instinctively sensed that Colonel Spier was not about to clear her name of suggestions of disloyalty, and that meant her future in Germany was tenuous. She had learned from the party officials she had slept with that Adolf was already gloating over his idea for a new Germany.

What she had overheard in the bedrooms and corridors of power would not have disturbed Erika except now she was also adversely reported on SA files. She knew well enough that once she was on their list of suspected persons she would always be under a cloud of suspicion, even if she were proved innocent. That was the way in a Germany where the people still blindly believed Adolf would lead them into a golden renaissance, showing the French and English that Germany was once again a power to be reckoned with. The humiliation of the Versailles Treaty still lingered in the minds of a generation that remembered the last terrible days of the war.

But Erika was not so naive to believe that the probable future leader of Germany cared for anything more than power and personal grandeur. The war clouds were on the horizon and she knew that the storm would engulf her as well. She had to get out of Germany and once again she had to rely on Gerhardt to save her. The fool had been easy to manipulate, she reflected. If Gerhardt thought that she was about to live in some godforsaken place at the end of the earth with her prissy sister-in-law and brother then he was in for a shock. All she needed to do was reach Australia and establish herself in Sydney. She had secretly accumulated a considerable amount of money from selling the many expensive presents she had received for her carnal services to the party. Fortunately, Gerhardt did not know about the hoard and she would use only a small portion of it to pay for their fares. Once in Australia she would leave him.

Erika had a perverse pleasure in inflicting pain. It had always been with her. Even as a child she had felt aroused by the sight of her father killing the goose for the Christmas dinner. The bird's terrified honking call as it sensed its danger and the splashing of blood as it bled to death had excited her. When she crept to her bed that night she had fantasised that she was a beautiful sleek leopard tearing down a helpless fawn, and the image brought on a powerful surge of erotic feelings. Blood and pain had been key elements in her fantasies from then on.

Erika did not think of it as prostitution. After all, she was only being paid to do what she liked most in the world: dominate others with her sexuality. When the time came, perhaps she could train her daughter to perform for men as she did. At least the girl would be useful for something.

But for now she had to rely on her naive husband to get them out of Germany and the reach of the all-powerful Nazi Party. Australia was a good choice. It was far from Europe and not likely to be involved in any possible conflict in the future. After all, the Australians had lost a significant proportion of their young men fighting for the British Empire. No, the Australians were not stupid enough to do the same again, she thought.

THIRTY-ONE

The *Erika Sarah* sailed with fair winds to Papua in two months. She could have done better time but they were delayed by stopovers along Queensland's coast. It was all too tempting to go ashore and spend some time lazing on the golden beaches under coconut trees.

After clearing customs in Port Moresby, Jack decided they should sail to Paul Mann's plantation and surprise them. All that Paul had known from a short telegram sent from Sydney was to expect them in the months ahead.

Karin was sitting on the verandah reading with her daughter when one of the *haus meri*s sweeping the yard paused to stare out to the small inlet. 'A boat comes,' she said.

Karin glanced up from the pages of the book. She could see the lugger slowly motoring in as her sails were being hauled down. 'Whose boat is it?' she asked the young native girl.

'Don't know, missus,' the girl replied as she shielded her eyes against the glare shimmering off the surface of the placid waters. 'Not a copra boat.'

Karin stood and walked to the edge of the verandah to get a better look at the lugger, now obviously seeking a berth at the newly built jetty that stretched out into the sea. A sun-bronzed man stripped to a pair of shorts stood at the bow. 'Jack!' she exclaimed softly and dropped the book to rush down to the jetty. Angelika followed her mother.

'Well, if it isn't the love of my life,' Jack said as he leapt from the lugger to the jetty and embraced Karin in a big bear hug. 'And little Angelika who is growing up so fast.'

'Jack Kelly! What are you doing here?' Karin demanded as she stepped back to gaze at Lukas who stood proudly at the helm. He carefully revved the engine to settle the hull close in whilst his father expertly secured the berthing ropes to stumps on the wooden jetty.

'Hello, Aunt Karin,' Lukas called. 'Can't talk until my useless deckhand gets the boat ropes in place.'

'I heard that!' Jack called up from the jetty. 'If you are not careful I will revoke your captain's licence.' The boat berthed and the two men stood on the jetty beaming smiles at Karin and Angelika. 'Where's that big oaf you married?' Jack asked.

'He is up on the Laloki River with Karl for the day, visiting a planter,' Karin replied. 'But he will be returning before nightfall. Come inside and tell me everything. Whose boat did you steal and why haven't I received any letters from either of you for almost half a year now?'

Jack and Lukas each placed an arm around Karin's shoulders and walked either side of her to the house. Angelika followed with a frown. The boy who had once stolen her mother's dumplings was back. One of the first to greet them at the house was Dademo. Jack felt that he was finally home.

Paul and Karl arrived just after sunset that evening. Jack rose with a broad grin. 'Paul, you old bastard. How the hell are you?'

The normally reserved German allowed a back-slapping hug and returned Jack's broad smile with his own. Lukas and Karl engaged in some friendly sparring and insults by way of renewing contact after such a long time apart. When all the rituals of greeting were over, Karin poured her husband a coffee and brought out a bottle of schnapps, knowing this was a time for the men to catch up. Excusing herself, she went inside to go over the lessons she had set that day for Angelika.

'So, you are broke again,' Paul said as he poured a glass each of the fiery clear liquid. 'What are you going to do?'

'Kind of hoping to pick up a bit of work around Papua with the lugger.'

'Since when have you been a man of the sea, Jack Kelly?' Paul asked with a wry smile.

'Since my son talked me into it.'

'So Lukas is the sailor in the family.'

'As far as I know we never had any nautical tradition,' Jack mused, studying his glass against the light of the hurricane lamp hanging a short distance away. He wanted to make sure that no Papuan creatures had decided to drop in and taste the German drink.

'I have heard that there is an American film crew in Moresby at the moment asking around about a charter,' Paul said as he took a sip of his drink. 'I don't know much more than that, but if you are available I can get more information for you.'

'I don't exactly know what a charter is all about but I would be interested. Being Yanks, they are sure to be fairly generous in paying for the services of the *Erika Sarah*.'

At the mention of the lugger's name Paul frowned. His old friend had not forgotten the woman who had deserted him so long ago. 'I have heard that Erika is on her way out here from Germany with her husband and daughter, Jack,' he said quietly.

'No real concern of mine,' Jack said dismissively. But Paul could see the change in his friend's expression. 'How about this Yank?' Jack asked, changing the focus of the conversation. 'I would like to start making a bit of money. I have to admit the trip north cost us a bit on incidental expenses.'

• • •

The next day Jack, Lukas and Paul drove into Moresby. In town Paul tracked a middle aged American film producer down to a boarding house. His name was Joe Oblachinski, and he was a portly man, built like an English bulldog. The heat of the tropics had soaked his white suit. As he stood sweating on the verandah greeting his visitors, he wiped his forehead with a big red bandana.

'I'll be goddamned glad to get back to the States when this job is over,' he said as he took Paul's and then Jack's hand. 'Mr Mann tells me you have a boat available for a charter.'

'That's right,' Jack said, eyeing a cumbersome camera. A clean-cut young man was seated a short distance away polishing a lens. Lukas had wandered over to the young cameraman and introduced himself, leaving the negotiations to his father – movies fascinated him as gold once had his father. Many afternoons had been spent sneaking away from school with Karl to sit in the dark and watch a world of action, adventure and romance unfolding in the flickering images on the silver screen.

'A lugger to be precise,' Jack continued, 'easily take you and your film crew anywhere in these waters you want.'

'You know the Fly River, Mr Kelly?' Oblachinski asked.

'I do,' Paul cut in. 'I was on an expedition up the Fly about ten years ago.'

Jack glanced at Paul as he continued, 'I could go with Jack at no extra cost to add my knowledge of the region.'

Oblachinski glanced back at Jack who said, 'I would rather Mr Mann was paid to accompany us if you charter my boat.'

'We can do that,' Oblachinski said swiping at his brow with the bandana. 'So long as the fee is reasonable.'

'Shall we talk money?' Jack asked and the American nodded.

The details were thrashed out over gin and tonics and a handshake between the American and the Australian sealed the deal. 'So what's the charter all about?' Jack asked when they had reached the end of the negotiations. He had warmed to the no-nonsense Yank.

'Hollywood has gone crazy over jungle movies lately,' Oblachinski said. 'We go out and get footage of genuine cannibals and head hunters to edit in. Papua and New Guinea give us the opportunity to can a few miles of film. A friend of mine, Joe Swartz, was over this way a couple of years back and chartered a young fellow by the name of Errol Flynn to take him around to the Sepik to get some footage.'

'I met Errol in Sydney,' Lukas said unexpectedly. Until now he had remained silent, as he knew his father would want him to. 'He was in Sydney with a troupe of Papuan natives and his film was being shown at the same time. Karl and I had a chance to introduce ourselves at the theatre when he came out dressed in a wig and British naval uniform before the screening of *In the Wake of the Bounty*. We told him that we were from up his way. He is a really nice bloke and said to keep in contact.'

'He was almost a neighbour of mine,' Paul added. 'He tried growing tobacco up on the Laloki River. That's where he got his kanakas to take to Sydney.'

Joe Oblachinski's face widened with a smile. 'Seems you guys are all related in this part of the world,' he said as a joke. 'Joe Swartz predicts that Flynn might have a future in the movies – if he ever makes it to the States.'

Jack remained silent, thinking that there was a lot he did not know about his son and his life in Sydney. But then, his own father seemed to know very little about him at the same age.

After final handshakes they left the American and his film crew, Jack having arranged to set sail the next day for Moresby to pick up the Americans.

'So why in hell would you volunteer to come on the expedition?' Jack asked as soon as they were in the truck, which was whining its way down the track back to the plantation. 'And you didn't tell me that you knew Mr Flynn,' he said to Lukas beside him.

Lucas answered first. 'You never asked.'

Then Paul replied, 'I'm your mate,' he said. 'And I know the waters pretty well. I doubt that you two are truly master mariners yet.'

Jack had to agree. Most of what he had told the American producer had been aimed to deflect from his and Lukas's lack of experience. Not that he lied, but he was careful to steer away from subjects such as other charters they had done. At least he had negotiated payment for Paul as a deckhand and assistant navigator. And he could not foresee any real danger in what they were doing. At least he could face Karin this time.

Ironically when Paul informed his wife that he was going away for a month with Jack on the American film expedition to the Fly River she made it firmly known that Paul was to ensure neither Jack nor Lukas were to come to harm. Paul shook his head as he walked away. Women, he thought. Why had she not expressed her concern for him?

Needless to say Karl insisted on joining the expedition with the argument that Dademo was more than capable of running the plantation. In the end it was his mother who interceded on his behalf and convinced her husband that he should take his son. Paul selected a young man named Malip from amongst his plantation workers to be an interpreter. He was from a village not far from the Fly River.

The next day when the lugger berthed in Port Moresby, a truck and a car drove down to the wharf to meet the *Erika Sarah*. Joe Oblachinski's film crew, three relatively young men, carefully unloaded their precious film equipment from the truck. The door of the car opened and out struggled Joe followed by the most beautiful woman either Lukas or Karl had ever seen outside a movie cinema. She was around five foot five inches tall, slim and had dark black hair and eyes that reminded the two boys of an Indian princess. She appeared to be in her mid to late twenties. Her hair was cut short and bobbed and she wore riding jodhpurs and a flowing long sleeved silk shirt of pale cream. The two boys stood gaping from the deck of the lugger as she thanked the driver and glided down the wharf.

'Got to be a movie star,' Karl muttered when he was able to close his mouth.

'I reckon,' Lukas agreed. 'But I don't know which one.'

'Good afternoon, gentlemen,' the Indian princess said with a sweet smile. 'Isn't it a beautiful day?'

Both boys mumbled their greetings and rushed to help her step aboard, suddenly struck with awkwardness in the presence of such a beautiful young woman.

Jack stepped forward to relieve the boys of their clumsy attempts to assist. 'We didn't expect female company,' he said as his hand went past the boys. 'Mr Oblachinski didn't mention you.'

'My name is Victoria Duvall,' she said with a smile and glanced at the boys. 'I expected that you would have native deckhands.'

'My son Lukas and my business partner's son Karl,' Jack said introducing the boys. 'My name is Jack Kelly.'

Victoria's face brightened at the mention of Jack's name. 'Would you be the same man who once was a gold prospector in these parts?' she asked.

'Depends on who wants to know,' he frowned. 'But I suppose since it appears the question is yours then I am probably the same man.'

'Oh, what a pleasure to meet you, Captain Kelly,' Victoria exclaimed in her delight. 'Whilst I have been in Port Moresby I have heard so many interesting stories about your adventures over the years. You seem to be a real honest to good adventurer in the tradition of Douglas Fairbanks' movies.'

'Don't believe everything you hear, Miss Duvall. And would I be right in presuming that you are the star of this adventure? It seems the two boys are under that impression.'

Victoria smiled. 'Thank you, but I am afraid not,' she said. 'I have no real association with Hollywood other than enjoying the movies. Joe has allowed me to accompany him on his project as a favour, to keep a diary of events. You could say that I am a kind of girl Friday.'

Jack smiled at the look of disappointment on the boys' faces. Still, she was pretty enough to be a movie star.

When all was secured aboard they cast off with Lukas at the helm. Jack went below to vacate his cabin for Victoria, who protested at his chivalrous gesture. 'You get the most privacy here,' he simply grunted, leaving her to unpack the single bag she had brought for the voyage. Jack was impressed with her economy; it was not often, from his past experience, that a woman could make any kind of trip without packing suitcases full of shoes and dresses – just in case.

After he was satisfied that his passengers were comfortable and settled in for the journey he went above decks. Paul sat at the bow and gazed at the gentle roll of tropical waters as the lugger cut through the water with a soft hiss. Karl was in the engine room checking that it was all working well and Lukas remained at the helm, issuing orders to the native crew. Jack sat beside Paul to take in the vista of gently rolling sea.

'If the weather holds up,' he said to Paul, 'then it should be a good trip.'

'You know, Jack,' Paul said, without looking at his friend, 'it's a funny feeling to be going back to a place I never thought I would see again.'

'So why did you step in and volunteer to come with us?'

'I don't know,' Paul replied. 'Maybe I needed a bit of adventure before I grew too old on the plantation.'

'Kind of hope we don't get too much adventure,' Jack laughed softly. 'All I want out of the end of this trip is the Yank's money and a cold beer at the Moresby pub.'

'That's the funny thing about life,' Paul said philosophically. 'We make plans and something happens out of the blue to alter our lives forever. When we look back the smallest and seemingly insignificant thing that happens to us becomes the catalyst for much bigger things. Like you and I meeting that day in September 1918. How could we have ever guessed that our lives would become so entwined?'

Jack knew just what his friend meant. As much as you planned for the future, something always came along to make you reassess your life. He had never considered buying a boat to make his living until the idea came to his son on a ferry trip after being jilted by a young lady. Lukas had told him the story on the voyage to Papua and Jack had been bemused by his son's approach to adversity.

That evening Paul pleasantly surprised Jack by cooking up a very good fish curry and rice for the crew and guests. As part of his contribution to the expedition he had volunteered to relieve Jack of catering duties but Jack had no idea that his friend could cook as Karin had always prepared the meals.

It was a calm night and they had anchored off-shore not far from the fire lights of a native coastal village. The evening air had just the touch of a chill in it. Jack went above, leaving the crew and guests listening to a collection of jazz records on Lukas's gramophone. The cameramen engaged in cards and conversation. Jack sat on the deck holding a big mug of coffee between his hands and gazed at the distant village nestled at the edge of the jungle.

'I thought you might be here,' he heard a voice say from the hatchway. Victoria climbed up to join him. She wore an oversized woollen jacket and a pair of slacks.

'Plenty of room,' Jack said. 'Just pull up a bit of deck.'

Victoria laughed softly as she sat down with her knees up and stared out at the landward side of the lugger. 'I just wanted to thank you for giving up your cabin,' she said. 'But I have travelled rough before and would be just as happy to sleep on the deck or in the galley.'

'Lady's privilege aboard the *Erika Sarah*,' Jack said. 'It would be bad luck not to, considering the name of the good ship.'

'Was that your wife's name?' she asked and added, 'I heard a lot of tales about you from the old hands in

375

Moresby. They call you the Captain. I also heard that your wife died back in '19. I am sorry for that.'

'So they call me the Captain,' Jack chuckled and Victoria turned to look at his profile in the dark. She could not consider him dashingly handsome but he had the looks of a man with a sense of humour, despite what she had learned of his hard past.

'Is that because you are the captain of the boat?' she asked and he shook his head.

'It was my rank as an officer in the army during the war,' he replied. 'Aussies always seem to find a name for you other than the one you were born with. Usually it has an irony, like calling a red-haired man Bluey. I like to think that my son is captain of the boat although I may own it.'

'I also heard that you once went into unexplored territory with an English lord and discovered a gold mine. But then your partner was killed by the natives, and you later turned the find into a fortune, until recently when it all went bust.'

'Sounds about the extent of it,' Jack said. 'Easy come, easy go. But since you seem to know so much about me how about you tell me something about yourself. For a start, Victoria is not a name I would consider being very Yank.'

The young woman ducked her head and smiled. 'My mother was a great fan of the English royal family. We republican-minded people rid ourselves of royalty but secretly yearn to have a royal family of our own. My mother admired Queen Victoria for all her virtues and named me in her honour when I was born twenty-eight years ago.'

'Thought you were younger,' Jack grunted matter of factly.

'Well, thank you, sir,' Victoria replied, laughing. 'Any lady over twenty-one wishes to be thought of as younger than her actual years. You know, I have noticed that you Aussie men are not as prone to flattering a woman as American men are, so I accept your observation as a real compliment.'

'So tell me a bit about yourself then,' Jack said, sipping his coffee and turning back to stare at the village.

'Well, there is not much to say really. I am the daughter of a lieutenant colonel in the American army and have spent most of my childhood on army bases in the Far East. I attended college in California and speak French and Japanese.'

'Japanese,' Jack mused. 'An unusual language for a woman to speak. Not much call for it in these parts of the world unless you are trying to negotiate with old Isokihi to charter his boat. So why Japanese as a language?'

Victoria seemed surprised at the Australian's interest in what she had achieved – most men preferred to shower her with sweet words than engage in meaningful conversation. She knew others considered her very beautiful but she was intelligent enough to know that life soon enough took its toll on beauty alone. Travelling with her father after her mother had died of cholera in China when Victoria was still very young had given her an independent outlook as well as an insatiable taste for travel and adventure. She had come close to marrying and settling down with successful and handsome young men on two occasions but realised in the end that they considered her little more than an ornament on their arm. So it was nice to be in the company of a man who actually seemed to consider her a person first. But his question about her interest in the Japanese language went beyond an answer she was in a position to give.

'Oh, it was just one of those things,' she said lightly. 'There are many Japanese living in California and it was easy to practise speaking the language.' She noticed that Jack was staring at her intently and could see the slightest smile in his expression.

'So you are not a girl Friday after all,' he said bluntly and she shifted nervously. 'And Joe Oblachinski is not really a film producer from Hollywood. My guess is that you are both here to collect a bit of information about this part of the world. I suppose you can say I am playing what you Yanks call a hunch.'

Victoria pulled away from his steady gaze. 'Oh, what the hell!' she blurted. 'I can't see why you shouldn't know a few facts. You are, after all, a patriot to your country from what I have learned about you, I suppose you have a right to know. Joe really is a film producer and I am acting as his secretary for this trip. But we are also taking footage for our Defense Department who want to get an idea about the terrain in this part of the world.'

'Here?' said Jack in disbelief. 'What the hell do they reckon is going to happen out here? I thought we'd be the bottom end of the world to you Yanks.'

Victoria continued, a little reluctantly. 'There are some military analysts who believe that we could be at war with Japan over control of the Pacific and Papua is part of the Pacific. A kind of bottom hinge to a door that controls who gets to own the big water between you and us.'

Jack burst into a soft laugh and raised his mug. 'You are definitely a very interesting lady and I salute you for what you are doing.'

'I am not a spy,' Victoria quickly added. 'I just volunteered to pick up a bit of information while I was over this way. My father works in Washington and I am doing this more as a favour for him. What I am actually doing is writing a book about this part of the world.'

'Yanks don't even know that Papua and New Guinea exist,' Jack said in a teasing tone. 'So why would anyone in your country be interested in your book?'

'Well, it's not exactly about Papua,' Victoria replied. 'I am writing a novel about people who live on the edge of life itself in exotic places. Papua is a perfect place to research. It still has lost tribes and the people are as savage as the tribes were in Africa half a century ago. I am writing a kind of adventure story like those written about Africa by Rider Haggard and Edgar Rice Burroughs.'

'You strike me as a young woman who knows where she is going and knows what she wants,' Jack said softly.

'You got that right, buster,' Victoria said. 'Now how do I go about getting a cup of coffee around this joint?'

Jack laughed and went below decks. For the next few hours as the Southern Cross wheeled slowly overhead, they talked about their lives until they were aware that the low din of voices had ceased and both passengers and crew were asleep. Victoria bid Jack a good evening and went below to the cabin whilst Jack continued to sit, wondering about the future and whether or not the lugger would make them a respectable income. But his musings were occasionally interrupted by thoughts of the woman who had sat beside him with her knees under her chin and had talked so easily about everything and nothing. He looked down at his unfinished coffee, now cold, then stood and stretched his legs to go below.

'Bloody women,' he growled softly as he tossed the contents of his mug over the side where its splash disturbed the calmness of the tropical night. It seemed that a woman was always the turning point in his life — and not always for the better. But why put Victoria in the same category, he chided himself. After all, she might be a woman of culture and with a vision of what she wanted, but he hardly knew her.

THIRTY-TWO

The missing file was not discovered until Gerhardt, Erika and Ilsa were somewhere in the Indian Ocean, steaming for the port of Fremantle in Western Australia. Colonel Spier sat at his desk with his head in his hands trying to puzzle out how the file had disappeared. And for some reason, his thoughts kept returning to Gerhardt Stahl. A tiny flame of suspicion was rapidly becoming a raging fire of anger at himself for falling so easily for the man's cunning.

'Neumann!' he bellowed down the corridor. 'Report to me immediately.'

The information officer scrambled from his desk and was soon standing stiffly in his superior's office.

'About six weeks ago you took a report on Frau Stahl, did you not?'

Neumann appeared puzzled. 'No, sir,' he replied. 'If I had I would have remembered, considering her husband works for us.'

Spier let out a breath of exasperation. Why hadn't he followed up on his gut reaction at the time that something was amiss about the whole matter? A husband, no matter how dedicated to duty, does not allow such a report to pass so easily through his hands. And now he suspected that Stahl had cunningly manoeuvred him to Erika's bed when . . . Speir instinctively touched the scrap of paper in his pocket. So that's how he did it!

'Bring me the nightwatchman's report from . . .' He thumbed through his diary to ascertain the night he had visited his subordinate's house and Neumann hurried away to find the log sheets. When he returned with them, Spier scanned the spidery handwriting of the old man. There was nothing in the report about a visit from Stahl but that did not surprise Spier. The old man was probably senile and forgot to record it. If Stahl knew the contents of the missing file they were both in serious trouble, Spier for his negligence if it was ever discovered how Stahl had stolen the foolishly recorded safe combination. Fortunately he had thought to have Stahl's movements monitored between his going on leave and departing on the ship from Hamburg. Even on a stopover in England agents had kept an eye on him but had nothing unusual to report. Stahl had not left the ship nor had any visitors.

God in heaven, Spier thought. New Guinea was at the other end of the world. But many German citizens still worked in the country as Lutheran missionaries and gold miners – surely it was only a matter of activating one of the contacts and having him eliminate the troublesome former employee. As it was, the killing would be sanctioned at the highest level anyway. That was not a problem.

A telephone call to the right person would identify the most appropriate agent to set up the execution in New Guinea or Papua when Stahl arrived. Ah yes, Spier thought. I remember the man who is our contact in that part of the world. Under the circumstances a rather unusual and interesting person, so trusted and apparently insignificant to the Australian administrators that they allowed him to work freely amongst them during the war. But Spier frowned when he recalled a recent report on the unreliability of their Papuan contact and the possibility that he could even be a double agent. Still, he had his own weakness – if it ever leaked out that he had been working for the Kaiser's interests during the war he would be ruined. He would cooperate, even if it took blackmail to persuade him.

It was time to activate him again, time to send the telegrams in the old code. He was sure that the agent would remember his briefings of just over twenty years earlier. After all, without the assistance of the former Imperial Intelligence system the man would not be as wealthy as it was reputed he was.

And there were those sympathetic to the Nazi ideals even amongst the Australians. Another very important file in the safe had the names of such people and organisations scattered across the globe. He did have a vague recollection of a name in Australia with commercial links to German industry. He took the file from the safe and thumbed through the folder. There was the name, Quentin Arrowsmith. Yes, it was still possible to reach across the ocean to faraway Australia and eliminate a potential traitor. Stahl could not escape from the reaches of the Nazi party. There were even many non-Germans who were sympathetic to the ideals of Adolf Hitler.

As he stood on the deck of the passenger ship, gazing at the unfamiliar night sky, Gerhardt was blissfully unaware of the telegram transmitted by the undersea cable on its way to Papua. But he was aware that his old colleague Adolf Hitler was now chancellor of Germany as the news had reached them on a stopover in Ceylon. What he had dreaded had come to pass, and he breathed a sigh of relief to have managed to leave Germany before the state apparatus was Adolf's to use for his own ends.

Erika was her old self again towards him and had insisted on separate cabins. Ilsa shared a cabin with her mother whilst Gerhardt was with three others. They were young British men on their way to Melbourne to take up posts with an English bank that had offices in Australia. He found them rowdy and preferred to return to the cabin after they had retired so he did not have to associate with them.

The passenger ship was steaming towards the west of the Australian continent, a day away from soil and safety. Even as Gerhardt considered how he would pass on his information to the Americans via the Australian government, another man was being sought by a code almost forgotten to him.

The Papuan agent had agonised over the mission, but knew that rejecting it would mean that his German controllers would somehow make it known that he had been a spy for them. He knew he had too much to lose, and so now stood in the Port Moresby post office and handed the letter to the postmaster.

'Haven't seen you in town for a while,' the post-master said as he took the letter. 'I heard a rumour that you might be leaving Papua, is that right, Mr Sen?'

Sen nodded as the postmaster gave the address on the letter a careful look. It wasn't such an unusual destination. And business dealings with the Dutch who controlled the territory west of the Papuan border were common enough.

Sen prayed that he would be able to report that his mission had failed, despite his best attempts to contact the man who would be the assassin. This assignment was too close to home, involving people he personally knew and respected. But he had taken the silver as had Judas Iscariot almost two millennia before.

The man who would receive the coded letter via a Dutch official, sympathetic to the Nazi cause, was a man the sender despised. He was a cold-blooded killer of Irish descent by the name of Tim O'Leary. Both men had worked together during the war to spy on the Australians in Papua and New Guinea and it seemed to Sen that he would never be free of this unholy alliance.

THIRTY-THREE

'There was an old canoe builder I met when I was up the Fly River years ago,' Paul said across the small table bolted to the floor in the airy cabin. 'He might still be alive.'

Joe Oblachinski steadied his cup of coffee between his hands as the *Erika Sarah* rose and fell on the gently rolling waters of the Gulf of Papua. They were off the mouth of the mighty river and the normally blue and clear salty waters were now littered with the brown and green detritus of the jungle. 'From what you have told me about him, he sounds like an interesting character,' he said as he took a sip. 'You think you could find him after all these years?'

'I can try,' Paul answered with a shrug. 'From my knowledge of these people they are territorial. If he is anywhere he will be around the area I was in.'

Jack unrolled a chart on the table and the three men stared at the series of islands that marked the wide mouth of the river. Paul used the stem of his pipe to indicate a point upriver. 'I made my first contact with him around here,' he said. 'His village had been razed to the ground during a raid by a rather evil bunch of people.'

'Other natives?' Joe asked.

'A European,' Paul replied and left the subject at that. He still felt pangs of guilt for not saving Iris and knew that by even going up the Fly River he was inviting old and bitter memories of failure.

'Well, guys,' Joe said leaning back against the bulkhead behind him, 'if we get lucky and meet this guy you know he could be the key to us making friendly contact with the locals and getting some great footage.'

Jack rolled up the chart and glanced at Paul. He could see the pained expression in his face and knew why. It should have been me who went after O'Leary, Jack thought.

On deck Jack stretched and stared at the distant rise and fall of the jungle covered shoreline. Lukas was at the helm, looking confident. Jack smiled to himself as he knew that his son was holding a noble pose for Victoria, who sat on the cabin roof taking in the warm sun and sea breezes. She wore a shirt tied at the waist and a pair of shorts that showed off her figure. The days at sea had tanned her and brought out a spray of freckles across the upper part of her cheeks. Somehow it made her look much younger. He knew Lukas was smitten by the beautiful woman, despite her being a good ten years older, and so too was Karl. Jack had noticed some prickliness in their friendship as both boys vied for her attention.

'Have you come to join me?' Victoria asked when she saw Jack on deck. 'It is a beautiful day.'

Jack returned her request with a broad smile. The sun had tanned him too and the hard physical work of sailing had toughened his body, so that he now looked like a slightly older version of his son.

'For a short while,' he said and sat beside her, ignoring the scowl on his son's face. 'I have to get some things sorted out before we head upriver. Paul thinks we might be able to make contact with a native he met here years ago.'

'That would be wonderful if we could,' Victoria said. 'I would love to meet a real live man from the Stone Age.'

'Not that romantic,' Jack said with a twisted grin. 'A lot of their practices aren't that savoury, unless we're talking cooked human meat. As for being Stone Age, you could be right in saying that their only technology is of wood and stone. But I figure the introduction of steel into their lives is going to change everything in the years ahead. The kanakas who have made contact with us in the rest of Papua and New Guinea have quickly learned the lesson of metal coins as exchange. Lately it's got to be a bit more lucrative than the traditional sea shell currency.'

'Do you like living in Papua?' Victoria asked, looking Jack directly in the eyes.

He sometimes asked himself the same question. 'I tried living in Sydney,' he said with a frown. 'Thought I was doing well but it's a jungle I don't understand. At least here I know where my enemies are and can take measures to protect myself. Yeah, I suppose I like it here.'

Victoria sighed and turned away at his answer. 'Why do you ask?' Jack continued.

'Oh, no reason.'

Jack shook his head and stood to make his way back to the cabin. He passed his son who was still scowling at his father.

'She's a bit young for you, Dad,' Lukas said from the corner of his mouth.

Jack stopped in his tracks. 'How old do you think I am?' he quizzed.

'Really old,' Lukas replied with the cheeky naivety of youth. 'Even ancient.'

Jack grinned and walked away. He rarely thought about his age. Maybe his body was ageing but his mind still carried the thoughts of a twenty-year-old man as he approached his fortieth year. But his son had nothing to fear concerning his behaviour towards Miss Victoria Duvall. She was a classy lady used to the comforts of the USA. He was a man of the wild frontiers. There could be no attraction.

Victoria noticed the interaction between father and son and smiled to herself, aware of Lukas and Karl's attempts to attract her attention. But Jack was different. Her inward smile turned to a frown when she thought about him. He was so unlike the many men she had known in her life. He was not a suave lawyer or wealthy stockbroker. Nor was he a man whose preoccupation was fame and fortune. But he had touched both in former years as she had learned from the stories told around Port Moresby by those who knew and respected him. Yet here he was now, for all to the world a beach bum drifting in the tropics, in many ways like the Papuan natives themselves: a warrior and chief. He would definitely be a colourful character in her book, she thought, a kind of Jungle Jim. Or in this case, Jungle Jack. She smiled at the name she had coined for him.

Victoria was not a woman who believed in torrid affairs and she suspected that Jungle Jack was not a man who would entertain such notions either. But a wicked thought crept into her mind as she considered what it would be like to feel those muscled arms around her, his strong, capable hands touching her in places that only a lover would. Victoria rose and walked unsteadily past Lukas to her cabin, aware that her idle thoughts had gone too far. But she had nothing to fear as Jack had never even made a pass at her – in fact, she was almost a little annoyed that he had not. All they had shared were gentle, intelligent conversations above deck at night when she often experienced a strange feeling, as if he had the power to touch her soul and see inside her. She would be glad when the expedition was over and she was on the boat back to the States. Any longer in the Australian's company could cause her to lose her composure, maybe say something really stupid like, 'I think I could be falling in love with you, Jack Kelly.' All because she was growing to want him. At least she did not need him. She was a modern and independent lady with means.

He was a big man with a scarred face. The Dutch official stamping his papers noted that the man was an Australian citizen born in Ireland.

'Mr Farrell,' the Dutchman said as he passed back his papers. 'You may depart now.'

O'Leary stuffed the falsified papers that gave him possession of the schooner into his pocket. The Germans had been generous and the boat would remain his after he completed his mission in Papua. Needless to say he would sell the boat and pocket the money. The sea was not a place where he felt comfortable. He gazed around the port of Merauke searching for his crew of three men who he had recruited in the bars of the town in Dutch New Guinea – a mere fifty miles or so from the Australian-administered side of the island. Sweat streamed down his face to be diverted by the deep scars either side of his now clean-shaven face – scars that were a bitter reminder of a confrontation with a brash young Australian by the name of Kelly.

O'Leary had been contacted by a Eurasian of Dutch and Indonesian blood who worked in the postal service and was paid by the Germans to hand deliver mail posted to certain residents of the west New Guinea territory under the control of Holland. O'Leary was one of the names on the list and the man had scoured the bars of the town to find the Irishman and deliver the envelope to him. O'Leary had scowled as he read the contents. The Eurasian was pleased to leave the seedy bar and the evil dispositioned Irishman. Whatever was in the letter was of no concern to him.

It took some time to decipher the code. O'Leary had not seen it in over fifteen years, not since the war ended and his role as a spy for the Kaiser terminated. But it was obvious that his name had remained in the efficient German filing system to be reactivated by his new masters – the Nazis.

O'Leary had volunteered to work for German interests after the Easter Rising in Dublin during the war. He had been motivated not so much by patriotism for the cause of his cousins in Ireland but by the chance to earn extra money for grog and women. He knew that there were Irishmen working with the Germans to destabilise the British war effort just off the English coast. Not that he had to do much for the money, just provide the occasional bit of information on military matters that he came across whilst undertaking his recruiting tasks for Sen.

Unlike the German citizens who had fallen under Australian control after New Guinea was invaded at the beginning of the war, he had been able to move freely from New Guinea to Papua. Fifteen years later he was being reactivated – but this time to kill a man. He felt confident enough to get in quickly and leave just as fast. The man to be killed would most probably be staying at the Mann plantation, just down the coast from Port Moresby. The instructions in the coded letter spelled out everything he needed to know to complete his task; it was all too easy. The three men he had recruited were like himself, ruthless and very dangerous, the flotsam of European and Indonesian society living on the fringes of the law.

The idea of killing did not concern him in the slightest. But returning to Papua did. He suspected someone may have connected him to the disappearance of the Eurasian woman Iris, sister-in-law to a man who now hated him with a vengeance. O'Leary was smart enough to realise that Sen would just as happily have him killed as blink. Only the terrible fear of being exposed as a traitor to the Australians must have forced the Chinaman to seek him out for the job in Papua. Or was it some kind of elaborate trap to lure him back to an ambush? But to find him in Merauke could only have meant that Sen had been contacted by the Germans – as far as O'Leary knew, they were the only ones who had any idea where he was. The Irishman scowled as he swallowed the last drop of fiery schnapps.

His crew were late and when they eventually arrived they were hungover and surly. O'Leary snarled at them to board and waited for the captain of his schooner to come above decks from below, where he had been inspecting the auxiliary engine.

'Fuji, are we ready to get under way?' O'Leary asked when the young man appeared, stripped to the waist and wiping his oil-covered hands with a rag.

The Japanese man nodded. 'When you are ready, I am,' he replied in perfect English.

O'Leary grunted and turned his back on his young skipper. He had confidence in the Japanese sailor's abilities as his father Isokihi had chartered many expeditions along the Papua and New Guinea coasts with Fuji at his side. Fuji had grown up with Papuan water in his veins as well as a deep grudge against all Europeans – including O'Leary. But O'Leary had promised to pay him generously for an expedition that might include working beyond Australian law. Fuji had not hesitated in taking the charter as O'Leary had also agreed to sell him the schooner after the expedition was over for a good price.

On shore the Dutch official wiped his brow as he watched the schooner glide away from the wharf under the power of its engine. Turning to walk away, he wondered why the mad Irishman would hire three well-known cut-throats on a charter for the Torres Islands. They were definitely not sailors, but that was not his worry. The port of Merauke was not short of men one step beyond the law.

THIRTY-FOUR

Sydney was a pleasant surprise to Gerhardt. Although it was winter in the southern hemisphere, the weather seemed magnificent after the bitter chills of a European winter. The ship had steamed into a beautiful harbour fringed by little sandy beaches and yellow eroded rock inlets backed by scrub trees and houses. The great single span bridge was a bow tying the two shores of the harbour together.

Ilsa was wide eyed at the sights as the ship made its way up the harbour and even Erika was strangely quiet. They disembarked and Gerhardt let his wife be their guide – after all, she had lived here once before. She knew a pleasant hotel not far from the city centre. Soon after the suitcases were dropped on the separate beds, Erika went to the reception to place a telephone call.

'I have an appointment,' she said, applying lipstick when she was back in their room. Gerhardt knew he would be wasting his time to ask with whom. She had continued to remain aloof. At least she had paid their way and for that he was grateful. 'You will look after Ilsa while I am away.'

With her parting words, Erika closed the door behind her.

'Well, my little love,' Gerhardt sighed as he sat on the bed next to his daughter. 'What would you like to do?'

Ilsa knew exactly what she would like to do. She had always wanted to see a kangaroo and koala. It was just a matter of finding out how they could do this. Gerhardt was pleased to make inquiries at the reception desk where the amused clerk suggested Taronga Park Zoo. 'Not many left around Sydney anymore,' the man chuckled. 'At least I haven't seen any 'roos hopping around in Pitt Street lately.'

Gerhardt thanked the man in his heavily accented English and returned to tell Ilsa the result of his inquiry. He now felt as far from Germany as any man could be and comfortable enough to carefully plan his next move. He would make contact with the right people in government and hand over the damning evidence against the new German chancellor, Adolf Hitler. His old friend and colleague would have to answer to the Americans now. The esteemed German–Jewish scientist was presently at Princeton University in America and news of a file marking him for assassination would cause a furore. As well as the satisfaction of revenge, Gerhardt also expected a substantial reward from the Americans along with sanctuary. He no longer had any reason to keep up a pretence of going to Papua with Erika to meet her brother, nor spy on the Australian administration in the territory for his old masters. Whatever his wife chose to do with her life was her business alone – all he desired was custody of their daughter. He would approach the American consulate in Sydney with his proposal and evidence and the rest was in their hands. Erika could play her game of mysterious rendezvous as he played out his of international intrigue.

For a brief moment Gerhardt had a thought that his estranged wife may be going to see the father of her child. He did not know why he should think this but he felt a cold chill. What if she was and the man came to visit his daughter? So far Gerhardt had been able to convince the only person he truly loved that her mother had been lying to hurt them both when she said that he was not her real father.

When she opened the door to her harbourside mansion Caroline greeted Erika with genuine warmth. 'It is good to see you again after all these years,' she said, ushering her inside.

'You are expecting,' Erika commented. 'I must congratulate you.'

'I will have coffee sent to us in the garden,' Caroline said abruptly, and for a moment Erika thought she saw a dark cloud in her face. Was the pregnancy not going well, she wondered, to cause such a thinly veiled look of concern? She followed Caroline to the garden where all seemed to return to normality.

'Do you have any children?' Caroline asked when they were seated.

'I had Jack's daughter,' Erika answered honestly, as she knew that Caroline was already privy to that information. After all, that is why she had been encouraged to return to Germany.

'And are you married?' Caroline asked rather abruptly.

'I married when I returned to Munich,' Erika replied. 'Two months before my daughter Ilsa was born. Do you have any other children?' Erika asked quickly, to avoid any reference to Gerhardt.

Caroline shook her head.

'I did not want any children at all,' Erika said, gazing across the harbour. 'Ilsa was a mistake I will always regret.'

'Surely you cannot say that,' Caroline exclaimed. 'She is your daughter.'

'No, she is Jack Kelly's daughter, not mine.'

Caroline could not understand Erika's attitude to motherhood. Despite her promiscuous ways as a younger woman, she had always felt that strange urge to be a mother and had deeply resented her husband for initially failing her in the matter. Only the agreement that she could look elsewhere for a father to her child kept them together, not that Quentin would ever sanction any talk of divorce or separation. It was not the done thing in their social circles. 'I am hoping for a son,' she said to alter the mood of the conversation. 'Quentin is also.'

'I did not come here to talk of babies,' Erika said, changing the subject altogether. 'I need your help in a matter.'

Caroline glanced at Erika with a hint of suspicion. She had changed since they last met, she thought, and she sensed a very ruthless woman beneath the cool, dark beauty that still remained. 'What help do you require?' she asked guardedly.

'I need your husband to use his contacts to grant myself and my daughter British citizenship in this country.'

Caroline relaxed. Such a request was not difficult. Quentin had many contacts in the government. 'I can do that for an old friend,' she replied. 'Anything else? Citizenship for your husband?'

'No,' Erika said quietly. 'He is now on his own. I do not care if I ever see him again. We have never really been husband and wife.'

Somehow Caroline was not surprised at Erika's reaction. She was a truly selfish and self-centred woman. 'What will you do in this country?' she asked, more from curiosity than concern.

'I have plans . . . but I will tell you about them later,' she replied.

The coffee was brought to the garden and in the time it took to consume the pot the two women spoke of social matters as if the years had not existed between them. In many ways Caroline was pleased to see her again. She also had plans for her social life after she recovered from the birth of her child. Caroline was even a little amused to think that Erika was not aware of how much they shared. She wondered how she would have reacted to the knowledge that she was carrying Jack Kelly's baby.

In many ways dealing with the Americans felt very much like working back in his old office in Germany. A small, windowless room in a basement with little else than a table and chair. Even the two men who interviewed him reminded Gerhardt of Spier and Neumann: menacing, taciturn and suspicious of all he said. One was middle aged, grey and serious, and the other in his late twenties, sharp and fluent in German. Neither introduced themselves by name and Gerhardt guessed that they were no ordinary diplomatic staff. More like members of some very secret American organisation working as counter German intelligence agents. He had been wise to not bring the negatives; once the contents of the files were handed over he would be of no use to the Americans.

'We need to check out who you say you are, Mr Stahl,' the younger of the men said as his partner deliberately perched himself on the edge of the desk where Gerhardt was seated. It was a form of intimidation he knew was intended to unsettle him, but he had played this game before in Germany when he was the one questioning informants.

'I understand,' Gerhardt replied with a drier mouth than he thought was possible, despite his experience.

'But if you would leave us with the film you say you have,' the younger interrogator said, 'we would take that as an act of good faith.'

'You know as well as I that this cannot happen until we come to an arrangement,' Gerhardt said firmly. 'Then I can promise you information that may be vital to your national interests.'

The men glanced at each other. The one sitting at the edge of the desk shrugged. 'Leave an address, Mr Stahl, and we will be back to you in the future. In the meantime, you know where to reach us.'

Gerhardt was annoyed as he pushed his chair away and rose to leave. He even had a little sympathy for the people he had interrogated in a similar manner in the past.

'You wouldn't happen to know where I can see a koala and kangaroo outside a zoo by any chance?' he asked, bringing a puzzled look to the men's faces. 'No matter,' he shrugged. 'I will find them myself.'

Out on the Sydney streets he once again entered a pleasant world where the only worry people seemed to have was trying to make enough money to keep a roof over their heads and put food on the table. It was far from the dirty arena of international intrigue, where failure could mean the termination of a man's life. Maybe Sydney wasn't the safe place he thought. Australia had a substantial population of German immigrants that had come to the country over many decades. He was still not beyond the grasp of the Nazis and the idea of continuing to Papua was sounding better all the time if the Americans failed to be interested in his knowledge of the new German Reich.

•   •   •   •

Jacob Schmidt was young to be a secret agent. He spoke fluent German, as his parents had immigrated to the United States before the Great War. They had opposed the militarism of the Kaiser, putting their lives at stake. Growing up, Jacob was a true patriot of American democracy and enlisted in his country's service when he had graduated from university. Employed by J. Edgar Hoover's United States Federal Bureau of Investigation as an agent, he had been dispatched to Australia to secretly investigate the possible link between the fascists of Europe and a shadowy organisation in Australia called the New Guard, an organisation led by a former Australian military man named Eric Campbell.

Hoover had briefed him personally on his mission. Since the bloody riots in Washington brought on by a protest march of former soldiers from the Great War, the head of the US FBI had shown a personal interest in the rise of neofascist organisations. Not that the 'Bonus March', as the protest was known, had anything to do with fascism. Rather it had been a march by desperately poor men requesting a 'soldier's bonus' for service to their country in war. But it had sparked the federal agency director's concern that a body of men with formidable military experience had the potential to organise and use their martial skills against the government. The director had made it clear to Jacob that his mission to investigate and report on the Australian neofascist movement was not on record. To do so might upset the Australian government with perceptions of spying on a friendly nation. Jacob and his partner were to work from the American embassy under the guise of businessmen seeking market opportunities. When Gerhardt had made his contact with the Americans, Jacob had taken control of the interrogation.

'What do you think?' Jacob asked his partner. 'Think he is on the level?'

'If he has what he says he does then I think we need to take him seriously,' he replied. Bill Havers had been an experienced police officer in Chicago before he resigned over his disgust at the power the bootleggers had with his department. He had served in the war in France, including military intelligence experience. It was one of his old army contacts who had wrangled him the job in the FBI. He also spoke German, but not as fluently as his younger partner. 'I think we need to see if our friend had as much contact with the new German chancellor as he says. If he did, then I think we can parley again. In the meantime, we need to cable Washington.'

Jacob nodded. This Adolf Hitler was a man well worth keeping an eye on. He suspected that where the Kaiser had left off in 1918 Herr Hitler was planning to take up the sword. Jacob Schmidt did not just think that war was inevitable – he knew it, with all the certainty of a man who had Jewish relations in Germany. All the reports coming out of Germany had the political indicators of a dictatorship in the making, one geared for military supremacy of Europe.

When Caroline broached the subject of Erika over dinner Quentin grew angry.

'Why does she want British citizenship?' he demanded with a fork full of smoked salmon halfway to his mouth.

'I did not ask,' his wife replied sweetly. 'But I would like it if I could see her after our baby is born.'

Quentin placed the salmon back on his plate and wiped his mouth with a linen napkin. 'You must realise that I have substantial business interests in Germany,' he said as he toyed with the stem of his crystal goblet. 'It appears that your little toy may be a person who has upset the new government. And if that is so then I do not want to be seen aiding her in any way. To do so might put my interests at risk.'

Caroline could see her husband's point of view. She was vaguely aware that Quentin had made it discreetly known to German visitors that he would support Hitler as his fellow entrepreneurs in Germany already had. Although he considered the new chancellor a raving idiot, Adolf at least advantaged the powerful industrial class of Germany with whom Arrowsmith had strong contacts. It was agreed by all that Hitler would easily be controlled by them once he was in power. He had, after all, promised to curtail the labour unions and stamp out the threat of Bolshevic interference. Arrowsmith also knew that his quietly held opinions were shared by many powerful people in England. Hitler was just what Germany and Europe needed to provide a strong bastion against Stalin's Soviet Union.

'Well,' Caroline sighed as she sipped her wine. 'I will tell my little pet that you cannot help her. A pity,' she added. 'I was so much looking forward to sharing her with you.'

When Erika received a telephone call at the hotel from Caroline to explain the difficult circumstances, she slammed the phone down. Damn her, she thought. She would find someone else to support her claim for British citizenship. The need to do so was now a matter of life and death. Hitler was in power and she well knew the lengths his government would go to in the future to eliminate anyone they felt was the slightest threat to them. Since her husband had planted her name in the files she knew there was no going back, despite her innocence. Damn him for taking away all that she had gained with her body. He deserved the worst she could think of. She had always plotted her revenge but had fooled him for the moment into thinking she had changed. It was time to take from him the only thing he considered precious and worth dying for.

Erika had not planned on continuing her journey to Papua. But getting citizenship of a country not under German influence was not to be. Suddenly the thought of continuing their journey to Papua had a great appeal. Erika had been told by Caroline that Jack Kelly was in Papua – around the Port Moresby district, she'd been informed when she had casually asked of his whereabouts. Caroline also told her of Jack's rise to wealth in Sydney and his sudden financial collapse. Caroline had given Erika an enigmatic look when she had asked about Jack.

But Erika had an idea of why Jack Kelly would support anything she proposed.

THIRTY-FIVE

The *Erika Sarah* lay at anchor in the broad waters of the Fly River. With his son at the helm Jack had navigated through a maze of islands to a point Paul remembered as close to Serero's village. Joe Oblachinski's cameramen had been filming the river at intervals while Victoria was busy making notes in her journal. Joe himself had relaxed on deck, puffing on a fat cigar, which he also used as a pointer to direct his cameramen to specific shots. 'It would be a real bonus if we could get some of the natives to come out of the bush and fire some arrows at us,' he said to Jack. 'Got a few Tarzan movies in the works where it sure would be great background stuff.'

'Probably on the cards,' Jack said dryly, 'from what Paul says about O'Leary's activities in this part of the world.'

'Who's this O'Leary guy you mentioned?'

'Someone you wouldn't want to know,' Jack replied as he scanned the jungle-covered shoreline for a place to land the rowboat.

'Well, time to go ashore and see if we can make contact with this canoe builder your German friend has told us about,' Joe said launching himself to his feet.

'I will be coming too,' Victoria said as she emerged from below decks wearing her jodhpurs and a clean cotton shirt.

'Not a real good idea,' Jack grunted. 'We don't know what kind of reception we might get ashore.'

'Too bad,' the young American woman countered, staring Jack directly in the eyes. 'You are being employed by Joe and I have full rights to go wherever he chooses to.'

'Okay,' Jack replied and turned his back on her to prepare the small boat.

'Lukas, you remain with the *Erika Sarah*. Karl can come and issue arms.'

Lukas was disappointed that he was not going ashore, but he also realised that someone had to look after the lugger. Karl grinned at his friend standing at the helm as he took a .303 rifle handed to him. 'See you when I see you,' he said and glanced at Victoria who was stepping down into the rowboat at the side of the lugger. Two cameras were then carefully lowered and when all were aboard Jack and Karl took the oars while Paul stood at the rudder to steer. The river was running and after ten minutes of hard rowing they reached the shore. As soon as they stepped ashore the drums began to beat.

'Looks like we might get a few arrows sent our way after all,' Jack muttered within hearing of Joe Oblachinski, who only beamed a smile as he prepared another cigar. Jack had to admire the man. The humidity onshore was extreme, as was the heat, but the American seemed to take it all in his stride. Nevertheless, he was sweating profusely and the extra weight he carried around his midriff could not have helped in the jungle.

'This is exciting!' Victoria exclaimed. 'It's just like a Johnny Weismuller movie.'

Jack did not comment but checked the safety catch on his rifle. He was no expert on the meaning of the drums but hoped they were peaceful messages being passed up and down the river.

'The village was around a quarter mile from here,' Paul said, hefting his rifle over his shoulder. 'At least it was ten years ago.'

He stepped forward and the others fell in behind him. Victoria seemed to stay close to Jack and within a short time they had slashed a track to where Paul remembered the village to be. But the jungle had long reclaimed what had once been a place of habitation. Just a faint outline of the logs that had once supported thatch huts remained in a clearing of high grasses.

'What next?' Joe asked, with a note of disappointment.

'We just sit and wait,' Paul replied. 'It is the way of the people in this country to come to you.'

'How long?' Joe asked and Paul shrugged his shoulders.

'Who knows,' he replied. 'But we will wait until near sunset and if they have not made contact by then we will leave the box of trade goods for them. Then we can come back tomorrow and they will see that we have come to talk and not make war.'

They settled down in the shade of a great rain-forest giant that had stood long before the now deserted village had existed. Jack prepared a billy of tea and Karl opened cans of bully beef to be handed around as their meal for the day. Victoria took one look at the gooey pink meat melting in its own fat in the tropical heat and passed it to Malip who grinned his appreciation at the extra rations. The men ate from the cans with their fingers and waited whilst the smoke from Joe's cigar curled in lazy clouds in the still air of the clearing.

In the mid afternoon they came. 'God almighty!' Joe swore as he raised himself into a sitting position to stare at the fully armed warriors emerging from the tree line on the far side of the clearing. 'I didn't think that there would be so many!'

Paul stood and shaded his eyes with his hand. They were a formidable force with their bows and long, deadly barbed arrows. They stood in curious silence as if considering whether to string their bows and release a volley down on the white men. Jack released the safety catch on his rifle and glanced at Victoria to check that she was near him if it came to a fighting retreat back to the boat.

The seconds that ticked by were tense with fear for what might happen next. But at the front of the line of warriors with their bows and plumes was one man with a very battered pipe in his mouth. 'Serero!' Paul Mann called, hoping that he had identified a friendly face. 'Serero, is that you?'

The man with the pipe walked forward and burst into tears. It was indeed Serero the canoe builder and he was overjoyed to see that his long dead brother was once again visiting him in his old age. The two men met in the centre of the clearing to embrace and the warriors swarmed forward to surround the party.

Victoria was the centre of their attention. She had to remind herself that she was doing all this for her country as they poked and probed her to ascertain whether she was in fact a female. Jack stood very close by and watched for any sign of distress from her. She glanced at him and saw the concern in his face for her predicament but shook her head to indicate he was to do nothing for the moment. Reluctantly he stepped back.

Serero began his high warbling speech of welcome and warned his fellow warriors to give the white woman space to move. His dead brother had returned to give him tobacco for his pipe, as he knew he would. They obeyed and Paul handed out the few trade goods that he had brought to the clearing as the cameramen frantically worked their cameras to record the moment. These were a people whose exposure to Europeans was negligible. It would make for rare footage indeed, back in Hollywood.

'Malip, you tell Serero that our friends from across the sea have many such gifts for all of them if they will do some things for him,' Paul said and Malip translated as best as he could.

Serero understood and held Paul's hand in his as he nodded.

'Mr Oblachinski,' Paul said, 'we have been very lucky and I think you will get the finest footage for your friends in Hollywood that can be taken.'

Jack supervised the pitching of the camp. With Malip's help in translating he had some of the warriors return down the track and stores were ferried from the *Erika Sarah*.

Victoria was photographing the events and found herself snapping many of Jack as he stood in the clearing and went about the task of setting up a base for the American film-maker and his crew. He was stripped to the waist and his tanned and muscular body reflected his hard life. With his rifle slung over his shoulder and a revolver at his waist, he well and truly fitted the Jungle Jack title that Victoria had secretly bestowed on him. The sight of him working amongst the colourfully plumed warriors was uncomfortably attractive for her and she tried to dismiss the next thought that came to her: the two of them making love. She knew that to do so would be to make a commitment to this man whom she had already guessed was not willing to be taken from this savage yet beautiful world of warriors and jungles. She clicked off another photograph of Jack attempting to communicate his orders to a couple of bemused warriors carrying bows and stone axes and shook her head. 'Girl, what are you thinking?' she muttered to herself. Whatever it was, it was tinged with sweat and passion.

By nightfall the camp was set up and Karl had hiked back to relieve Lukas on his watch aboard the anchored boat. A fire was lit and the night sky filled with sparkling stars. A haunch of beef that had been kept in the refrigerated locker of the lugger was cooked in a camp oven with fresh vegetables and served with a few precious bottles of wine hoarded for the occasion. The sumptuous meal – by expedition standards – was washed down with good coffee and tea. There was soft laughter and risqué yarns spun about Hollywood celebrities under the sparkle of tropical stars until the rain came in a sudden, violent downpour, forcing all to the tents that had been erected in the late afternoon.

Victoria grabbed Jack by the hand as she sat by him on a log near the fire which was now sizzling under the weight of water. 'Quick,' she said with a laugh, 'we can get to my tent before we drown.'

Jack let her lead him and they both burst inside her tent drenched to the skin. She collapsed on her camp stretcher in the dark and Jack fumbled for the lantern which he found and lit. The soft light flooded the tent as the rain pounded the canvas and ran in little rivulets across the earthen floor. He hung the hurricane lantern on a post and wiped his face with his hands. 'Don't think we were very successful,' he said with a smile as he sat in a portable camp chair and gazed at Victoria stretched out on her bed.

'I do,' she answered quietly. 'I have you alone on a night when I doubt that anyone is going to come visiting.'

It took a second for the meaning of her reply to dawn on the tough Australian. He stared into her eyes and saw a strange softness that he had not noticed before. 'Victoria?' he asked, and she reached up to draw him down to her. Without further conversation she slowly undid the buttons of his shirt. He felt her lips on his and her tongue probe his mouth. Then she pulled him down on her and he felt the softness of her breasts against his chest. His head was spinning at the suddenness of events unfolding as the rain roared in his ears. He was barely aware of her whispered words but found that he was reacting, as she had wanted him to. His hands were inside her shirt and he found her nipples under his fingers, large and erect. Then he was kissing her back with the intensity of long concealed desire. But he was also tense for reasons he could not fathom. Yes, he admitted to himself, he had wanted her from the day he had laid eyes on the beautiful young woman stepping out of the car on the Moresby wharf.

'Are you sure?' he asked somewhat obtusely, and she smiled at his words. Any other man would have taken advantage of the opportunity she was providing.

'Of course I am sure,' she laughed softly. 'You are such a maddeningly desirable man, Jack Kelly.'

He felt himself relax and they undressed each other under the yellow glare of the lantern. Jack marvelled at her perfectly smooth skin while she touched the welts and raised skin where bullets and shrapnel had scarred his body. They told her so much about him: the pain he had suffered as a younger man in war and the way he had lived with the memories of another time. How many other women, she found herself wondering with just a touch of jealousy, had also touched those scars and felt his hard body covering theirs? But his kiss and his hands holding her face swept away the thoughts as she felt her arousal heighten. Very gently she lay back and spread her legs to allow him to become part of her. She gasped the moment she felt him enter her. Their lovemaking lasted until she was exhausted. He was like a wonderful, tireless machine. But in his intensity, she also experienced the great depths of his innate tenderness.

When they had finished she lay back and felt his kisses on her stomach, thighs and between her legs. The storm outside continued to rage and she felt so content that she fell asleep as he held her in his arms without any further words being spoken.

That night Victoria slept as soundly as she could ever remember. She only awoke when she smelt the earthy scent of damp wood burning and heard the low murmur of a camp coming to life in the early hours just on dawn. Jack had gone but this did not surprise her. She guessed that he was the kind of man who would not want their time together to be known to anyone but themselves.

But perhaps it had all been just a dream. As Victoria dressed she realised that she could still feel his wetness in her. Definitely no dream, she muttered to herself as she stepped from the tent into the rising and oppressive heat of another day in the tropics.

Jack was squatting by the fire with a mirror, cut-throat razor and some hot water. His face was lathered in soap as he prepared to shave and he glanced up at her with a gentle smile. She returned the smile and stepped from the tent entrance to pour a cup of steaming coffee from the pot that the cameramen were brewing to one side of the campfire. Only Lukas noticed the subtle exchange of looks and glowered his disapproval. He had seen his father going to Victoria's tent the night before and he had not returned to their tent for some hours. What could such a beautiful young woman see in an old man like his father? Lukas shook his head. He wondered whether he should tell Karl that they no longer had any reason to compete for the American girl's attention. But on the other hand, maybe Victoria would realise that she could have a much younger and more virile version of his father in him. It was not all over yet.

Lukas found an opportunity to corner his father later that morning as they walked back down the track they had cleared to the shoreline. 'It looks like you are a bit keen on that Yankee sheila,' Lukas said and Jack glanced at his son.

'What business is that of yours if I am?' Jack asked defensively.

'Just that I am your son and it's my duty to look after you,' Lukas said in a school master's voice. 'Dad, you are pretty old and you do not know about young women, like I do.'

Jack burst into a laugh that pealed through the steaming jungle. When he finished laughing he placed his hand on his son's shoulder. 'I suppose the

417

next thing you are going to do is give me a lecture on the birds and bees.'

Lukas reddened and tried to maintain a stern demeanour. This was no laughing matter and he did not want his father to get hurt – or worse, make a fool of himself. 'She is a lot younger than you, Dad,' he said in a strained voice. 'Modern women have different ideas to the ones you knew in the olden days.'

Jack could not help himself and commenced laughing again. 'How old do you think I am?' he finally asked. 'A hundred?'

'This is serious, Dad,' Lukas protested. 'I love you and don't want you to get hurt.'

'Or is it that you feel Victoria is more suited to you?' his father responded light heartedly. 'Even if she is an older woman?'

Lukas cast his father a pitying look. 'That was never on my mind,' he lied. 'It's just that she will be returning to the United States after we return to Moresby.'

The jovial expression on Jack's face rapidly faded. 'I know,' he said quietly, and Lukas sensed that his father was truly aware of the impossible situation that existed in such an affair. But he also hated to acknowledge that he was also frightened that Victoria might come between them. A part of Lukas was beginning to resent the beautiful American and in his dark thoughts was the savage consolation that within a short time events would sweep her from their lives. No, his father did not know what was best for him, he thought. He would be more than happy to see the back of Miss Victoria Duvall.

• • •

Fuji stood at the wheel of the schooner and gazed up at the canvas flapping in the light breeze. The strong winds appeared to have been replaced with little more than a gentle zephyr playing in the tops of the boat's twin masts.

'What the bloody hell is going on?' O'Leary yelled at him from below decks. 'We don't seem to be moving.'

'Wind is down,' Fuji yelled back. 'We will have to go to the engine if we want to continue.'

Fuji did not like O'Leary. In fact the young Japanese sailor did not like any Europeans – or any other race for that matter. He held a grudge about the way his people had been viewed by the west as inferior because they were Oriental. And he was very aware of the way the Europeans in Papua regarded him as something from the *Mikado,* a joke. Well, the recent invasion of China by the Emperor's armies had taken some of the mirth out of the way men like O'Leary and others viewed the Japanese nation. And had they not beaten the mighty Russian empire only thirty years earlier at Port Arthur?

O'Leary appeared on deck in a foul mood. Earlier he had been drinking with his men and had to discipline one of them for insubordination by beating the slightly built Eurasian half to death with his fists then kicking him in the face breaking his jaw. The show of brutal force had its effect and the other two hired men did not dare question the big Irishman's authority again with their surliness. But mostly O'Leary was in a foul mood because the coded telegram from Sen that was meant to be delivered to the Thursday Island post office had not arrived. It was supposed to give the time and date when the target was to arrive at the Mann plantation so that he could do the job and claim his financial reward for services rendered to Berlin. And now they were stuck, becalmed in the Gulf of Papua en route to the Moresby district. 'How long do you think the wind will be down?' he growled at Fuji, who still stood behind the big spoked wheel of the schooner's rudder.

'Who knows,' Fuji shrugged. 'Only the spirits of the sea have the answer to that.'

'You talk pretty good English for a Jap,' O'Leary said belligerently in Fuji's face. 'Where did you learn to speak so good?'

'Mission school in Papua,' Fuji replied, not intimidated by the larger man whose breath stank of whisky. 'What about you?'

It took a second for the Irishman to comprehend that the Japanese was insulting him but when he did he saw red. For a moment Fuji thought O'Leary might attempt to hit him, but his insolence had been a test. Fuji wanted to ascertain just how much power he had as skipper of O'Leary's schooner. He was not afraid of the bigger man. He knew his own skill with the razor sharp knife tucked in its sheath at his hip. The Irishman glared at him with eyes reddened by drinking and unclenched his fist. He too had realised the Japanese skipper's motives.

'Smart arse for a Jap,' he muttered and stormed away.

Fuji felt the sweat on his hands despite his show of bravado. It could have gone against him. But at least now he knew that for the moment he was immune from the Irishman's unpredictable bouts of rage. He gazed up again at the sails that now lay limply against the masts and sighed. The spirits of the sea were not on their side. He wanted to get the mission over so that he could take possession of the schooner then sell it for a ticket to a country he had never visited. And when he stepped foot on the soil of his ancestors he would enlist in the Japanese navy. He did not want to miss out on the glorious future of a land he knew only from his father's stories when he was growing up in Papua under the oppressive heel of the hated Europeans. The land of his ancestors was destined to rule Asia and one day he would return to Papua and wipe the sneering smiles from the faces of the Australians. But for now he was on a mission to kill a European and that was satisfying in itself. He knew the Mann family personally and remembered how he had lost face in front of his father that day on the beach at the plantation. When he had returned to the coastal trader his father had refused to speak to him. He had been shamed in his defeat at the hands of the barbarians and blamed his son for that. So this mission was a personal vendetta and Fuji prayed to the ancestors that Karl Mann would be on the plantation when they struck from the sea. Then he would settle his score permanently and his father would once again hold his head high.

THIRTY-SIX

Gerhardt felt a chill of apprehension when he returned to his hotel from a sightseeing trip around Sydney Harbour with Ilsa. The two American agents were waiting in the foyer and for a moment Gerhardt was reminded of a Hollywood film about Chicago gangsters.

'Ilsa, go to the room,' he said quietly to his daughter. 'I will be up soon.'

The two men moved forward to meet him when Ilsa left.

'Mr Stahl,' Jacob Schmidt said in German. 'We would like to talk to you somewhere less public.'

Gerhardt could not detect any menace in the young American's tone and relaxed just a little. 'Do you mean your office?' he asked.

'I think that you should tell your daughter that you have to go out for a short time,' Jacob said. 'Oh, don't worry,' he added when he noticed the expression of fear that flitted across Gerhardt's face. 'This is not Germany. It's just that we needed time to make some inquiries about you. Our questions have been answered and we are ready to talk.'

Gerhardt glanced at the young man's companion but could detect no malice in his demeanour. Either they were very good actors or they were genuinely friendly, he thought. Whichever way it went he knew he had little choice but to comply with their directions.

When he went to the hotel room and spoke to Ilsa, the Americans did not follow him but remained downstairs. Another good sign. If they had meant him harm then they would have not let him out of their sight. This was definitely not Germany, he reassured himself.

'Did you get to see a kangaroo?' Jacob asked when Gerhardt returned to the foyer. Gerhardt cast him a quizzical look until he remembered his question at their first meeting four days earlier.

'No, I am afraid that I have not as yet,' he replied as he walked with the two men to the street.

'I understand that you first met Adolf Hitler just after the war,' Jacob began when they were out of earshot of passers-by. 'We would like to know as much about him as possible and have been led to believe that you may be the man to help us. We also understand that your wife was intimate with many high ranking Nazi officials and could also be of assistance.'

The unexpected mention of Erika sharply brought her back into Gerhardt's life again. He had not seen or heard from her since their first day in Sydney but this did not surprise him. After all, she had lived in Sydney before and no doubt had friends. 'I am sorry, gentlemen,' Gerhardt apologised, 'but I do not know where my wife is.'

Bill Havers glanced at his younger partner with an expression of surprise. 'A bit odd that you do not know where your wife is, Mr Stahl,' he said. 'I thought you would be concerned for her whereabouts.'

'We do not have a normal marriage,' Gerhardt replied. 'My wife does as she likes.'

Jacob frowned. The information he had received from Germany had failed to mention the estrangement and he did not like to be in the dark. 'You mentioned in our first meeting that you had film of a file kept by the people you worked for that was of a national interest to America. Do you think that you would be prepared at this stage to share that information?'

As they strolled casually along the city street like friends involved in a conversation, stopping to cross the road as they approached Hyde Park, Gerhardt considered his words. 'I think that the information warrants your government providing me and my daughter with sanctuary in America. With that goes a ticket for us both to sail as soon as possible for the United States.'

'Give us a sample of what you have and we will give you an answer,' Havers said.

'Do you know of the physicist Albert Einstein?' Gerhardt questioned, knowing the name would get their attention.

'Of course,' Jacob replied. 'Who doesn't?'

'His name is on a list for assassination should he ever return to Germany. Failing that, he is to be eliminated wherever he is if Germany ever becomes involved in a war with America.'

'You can prove this?' Havers asked and Gerhardt nodded. 'Jesus,' the American breathed. 'Einstein is planning to return to Germany this year.'

'Better that he does not,' Gerhardt cautioned, 'or he will have an accident.'

'Give us the proof and you will get your ticket to America on the first boat out of here,' Jacob said as they entered the expansive parklands at the heart of Sydney.

'You will have it,' Gerhardt concluded.

He turned to walk back to his hotel. All he had was his trust in the two men. But already he was learning that there were still places outside Germany where trust was more than just a word. And after all, he had split the film so that they received negatives of only half the files – the other half was his insurance. The Americans would need the complete file to make sense of the fragment they would be given.

When Gerhardt went to his room Ilsa was not there, unusual for his normally obedient daughter. Noticing with growing alarm that all her personal possessions were missing as well, he went immediately to the foyer.

'My daughter is not in our room,' he said to the man at the desk. 'Have you seen her?'

'It's all right, Mr Stahl,' the man behind the desk replied. 'Your wife came and picked her up.

She left a message that she would contact you a bit later.'

Gerhardt felt his alarm turn to a sickening dread. He had not seen Erika in days and suddenly she comes to the hotel when he is occupied and takes their daughter?

'Did she leave an address or telephone number I could contact her?' he asked.

The man frowned. 'Come to think of it she didn't, sir. Just said she would contact you, that's all.'

Gerhardt felt ill. Something was terribly wrong. But he had no one in this foreign land who he could turn to. Never before had he felt so alone. Worse still was a small fear that was growing by the moment that the dangerous tentacles of the Nazi party had already reached across the ocean to seek him out.

Quentin Arrowsmith was reluctant to get himself tangled in international politics, but the approach that came through one of his German business contacts had been persuasive. At least, his threat of discontinuing business with Quentin's company agents in Germany had been persuasive. The new chancellor was promising a prosperous nation for the industrialists and the Arrowsmith companies had a branch office in Berlin to promote his enterprises. All he had to do to placate his persuasive visitor from the German embassy was convince Erika Stahl to have her husband continue his journey to Papua.

• • •

Gerhardt waited less than a day before Erika knocked on the door of their hotel room. She stood before him with dark shadows under her eyes. Her face reflected days of concern and nights of little sleep.

'Where is my daughter?' Gerhardt asked abruptly, ignoring her distress.

Erika pushed her way past him and slumped into a chair. 'They know that you stole a very sensitive file,' she said. 'And they have Ilsa.'

'Who is "they"?' Gerhardt asked as he closed the door.

'The Nazis have many sympathisers in this country. Your old boss Spier was able to link me with an Australian who arranged to place Ilsa in his care until you return the file that is missing.'

'What file?' Gerhardt bluffed.

'The one that you are planning to give to the Americans.'

'How do you know about the Americans?' A pretence of ignorance was futile, he now realised.

'I know and that's all you have to know,' she replied.

A naval liaison officer from the German embassy had overheard a conversation at a cocktail party about the presence of two FBI men in town. The matter was of great interest when passed on to German intelligence as they knew that the Americans were not permitted to spy on their friends across the Pacific. From then on, German counter intelligence had assigned a shadow team to the American agents. The meeting of Gerhardt and the American agents was noted, and it had not been hard for the German agents to trace Erika. At a rendezvous in a café they had easily turned her with promises of redemption. She had wanted acceptance back into the party fold and the offer to pay her as an agent in foreign lands was welcomed by her. It meant being financed to continue what she was good at – sex and intrigue. Erika was briefed on the current situation concerning her estranged husband. It was reassuring for her to be told as much. What was important, however, was that Erika convince Gerhardt that he must continue his journey to Papua. The operation to kill him had been put in motion from far off Berlin and for his death to take place far from the spotlight of the Australian newspapers would mean even less attention to the whole matter. Papua was, after all, a frontier where such things as violent death could be taken for granted.

'Where is Ilsa?' Gerhardt asked.

'They will tell us when you hand over the file to a man in Papua, at my brother's plantation there,' Erika answered, feigning distress. 'Then you can have Ilsa back.'

Gerhardt did not want to believe that his wife was involved in a conspiracy, but her taking of his daughter from him and something in her last words made him think that she was very much part of a plot. 'If anything should happen to my daughter then I will come looking for you,' he said calmly. 'Make no mistake in thinking that I would not kill you.'

Erika stared at him with a mixture of pity and contempt. It did not matter that he believed that she was a part of Ilsa's pseudo abduction. She knew that her daughter was staying with the Arrowsmiths and would come to no harm, but Gerhardt did not know that. It had been Quentin Arrowsmith himself who had contacted her to set up the meeting with the German agents in the café. He had done his part to retain his German industrial contacts in Berlin and the rest was up to Erika.

'You can threaten me as much as you want,' she retorted, 'but the bottom line is that the file must not go to the Americans or anyone else other than the man who is to meet you in Papua.'

It was obvious to Gerhardt that his wife did not know the file had been photographed and the original papers burned in the fireplace. What concerned him was that even Australia was not safe anymore. He doubted that the two Americans who had kept in contact with him would be interested in continuing talks if he did not have the contents of the file to corroborate his story. He had to weigh the outcomes of his decision: to continue to Papua and comply with the Nazis' demands most probably meant he would see Ilsa again. They would not harm a child on foreign soil if they could avoid it. To deal with the Americans meant losing the only person he had grown to love.

'I will go to Papua,' he said after a moment of indecision. 'But I have no proof that you and they will honour the bargain.'

'I have no use for Ilsa,' Erika said coldly. 'You can have her back as soon as I receive confirmation that you have handed over the file and not made any deals with the Americans.'

'Do you know what is in the file?' he asked.

'I was not told and I do not care,' she answered. 'I will be staying on in Australia.'

'So you have my old job,' Gerhardt smiled without humour. 'Gathering intelligence against British interests in Australia.'

Erika did not react to his accusation but Gerhardt knew he was right. Somehow she must have struck a deal with the new government in Berlin to work for them in exchange for betraying him. She must be less than human to use her own daughter to achieve her own selfish means, he mused, wondering how he could have ever loved her. Worse still, he wondered at how easily she had fooled him just before they left Germany. She was far more dangerous than any man he knew.

'You will get your way,' he conceded quietly. 'But I will keep my promise if anything happens to Ilsa.'

'She is safe,' Erika reiterated, walking to the door. 'So long as the file is returned to Berlin.'

Gerhardt was in a terrible quandary. He had just sentenced himself to a life on the run if he could not obtain refugee status outside of the grasp of the Nazis. Maybe he could save Ilsa by going on to Papua but he also knew he might not live to see her grow to be a young woman.

He sat on the bed and stared at the walls of the hotel room. After a time he roused himself and wrote a long letter, addressing it to Erika's brother in Papua. At least in time Ilsa would know the truth. In the letter he confessed that he was not her biological father, not that it had mattered to him. Her real father, he wrote, was a former Australian soldier called Jack Kelly, who was, he had since learned, a friend of her uncle, Paul Mann. Erika had let the relationship between the two men slip during a conversation they had on the voyage to Australia. At first the knowledge worried Gerhardt but now he wrote that if anything happened to him Ilsa was to seek out her real father through her uncle. Gerhardt hoped that at least he would have some concern for the young girl who was part of his own flesh and blood, even if her mother did not.

Gerhardt knew that his only real alternative was to once again work with the Americans. Oh yes, he would deliver the file to the contact in Papua. But first he would make a deal with the agents to seek out his daughter, using every means at their disposal. For that he would give them not only a copy of the file but also the name of an agent working in Australia. Erika was not as smart as she thought. If she had not used their daughter to achieve the aims of her masters in Berlin, then it may have been a different matter. In a way it was a satisfying and bitter revenge for the years of humiliation he had suffered at her hands. No doubt the Americans would pass on to the Australian government the information that they had an active Nazi agent in their country. And no doubt that would lead to others if they did their work properly. It was strange how circumstances had forced him into the camp of his former enemies.

Gerhardt finished the letter and sealed it. Now it was time to make contact with the Americans. But he knew that he must be very careful. He assumed now that he was being watched. First he must go to Martin Place to the General Post Office and send the letter to Papua.

THIRTY-SEVEN

Timing would be all-important. But O'Leary still had not been given a time to strike. All that followed the original coded letter from Papua was a complete silence; no letter indicating the arrival of the German Gerhardt Stahl had been sent to Thursday Island. O'Leary had wasted a week before giving up and sailing north into the Gulf of Papua only to be becalmed. The Irishman fumed about the breakdown in communications as he stood on the deck of his schooner and waited for a wind to move them on a northeast bearing to the Port Moresby district. A niggling suspicion began to eat away at him. He knew that Sen hated him enough to kill him if the opportunity arose. Was he was being set up in an elaborate ambush?

'Fuji!' he bellowed from the bow. 'How far are we from Moresby?'

The Japanese sailor did not have to refer to a chart to answer. He knew these waters like the back of his hand. 'Forty-eight hours if we get a wind.'

'Use the bloody engine,' O'Leary commanded. 'Just get us there in forty-eight hours.'

Fuji went to protest. Using the engine would quickly consume their limited supply of fuel. But he shrugged and decided to obey. Hopefully they would not use all the fuel before the winds returned.

Within minutes the schooner was again under way and a few hours later they were fortunate to pick up a good breeze. O'Leary was not a patient man. If he was being lured into a trap by Sen, he wanted to know. Or perhaps the Chinaman had fallen silent for reasons known only to himself. The Irishman had not survived for so long on caution alone. Sometimes it paid to make the first move. The Mann plantation was on a secluded part of the coastline and a strike from the sea would be the best way to achieve his ends.

Joe Oblachinski was more than satisfied with the footage that he had been able to film. Serero had coordinated the mock battles but some blood had still been spilled in the enthusiasm of the warriors to show off their prowess, although fortunately none of them had been killed when the arrows flew. It was in the can, as Joe said, and he was ready to pack up and return to Port Moresby.

Jack Kelly was puzzled at Victoria's apparent avoidance of him after the wonderful night they had shared. It was as if nothing had happened. He tried to convince himself that the night of passion had been brought on by the excitement of making contact with Serero's clan and was not to be repeated. He would be wise to dismiss her from his life. But as much as he tried to forget her, Victoria haunted his thoughts. He reacted to her seeming indifference with his own but found that he had to restrain himself from displaying any sign of emotion when he noticed his son and Victoria flirting with each other. Well, easy come, easy go, he told himself.

'Got everything aboard?' Paul asked as he stood at the stern pondering the beautiful and intriguing young American woman.

'Yeah,' Jack answered absent-mindedly and sighed. 'Time to head back.'

Paul left his friend standing alone and staring vacantly into the brown swirling water at the river mouth. He sensed Jack's preoccupation but did not suspect that it was about a particular woman. In all the years he had known Jack, though, he had never seen the man looking so gloomy. Even during the toughest of times when they had gone in search of gold in the Morobe province years earlier, Jack would remain calm and cheerful in the worst of situations. Although things were going well for Jack's first charter, his friend was noticeably a different man to the Jack Kelly who had set out on this trip.

'Ready to pull up the anchor?' Paul asked Lukas as he scrambled across the top of the lugger to the cockpit.

'Ready to sail,' Lukas replied with a grin. He had grown so comfortable with the *Erika Sarah* that it now felt like a part of his own body. The anchors were weighed and the lugger pulled out into the channel under the power of her auxiliary engine. Once she was in the channel the sails were unfurled and the lugger was set on her course back to Moresby.

After supper Victoria left the men to go above decks where Jack was at the helm, guiding the lugger through the gently rolling tropical seas. She knew that the next morning they would be berthing in Port Moresby and within days she would be on a ship back to Australia and then en route to the United States. She watched the Australian standing behind the great polished timber wheel, a glowing cigar clamped between his teeth. It had been sent up to Jack earlier by Joe from his store of fine Havanas to celebrate the end of a successful expedition.

'Thought you would be with the boys celebrating,' Jack said mildly when Victoria appeared in the cockpit.

'I thought that you might like some company since your watch has denied you the pleasures of Joe's stories and whisky.'

'I'm sure that Joe will pay enough to buy one or two bottles for me to celebrate when we reach Moresby in the morning,' Jack replied. He puffed on his cigar which was being rapidly whittled away by the stiff night breeze.

'You have said very little to me since we spent that night together,' Victoria said. 'I was wondering why.'

Jack took the cigar from his mouth and gazed into the velvet depths of the night. The stars had disappeared behind a heavy cloud cover and apart from the lantern swinging beside him, they seemed alone to the rest of the world. 'Didn't think it meant much to you,' he said, softly enough for his words to be almost swept away by the wind. 'You head back to the United States soon to make your report and write your book. But I promise you that I will be the first Aussie to buy a copy when it comes to Papua.'

'I . . .' Victoria was at a loss to say something that would make sense to not only him but also to herself. She glanced away, staring into the same darkness that held Jack's gaze.

'I think you will write a great yarn,' Jack said gently. 'You are truly the most extraordinary woman that I have ever met.'

Victoria turned to him, her face an enigmatic mask. 'I just wanted you to know that I will never forget that night. I . . .' she choked on her words and turned away lest he see the depth of feelings she was so desperately trying to suppress. 'I think I should go back and join the party.'

Victoria made her way down to the cabin where the bottles were almost empty and the drinkers mostly full. Even Paul had imbibed more than usual and both Lukas and Karl were already feeling the nauseating effects of too much strong liquor. They hardly noticed Victoria as she passed by them to go to her cabin.

With the door closed she fell on the bunk and stared at the low ceiling. What was it about Jack Kelly that preoccupied her? She knew time was running out. Soon they would be in Port Moresby and shortly after that Jack Kelly would no longer be a part of her life except as the main character in her book.

At the helm Jack watched the compass shifting in its glass dome as the boat rose and fell against the sea. South on the horizon a tiny light was also rising and falling. He knew it must be another boat – any village lights would have been on the landward side to the north – but this was not unusual as many boats used these waters. Little did he know that Tim O'Leary was at the helm of his schooner and had also noticed a boat's light to his north. And like Jack Kelly, he did not think the sighting of any significance either.

As he stood in Gerhardt's hotel room Jacob Schmidt examined the grainy photographs, handing each one on to his partner Bill Havers. Gerhardt sat in a chair in the corner of the room, waiting patiently for their reaction.

'We will need you to corroborate the authenticity of what we have here,' Bill Havers said as he passed the photographs of the stolen files back to Jacob.

'You will have that,' Gerhardt replied in a tired voice. 'As soon as I complete my deal with the Nazis.'

'You realise that if you go to Papua you may be travelling to your death,' Jacob pointed out sympathetically. 'As far as the new German government is concerned, you are a traitor and therefore can expect no mercy at their hands.'

'At least what they do on Australian territory will be considered murder,' Gerhardt answered bitterly, 'no matter how the German government tries to justify my death.'

Jacob glanced at his partner. They had worked together long enough to understand what such a look meant. 'We would rather you did not make the appointment in Papua but returned with us to the States to assist in our future investigations.'

Gerhardt realised that the American's offer was not motivated by any humane concern but rather by the value of what he knew, but it was reassuring in any case. 'My daughter is more important to me than my life,' he said. 'If there were any way I could get her back other than honouring my pact with my former government, then I would.'

A slow smile developed on Bill Havers' battered face. 'I think we can do that,' he said and Gerhardt glanced at him sharply.

'How? I have no idea where my daughter is.'

'Jacob and I have been involved in a discreet investigation into a group here called the New Guard. It has worried Uncle Sam because it seemed to be somewhat similar to Mussolini's Fascist party and your Nazis in Berlin. Along the way we have had the cooperation of the Australian government in information sharing. They are also concerned. The organisation is made up of former military men who could possibly provoke a civil war in this country. So far we cannot find any links with Hitler or Mussolini, but one thing we have discovered is a New Guard link with one or two prominent businessmen. Our counterparts in the Australian government have been keeping track of your wife's movements. We know where your daughter is.'

Gerhardt leapt from his chair and crossed the room to Havers. 'Why did you not tell me before? Is she safe and well?' he demanded. 'When can I go and take her back?'

'As soon as you agree to return to the States with us.'

'You have my agreement. Where is my daughter?'

'Not far from here, Mr Stahl,' Jacob said. 'We can make contact with our Australian friends and arrange for the appropriate people to come with us.'

Quentin Arrowsmith was outraged by the intrusion of a couple of burly New South Wales policemen into his house at one o'clock in the morning.

'We have reason to believe that there is a young German girl here by the name of Ilsa Stahl, sir,' the uniformed sergeant said as he stood over Quentin who wore only his dressing gown.

'You realise who I am, Sergeant?' Arrowsmith replied. 'If so you must realise that I have friends in government.'

'That may be, Mr Arrowsmith,' the big sergeant said, unfazed. 'But as I understand it these couple of Yanks with me are acting with the government in this matter. The Premier's department personally informed me this evening that I was to act on their behalf in this matter.'

Quentin glanced past the policeman to the two men dressed in grey suits standing in his foyer. One was young with an intelligent expression whilst the other was a tough looking older man whose face spoke of rugged times. Behind them he could see another man who he guessed to be in his early forties. He looked worried, not like a police or government officer.

Outraged as he was, Arrowsmith was not about to involve his name in any public scandal. He had done all that was asked of him and handing over Ilsa was of no great concern. 'Ilsa is a guest in this house, Sergeant,' he said. 'But if you have the authority to take her with you then I will not stand in your way.'

'I thank you for your cooperation, sir, and apologise for disturbing you at this hour of the morning. Now if you could fetch the young lady we will let you all get back to bed.'

Quentin led the men upstairs to a bedroom, opened the door and turned on the light. Ilsa stirred under the blankets, then sat up and blinked at the fuzzy picture slowly focusing before her. The first face she saw was that of her father. 'Papa!' she cried out as Gerhardt swept her up in his arms. 'Mama said that you had gone back to Germany and that I would never see you again.'

By his daughter's innocent words Gerhardt knew that Papua had been a trap. 'I would never leave you, my little love,' he said with tears in his eyes. 'You and I are going to America with these nice men. You will get to meet Shirley Temple and all the other movie stars.'

'Where is Frau Stahl?' Jacob asked Arrowsmith outside the bedroom.

Quentin did not ask the young American to identify himself and would be glad when they were all gone from his house. But his reply was prompt. 'Mrs Stahl is currently at the hospital with my wife. And I would suggest that you don't go bothering either one of them at the moment as my wife has gone into labour.'

Jacob frowned at the aristocratic looking Australian. 'Thank you for your help, Mr Arrowsmith,' he replied and turned his back on the man in disgust.

When they left the Arrowsmith mansion Gerhardt suddenly remembered his letter to Papua. Now that he was safe with the Americans and had Ilsa back, there had been no need to send it. But what would happen when Erika's brother received the letter and read its contents? He reassured himself it would not matter as he and Ilsa would be well and truly on their way across the Pacific Ocean to their new home in the United States of America. Even if this Jack Kelly – if he was still alive after all these years – did learn that he was the real father of Ilsa, there was little he could do.

THIRTY-EIGHT

It was mid morning when Fuji ordered the anchor to be dropped in the picturesque bay. O'Leary scanned the shoreline and noted the layout of buildings. He had the semblance of a plan but knew that he required a reconnaissance to ensure that all went smoothly. 'You think that you could go ashore and have a look around without anyone getting suspicious?' he asked the Japanese sailor.

'They would not suspect me,' Fuji said. 'I can ask them if they have any fuel to spare for the boat.'

'Good. Take one of the boys with you.'

There was nothing else to do until Fuji returned with his report. The Irishman went below to break out the guns.

• • •

The *Erika Sarah* glided to a stop beside the wharf in Port Moresby behind a Burns Philp steamer. Lukas was at the helm and Jack leapt onto the wharf to tie the ropes. When they were secured Lukas cut the engine and Jack helped his passengers disembark. Last to leave was Victoria. Jack held out his hand to her to assist as she climbed onto the wharf. Her hand felt soft and warm in his and for a moment he felt the pain of losing her from his life.

'What are you planning to do now?' she asked as they stood together.

'Try and rustle up another charter or some cargo work,' Jack said.

'I mean what are you going to do today?'

'We'll leave the boat here and travel back to Paul's place in his truck.'

Victoria glanced away so Jack would not see her expression of disappointment. She had hoped that he might stay around until she caught her boat south to Australia. 'I guess we should make our farewells now then,' she said.

Jack held out his hand. 'It was a pleasure knowing you, Miss Duvall,' he said. 'I know all will go well for you.'

'Is that it?' Victoria glared. 'A brief handshake and the best of wishes?'

'What else could there be?' Jack asked with just a hint of pain in his voice. 'You are a lady destined for important things back in your world of concrete and tall buildings. Me? Well, you have seen my world.'

'I suppose you are right,' Victoria sighed. 'Well, I'll be seeing you, Jack.' She turned and walked down the wharf into the crowd of natives and Europeans.

Jack watched her leave. Never before had he felt so alone. He wanted to stop her reaching the end of the wharf, but he wasn't sure enough that she would want to explore what they may have felt about each other.

'Dad?' Jack was hardly aware that Lukas was now standing beside him. 'Are you okay?'

'Yeah, I'm okay,' Jack sighed. 'Why shouldn't I be?'

'Just asking,' Lukas said with a shrug. 'I was under the impression that you were a bit keen on Victoria.'

Jack glanced at his son. 'Put it this way, son,' he said. 'If we ever rename the *Erika Sarah* we can call her the *Victoria Sarah*. Maybe that answers your question.'

Lukas wanted to comfort his father but knew this was not the time. 'Uncle Paul is going into town to pick up the truck. He says that he can finish up with Joe for you.'

'That would be good,' Jack said. Victoria was now out of sight and out of his life. 'Maybe his brother-in-law from Germany has arrived while we have been at sea.'

Jack could not bring himself to mention Erika's name. He had not thought about her until now. A woman he had grown to know and feel so strongly about had just left his life and another he had once loved and lost was possibly in Moresby at the moment. Life certainly had a way of weaving complicated knots.

'Uncle Paul said he was going to ask the shipping clerk if Mr Stahl and his wife had arrived while he was out picking up the truck,' Lukas said. 'In the meantime, I'll grab a few things off the lugger to take to the plantation. It will be great to see Aunt Karin again.'

'Yeah,' Jack replied hollowly. 'Should be one hell of a day.'

Fuji was met on the beach by Dademo who had watched the unfamiliar schooner enter the bay. When he recognised the young Japanese sailor he greeted him with a grudging, wary familiarity. The violent incident on the beach some months earlier was still fresh in his memory.

'Why are you here?' Dademo asked as he helped bring the dinghy onto the sand. 'And whose boat is that out in the bay?'

As Fuji climbed out of the dinghy, Dademo eyed his companion with suspicion. From the stranger's appearance he was likely from the Dutch side of New Guinea. He was a surly, evil looking character who carried a curved knife in his belt. The man said nothing but returned Dademo's appraisal with an expression of contempt. The stranger was at least half-European and it was obvious to Dademo that he looked down on people of full blood as inferior. Fuji did not bother to introduce his companion.

'Mr Mann up at the house?' he asked, ignoring Dademo's questions. 'I am low on fuel for the schooner's engine. Thought he might have some spare for sale.'

'Master Paul not here,' Dademo replied. 'Only his missus.'

Fuji looked sharply at the plantation boss boy. 'Where is Mr Mann?' he asked.

'Gone with Mr Jack Kelly on a trip up the Fly River with some movie people,' Dademo replied as the three men walked up the beach towards the house. 'Not sure when he will be back but it should be pretty soon.'

'So it's only you and Mrs Mann looking after things then,' Fuji said casually, glancing around at the native labourers busy at work in the packing sheds and coconut groves. Too many questions might arouse the boss boy's suspicions and he did not underestimate either Dademo's intelligence or his loyalty. He also knew that asking about guests from Germany might arouse just enough suspicion to put Dademo on full alert. There were enough villagers working around the plantation armed with their traditional bows and arrows as well as steel axes and knives to make any operation risky if they turned on himself and his companion. They had not come armed with firearms. But he had enough information to take back to O'Leary.

Dademo arranged for a small drum of fuel and Fuji paid him. Bidding Dademo farewell, he took the drum down to the boat at the beach. Dademo watched the two men row back to the schooner anchored in the bay. He frowned and shook his head as he turned to walk back to the packing sheds. Maybe he was just being overcautious, but something about the Japanese sailor made his skin crawl.

Dademo had never liked him. Fuji had a reputation for being a young man with a chip on his shoulder.

'There was no mention of any visitors staying at the house,' Fuji briefed O'Leary aboard the boat. 'Just Mann's wife.'

O'Leary stared in silence out the porthole.

'What are you going to do?' Fuji asked to break the silence.

'We are going ashore tonight when the kanakas go back to their village,' O'Leary growled. 'I haven't come this far not to find out whether that bloody former houseboy of Sen's failed to mention visitors staying on the plantation. One way or the other I am not leaving here until I know.'

Fuji shrugged. He was disappointed that Karl was not around – he would have liked to finish him off before leaving for Japan. At least he would get ownership of the schooner as soon as the operation was over and they were safely back in Dutch territory.

Before leaving Port Moresby to drive to Paul's plantation, Jack discovered that his friend Sen was no longer in Papua. The locals said that he had sold up and travelled to Singapore with his family. Jack shook his head in his puzzlement. He knew that Sen was planning to re-establish himself in Singapore but was surprised that he had not passed on his farewells to Jack in some form or another.

Lukas had bundled together a few possessions from aboard and gave instructions to Malip to guard the boat while they were away for a day or two. The

Papuan grinned a betel nut stained smile by way of acknowledging the responsibility he had thrust upon him. Mr Jack was generous in his pay and would receive good service in return.

Paul, Jack and the two boys drove out of Moresby just on sunset after a day of refurbishing the lugger and its supplies. Oblachinski had paid them in cash and the money was safely in the bank. Only Jack remained relatively silent on the noisy journey filled with talk and laughter as Paul's truck jarred its way along the dirt track to the plantation. Paul hoped to be home around midnight and had spent some of his money on new dress material for Karin and Angelika. He swore to himself that this would be the last time he would be away from his wife's side. He had missed her gentle touch and good cooking as much as he had missed lying beside her with his arms wrapped around her as they slept.

O'Leary and his men came ashore just before midnight. The four men each carried a rifle and only Fuji had remained behind to keep watch over the schooner. As Karl would not be ashore he did not mind staying out of whatever might occur, it was not his concern.

Karin had sat up late that night reading a novel. Normally she would have retired to bed around ten o'clock but the book had her hooked. Outside, she heard the dogs barking furiously and was annoyed to be disturbed by a visitor so late at night. Still,

Dademo would deal with whoever it was; his quarters were less than fifty yards from the main house.

Dademo was indeed roused by the sound of the dogs. Springing from his camp stretcher he snatched the rifle leaning against the wall of the single room he occupied in the corner of a packing shed. He immediately suspected that the disturbance had something to do with Fuji's boat, which at sunset had still been anchored in the bay. He found a hurricane lamp and lit the wick. When it flared he stepped warily into the dusty yard to peer into the night.

O'Leary saw the light flare as they approached the house from across the yard. 'Bloody hell,' he swore when he saw the outline of a rifle gripped by the shadowy figure holding the lantern.

'Who is that?' Dademo called nervously.

His answer was the explosive crack of a rifle. The bullet tore through his chest, just missing his heart. The lamp flew from his hand and the yard was once again in darkness except for the soft light from the house spilling onto the verandah.

Karin jumped in fright at the sound of the rifle shot but her instincts took over. She ran to the room where Paul kept the plantation firearms locked away, foraging frantically in a desk drawer for the key to the gun cabinet. But before she had the opportunity to retrieve one of the firearms she heard a shattering of glass. She swung in the direction of the noise to see a huge burly man standing in the doorway with a pistol in his hand pointed at her. Although Karin had never seen this man before, his first words revealed his identity, and the name increased her terror.

'Me name's Tim O'Leary, missus,' he said. 'And me and my men are not here to have a cup of tea. Where's Gerhardt Stahl?'

Karin's thoughts were in a whirl. The gun cabinet was so close and yet she knew she had no chance of opening it now. And there was Angelika only a room away in her bed. 'Herr Stahl is not here,' Karin croaked in fear. 'And I think you should leave immediately, Mr O'Leary.'

O'Leary merely smiled and walked towards her. He had lowered the pistol and replaced it in a holster at his side. He knew that he would only be encumbered by it given what he was about to do. It had been a long time since he had a European woman and this one was very pretty. He waved away one of his men who had entered the room to see what he could loot while his comrades went through the house like a plague of locusts. Karin heard her daughter's scream from the next room as one of the men burst in. She turned to the Irishman. 'Please, I beg in the name of God that you leave my daughter,' she pleaded. 'Do anything you wish to me but by all that is sacred please don't harm my daughter. She is only eleven years old.'

O'Leary frowned. 'I didn't know that you had a daughter,' he sneered. 'But in this country if she were a kanaka she is old enough to be married. So whatever my men have in mind is okay by me.'

In her desperation Karin slashed out at the burly man with her nails. But he was fast and ducked as he retaliated by slamming his fist into her face. As Karin's world faded she did not remember anymore except Angelika screaming for her.

O'Leary was disappointed that she was unconscious. He preferred women to be awake and aware when he took them. At least the mission was not a complete waste of time. They would grab anything of value and leave before first light to sail back to Dutch territory. Needless to say he could not afford to leave any witnesses alive – young or old.

Dademo lay on the earth and felt the numbness throughout his whole body. He was having trouble breathing and when he attempted to move the pain came in an intensity that shocked him. The rifle lay somewhere in the dark. He could hear the screams coming from the house and was vaguely aware that he had seen at least four men enter. He must find the rifle then crawl over and kill the intruders. But he felt too weak to move and knew he was probably dying. The missus and little missus were in his care and Dademo knew about responsibility. In agony he began to drag himself on one elbow across the yard until he bumped into the reassuring metal and wood of his rifle. Unable to raise himself to his feet, he lay on his back with the rifle across his chest. Maybe his only hope was to shoot the men when they came out of the house. Whatever they were doing to the missus and little missus, he knew it was too late to stop them but at least he could avenge them. In the distance he thought he could hear the sound of a truck engine grinding and groaning. The sound grew and he knew it well. Dademo had one last idea.

He pulled the trigger of the loaded rifle. Its sound was loud and with great effort he ejected the empty shell to reload another round. He fired a second time in the air.

Jack had been dozing in the front seat of the truck as it approached the plantation, but the distant cracking pop of the rifle brought him awake. It was a sound he knew all too well. 'You hear that?' he asked Paul, who was driving.

'Hear what?' Paul frowned.

A second shot. 'I heard that,' Paul said as he brought the truck to a stop.

'We thought we heard a couple of shots,' Karl called down into the cabin from the tray where he and Lukas were sitting.

Then there was a third shot, followed by the silence of the jungle.

'Something is wrong,' Paul said as he reached for his rifle jammed down the side of the seat. Jack grabbed for his own gun, but Lukas and Karl were unarmed, having left their firearms aboard the lugger.

'What do you think is going on?' Jack asked.

'I don't know,' Paul answered as he grabbed a box of .303 cartridges from under the seat and tore the cardboard open. 'But any shooting this time of night has to mean something bad.'

Jack took a handful of the brass cartridges from Paul and shoved them in his pocket. Both rifles had fully loaded magazines and spare rounds. Lukas and

Karl jumped from the truck and stood with worried faces beside their fathers.

'You two boys are to stay with the truck,' Jack said without any invitation to argue. 'We'll go ahead on foot to have a look around. When it is clear we will come back.'

The boys reluctantly nodded and the two former soldiers moved quickly along the track towards the plantation. The night covered their approach and in the distance they could see the lights of the house through the trees.

O'Leary had also heard the shots. He had only succeeded in stripping away Karin's nightdress as she slowly regained consciousness. 'Go and see who the hell is firing off the rifle,' he bellowed to his men in the adjoining room. He could hear their reluctant cessation of activities with the young girl. 'And I mean all of you go, or I will shoot you myself if I come in there and you haven't.'

The three men picked up their rifles and left the naked girl lying on her bed in a state of shock.

Jack and Paul had reached the edge of the bush opposite the house and taken up positions side by side in the dark. They had hardly positioned themselves when they saw the first of the Indonesians move cautiously through the front door of the main house with a rifle in his hands. No matter which way they looked at it, Paul and Jack knew that the man had to be a threat. Paul raised his rifle and slipped off the safety catch.

'Not yet,' Jack hissed. 'We need to know if he is alone.'

Paul kept his finger on the trigger and the man in his sights. He knew Jack was right but every instinct in him screamed out to kill the armed stranger who had emerged from his house. The foresight of the rifle followed the indistinct outline of the man as he stepped off the verandah and moved stealthily across the yard. From the way he moved Jack guessed that he was hunting someone in the dark, but there was just enough light from the house to make the man a target for them.

'Two more!' Jack hissed again, and Paul glanced away from his target for a brief moment to see two more armed men emerge from the house to stand on the verandah. Jack raised his rifle to cover them.

The first to emerge from the house yelled something in an unfamiliar language and his comment brought a burst of nervous laughter from the two men on the verandah. Paul's eye was trained on the man in the yard, trying to ascertain what had caught his attention. He cursed the lights of the house that prevented him gaining his night vision, but by looking from the corner of his eye he could vaguely make out a shape lying in the yard. When the shape moved he knew it was Dademo. Only Dademo knew about the three shot signal for emergencies. As the intruder raised his rifle Paul guessed that Dademo must still be alive. Paul fired and his aim was true, the intruder screaming as the heavy calibre bullet tore through his body.

A split second later Jack fired at one of the men on the verandah. He was thrown back against the wall by the impact. The third man stood in a state of shock, staring into the night that had suddenly turned deadly. His hesitation cost him his life as Paul swung the foresight onto him even as he worked the bolt to eject the spent cartridge and chamber a fresh round. The second shot blasted through the third man's head and Paul cursed himself for the bad shot. He had expected to hit the man in the centre of the body. All his training had taught him to do so. A headshot was something for snipers, not former infantrymen.

O'Leary heard the gunfire and the screams of dying men as he stood with Karin at his feet. He was momentarily confused as he knew the local natives would not have firearms. But there was no mistaking the fact that someone outside the house had just opened fire. He quickly extinguished the light and drew his revolver. It was time to assess his situation. Moving through the rooms he killed all lights so the house was in complete darkness. Then he took cover behind a window that commanded a view of the yard. Scanning, very carefully, he saw the fluttering shadow of a figure sprinting to the packing sheds. He sensed that it was not one of his own men and felt fear for the first time in many years. Whoever was out there knew what they were doing. He could see one of his men sprawled on the verandah in a pool of blood. Maybe the Chinaman had set him up after all. But since he had not heralded his arrival at the plantation he did not think that could be the explanation. The German planter must have returned, alerted by the gunshots, he deduced. If that were true the Irishman knew he had a chance of extracting himself. But to do so would require the most ruthless of solutions.

THIRTY-NINE

The stern nursing matron had not permitted Erika to see Caroline until the baby was safely delivered and Caroline had been trundled to a bed in the hospital ward. But she did allow Erika a glimpse of the baby in its crib in the nursery section of the hospital.

'You have a beautiful daughter,' Erika said as she sat by Caroline's side in the early hours of the morning. 'What will your husband think of having a daughter instead of a son?'

Caroline was still in a daze and weak from the delivery. She turned her head to focus on Erika. 'I don't care what he thinks,' she said with a weak smile. 'It's not even his flesh and blood. My daughter's real father is Jack Kelly.'

Erika gasped at the revelation. Possibly it was the euphoria of birth that had loosened Caroline's tongue or perhaps she no longer cared to keep her secret. Only Caroline knew.

'The ironic part,' Caroline continued, 'is that Jack does not know about either.'

Erika stared at Caroline. Was she aware of what she was saying? Was this the truth or was she in some sort of confused state? Erika gazed into the eyes of her friend. 'How could this be?' she asked, feeling a strange hatred for Caroline. Whatever contempt she had held the Australian adventurer in, it was as if she had stolen something from Erika. For the first time in years, Erika was feeling a sorrow for what could have been. But regrets, she knew too well, were also emotions without purpose.

'As Quentin was not capable of being so himself, I needed a father for my child,' Caroline continued in a tired voice. 'Jack was easily seduced and his virility did the rest. Now all Quentin has to get used to is that a woman will inherit the Arrowsmith fortunes in the years ahead. Somehow I think he will have to change his thinking about us weak females.'

Erika's antagonism towards Caroline seemed to dissipate and she reached out to take her hand. 'You should get some rest,' she said softly. 'I am pleased for you.'

Caroline squeezed her hand in gratitude. 'You were here with me when even my husband didn't think it was important enough to be at the hospital,' she said with an edge of bitterness. 'That means a lot more to me than you could possibly know.'

Erika rose from her chair and leant over to kiss Caroline on the forehead. 'We are now sisters in life,' she whispered. 'Our lives are entwined forever.'

Caroline smiled and nodded her head. She sighed and turned her cheek against the pillow. Sleep came to her as Erika left the hospital to return to the Arrowsmith house where she would remain a while longer as a guest.

It was not a high class passenger ship that left Sydney Harbour just after midnight, but to Gerhardt the ship represented freedom and safety. Jacob Schmidt and his older partner Bill Havers had come aboard the cargo vessel destined for San Francisco to bid Gerhardt and his daughter farewell. Gerhardt felt the strength of the young agent's grip as they shook hands. 'We will have to work together, Herr Schmidt,' Gerhardt said, looking the young American straight in the eye. 'Hitler is a madman who has fooled my countrymen into believing his lies. I know in my heart that he will not stop until he takes the world into another terrible war.'

'I am afraid you and I know that,' Jacob said, 'and I also know that there are Brits like Mr Churchill who also share our views. But I am also afraid that the rest of the world will not listen to us until it is too late. Your assistance will help them to hear. You will be a true patriot to your country.'

Gerhardt smiled sadly. 'Once I was young and foolish and prepared to lay my life down for my country in the Great War. Now I am older but still just as foolish. My only regret is that I followed that madman. But that is now something that I can use against him in the future. I know him. And what I know of Hitler, you too will know.'

'Well, be careful, Herr Stahl,' Jacob said as he let go Gerhardt's hand. 'We have made arrangements for you to be met in the States when the boat docks. Your residency in America comes at a price. We will call on you again.'

A crewman arrived to show Gerhardt and Ilsa to their cabin. The two Americans went ashore but not before Bill Havers gave Ilsa a small brown paper parcel with instructions that she was not to open it until the ship had passed through the sandstone cliffs that stood either side of the harbour. But Ilsa could not help herself, ripping open the paper just as the ship pulled away from the dock. Inside she found a tiny stuffed kangaroo and an American teddy bear. Bill Havers had come to like Australia and its people, who he found very much like Americans in many ways. The gift was symbolic of what he saw in the years ahead. He hoped Ilsa too would come to see it as so.

When Erika returned to the Arrowsmith residence in a taxi just before dawn she was told of the police visit earlier that evening by a very irritated Quentin. 'Was it a boy or a girl?' he asked, almost as an afterthought, when he made to leave her alone in the spacious living room.

'A girl,' Erika told him and saw the bitter look of disappointment on his face as he turned away to go back to bed.

She slumped into a chair as she took in the news, her thoughts whirling. Gerhardt had outsmarted her. How was she going to explain this to her masters in Berlin? The sun was rising over Sydney and the new day promised warmth on the ancient continent. For Erika she had not only lost her daughter but possibly the confidence of the party. She felt very much alone and frightened. At least she had Caroline whom she knew would stand by her. After all, they both belonged to Jack Kelly's unwitting harem. What would he think if he ever found out about his two daughters? The possibility was unlikely but nonetheless it amused Erika at a time when little else did.

FORTY

Paul and Jack decided to split up after they had eliminated the three men. They did not know how many more intruders were in the house or even in the compound. All they knew was that they had at least reduced their opposition. Paul chose to make his way to the rear of his house whilst Jack kept the front covered. When the house suddenly went dark he knew that there was at least one other inside, if not more.

Paul was desperate with fear for Karin and Angelika. There had been no sound of their voices and by now he was certainly close enough to hear if they spoke or called out. The dogs were still barking but quietened when he neared them in their kennels at the back of the house. Their silence was not lost on whoever was in the house, however.

'Is that you, Mann?' a man called from inside.

Paul did not immediately recognise the voice but Jack Kelly did. He knew it well and the years had not diminished his hatred of the Irishman. Then a vague memory from Paul's past now brought the terrible realisation of who he was dealing with – a recollection of the Fly River and a callous killer who had transported Sen's sister-in-law into slavery. His anger turned to a blinding need to kill O'Leary before he could take two of the most precious people from him. 'It is me, O'Leary,' Paul called out. 'Are my wife and daughter unharmed?'

'For the moment,' O'Leary called back, and Paul thought he heard a muffled sound, like the stifling of a call by a gag or hand over the mouth.

'Who is with you?' O'Leary asked.

'I am on my own,' Paul bluffed.

But the Irishman was not fooled. 'You are lying, Mann,' he said. 'One man alone couldn't take out three of my men so easily. So I will ask again who is with you and if you don't answer truthfully I will use my knife to slice off a piece of your wife or daughter – I will let you decide which one.'

Paul knew that O'Leary meant what he said. He had seen first-hand what cruelty the former recruiter of native labour was capable of. 'Jack Kelly is with me,' he answered in his desperation.

'Kelly!' O'Leary exploded. 'Tell him to show himself.'

'I will show myself,' Jack called from the front of the house, 'when you send out Mrs Mann and her daughter unharmed.'

'I will make a deal with you, Kelly,' O'Leary said. 'I will send the kid out unharmed if you stand at the foot of the steps to the verandah without any weapons.'

'It's a deal,' Jack replied. Paul cursed his friend but knew he was helpless to stop him. He was virtually sentencing himself to death and must have known it. He was sacrificing his life for one of his family and Paul felt tears of frustration wet his cheeks. 'Don't do it, Jack,' Paul cried out. 'The bastard will kill you.'

'Old Tim and I go back aways,' Jack said loudly. 'If nothing else he knows I will honour my word, and he also knows that if he doesn't I will kill him.'

Jack's bravado did not fool Paul. He knew that Jack was prepared to sacrifice himself for people he considered his family. When a light went on in the house, flooding the verandah with its yellow glow, Paul hoped that this was an opportunity to see if there were others inside. Perhaps the Irishman was setting them up for an ambush?

Jack laid his rifle down and walked towards the house, feeling the fear grip his stomach like a knot. He knew what he was doing was suicidal but he was desperate to get Karin and Angelika out of there. And there was a slim chance O'Leary would honour the deal. As he came to a stop at the foot of the steps to the verandah, little Angelika appeared shivering with a sheet wrapped around her, staring at him uncomprehendingly. Behind her O'Leary held Karin who was gagged with a piece of sheet, her hands bound behind her back. She wore the tattered remains of a nightdress, the front of her body exposed. The Irishman pressed a revolver against Karin's head.

'Come to me, little angel,' Jack said gently as he held out his hand to Angelika.

His nickname for her seemed to work. 'Uncle Jack,' she cried out, 'help Mama.'

'I will,' Jack said, glancing past Angelika to catch Karin's eyes pleading for him to get her daughter away.

Angelika took his hand and Jack turned to walk with her across the yard. From the corner of his eye he could see Dademo lying on his back with his rifle across his chest. Jack was very aware of O'Leary behind him in the doorway of the house. He felt the bullet before he heard the sound of the shot from the revolver. Jack pitched forward into the dust. 'Run,' he croaked up at Angelika who stood over him. 'Run down the track to Karl. He's waiting for you.'

Jack lay face down, vaguely aware that it was very dark. Whether that was because O'Leary had turned out the lights of the house again or he was just dying did not matter anymore. He could taste the soil of Papua in his mouth and thought that it might have been the taste of French soil if he had been killed on the Western Front years earlier. At least it was the soil of his adopted country that he would taste as he died.

'O'Leary, you murdering bastard!' Paul roared, now concealed at the side of the house. 'You said you would not kill him.'

'I said I would release your kid if Kelly appeared unarmed at the foot of the verandah,' O'Leary replied from the depths of the again darkened house.

'I never said I wasn't going to shoot him. You see, I *am* a man of my word.'

Paul had not been able to see O'Leary when he came to the door. His only view had been of the yard and Jack approaching from the treeline at the edge of the compound. He had felt his heart skip a beat when he saw Jack walking away with his daughter who appeared relatively unharmed. But to his horror he had also seen Jack flung forward by the bullet from O'Leary's pistol. Even now he could see the dark patch spreading to soak Jack's shirt. If he was still alive he would not be for long given how much blood was seeping from him.

'It seems that with Kelly gone,' O'Leary said from inside the house, 'that leaves only you, me and your missus to work out a deal. And the deal is simple. You do not attempt to shoot me and I will not attempt to shoot your wife. So I expect you to come forward without any weapons and you get the same deal as Kelly, except this time I promise I won't shoot you or your missus.'

'I don't trust you,' Paul replied. 'But if you let my wife go I will put down my gun and you can use me as a hostage instead.'

'Ah, but that means I have to trust you and I am by nature not a trusting man. So you will have to believe me when I say your wife and I will go down to the beach and across to my boat together. When I am sure I am safe I will release her.'

Paul knew the Irishman had the upper hand. While Paul was still armed he knew O'Leary could not kill Karin without being killed himself. And to put down his gun before the Irishman meant certain death for him and Karin. And if O'Leary was intending to take Karin to a boat in the bay then there was a good chance he would still kill her, or worse – send her to wherever it was that he had sent Iris many years earlier. The situation was looking hopeless. 'We go to the beach together,' Paul finally answered. 'But I do not put down my gun.'

'Fair enough,' O'Leary replied.

Paul stepped out warily from beside the house when the lights once again went on inside. He held the butt of his rifle into his shoulder and kept his finger on the trigger, just in case O'Leary had more men waiting to ambush him. But only the Irishman emerged with Karin, still gagged and tied.

'You know,' Paul said quietly as he approached O'Leary. 'I once had you in my rifle sights when you were taking Iris aboard that Arab dhow a few years back.' He could see O'Leary's surprise. 'I had you in my sights and spared you for reasons I wish I had reconsidered. If I had killed you then my friend Jack Kelly might not have become another of your victims nor would my family be threatened as it is now.'

'You were up the Fly back in '23? Or was it '22?' O'Leary asked. 'Not that the past matters anymore. Just worry about what is going to happen in the next few minutes if you are not very careful.'

'You know if you shoot my wife you are a dead man,' Paul said calmly. 'But I can promise you that all I am concerned about is that I have Karin alive and well. Then you have your safe passage out of here. One day though you and I will settle up.'

'That it will probably come to,' O'Leary replied as he stepped off the verandah with the revolver at Karin's head. 'Too bad old Jack is dead,' he commented, glancing across the yard into the far reaches of the light from the house to where Jack lay in the dust. 'I could have told him where that Chinese sister-in-law of old Sen is right now. I heard that if Jack could have found her he would have inherited a fortune. He would have never needed to work again in this stinking place.'

'You know where Iris is?' Paul asked.

'She is with my old mate, the Froggie,' O'Leary said, pushing Karin ahead of him but keeping her between himself and Paul as a shield as Paul walked backwards in front of them. 'He decided that he needed a wife to help him run his little business. I don't suppose it matters if I do you a favour and tell you where she is now.'

Paul was not a religious man but in the next few seconds found himself praying. For behind the Irishman's back Paul had seen a figure emerge from the shadows at the edge of the bush and move stealthily over to Dademo's prone figure. He could tell it was Lukas and saw the young man pick up the rifle. Lukas would require absolute skill and raw nerve, but he was now walking towards them, carefully chambering a round so that the metal parts of the breech did not make a sound as the bolt closed into place.

Maybe it was a subtle change in Paul's demeanour but the Irishman suddenly sensed danger and shifted his attention to glance over his shoulder.

Lukas was still at least four paces away but in desperation brought the rifle up with one hand as if it were a hand gun until the end of the barrel was only inches from O'Leary's head. The Irishman snarled as he swung on Lukas with his pistol, but had little chance as Lukas pulled the trigger, the high velocity round blasting through the Irishman's head.

Paul leapt forward to grab hold of his wife, who had stumbled in the dark. It was over.

FORTY-ONE

Fuji did not wait any longer for O'Leary to return. The sporadic gunfire told him that the Irishman's luck had finally run out. He hauled up the anchors and under the power of her engine the schooner slid through the placid waters to the Gulf of Papua. He knew where he could find a buyer for the boat in the Torres Islands and expected to soon find a berth on a cargo ship steaming to Japan. There he could realise his dream and enlist in the Imperial Japanese Navy.

Dademo's body had a blanket placed over it as a sign of respect for the courageous boss boy. He would receive a funeral worthy of a warrior in his village outside of Port Moresby.

Jack lay bleeding on the floor of Paul's house where he had been carried by Lukas and Karl. He was semi-conscious, floating in and out of a world of shadows and lights.

Paul sent Karl back to Moresby in the truck to fetch a doctor whilst Karin tended to Jack's wound. From what she could see the bullet had entered the upper left of his back and lodged itself somewhere in his chest. Jack was breathing hard and Karin guessed that the bullet had damaged a lung.

'Do you think he will live?' Karin whispered.

'Jack will live,' Paul said without hesitation. 'He suffered worse wounds during the war.'

'But he is not a young man now. Will his body take the shock of losing so much blood?'

'Jack?' Paul asked as he bent to speak in his friend's ear. 'Are you going to die and cause a big mess that I will have to clean up?'

Jack heard the words and forced a grin. 'Wouldn't put a mate to any inconvenience,' he croaked with some effort. 'Of course I am going to live.'

'See,' Paul grinned. 'I told you.'

Karin shook her head in her confusion. How could men be so insensitive to another's pain? Their humour must be born out of a war where they were forced to live with such conditions on a daily basis. It was a way of staying sane.

'Where is Lukas?' Jack asked with difficulty.

Paul looked around. He thought that he was somewhere in the house but he had seemed to have disappeared.

'He must be looking after Dademo's body,' Paul answered. 'I can go and fetch him if you like.'

'No matter,' Jack whispered. 'I will talk to him later about disobeying my order to stay with the truck.'

'He saved our lives,' Paul consoled. 'Had he not killed O'Leary I don't know what may have happened.'

Karin had been able to quell the bleeding but dared not move the Australian lest she caused him further damage. Jack was pale and she was frightened that he may not survive through the night. If only the doctor would arrive. But that now depended on her son Karl getting to Moresby and back again safely.

The hours seemed to crawl by and the sun was just below the horizon when Karin heard the grind of the returning truck. She snapped from her dozing sleep beside Jack. 'Is that Karl returning?' she called out to her husband.

'It is,' he replied as he flung open the gauze door to the verandah. 'God in heaven,' he gasped when he saw the truck pull into the yard. 'No wonder I couldn't find young Lukas. He went off with Karl.'

Karin was slightly confused at the number of people who spilled from the truck. Along with her son, Lukas and the doctor, there was a portly man with a cigar who she did not recognise, and a pretty young lady. 'Who are these other people?' she asked Paul.

'That's the American film man we were working for,' Paul said. 'And Miss Duvall.'

Karin's female instincts told her that the young woman had a great interest in the welfare of Jack. It was written in the concern on her face as she quickly pushed her way into the house. Introductions would have to wait.

Victoria came to a stop when she saw Jack lying amongst a pile of bloody rags. She dropped to her knees beside him and cradled his head in her lap. Jack opened his eyes at her touch. 'Must have died,' he murmured with a grin. 'Because against all odds I've gone to heaven and met an angel.'

'Jack, darling, you are far from dead,' Victoria said, forcing back the tears. 'Lukas came to the hotel to tell us what had happened. He said that you had asked to see me.'

Jack did not blink at his son's lie but turned his head slightly to seek him out. He was standing a short distance away, looking guilty. But Jack smiled at his son with an expression of gratitude and love. 'That's right,' he said. 'I didn't want to leave this world without seeing your beautiful face just one more time.'

Victoria gently hugged him to her. 'You have to take me with you to that place in Australia you once told me about that you like so much.'

'I would except Lukas is now the captain of the *Erika Sarah*,' Jack said, his pain exacerbated by Victoria's loving embrace. 'He will need the boat to make us a living.'

'There is something I have to tell you, Dad,' Lukas said sheepishly. 'Joe has a friend in the States who will teach me to fly. I will have to leave the boat with you.'

'You are going to do *what*?' Jack asked.

Lukas shuffled his feet. 'Joe thinks I would be a natural and I reckon the future of this country is going to be in the air.'

'So how do I operate the lugger with you off in the States?' Jack growled, wincing with the effort. 'We still have a living to make.'

'I will be your first mate,' Victoria said. 'I have a hankering to see more of this part of the world. And I think I am capable of looking after a crotchety old war horse.'

'Guess I'd better not die on you then,' Jack grinned.

'I think that I have always loved you, Jungle Jack,' Victoria blurted.

'Who the bloody hell is Jungle Jack?'

'I will tell you about that when you are better,' Victoria said with a tearful smile. 'In the meantime I guess I should let the doctor look at you before he hands you over to my care. I hope you like chicken soup because you will be having a lot of it.'

Jack tried to smile at her offer. He did not have the heart to tell her he hated chicken soup.

FORTY-TWO

Standing beside Victoria with his arm in a sling, Jack waved to his son who stood on the deck of the Burns Philp steamer, sailing to Australia. Beside Lukas stood Joe, his ever-present cigar in his mouth.

'He will be all right?' Jack asked.

Victoria squeezed his arm affectionately. 'Joe will look after him and he will be back before you know it. Joe has a lot of friends in many places and Lukas will have the best flying experience in the world. You will be proud of him.'

'I am already proud of him,' Jack said. 'As proud of him as I ever could be.'

'Well, Mr Kelly,' Victoria said, 'where are we going for your recuperation?'

'I thought maybe a sea voyage on a slow boat to Queensland,' Jack answered with a slow smile. 'We might spend some time in a little village I know on the New South Wales border. The fishing is great and you don't have to worry about crocs and malaria. There are some beautiful mountains there. Oh, I happen to own a piece of land with a wonderful view of the ocean.'

'You'd better not leave all the cooking aboard to me,' Victoria sighed as the ship pulled away from the wharf.

'But,' Jack asked with a lazy grin, 'isn't that a woman's thing?'

Paul Mann reread the letter addressed to him. It was from the brother-in-law he had never met.

'What is in the letter?' Karin asked. 'You look so worried.'

Paul carefully folded the letter. 'Nothing of importance,' he replied. 'Nothing that will do anyone any good in the future.'

Karin knew that if Paul had chosen not to tell her what Erika's husband had written then he had good reasons to do so. She returned to her task of sewing a dress for their daughter as Paul placed the letter in his pocket and went out to the verandah. It was another beautiful day of balmy weather and blue skies dotted with white clouds. This was the Dry season before the torrential rains would come to drench the earth.

His earth and his people, Paul reflected. Jack was a complex man, despite his seemingly easy-going ways. To learn now that he had a daughter would not be good for a man who had been brought back from the brink of death. In his opinion, Jack deserved to continue his life without this added complication. No, this was not the time to burden his friend with the surprising revelation. A good mate was someone who watched his friend's back, Jack had often said. And Jack Kelly was his best mate.

EPILOGUE

A cool breeze wafted through the elegant house on Singapore Island. Kwong Yu Sen paused in writing his report to reflect on the carefully coded words. He would convey the facts as he knew them for his Nazi masters. As for how the mission to kill Gerhardt Stahl had failed because of O'Leary's impulsive impatience he would say nothing.

The Chinese businessman sighed. Although he was not by nature a gambler, in this instance he had gambled everything on his understanding of the ways of man. If anyone was capable of carrying out his personal revenge on the Irishman it would be the combined force of Paul Mann and Jack Kelly. The abduction of Iris was neither forgotten nor forgiven. Sen had not planned anything further after activating his former colleague for the mission but instead allowed fate to take its course. By his deliberate silence he had allowed luck to play its part. Now O'Leary was dead and no longer a possible source for the British to learn of Sen's espionage activities in the Great War. His faith in the abilities of the two remarkable men had been vindicated. The fate of his sister-in-law remained the only ghost in his life. Where she was, and what had been her fate, would forever haunt him.

She sat in front of the stone building and gazed without seeing the noisy crowds of dark skinned people passing her by. It was not yet time to open her husband's bar and cater to the thirsts of the Legionnaires from the fort. She did not like these men who pawed her after drinking the cheap wine and spirits that her husband sold them. Nor did she like this land. It was a lonely place of sand, searing heat and flies. It was a land of barrenness to Iris who had once known the beauty of the rainforests of Papua and before that the snows of her native China.

But Pierre had made his deal with his former boss who had traded her for a year's worth of work for him. She often thought that she may have been better off in Arabia where at least the English had contact with the local tribes, growing rich on the oil beneath their sands. In North Africa the people either spoke their native tribal dialects or French. Her grasp of French was improving but she had also learned that no one was interested in the mad ramblings of a Eurasian woman claiming to have been abducted from Papua. She had become like the people who passed her by each day as she sat in front of the bar, waiting and watching for just that one face that she might trust – that one person who might take her away from her slavery, and return her to her family.

The desert was brewing a storm outside the garrison town for the French Foreign Legion. Within a few short years the storm would turn to a war that would sweep North Africa with steel and fire.

AUTHOR'S NOTE

Enau wantoks!
It is not my intention to write a history of Papua. There are sources available in most libraries that will give those interested in the history of the great island to the north of Australia the information they require.

Today the island is divided into the democratically governed Papua New Guinea on the east and the former Dutch administered territory Irian Jaya on the west, now under the control of Indonesia.

New Guinea (the northern half of the eastern side) was under German control until 1914 when it was occupied by Australian Armed Forces. Papua (the southern part on the eastern side of the island) has been under Australian control since the early part of the twentieth century. In 1975 Papua New Guinea raised its flag as a fully independent nation.

Papua New Guinea is a land of great beauty with tall, jungle covered mountains that reach into the clouds; there is even a peak that is snow covered at times during the year. The land is so rugged that for over forty thousand years many tribes evolved in complete isolation from their neighbours in the next valley. This has led to a plethora of languages. One estimate puts the number of languages originally spoken at around nine hundred. Needless to say the culture of the island has been a paradise for anthropologists and tribes were still being 'discovered' into the latter part of the twentieth century. Cannibalism and head hunting have been the way of life for many of the tribes and their men constitute a true warrior class.

I had the honour of working with the Royal Papua New Guinea Constabulary in the early 1990s and have been humbled by the courage shown by the men and women who battle every day to maintain peace in a land that still retains a greater part of its warrior culture. It is one of the most beautiful and exotic places on the planet and one that to this day is truly a frontier land, despite the incursion of western technology.

For ease of reading I have anglicised the language spoken in this novel. My characters would have spoken German, English, Police Motu, pidgin and tribal dialects. Today English is the official language of government but the people prefer to communicate in the island's universal language of *tok pisin*. It is truly a wonderful language, one still evolving with creative colour and derived from a mixture of German, English and indigenous words.

The men and women who pioneered Papua from the end of the nineteenth century and into the twentieth were even more colourful than I could describe in this novel. Government officials, military personnel, missionaries, precious minerals prospectors, traders, charter boat operators, fauna hunters – these are just a few of the sorts of people who went to Papua to seek adventure or fortune, or just simply escape from murky pasts. I would recommend a couple of great writers on the days of adventure in Colin Simpson and James Sinclair. Both authors' works I drew heavily on for the historical facts and details of the way of life. A wonderful book that provided me with a strong sense of European life in early Papua was that of Dr Jan Roberts, *Voices from a Lost World*. There are many others that I read in the course of my research and I am indebted to them all.

As for the 'file' referring to the planned assassination of Albert Einstein, that is just a work of fiction.

Em tasol
Peter Watt
Tweed Heads, Australia

Peter Watt
Cry of the Curlew

Squatter Donald Macintosh little realises what chain of events he is setting in motion when he orders the violent dispersal of the Nerambura tribe on his property, Glen View. Unwitting witnesses to the barbaric exercise are bullock teamsters Patrick Duffy and his son Tom.

Meanwhile, in thriving Sydney Town, Michael Duffy and Fiona Macintosh are completely unaware of the cataclysmic events overtaking their fathers in the colony of Queensland. They have caught each other's eye during an outing to Manly Village. A storm during the ferry trip home is but a small portent of what is to follow . . . From this day forward, the Duffys and the Macintoshes are inextricably linked. Their paths cross in love, death and revenge as both families fight to tame the wild frontier of Australia's north country.

Spanning the middle years of the nineteenth century, *Cry of the Curlew* is a groundbreaking novel of Australian history. Confronting, erotic, graphic, but above all, a compelling adventure, Peter Watt is an exceptional talent.

Peter Watt
Cry of the Curlew

Peter Watt
Shadow of the Osprey

On a Yankee clipper bound for Sydney harbour the mysterious Michael O'Flynn is watched closely by a man working undercover for Her Majesty's government. O'Flynn has a dangerous mission to undertake . . . and old scores to settle.

Twelve years have passed since the murderous event which inextricably linked the destinies of two families, the Macintoshes and the Duffys. The curse which lingers after the violent 1862 dispersal of the Nerambura tribe has created passions which divide them in hate and join them in forbidden love.

Shadow of the Osprey, the sequel to the bestselling *Cry of the Curlew*, is a riverting tale that reaches from the boardrooms and backstreets of Sydney to beyond the rugged Queensland frontier and the dangerous waters of the Coral Sea. Powerful and brilliantly told, *Shadow of the Osprey* confirms the exceptional talent of master storyteller Peter Watt.

Peter Watt
Flight of the Eagle

No-one is left untouched by the dreadful curse which haunts two families, inextricably linking them together in love, death and revenge.

Captain Patrick Duffy is a man divided between the family of his father, Irish Catholic soldier of fortune Michael Duffy and his adoring, scheming maternal grandmother, Enid Macintosh. Visiting the village of his Irish forbears on a quest to uncover the secrets surrounding his birth, he is beguiled by the beautiful, mysterious Catherine Fitzgerald.

On the rugged Queensland frontier Native Mounted Police trooper Peter Duffy is torn between his duty, the blood of his mother's people – the Nerambura tribe – and a predestined deadly duel with Gordon James, the love of his sister Sarah.

From the battlefields of the Sudan, to colonial Sydney and the Queensland outback, *Flight of the Eagle* is a stunning addition to the series featuring the best-selling *Cry of the Curlew* and *Shadow of the Osprey*, with master storyteller Peter Watt at the height of his powers.

Peter Watt
To Chase the Storm

When Major Patrick Duffy's beautiful wife Catherine leaves him for another, returning to her native Ireland, Patrick's broken heart propels him out of the Sydney Macintosh home and into yet another bloody war. However the battlefields of Africa hold more than nightmarish terrors and unspeakable conditions for Patrick – they bring him in contact with one he thought long dead and lost to him.

Back in Australia, the mysterious Michael O'Flynn mentors Patrick's youngest son, Alex, and at his grandmother's request takes him on a journey to their Queensland property, Glen View. But will the terrible curse that has inextricably linked the Duffys and Macintoshes for generations ensure that no true happiness can ever come to them? So much seems to depend on Wallarie, the last warrior of the Nerambura tribe, whose mere name evokes a legend approaching myth.

Through the dawn of a new century in a now federated nation, *To Chase the Storm* charts an explosive tale of love and loss, from South Africa to Palestine, from Townsville to the green hills of Ireland, and to the more sinister politics that lurk behind them. By public demand, master storyteller Peter Watt returns to his much-loved series following on from the bestselling *Cry of the Curlew*, *Shadow of the Osprey* and *Flight of the Eagle*.

PHOTO: DEAN MARTIN